District Nurse On Call

Donna Douglas

arrow books

1 3 5 7 9 10 8 6 4 2

Arrow Books
20 Vauxhall Bridge Road
London SW1V 2SA

Arrow Books is part of the Penguin Random House group of companies
whose addresses can be found at global.penguinrandomhouse.com.

Penguin
Random House
UK

First published in Great Britain by Arrow Books in 2017

www.penguin.co.uk

A CIP catalogue record for this book is available from the British Library

ISBN 9781784757151

Typeset in 10.75/13.5 pt
by Jouve (UK), Milton Keynes
Printed and bound in Great Britain by Clays Ltd, St Ives Plc

MIX
Paper from
responsible sources
FSC
www.fsc.org FSC® C018179

Penguin Random House is committed to a
sustainable future for our business, our readers
and our planet. This book is made from Forest
Stewardship Council® certified paper.

Acknowledgements

This book almost never saw the light of day due to me being struck down by illness halfway through. I'd like to thank the following people for their patience and their persistence.

The team at Random House, especially Selina Walker, Susan Sandon, Cass Di Bello and my new editor Viola Hayden, who must have wondered at times what kind of author she had been landed with. I'd also like to thank the sales team for dealing so well with the ever-changing schedules and deadlines.

My agent Caroline Sheldon, for being so understanding and for dealing with all the difficult stuff. And there was a lot of difficult stuff.

My friends and family for rallying round me and bolstering my spirits. Plus, of course, the amazing people who helped me get well again, especially Dr Geddes and Dr Sinclair, Ranza, Amanda, Marji and a guy called John in Boots who will never know what his quick-thinking advice did for me.

To my very good friend June Smith-Sheppard,
for always being there

Chapter One

1926

'Well, here it is, my dear. Your new home.'

Philippa stopped the car on top of a ridge overlooking the valley and peered through the windscreen. 'It doesn't look very promising, I must say.'

Agnes Sheridan got out of the passenger seat, struggling against the chilly March wind that threatened to tear the cap from her head. She clamped it in place with one hand and pulled her navy blue overcoat more tightly around her with the other as she gazed down into the valley.

Phil was right, it wasn't promising. The village of Bowden settled like grey sediment in the bottom of the shallow valley bowl, surrounded on all sides by the rolling bracken-covered Yorkshire moors. From her viewpoint, Agnes could make out a collection of solid-looking buildings in the centre of the village, a school, some shops and the spire of a church. But it was the colliery that drew her eye. It lay to the east of the village, a sprawl of yards, outbuildings, railway lines, black spoil heaps, and the tall, stark shapes of the winding machinery, towering over the tight grids of terraced cottages clustered in their shadow.

Bowden Main Colliery. The reason the village – and she – was here.

Behind her, she heard Phil get out of the car.

'Just imagine,' she said, coming to stand beside her. 'You're going to be responsible for all these people now. All those hacking coughs and sore eyes and injured limbs and bad chests. Coal miners aren't known for their good health, are they? I expect most of them will be on their last legs.' She lit up a cigarette. 'And the children ... malnourished and crawling with lice, I should imagine.'

'It can't be any worse than Quarry Hill,' Agnes said.

Phil shuddered. 'God, no. Nothing could be worse than Quarry Hill.'

As part of their district nursing training, they had both spent time in the rundown Leeds slums. At the time, Agnes couldn't wait to get her badge and escape to a district of her own. Now she wished she was back there, still safe under the watchful eye of her mentor, Bess Bradshaw.

As if she could guess her thoughts, Phil suddenly turned to her and said, 'Are you sure you're ready for this, my dear?'

It was a question Agnes had asked herself several times over the past few weeks, ever since Miss Gale, the Nursing Superintendent at Steeple Street, had given her the news. Bowden was to be her first official placement as a Queen's Nurse, and the responsibility lay heavy on Agnes' shoulders. She hadn't been able to sleep at all the previous night for thinking about it.

What if it was too much for her? What if she couldn't cope?

But in the light of day she refused to give in to such fears.

'Of course.' She gathered her coat more tightly around herself and looked down at the village, nestling below. 'I'm looking forward to it.'

'You always did like a challenge, didn't you?' Phil said. 'Not like me. Give me my nice rural patch any day. Healthy farmers' wives giving birth like shelling peas, and rosy-cheeked children, and nothing more serious than the occasional cow stamping on a milkmaid's foot.'

2

Agnes smiled. 'You never used to say that when you had to cycle thirty miles and back every day!'

'That was before Veronica came along.' Phil lovingly stroked the bonnet of her Ford. For as long as Agnes had known her, Phil had been pestering the District Association for a motorcycle, and finally – probably hoping to keep her quiet for good, Agnes thought wryly – they had given in and allocated her a car. Phil adored Veronica, but her driving left a lot to be desired. Agnes had kept her eyes closed all the way from Leeds, her fingers gripping the edge of the leather seat as they sped along the twisting country lanes.

'Anyway, we'd best get going.' Phil stubbed out her cigarette and started back to the car. 'You want to make the right impression on your first day, don't you?'

They headed downhill and soon the open farmland and fields gave way to a patch of straggly woodland before the road flattened into the village.

On closer inspection, Bowden wasn't quite as bad as Agnes had thought. Away from the pit, and the tight knots of colliery cottages clustered around it, there were a couple of streets of larger, more well-to-do houses, a patchwork of neatly kept allotments, a recreation ground, a few plainly built chapels and a row of shops, all empty and locked up on this late Sunday afternoon.

Agnes gritted her teeth as Veronica bumped along the narrow, deeply rutted street.

'Don't you think we should go a little slower?' she said.

'Nonsense, there's no one about,' Phil dismissed, peering through the windscreen. 'Now remind me again what we're looking for?'

'The Miners' Welfare Institute. Miss Gale said it was just behind the Co-op.'

'We must have passed it. I'll turn round.'

3

'Be careful,' Agnes begged, as her friend wrestled with the gearstick, throwing Veronica into reverse.

'Oh, do stop fussing, Agnes! Honestly, you're starting to make me nervous, the way you go on—'

'Look out!' Agnes caught a flash of movement behind them as Veronica jerked backwards. A second later there was a bump and an almighty clatter.

Phil slammed on the brake pedal, her face ashen. 'What was that?'

'I think you hit something.'

'Oh, Lord, no!' Her friend's face paled as she sat frozen behind the wheel. 'What if I've damaged Veronica? The District Association will take her away for sure.'

'Never mind Veronica!' Agnes jumped out of the car and ran to the rear of it. A man lay sprawled on the pavement, tangled with a bicycle that was half hidden under Veronica's back bumper.

She bent down beside him. 'Oh, my goodness, are you all right?'

'What do you reckon?' A pair of snapping slate-grey eyes met hers. 'What the hell do you think you're playing at? You could have killed me.'

'Yes, well, you shouldn't have cycled behind me while I was reversing, should you?' Phil said, getting out of the car.

The man glared at her. 'Are you trying to say it were my fault?'

'Well—'

'Of course not.' Agnes shot a warning look at Phil. 'Now, can you move? Are you in any pain?'

'I'll live, no thanks to you.' He started to extricate himself from under his bicycle. Agnes made a move to assist him, but he shrugged her off.

'I only want to help you.'

'I reckon you've done enough.'

4

He struggled to his feet and brushed himself down. His jacket was threadbare at the elbows, Agnes noticed, and his grubby collarless shirt had seen better days. He was in his thirties, with black hair and a lean, unsmiling face.

He reached down and started to disentangle the bicycle from under Veronica's bumper.

'Careful,' Phil said. 'Don't scratch my paintwork.'

Agnes saw the man's dark frown and stepped in again. 'Is your bicycle damaged?' she asked.

'If it is, you'll owe me for a new one.'

He took a long time to inspect his bicycle, spinning the wheels and testing the handlebars. Agnes looked at her watch and agonised over the time.

'Will you be much longer?' she asked finally. 'Only I have an appointment.'

He gave her a grim look. 'Aye, I could tell you were in a hurry.'

Finally, after what seemed like an unbearably long time, the man seemed to decide his bicycle was roadworthy after all.

'I'm glad it's all right,' Agnes said, relieved.

'Time will tell, won't it?'

'Are you sure you're not injured? I'm a nurse, you see, and—'

'You're a ruddy menace, that's what you are!' He swung his leg over his bicycle and was gone.

Agnes watched him as he cycled off down the road, muttering to himself. She couldn't make out what he was saying, but something told her she wouldn't have wanted to hear it.

'What a charming man,' Phil commented dryly. 'I do hope for your sake they're not all like him.'

'You can't really blame him, can you?' Agnes sighed. 'So much for making a good impression!'

Phil giggled. 'We certainly made an impression on his bicycle!'

'It's not funny, Phil. I told you not to drive so fast. I'm supposed to be here to nurse people, not put them in hospital!'

'It was an accident.' Phil shrugged. 'Anyway, you saw him. He was perfectly fine. Now, shall we go?'

'I think I'd prefer to find my way to the Miners' Welfare Institute by myself,' Agnes said. 'It might be easier on foot.' And safer, she added silently.

'But what about your things?'

'It's only one suitcase and my medical bag. I should be able to manage them on my bicycle.'

'Well, if you're sure?' Phil opened the boot and helped Agnes unload her bicycle and suitcase. Then they stood for a moment, looking at each other awkwardly.

'Well, cheerio, my dear.' Phil lunged forward and hugged her fiercely. 'I'll miss you, old thing,' she mumbled into her shoulder.

Agnes hesitated, too surprised to respond. Phil had always been an unsentimental type. In fact, she could be positively hard-faced at times.

'Steady on!' She tried to make light of it, disentangling herself from her friend's embrace. 'I'll be coming back to Steeple Street soon. I have to report regularly to Miss Gale, remember?'

'I know. But it won't be the same, will it?'

No, Agnes thought a moment later as she watched Phil manoeuvring Veronica haphazardly back down the narrow high street. It won't be the same at all.

Chapter Two

After cycling around the deserted streets a few times, Agnes finally found the solid, red-brick building with a sign over the door reading 'Miners' Welfare Institute and Reading Room'.

There was an elderly man waiting on the step, his tall, thin frame stooped over a walking stick. He approached Agnes as she climbed off her bicycle.

'Miss Sheridan? I'm Eric Wardle, from the Miners' Welfare Committee. I'm the one who's been in correspondence with your Miss Gale.'

'Oh, yes, Mr Wardle. How do you do?' As she went to shake his hand, Agnes found herself looking up into a pair of bright blue eyes and realised she had been wrong about Eric Wardle. In spite of his lined, weary face and bent frame, he was no older than his late forties. She wondered what terrible illness had aged him before his time. 'I'm sorry I'm a little late. It took me a while to find this place.'

Eric Wardle waved away her words. 'No matter, lass, tha's here now. Come wi' me, I'll take you up to the committee room. They're all waiting for thee.'

The Miners' Welfare Institute had an unmistakably masculine air about it. The walls of the long passageway were lined with photographs of various sports teams, arms folded, posing proudly in football shorts or cricket whites, and groups of older men cradling pigeons outside their lofts. The lingering smell of cigarette smoke hung in the air mingled with the musky scent of stale sweat. From a half-open doorway at the far end of the long passage, Agnes could hear the distant sound of a piano playing.

Eric Wardle hobbled ahead of her past a glass cabinet full of gleaming trophies, and up a narrow staircase to a door marked with a brass sign saying 'Committee Room'. From beyond the door came the sound of men's voices, raised in what sounded like a heated debate.

'Here we are.' He turned to smile at her as he pushed the door open. 'No need to fear, lass. They won't bite you. Well, most of 'em, anyway.'

'Oh, I'm not afraid,' Agnes assured him, adjusting her cap and squaring her shoulders.

Eric Wardle sent her a considering look. 'Nay,' he said. 'Tha doesn't strike me as the fearful type.'

Four men sat at a long table in front of the window. They stopped talking when Agnes walked in, and rose to their feet, but only three pairs of eyes turned to look at her. The man at the far end of the row kept his gaze fixed on the papers on the table in front of him, as if he had more important matters on his mind than greeting a lady.

'Now then,' Eric Wardle said. 'This is Miss Sheridan, who's to be our new district nurse.' He pulled out the solitary chair on the opposite side of the table for Agnes to sit down, then shuffled slowly to join the other men, taking the seat that had been left for him in the centre of the row. Agnes noted the quietly respectful way the others moved aside to make room for him. 'Miss Sheridan, this is Sam Maskell, one of the overmen at the pit, this is Reg Willis, Tom Chadwick – and this is Seth Stanhope, the union branch secretary.'

'We've met.' Seth Stanhope lifted his scowling grey gaze from his papers at last and Agnes felt an unpleasant jolt of recognition.

'Now then,' Eric Wardle continued, 'as Chairman of the

8

Welfare Committee, I'm calling this meeting to order. Let's be as quick as we can, shall we? We've all got homes to go to, and I daresay Miss Sheridan will be worn out after her journey from Leeds.'

Agnes deliberately turned her attention from Seth Stanhope to the other men. They looked slightly uncomfortable, sitting at the table done up in their Sunday best suits. The small wiry man on the end, Reg Willis, kept running one finger around the inside of his starched shirt collar as if it was strangling him, while Tom Chadwick blushed furiously, as if he had never seen a woman before in his life. Only Sam Maskell seemed at ease, leaning back in his chair, his waistcoat straining over his portly belly.

'Now then, Miss Sheridan,' Eric Wardle said. 'As Miss Gale has probably told you, we've never had a district nurse in Bowden before, and I must confess we're at a bit of a loss as to what tha'll be doing in the village. Perhaps you could tell us?'

Agnes considered the question for a moment. 'Well,' she said finally, 'I suppose one of my duties will be to assist the doctor.'

'Assist him?' Sam Maskell laughed. 'Then tha'll have an easy life, since that lazy bugger niver does owt!'

'Shh!' Eric frowned at him. 'We'll have no pit talk in front of the lady, if you please. Go on, Miss Sheridan.'

'But mainly I'll be doing all I can to nurse the miners and their families, since my position is being funded by the Miners' Welfare,' Agnes continued. 'I'll be visiting the chronically ill patients, giving them whatever care is needed. I'll dress wounds, give help with feeding and bathing. I'll also be acting as a midwife, and advising mothers on the best way to care for their children—'

'My missus wouldn't thank you for that!' Reg Willis interrupted. 'She never takes advice from anybody.'

'Nor mine,' Sam Maskell agreed. 'And they don't need any advice on having babies, neither. They've been doing it for years.'

'I reckon mine needs advice on how not to have 'em,' Tom Chadwick said gloomily. 'Then maybe we wouldn't have so many mouths to feed.'

Sam slapped him on the shoulder. 'If tha doesn't know where all them bairns come from by now, Tom lad, then you're beyond help, even from t'nurse!'

'It's part of the nurse's job to prevent illness as well as treating it.' Agnes raised her voice over their laughter. 'That means giving advice and promoting good health and hygiene.'

'Oh, Lord, listen to her!' Sam Maskell guffawed again. 'Tha'll have a job on tha hands here, lass.'

'Sam's right,' Eric nodded. 'We don't care much for change in Bowden.' He smiled apologetically. 'I in't sure how we'll take to your new-fangled ideas.'

Agnes frowned. 'Then may I ask why I'm here?'

'Good question,' Seth Stanhope muttered from the far end of the table.

'The Miners' Welfare Committee decided it were time we had a district nurse in the village,' Eric Wardle said, glaring at Seth. 'I didn't say we didn't need thee, Miss Sheridan. I just think tha'll have a hard time winning people over.'

'I'll do my best to persuade them to my way of thinking,' Agnes said.

'I daresay tha'll have a good try.' Eric Wardle looked thoughtful. 'Now, I don't know about you, but I reckon we've heard enough. So if there are no more questions for Miss Sheridan . . . ?' He glanced quickly up and down the table. The other men shook their heads. 'Good. Then I daresay you'll be wanting to settle in to your new lodgings,

Miss Sheridan. We've arranged for you to stay with t'doctor, since you'll be working with him. Dr Rutherford is an elderly widower and his housekeeper Mrs Bannister lives in, so it's all quite respectable. I hope that suits?'

'I'm sure I'll be very comfortable there,' Agnes said.

'I wouldn't bet on that, not with that baggage Mrs Bannister in charge!' Sam Maskell grinned, showing several gaps where his teeth had once been. 'Stay on the right side of her, miss, that's all I'm saying.'

'Now then, Sam. Don't you go putting the poor lass off.' Eric turned to Agnes, his smile back in place. 'The doctor lives a fair distance away, and it's easy to get lost. One of us should go with you, show you the way. Perhaps Seth—'

Agnes caught his eye. It was hard to tell which of them was more dismayed at the suggestion. 'There's no need,' she said quickly. 'I'm sure I can find it if you give me directions.'

'Are you certain, miss? As I said, it's a fair distance.'

'I've got my bicycle.' Agnes ignored the dark look Seth sent her. 'And I'm quite good at finding my way around, once I've got my bearings.'

Eric Wardle rose to his feet slowly, and once again Agnes noticed how heavily he leaned on his stick. Pott's disease, she guessed, judging by the unnatural curve of his spine. He held himself so rigidly, she was sure he must be wearing a brace underneath his shirt.

'Tha can't miss it,' he said. 'It's right on t'edge of village, on t'opposite side to the pit. Tha, will have come in that way, I expect? The road from Leeds passes through that end of Bowden.'

'All the best people live out there,' Reg Willis said. 'As far away from t'pit as they can get. They don't like the smoke and the smell, y'see.'

11

'The doctor's house stands by itself, as the hill rises,' Eric continued. 'Just before the lane that goes up to t'big house.'

'The big house?' Agnes queried.

'Where the Haverstocks live,' Reg Willis put in. 'The pit owners,' he explained, as Agnes looked puzzled.

'They live up on t'hill. So they can look down on us all,' Tom Chadwick said, and the other men laughed. Except for Seth Stanhope, who once again failed to crack a smile.

Eric Wardle watched from the window as Agnes Sheridan cycled off up the road, then turned to his fellow committee members. 'Well?' he said. 'What did you think of our new district nurse?'

'I didn't expect her to be so young. Or so pretty.' Reg Willis leered. 'Might almost be worth getting sick to find her at my bedside.'

'She wouldn't get anywhere near you,' Sam Maskell said. 'Your missus would see her off with a rolling pin long before she caught sight of you in your combinations!'

'True,' Reg agreed gloomily.

'I don't suppose your missus will be the only one,' Tom Chadwick said. 'I can't see anyone in Bowden taking to her. She seems like a sharp little madam to me.'

'We'll have to see, won't we?' Eric looked down the table at Seth Stanhope. 'What do you reckon, Seth? You've been very quiet on the subject.'

Seth gathered up his papers. 'You know what I think.'

'He doesn't like her,' Reg said, grinning. 'He's taken agin' her, I can tell.'

'It's nowt to do wi' her. I just think the money could be better spent elsewhere, that's all. Especially when there's trouble coming.'

The other men shook their heads. 'Here he goes again,' Tom sighed.

'Anyone would think he were looking for trouble,' Reg muttered.

'You think I want another strike like the last one?' Seth turned on him. 'This colliery nearly went to the wall five year ago, and the rest of us with it. You think I want that to happen?'

'It won't come to that, lad,' Sam said patiently. 'There's no strike coming.'

'No strike? Have you been paying attention to what's going on? The government have said they want the mine owners to increase our shifts and cut our pay by thirteen per cent. Thirteen per cent! You think the miners will stand for it? Because I certainly won't.' Seth shook his head. 'I'm telling you, there's trouble coming whether we want it or not. And we should be putting the Miners' Welfare contributions towards that, not wasting it on bloody nurses!'

The other men fell silent. Everyone was wary of Seth Stanhope's quick temper, which never seemed too far from the surface these days. But Eric recognised the passion – and the fear – behind his angry words.

'Happen you're right, Seth lad,' he said. 'But it's all been decided now, and the money's been set aside, so there's nothing more to be said. Anyway, it's not as if we can't change our mind, if needs be. Miss Gale was very clear on that.'

'I'd be surprised if she don't turn tail and run herself, once she sees this place,' Tom said.

'I in't so sure.' Eric thought about the look of fearless determination in Agnes Sheridan's brown eyes. 'I don't think she's one to give in easily. She knows her own mind, that's for sure.'

'Aye, God help us,' Seth Stanhope muttered.

Eric smiled to himself. Agnes Sheridan had only been in Bowden for five minutes, and she'd already rattled Seth Stanhope's cage. He wondered how many more people she would manage to rattle.

Chapter Three

It was late afternoon by the time Agnes reached Dr Rutherford's house. As Mr Wardle had directed, it was right on the edge of the village, hidden from the lane by a high, ivy-covered wall. Dr Rutherford was a man who liked his privacy, Agnes decided, as she pushed her bicycle through the tall, wrought-iron gates.

The house was beautiful, big and rambling, with mullioned windows and mellow grey brickwork. Agnes propped her bicycle against the porch, brushed down her coat, straightened her cap and tugged on the bell pull. A moment later she heard a woman's voice from inside.

'Jinny? Jinny, there's someone at the door.' There was a pause, then, more impatiently, 'Jinny? Are you there? Oh, for heaven's sake! Where is that girl?'

Agnes waited, her hand hovering over the bell. She was just wondering whether to give it another tug when she heard footsteps approaching. A moment later the front door swung open and a woman stood before her.

Agnes' gaze travelled up to her unsmiling face. The woman was in her fifties, tall and upright. Her carefully curled light brown hair did nothing to soften her hard-boned, masculine features.

'Yes?' she snapped.

Agnes straightened her shoulders. 'My name is Agnes Sheridan. I'm the new nurse.'

The corners of the woman's mouth turned down even further. 'Oh, is it today you're supposed to arrive? No one mentioned it to me.' She let out a heavy sigh, then said, 'Well, in that case I suppose you had better come in.'

Agnes carried her suitcase over the threshold and stepped into the large, airy hall.

'You must be Mrs Bannister?' she said.

The woman's glacial eyes narrowed. 'Who told you that?'

She looked so put out about it, Agnes was slightly flustered, wondering if she had made a mistake. 'Mr Wardle at the Welfare Committee.'

'Oh, the Welfare Committee.' The woman's mouth tightened in disdain. 'Don't talk to me about them. Making free with people's houses, imposing on their good nature—'

Before Agnes had a chance to reply, a flustered-looking girl came rushing up the kitchen steps, wiping her hands on her oversized white apron.

'Were you calling me, ma'am?' she asked breathlessly.

Mrs Bannister turned to her, frowning. 'It's too late now, you silly girl, I've opened the door myself. But you must come the minute I call in future.'

'Yes, ma'am. Sorry, ma'am.'

Agnes looked at the maid with sympathy. She was a child, barely more than twelve or thirteen. A skinny little thing, with pale eyes and a narrow, washed-out face framed by a white linen cap. Agnes wondered what Dottie, the maid at Steeple Street, would have done if anyone had spoken to her like that. Taken off her apron and marched straight out of the front door, she suspected.

'Yes, well, never mind. Take Miss Sheridan's bag up to her room, if you please. And bring us some tea in the drawing room. And some sandwiches, too. I suppose you'll be wanting something to eat?' She made it sound like an accusation.

'That would be very nice, if it's not too much trouble?' Agnes replied politely.

'Too much trouble, she says!' Mrs Bannister rolled her eyes. 'Well, don't just stand there gawping, Jinny!' She clapped her hands and the girl instantly jumped to attention, grabbing Agnes' suitcase and hauling it towards the curving staircase. The case was heavy and Agnes could hardly bear to watch her skinny arms struggling to lift it.

Mrs Bannister peered out of the glass panel beside the front door. 'Is that your bicycle out there? It'll have to go round the back of the house. We can't have it cluttering up the porch like that. Dr Rutherford likes everything kept nice.'

'I'm sorry. I'll move it at once.'

'No need. I'll get Jinny to do it later, before the doctor gets home.'

'Oh. Is Dr Rutherford on his rounds?'

'On a Sunday? I should think not.' Mrs Bannister looked scandalised. 'Dr Rutherford has gone fishing with Sir Edward this afternoon. I am not expecting him home until later. Now, I'll show you into the drawing room.'

Agnes would have preferred to go up to her own room, but Mrs Bannister seemed so put out about everything, she didn't want to antagonise her further.

The drawing room, with its crackling fire and leather Chesterfield sofas, was almost too perfect to be homely. Everything was immaculately arranged, from the Indian rugs on the polished wooden floor, to the artful vase of chrysanthemums on the console table.

It reminded Agnes of the large, comfortable house in leafy North London where she had grown up. Her mother had always had such a sense of style and eye for detail, nothing was ever allowed to be out of place.

At one end of the room was a pair of French doors leading out to the garden. Agnes went over to look out of them. The garden too was perfect, with manicured lawns, flowering shrubs and trees, and an ornamental pond in the centre.

'Your garden is very beautiful,' she commented.

'It is, isn't it? The doctor is very particular about it.'

'We had a big garden at the district nurses' house in Leeds, but it was nowhere near as well kept as this.' Agnes thought of Steeple Street, with its overgrown grass, shrubs and roses allowed to run wild, and the wasps getting drunk on drifts of fallen apples and plums.

She turned away from the window, an unexpected lump rising in her throat.

The door opened and Jinny the maid came in, struggling with a silver tea tray. Mrs Bannister greeted her with a sour look.

'Ah, there you are, Jinny. You took your time, I must say. Well, don't just stand there, girl. Put it on the table before you drop the lot.'

Agnes bit her lip, hardly daring to watch as the tray wobbled dangerously in Jinny's hands. Miraculously, she managed to set it down without spilling anything.

Mrs Bannister took the lid off the pot and peered into it. 'How much tea did you put in?'

Jinny's gaze dropped to the rug. 'I – I can't remember, ma'am,' she mumbled.

'Can't remember? Good gracious, girl, it's a simple enough question! I suppose you were daydreaming again? How on earth can you hope to make a pot of tea correctly if you don't think about these things?' She put the lid back on the pot and scanned the tray. 'And where is the tea strainer?'

'I—' Jinny gulped. The poor girl looked near to tears.

Mrs Bannister tutted. 'Take it away,' she said, with a dismissive wave of her hand. 'And come back when you've managed to do it properly. I don't know,' she sighed, as

Jinny stumbled off with the tray. 'That girl doesn't seem to be able to do the simplest tasks. You would have thought she would pay attention and try to improve herself, wouldn't you? But I suppose coming from a family like hers . . . ' She shook her head, her expression sorrowful.

Agnes stared at Mrs Bannister's haughty profile and suddenly realised it wasn't just the house that reminded her of her mother. Agnes had seen the same curl of disdain on Elizabeth Sheridan's lips when something wasn't quite up to her standards. Nothing was ever right for her.

Including you. The thought flashed through Agnes' mind, the pain catching her unawares before she had time to steel herself against it.

She forced herself to think of something else. 'What time did you say Dr Rutherford would be home?' she asked.

'I didn't,' Mrs Bannister replied. 'But I daresay he will be invited to dine at Haverstock Hall, and then he and Sir Edward are bound to end up playing cards until well into the evening.'

'What a pity,' Agnes said. 'I had hoped he might be here to meet me.'

'Yes, well, I expect he forgot you were coming, just as I did.' Mrs Bannister sent her a scathing look. 'I suppose you think you are very important, Miss Sheridan, but I assure you the doctor and I have other matters to think about besides your arrival.'

At that moment Jinny returned with a fresh pot of tea, which mercifully passed Mrs Bannister's critical examination. Agnes found herself holding her breath as much as poor Jinny, until the housekeeper waved the girl away.

'So you've come from Leeds?' Mrs Bannister said as she passed Agnes her cup. 'You don't sound local.'

'I'm not. I'm from London originally.' Agnes avoided her gaze as she stirred her tea.

'London?' Mrs Bannister perked up, setting down her cup. 'Then you must know the Hollister-Bennetts?'

'I'm afraid I don't.'

'Are you sure? They're terribly well known in society. How about the Duvalls? Or Lord and Lady Penhaven?'

Agnes shook her head. 'I'm sorry. I've never heard of them.'

'Well, I must say, I am surprised. I thought everyone had heard of Lord Penhaven.' Mrs Bannister looked unimpressed. Agnes realised she had been found as wanting as poor Jinny.

'I myself spent a great deal of time with the aristocracy when I worked for the Charteris family,' Mrs Bannister went on. 'Their family seat was in North Yorkshire, but they kept a house in London so their daughters could do the Season. We met so many interesting people. Such wonderful parties.' She smiled fondly at the memory. 'So what kind of family do you come from, Miss Sheridan?'

Agnes' stomach sank at the question. 'Well, my father is a doctor. '

'What kind of doctor?' Mrs Bannister pounced.

'A GP. But he's retired now.' The Great War had seen to that. Charles Sheridan had returned from France a changed man. Unable to forget the horrors that he had witnessed in the trenches, he had withdrawn from his beloved practice, and from his family.

'And your mother? I suppose she does a great deal of work for charity?'

'I suppose so.' Agnes felt a chill in her heart, thinking about Elizabeth Sheridan.

'Suppose? You mean, you don't know?'

Agnes stared into her cup, afraid to allow Mrs Bannister to look into her eyes in case she gave herself away. She couldn't imagine what the housekeeper would say if she told her she hadn't seen or spoken to her mother in months.

'It's difficult to keep up with her . . . she's always so busy,' Agnes said vaguely.

'Hmm.' Mrs Bannister paused for a moment. Then she said, 'Are you courting, Miss Sheridan?'

Agnes looked at her, taken aback. 'I don't understand?'

'It's a simple enough question, surely? Do you have a young man?'

Agnes looked down at her left hand, where she had once worn Daniel's engagement ring. The imprint had faded long ago. 'No,' she said.

'I'm glad to hear it.' Mrs Bannister helped herself to another cup of tea. 'We have a certain position to maintain here, Miss Sheridan. I wouldn't want Dr Rutherford's good name being put at risk in any way.'

'Put at risk?'

'Oh, you know. This isn't London or Leeds, Miss Sheridan. Everyone knows everyone else's business here. If you were to have all sorts of gentlemen callers, it might cause people to gossip.'

'I think you'll find I'm quite respectable,' Agnes replied, tight-lipped. But even as she said it, she could see her mother's look of scorn.

You have disgraced this family, Agnes.

'We shall see, won't we? Although I must say, I am still not happy about the lodging arrangements. I can't think why Dr Rutherford agreed to it without consulting me first. Aside from all the extra work, it hardly seems proper to have a young unmarried girl living under the same roof as a widower.'

Agnes glanced at the display of silver-framed photographs on the side table. Several of them seemed to feature an elderly, white-haired man, whom she took to be the mysterious doctor. Could Mrs Bannister seriously believe she might have designs on him?

21

'I'm sure Dr Rutherford and I can maintain a perfectly respectable working relationship,' she said, trying to stop herself laughing out loud.

'Nevertheless, I would prefer it if we could establish certain rules from the start,' Mrs Bannister said.

'Such as?'

After five minutes, Agnes began to feel sorry she had asked the question. The housekeeper's list of rules and regulations made her head spin. At what hours she could use the bathroom, which rooms downstairs she could occupy and which she couldn't, which visitors to the house were considered suitable and when they could call.

Agnes listened carefully, but she could barely take it all in. Once again, she longed for Steeple Street, where Miss Gale had managed to keep a house full of district nurses in order with little more than mutual trust and good sense.

'I would like you to eat in the kitchen as Dr Rutherford prefers to dine alone,' Mrs Bannister was saying. 'Meals are included in your board and lodging, as is cleaning your room, but if you want Jinny to do your laundry for you, then you'll have to come to a separate arrangement with her. Please be clear, Miss Sheridan, that we are employed by Dr Rutherford. We are not here to skivvy for *you*.'

'I wouldn't expect it,' Agnes replied, stifling a yawn. She longed to escape and retire to her room.

Sam Maskell's words came back to her. *Stay on the right side of her, miss, that's all I'm saying.*

'I'm glad we understand each other,' Mrs Bannister said. 'Another sandwich, Miss Sheridan?'

Agnes looked at the plate that was waved under her nose. *Are you sure I don't have to pay for it?* she was tempted to ask, but was saved by the sound of the front doorbell.

Agnes looked up hopefully. 'Perhaps that's the doctor?' she said.

'I very much doubt he would be ringing on his own front door,' Mrs Bannister replied, nibbling at the corner of a potted meat sandwich.

The doorbell rang again.

'I don't mind waiting, if you need to go and answer it?' Agnes said, but the housekeeper shook her head.

'It is not my place to answer the door like a common maid,' she dismissed. 'Do calm yourself, Miss Sheridan. You're as jumpy as a cat.'

A moment later they heard the sound of Jinny's footsteps scuttling across the hall. Mrs Bannister was in the middle of instructing Agnes about when it was acceptable to speak to the doctor outside surgery hours, but her attention was tuned to the sound of the voices coming from the hall.

She could hear a child, high-pitched and agitated, and Jinny, sounding as if she was trying to calm him. Agnes longed to go and find out for herself what was wrong, but she was pinned in her seat by Mrs Bannister's steely, forbidding gaze.

Finally there was a knock on the door and Jinny appeared in the doorway.

'Laurie Toller's here, Mrs Bannister,' she said, looking anxious. 'He says his father's having another one of his coughing fits and can't breathe. He needs the doctor.'

'Yes, well, the doctor isn't here, is he?' Mrs Bannister looked annoyed. 'Besides, he should know Dr Rutherford never makes house calls on a Sunday.'

'But he says his dad's right bad—'

'Perhaps I could go and see him?' Agnes said, putting down her plate.

'You'll do no such thing!' Mrs Bannister snapped. 'Dr Rutherford wouldn't like that at all, I'm sure.' She turned back to Jinny. 'Tell the child his father will have to come to the surgery tomorrow morning.'

'But—'

'You heard me, girl.'

The maid bobbed her head and left. Agnes tried to listen to what was going on outside, but she couldn't hear for the sound of Mrs Bannister going on, complaining about people turning up unannounced outside surgery hours.

Finally, Agnes could bear it no longer. 'Are you sure I shouldn't go and see this man?'

Mrs Bannister's lip curled. 'Good heavens, no! If you do it for one, then the next thing you know we'll have people lining up at our door at all hours, expecting to be seen. And without a penny in their pockets, half the time!'

'As Queen's Nurses, we are told never to withhold treatment from a patient in need, just because they can't afford to pay us,' Agnes said.

'Then more fool you.' Mrs Bannister sent her a narrow-eyed, assessing look. 'I suppose you're one of those modern women, full of ideas about how the world should be,' she said. 'If you are, I can tell you now you won't get on very well in this village. The people here are cunning. They'll take advantage of you as soon as look at you.' She proffered the plate. 'Are you sure you won't have another sandwich? You've hardly eaten a thing.'

'I'm not hungry.' In truth, her stomach was gnawing, but Agnes would rather have starved than spend another moment in the housekeeper's company. 'I think I would like to go to my room, if you don't mind?'

'Already? But it's barely six o'clock.' Mrs Bannister frowned at the clock on the mantelpiece. 'Oh, well, I suppose if that's what you want ... We'll have to finish going through the rules in the morning,' she said, putting down her plate. 'Now please remember, breakfast is at eight o'clock sharp, and yours will be served in the kitchen. Morning surgery is at nine, and the doctor can't be disturbed before then ... '

Agnes left her talking, and went up to her room. She couldn't hope to remember all the rules, so why listen to them?

At least her room seemed pleasant enough. Agnes took her time unpacking her suitcase. Most of her case was taken up with her medical equipment and supplies, with little space given over to her few personal belongings.

How her old room mate Polly would envy all the empty cupboards in her new room, Agnes thought as she hung up her clothes. But even with endless amounts of space, Polly would probably still have her things strewn all over the place as usual ...

Agnes stopped, tensing herself against the painful memory. She had only been gone for a few hours, but she already missed Steeple Street dreadfully. The district nurses' house had become her home during the six months of her training. She longed for the steady routine of daily life there, the shared mealtimes gathered around the big dining table with the other nurses, telling stories about their rounds. No matter how badly the day had gone, there would always be sympathy and advice and someone to make her laugh off her troubles. The other nurses had become her family – Phil, Polly, old Miss Hook and her terrible poetry, and the entirely misnamed Miss Goode, the most spiteful gossip Agnes had ever known.

And then there was Bess Bradshaw, the Assistant Nursing Superintendent. She and Agnes had got off to the worst possible start, but over the months Agnes had come to appreciate her wisdom and her kindness.

It was at Steeple Street that Agnes had managed to rebuild her shattered life after her family abandoned her.

She had made friends and found hope for a future she never thought she would have.

She pushed the thoughts from her mind. Bowden was her home now, and she had to start thinking of it that way. Once again, she had to put the past behind her and look to the future.

Chapter Four

The insistent clang of a bell woke Agnes up with a start.

At first she thought she must be dreaming. She had heard the pit hooter sound at ten, calling the men to the night shift, just as she had put away her book to settle down for the night. But the sound of the bell was different, an urgent clamour that had Agnes springing out of bed before she even knew what was happening.

She hurried to the window and looked out. Dr Rutherford's house was on the other side of the village, but she could see a stream of bobbing lights heading off up the lane towards the colliery.

Agnes pulled on her dressing gown and hurried downstairs to find Mrs Bannister closing the front door. Even though it was well past midnight, the housekeeper was fully dressed, not a hair out of place, as if she hadn't been to bed.

She turned to face Agnes, her brows rising. 'Why, Miss Sheridan, what on earth are you doing up at this hour?' she asked.

'The noise woke me. What's going on?'

'It's the calamity bell. It rings when there's been an accident at the pit.' She looked Agnes up and down, her mouth tightening in disapproval. 'I must say, Miss Sheridan, I did mention in my rules that you shouldn't wander around the house in your night attire. What if Dr Rutherford were to see you?'

'I'm sure Dr Rutherford must have seen a woman in a

27

nightgown before!' Agnes snapped back. 'Where is he now?'

'Why, he's gone down to the colliery, of course. I've just seen him off a minute ago. And I'm sure he has seen many women in their nightgowns, but not under this roof – Miss Sheridan? Are you listening to me?' Her voice followed Agnes as she ran back upstairs to her room.

She dressed quickly, pulling on her blue dress and apron and jamming her feet into her stout black shoes. She hurried back downstairs a minute later, clutching her leather Gladstone bag in one hand and pushing her chestnut curls under her cap with the other.

Mrs Bannister was still in the hall, stiff with disapproval. Agnes hurried past her to fetch her coat from the hook.

'Where did you put my bicycle?' she asked over her shoulder.

'In the shed at the back of the house. Why? Where do you think you're going?'

'To the colliery, of course. Dr Rutherford might need me.'

The housekeeper sneered. 'I very much doubt that. What on earth could *you* do?'

'I won't know that until I get there, will I?' Agnes moved to the front door, but Mrs Bannister stepped in front of her, barring her path.

'You'll only be in the way,' she said. 'If Dr Rutherford had wanted you there he would have taken you with him.'

Agnes sidestepped her and hurried outside into the cold, windy night. It took her a while to find the shed, stumbling around in the darkness, and even longer to unearth her bicycle from where Mrs Bannister had buried it deep under a load of gardening equipment. Agnes' hands were scratched and filthy by the time she had dragged it out from underneath a wheelbarrow.

She didn't need directions. All she had to do was follow

the people streaming down the lane. In the distance, the stark shape of the pit winding tower was illuminated eerily against the night sky by the glow of dozens of lanterns.

A crowd of people had gathered around the pit gates when she arrived: mostly they were women with children and babies in their arms, wrapped up against the biting March wind. Some were talking quietly amongst themselves while others were silent, their attention fixed on what was happening in the pit yard. The light from the lanterns showed their pinched, anxious faces. All the while the bell clanged, filling the air with its discordant, ominous sound.

Agnes shouldered her way through the crowd and approached the stocky man who stood watch by the gates. As he turned around, she saw it was Sam Maskell.

He frowned when he saw her. 'Now then, Nurse? What are you doing here?'

'I came to see if I could help. What's happened?' she asked.

He glanced back at the men milling around in the pit yard, his face impassive. 'Been an accident. The rescue team's just gone down there. Fire damp, they reckon.'

'Fire damp?'

'Build-up of methane gas in t'pit. It only needs a single spark and the whole lot goes up.'

'Is anyone injured?'

'No one knows. There's still a few men not accounted for. T'doctor's down there now.'

'Is there anything I can do?'

'Not until they start bringing them up. Could be a while yet.'

'Should I go down too?'

He shook his head. 'The mine's no place for you, lass.'

'But I might be able to help. '

'Nay,' he said kindly. 'If tha wants to help, go over there

29

and see to t'women. There might be bad news for some of 'em before too long,' he said grimly.

Agnes looked past him. Beyond the gates, she could see men going to and fro, the light from their lanterns bobbing in the darkness. She had seldom felt so helpless.

'Let me know if you need me,' she said, her voice lost over the clanging of the bell.

'Aye,' Sam said. But he had already turned away from her.

She returned to where the women were standing, more of them now, pressed close to the gates, shoulder to shoulder. Babies were crying, the sound mingling with the toll of the bell.

Suddenly she spotted a familiar face in the crowd. Dr Rutherford's maid, Jinny, was standing by the gates with an older woman who had a baby wrapped up in her arms and three more small children clinging to her coat. But she barely seemed to notice them as her anxious gaze scanned the yard beyond the gates.

Agnes pressed her way through the crowd towards them, calling to the girl. Jinny swung round.

'Miss? What are you doing here?'

'I came to see if I could help.' Agnes nodded past her to where the other woman stood. Close to, she could see that they must be related. They had the same narrow, colourless faces and pale eyes. Even bundled under a thick coat and layers of shawls, Agnes could see the woman was as thin as the girl. 'Is that your mother?'

'Aye, miss. My dad and two of my brothers are down there.'

Agnes looked at her closely. Jinny's face was as impassive as her mother's. 'I'm sure they'll be all right,' she said.

'Yes, miss.'

Agnes glanced towards the gates. 'I tried to go down there myself, but they wouldn't let me.'

'Down the pit? I shouldn't think they would, miss.' Jinny paused for a moment, then said, 'You can come and stand wi' us, if you want to?'

Agnes followed the girl over to where her mother was standing. The baby in her arms was howling, but she seemed utterly oblivious to it. Jinny took the child from her, rocking it gently. 'Ma, this is t'new nurse, come to lodge with Dr Rutherford,' she said.

Some of the other women regarded Agnes with interest and started murmuring amongst themselves, but Jinny's mother didn't register her presence at all. Her gaze was still fixed beyond the gates.

'I don't like it,' she muttered. 'They've been down there too long. It must be bad.'

'You mustn't mind Ma,' Jinny whispered. 'She's always like this when there's an accident down t'pit. My uncle died there, not three years since, and she's never forgotten it.'

'Sent him home to his missus on the back of a cart, wrapped in an old bit of sacking wi' "Property of Bowden Main Colliery" printed on it,' Jinny's mother spoke up, not looking at Agnes.

The baby cried in Jinny's arms. As she tried to shift its weight, the shawl slipped, and Agnes caught a glimpse of a little head in a knitted bonnet.

'And who's this?' she started to say, but Jinny's mother seemed to come to life, snatching the baby from her daughter's arms and swaddling him back in the shawl.

'Cover him up,' she snapped. 'He'll catch cold.'

Close by Agnes, another child began to whimper.

'I'm n-nithered, Ma,' the little mite cried, tugging on his mother's sleeve.

'Aye, well, there's nowt I can do about that,' the woman replied briskly. She put her arm around the shivering child, pulling him closer to her. 'It won't be long now,' she said, gazing towards the gate.

'Here.' Agnes took off her coat and slipped it around the child's shoulders.

'Nay—' His mother started to protest, but Agnes shook her head.

'Please,' she said. 'I might as well be of some use, as I'm here.'

The woman gave her a quick, unsmiling nod. 'Much obliged, I'm sure,' she muttered.

There was a sudden flurry of activity from beyond the gates, and all the women surged forward, craning their necks and pushing to see what was going on.

'They're bringing them up!' someone said.

Over Jinny's shoulder, Agnes saw figures emerging from the main building, silhouetted against the pool of light that spilled from the open doorway. A moment later a set of metal doors clanged open and two men emerged, carrying a stretcher between them. Agnes could feel the tension of the women around her as they strained to see.

Then the tide of whispers began.

'Who is it?'

'Can't tell.'

'Is he dead?'

'Looks like it. They've covered him up, any rate.'

Others started to emerge after that, one more on a stretcher, others on their feet, leaning heavily on companions for support. They staggered out of the lift gates, their faces upturned to the night sky, gulping in the cold, fresh air. Agnes couldn't make out their faces, but every line of their bodies cried out their relief at being alive.

Behind her, one of the women let out a cry. 'I can see our Matthew!' But the rest remained stoically silent, their attention fixed on the gates.

Gradually, news began to ripple through, as women passed along the names of the men who had come up. Still no one seemed to dare to celebrate. Only the occasional reassuring pat on the shoulder or strained smile gave away their true feelings.

In the yard, a cart drew up outside one of the outbuildings. Agnes felt a collective intake of breath among the women as a stretcher was loaded on to it.

'One dead, then.'

'Who is it? Has anyone said?'

'Here's Mr Maskell. He'll know.'

Sam Maskell opened the gate and came out, but no one moved. They all seemed to stay as rigid as statues, their eyes cast down while the overman moved among them, as if by not catching his eye they could somehow avert the bad news they had been dreading.

Finally, he found who he was looking for, on the other side of the crowd. There were words exchanged, and a cry of anguish went up. Two women separated themselves from the crowd and followed Sam Maskell through the pit gates into the yard. One of the women was crying while the other comforted her, one arm firmly around her shoulders to hold her up.

The overman closed the gate behind him with an ominous clang, and straight away the whispers started up again.

'Reckon it must have been Harry Kettle.'

'No! Not Harry.'

'He was no age, was he?'

'Twenty-three, same as my George. They went to school together.'

'His poor mother.'

'What about his wife? They've barely been married a year. And her with a baby on the way, too.'

Some minutes later the pit gates opened again. Without a word, the crowd parted, heads lowering in respect as the cart rolled slowly out of them. Agnes lowered her head too, but out of the corner of her eye she watched the solemn procession. The two women followed the cart. The younger one, her pregnant belly evident under her coat, had regained some of her composure as she walked slowly beside her mother-in-law, their faces stiff, staring straight ahead. Only her eyes, puffy and swollen from crying, gave away the grief she felt.

They were followed by a line of men, the miners who had come up from the pit, their faces and clothes black with coal. Some were limping, clinging to their fellows for support. The stench of dirt and sweat filled Agnes' nostrils as they passed.

As the last of the men passed by, the women began to shift and talk amongst themselves.

Agnes kept her gaze fixed on the cart as it rolled out of sight.

'Miss?' Agnes turned to face the woman holding out her coat to her. 'Tha'll be wanting this back,' she said.

'Thank you.' Agnes took the coat, still staring down the lane. Should she go after the cart? she wondered. She didn't know the family, but she might be able to offer some comfort to them . . .

As if the woman could read her thoughts, she said, 'I daresay Hannah Arkwright will lay him out, if that's what you're wondering. She allus helps out at times like this.'

Agnes stared back at the woman, but she was already walking away, joining the tide of others who were drifting back towards the colliery cottages with their children, talking quietly amongst themselves, leaving the new nurse standing alone at the pit gates.

Chapter Five

'One dead, three burns and a fractured femur.' Dr Rutherford leaned back in his leather chair. 'All in all, I think it could have been a great deal worse.'

Agnes thought of the poor pregnant girl, distraught with grief in her mother-in-law's arms. 'I think Harry Kettle's widow might feel differently about that, Doctor,' she said.

Dr Rutherford's bright blue eyes met hers over the top of his wire-rimmed spectacles. He was in his sixties, with thick snowy white hair that contrasted with his ruddy cheeks.

'I suppose you must think me very harsh, Miss Sheridan.' His voice was deep and rumbling, with a hint of the Highlands in it. 'But I'm afraid death and injury are the way of life for us in Bowden. There's barely a family in the village who hasn't lost someone down the pit. Mining is a dangerous business.'

'I'm beginning to realise that, sir.' Agnes had spent the past few weeks studying mining injuries in preparation for her placement. She knew all about nystagmus and pneumoconiosis, and had looked at enough grisly photographs of inflamed joints and crushed limbs to believe that nothing could shock her.

But the sight of Harry Kettle's body, wrapped in sacking and thrown on to the back of a cart, had moved her to her very core. As had the pathetic dignity of the procession that had followed behind, the miners with their blackened faces and pit clothes, the watching women silently giving thanks that it was not one of their men they were taking home.

Agnes hadn't been able to sleep for most of the night, thinking about it. She had finally drifted off just before dawn, only to be woken by the pit hooter sounding at six o'clock in the morning, summoning the men to their shift.

'Surely it won't be safe for them to go back underground so soon?' she had said to Jinny as she waited for her breakfast in the kitchen that morning.

'Aye, I expect they'll have to close that shaft for the time being. But there's another one the men can dig,' Jinny had replied. 'Either that or old Haverstock will send 'em to one of his other mines, along the valley. He won't let 'em stand idle, that's for sure. Not unless it suits him.'

Agnes shuddered. 'I'm surprised anyone would be willing to go back down the pit, after what happened.'

Jinny had sent Agnes a wise look as she forked rashers of bacon from the frying pan on to her plate.

'Their families have to eat, miss. If they don't work, they don't get paid. My dad and my brothers were stuck down t'pit for two hours last night, but they'll be back on their shift tonight, you can be sure of that. It's best not to think about it, so my dad says.'

But Agnes couldn't seem to stop thinking about it as she sat in Dr Rutherford's pleasant, book-lined surgery. She felt almost guilty that the men had to put their lives in so much danger while she lived in comfort.

'Poor Miss Sheridan.' Dr Rutherford looked at her kindly. 'I'm afraid you've had rather a rude introduction to Bowden one way and another, haven't you?' He paused. 'I'm sorry I wasn't here to greet you when you arrived yesterday, but unfortunately I had already promised Sir Edward some time ago that I would go fishing with him.

And believe me, one doesn't refuse a summons from the Haverstocks!'

Agnes pulled herself together enough to smile at him. 'It's quite all right, Doctor. I managed to settle in very well.'

'I'm glad to hear it. And I suppose you had Mrs Bannister to help you?'

Agnes paused. 'Yes,' she said carefully. 'She was most – instructive.'

'I'm sure she was.' Dr Rutherford gave her a knowing smile. 'Dear Mrs B, she's been with me since I arrived in the village twenty-odd years ago. D'you know, I remember my first day as if it were yesterday ... '

Agnes shifted restlessly in her seat and glanced at the clock. Morning surgery should have started at nine o'clock, and it was now a quarter-past. Next door, the waiting room was full of poorly patients waiting to see the doctor. But Dr Rutherford seemed in no hurry to do anything, settling back comfortably behind his desk, ready to reminisce.

She cleared her throat. 'If you don't mind, sir,' she ventured, 'I'd like to get started on my round as soon as possible.'

Dr Rutherford's bushy brows rose. 'You're very keen, Miss Sheridan?' He was smiling when he said it, but it still sounded like a criticism.

'Yes, sir.'

'Well, as it happens I have prepared some names for you.' He drew a sheet of paper from the top drawer of his desk and consulted it over the rim of his spectacles. 'They're mostly elderly, chronic problems – rheumatics, bronchitis, that sort of thing. I don't suppose you'll be able to do much for them, but I'm sure they'll be glad of a chat.' He handed the list over to her.

Agnes studied it. 'Which of these are the men from last night?' she asked.

Dr Rutherford looked perplexed. 'I'm sorry, I don't follow you . . . '

'The men who were injured down the pit?' Agnes prompted. 'The burns and the fractured femur?'

'Oh, I see. Well, the fracture and one of the burns were taken to hospital. And as for the other two – well, I wouldn't worry about them. I daresay their wives will look after them. That's the way things are done here.'

'All the same, I would like to check on them.'

'It really isn't necessary.'

'I'm being paid by the Miners' Welfare, so I should be paying attention to the miners' health, don't you think?'

Dr Rutherford regarded her across the desk, his smile fixed. 'Very well,' he said. He snatched the list from her, picked up his pen and scrawled a couple of names at the bottom. 'Visit them if you must. But I'm telling you now, they won't thank you for it. Bowden folk don't care for strangers poking about in their business.'

'So I've been told.' Agnes took the piece of paper from him.

'And you might as well add another name, since you're so anxious to involve yourself in the wellbeing of the miners. Jack Farnley. He cut his hand nearly a week ago. I've been meaning to call on him for the past couple of days.'

Agnes wrote down the name. 'I assume he'll need the wound checked, and the dressing changed?'

'If need be, I suppose.' Dr Rutherford shrugged. 'But mainly I want you to see if he's fit to go back to work yet. He's a good man, according to the pit manager. And with a hewer laid up in hospital after last night, and young Harry Kettle gone, I daresay Mr Shepherd would like him back as soon as he's able.'

Agnes flinched at the bluntness of the doctor's words.

But as he said, death and injury were the way of life in the village. Perhaps after twenty years it no longer affected him.

Agnes decided to call on Jack Farnley first, since his case seemed the most urgent on her list.

The Farnleys lived on the far side of the village, in one of the many streets of colliery cottages. The wind that had gusted through the village the previous day had died down, and now a thick, yellowing veil of mist hung over Bowden, obscuring the top of the winding tower. But Agnes could still hear the engines churning as she cycled down the hill towards the colliery. As she drew closer, she could almost feel its malevolent presence, turning the air thicker, tainting it with smoke, coal dust and engine oil.

The earth road was deeply rutted with cart tracks, and mud spattered her legs as she cycled past the tall iron gates. Agnes averted her gaze, not wanting to think about the previous night, and the cart rolling slowly across the yard, bearing poor Harry Kettle's body.

She had no trouble finding her way, even in the mist. The cottages were arranged in neat grids, each row separated from a line of privies opposite by a narrow lane. The whitewashed houses were all alike, simple single-storey dwellings with two small windows, one on either side of a green front door that opened straight out on to the lane.

Humble though they were, they were neat and well kept, and appealed to Agnes' sense of order, unlike the dark, twisting alleys and courtyards of Quarry Hill, where it was far too easy to get lost. Even the streets in Bowden were sensibly named. There was Top Row, Middle Row, End Row and Coalpit Row, the road closest to the mine. They were crossed by several more lanes. These were in numerical order, with First Lane closest to the mine.

As in Quarry Hill, Monday was washday. A group of

women were gathered around the water pump at the top of End Row, their arms full of buckets and poss tubs. They all fell silent and turned to look as Agnes rounded the corner. She gave them a smile and a wave, but they stared back in silence.

She cycled the length of End Row, bending low over the handlebars of her bicycle to dodge the washing lines that criss-crossed the narrow lane. But it was difficult to see in the mist, and sometimes she felt the wet slap of a shirt or a pair of combinations hanging limply in her path.

Finally, she found the Farnleys' cottage and propped her bicycle against the wall. As she approached the cottage, a mangy-looking dog appeared in the open doorway, its teeth bared in a snarl that stopped her in her tracks.

'What is it now, you daft beggar?' A woman appeared, wiping her hands on her apron. She saw Agnes and her expression fell. 'Oh. What can I do for thee?'

'I'm Miss Sheridan, the new district nurse.' Agnes kept her wary gaze fixed on the snarling dog at her side. 'Dr Rutherford has asked me to come and see your husband.'

'Oh, he has, has he?' Mrs Farnley folded her arms across her chest, her expression grim. Three small, grubby-faced children gathered around her skirt. 'I bet I know why, an' all.'

For a moment Mrs Farnley glared at her. Then, just as Agnes had started to think she might never move, she turned away, muttering, 'Tha'd best come in.'

'Thank you.' Agnes inched her way past the dog, being careful to keep her Gladstone bag between herself and its jaws. It let out a low growl, but didn't move towards her.

Inside the cottage was small and simple, consisting of one room and what seemed to be a lean-to scullery off to one side, with another small room off to the other. A wooden ladder in the corner led up to the roof space. The air was damp and hot, a fug of steam billowing from the copper tank, which squatted on a low brick structure in the corner. Washing day was in full swing, with a galvanised tub set out on the stone-flagged floor, and wooden clothes horses arranged around the fire.

Jack Farnley was sitting in a chair by the fireplace, barricaded behind rows of drying washing, his heavily bandaged hand lying uselessly in his lap. Two more children sat on the floor at his feet, playing with a pack of cards. He looked up at Agnes, then at his wife.

'It's t'new nurse,' Mrs Farnley muttered in reply to his unspoken question. 'T'doctor sent her to have a look at you.' A meaningful look passed between them, which Agnes didn't quite understand.

'Hello, Mr Farnley. How are you feeling today?' Agnes satisfied herself that the table was clean, and set down her bag.

'Not too bad, Nurse.' Mr Farnley gazed at his hand. The dog plodded over and lay down beside him.

His wife shook her head. 'Not too bad!' she tutted. 'It were hanging off not a few days since.'

'I'll give my hands a wash and we'll have a look, shall we?' Agnes started to take her soap and towel out of the pocket at the front of her bag, but Mrs Farnley interrupted her.

'Afore tha' starts, I want to know how much it will cost us,' she said.

'Be quiet, woman!' Mr Farnley said, tight-lipped.

'Nay, I'll not. I know you lot, tha niver does nowt for free. That doctor doesn't leave without a shilling in his pocket.' She grimaced.

'It's quite all right, Mrs Farnley. Any treatment I offer is covered by your contributions to the Miners' Welfare Fund.'

'Oh, aye?' Mrs Farnley's chin lifted. 'That's all right, then.'

'Nay, I don't want charity,' Mr Farnley put in quickly.

'It in't charity, is it? You heard what she said, it comes out of your contributions. You've been putting in long enough, it's only right you should start taking out.' Mrs Farnley looked back at the soap and towel in Agnes' hands. 'Tha'll be wanting a bowl of hot water to go wi' that, I suppose?'

'Yes, please. And another bowl of clean water to clean the wound, if you don't mind?'

Once Mrs Farnley had fetched the bowls and filled them from the copper, she went back to her washing, rubbing at the collar of a shirt with a lump of strong-smelling green soap. But Agnes could feel the other woman watching her suspiciously from across the room as she set about carefully removing Mr Farnley's dressing.

The wound was so savagely deep and ugly, it caught her unawares. Agnes tried to brace herself, but she was too late.

'Not pretty, is it?' Jack Farnley said grimly.

'No, it isn't.' But it wasn't just the sight of the jagged, gaping flesh that made the bile rise in the back of her throat. There was a strange, sickly odour coming from the wound, like nothing she had ever smelled before.

'Hannah Arkwright gave us some of her special ointment to put on it,' Mrs Farnley answered her unspoken question. 'She's been coming round to change his bandages. She won't be too happy about you interfering in her treatment, I'm sure,' she added, looking nervous.

Agnes glanced over her shoulder. 'Who is Hannah Arkwright?'

'She heals people. She's got the gift.' Mrs Farnley nodded towards her husband. 'She made that ointment special for us. Got all sorts of rare herbs in it. She did tell me their names, but I can't recall them all now.'

It smells like cow dung, Agnes thought. She held her breath and grabbed a swab to clean the wound as quickly as she could. Mr Farnley noted her reaction with amusement.

'The pong takes a bit of getting used to, doesn't it, Nurse?'

'I'll say, Mr Farnley,' Agnes replied through clenched teeth.

'As long as it does some good,' Mrs Farnley said. 'Hannah reckons it's knitting together nicely.'

'What do you think, Nurse?' Mr Farnley watched her carefully.

Agnes examined the wound. 'It certainly seems to be healing well,' she said. 'You see where this part has turned pink? That's called granulation, and it's a sign that healthy tissue is growing.'

'That'll be the herbs Hannah put on,' Mrs Farnley said with satisfaction.

'I don't know about that,' Agnes said. 'Most wounds heal themselves in time, if they're kept clean. In fact, you're better off not putting anything on them, Mrs Farnley, just in case it causes infection.'

Mrs Farnley muttered something under her breath and attacked another shirt collar with the soap.

Agnes set about putting on a clean dressing, aware that she was being watched by the two small children at their father's feet. Agnes smiled at them, but they stared back at her with the same baleful, suspicious eyes as their mother.

'So when do you reckon I can go back to work, Nurse?' Mr Farnley asked, when she had finished.

'Not until you're fit,' his wife interrupted from the other side of the room.

'I am fit. I've still got one good hand, and I reckon I

can swing a pick with one as well as I can with t'other.' He flexed the fingers of his left hand as if to prove his point.

Agnes smiled, remembering what Dr Rutherford said. 'I'm sure the pit manager will be pleased to hear that—'

'I knew it!' Mrs Farnley interrupted her, throwing down the bar of soap. It landed in the tub with a splash. 'That's why you're here, in't it? He sent you.'

Agnes stared at her angry face. 'I—'

'Now, Edie.' There was a warning note in Jack Farnley's voice. 'Don't start.'

'Why not? Why shouldn't I have something to say about it?' Edie Farnley got to her feet, hands planted on her hips. 'You come here, making out you're on our side, but you don't fool me!' she sneered at Agnes. 'You're just like the rest of them. All you want to do is stop our money!'

'I don't understand?' Agnes looked from one to the other.

'What she means is my sick pay is due to finish in a couple of days,' Mr Farnley explained, shooting his wife a dark look. 'A week is all we're allowed, unless the doctor signs us off for longer.'

'Which he never does,' Mrs Farnley said. 'He's in the Haverstocks' pocket, and they don't like paying out for men who in't working, even when it's the pit that's made 'em ill.'

'I'm sure that isn't the case at all,' Agnes said.

'Aye, well, you don't know owt about it, do you? You've only been here five minutes. I've seen the state of some of those men old Rutherford's sent back down the pit. Coughing up coal dust, barely able to walk . . . He might as well be signing their death warrants as signing them off the sick. Well, you in't sending my Jack back to work. Not until he's fit.'

'And how will we manage without my money?'

'We'll manage,' his wife said firmly.

'If they stop my sick pay we'll have to go to the Poor Law—'

'I said, we'll manage,' Mrs Farnley cut him off. 'We've done it before, in't we? We can do it again.'

Agnes saw the look that passed between them. It was as if they had both forgotten she was there.

She cleared her throat. 'There won't be any need for that,' she said. 'Your wife is right, Mr Farnley. You can't possibly go back to work with that wound as it is. I'll speak to Dr Rutherford and get him to sign you off for at least another week.'

Mrs Farnley laughed harshly. 'And tha thinks that'll do any good?'

Agnes straightened her shoulders. 'If it's my professional opinion—'

'I told you, lass. I've known that fool Rutherford send men back down that pit on their last legs, just to save the Haverstocks a few bob in sick pay. I don't see why he should listen to you.'

'I've told you, I want to go back to work,' Jack Farnley said. 'I'd rather be down the pit than sitting at home feeling useless.'

His wife rounded on him. 'You'll go back to work when you're fit enough!'

'I'll speak to Dr Rutherford,' Agnes repeated. 'I'm sure he'll agree with me that you're not well enough to go back to work.'

Mrs Farnley went back to her scrubbing. 'And pigs might fly,' she muttered.

Chapter Six

It didn't take Agnes long to call on all the addresses on the list Dr Rutherford had given her, since they were clustered together in the various rows and lanes around the pit.

First she visited the men who had been injured the previous night. At the first cottage, she was met by a disgruntled woman wearing the same belligerent expression as Mrs Farnley.

'You tell that doctor to mind his own business,' one told her as she stood in the doorway wielding a broom. 'My Albert will be back at work when he's right, and not a minute before.'

'You don't understand, I only want—' Agnes tried to explain, but the door had already slammed in her face.

At the second house she was turned away again, this time with a polite, 'I'll look after my husband, thank you. It's a woman's job to nurse her mester.'

'But he needs special treatment,' Agnes said.

'Aye, I've already spoken to Hannah Arkwright. She says she'll come round later.'

With more of her special cow dung ointment, no doubt, Agnes thought sourly. She wondered how long it would be before she was having to deal with a severely infected wound.

It was the same story with most of the other patients she visited. Agnes would knock on every door with a smile on her face, only to be greeted by suspicion or downright hostility. By midday, she had only managed to bathe an infected eye, syringe two pairs of ears and treat a case of threadworms. Hardly a good morning's work, she thought as she headed back to Dr Rutherford's house. As she cycled past the end of Coalpit Row, heading back up the hill towards the surgery, Agnes noticed the cottage on the end had its curtains drawn closed, even though it was nearly midday.

It was a strange, silent contrast to the other houses on the row, which bustled with activity as women rinsed their clothes and worked their mangles and hung their flapping sheets on the line, all the while casting glances towards the closed curtains.

Agnes slowed her bicycle as the door suddenly opened and a heavy-set woman emerged, huddled in a black coat, a basket tucked over her arm. Agnes recognised her straight away from the previous night, her face blank with shock as she followed the cart carrying her son out of the pit gates. Agnes looked back at the cottage, just in time to see the curtain twitch and the pale, distraught face of a young woman briefly appear.

The black-clad woman had drawn level with Agnes now. She took a deep breath.

'Mrs Kettle?'

The woman stopped. 'Yes?'

As Agnes looked at her grim face, Bess Bradshaw's voice came into her head.

You need to learn to think before you speak, Miss Sheridan.

'I – I just wanted to say I'm sorry,' she mumbled. 'About your son.'

The woman nodded. 'Thank you.'

'How is your daughter-in-law?'

'As well as can be expected, thank you.'

Agnes glanced over the woman's shoulder towards the cottage. 'When is her baby due?'

47

Mrs Kettle paused, as if reluctant to speak. 'Not for another two months yet,' she said finally.

'When would be a good time for me to call on her, do you think?'

Mrs Kettle blinked at her. 'Call on her? Whatever for?'

'To introduce myself. Since I'm going to be delivering her baby, I'll need to make sure . . . '

But Mrs Kettle was already shaking her head. 'Nay, Nurse. Hannah Arkwright brings all our bairns into the world.'

'But . . . '

'Our Ellen wants Hannah. No one else,' Mrs Kettle said firmly. 'Now, if tha'll excuse me, I must be on my way. We're burying our Harry on Thursday, and I've a funeral to sort out.'

As she went to move past, Agnes blurted out, 'Is there anything I can do?'

Mrs Kettle frowned, and once again Agnes heard Bess' voice in her ear.

Honestly, Miss Sheridan, don't you know when to stop? You always have to push it too far, don't you? Why can't you ever leave things be?

'No, thank you,' Mrs Kettle said. She glanced over her shoulder, back at the cottage. 'It's best if we're all left in peace.'

'Of course. I understand. But do tell her if there's anything I . . . ' Agnes' words were lost as the woman stomped off down the lane.

Agnes returned to Dr Rutherford's house. She parked her bicycle round the back of the shed, carefully placing it well out of Mrs Bannister's sight, then let herself into the kitchen.

Jinny was at the stove. And she wasn't alone. Three small children sat around the kitchen table, dipping crusts of bread into a bowl of thick, creamy dripping.

Jinny swung round, her hand flying to her heart, then relaxed when she saw Agnes.

'Oh, thank goodness it's you, miss. I thought it were Mrs B, come back from Leeds early. She'd have a fit if she saw the bairns here.'

Agnes looked at the children. They all stared back at her, their eyes round above grease-smeared mouths.

'I had to bring them wi' me,' Jinny said. 'Ma needed them out of the house. You'll not say anything to Mrs Bannister, will you? She'll sack me for sure, and Ma says we need the money.' Her small face was screwed up with worry.

'I won't say a word,' Agnes promised. She went off to hang up her coat and put away her bag, then returned to the kitchen.

'You'll be wanting summat to eat?' Jinny said. 'I'm sorry, miss, I weren't expecting you back while one o'clock. What with having to keep an eye on this lot, I've fallen a bit behind.' She looked vaguely around the kitchen. 'I think there might be some cold cuts, if you fancy them?'

Agnes looked at the children's plates. 'This bread and dripping looks nice.'

Jinny's pale eyes widened. 'Oh, no, miss, I couldn't give you that!'

'Why not? We used to eat it all the time at the hospital when I was training in London.' Agnes pulled out a kitchen chair, keeping a careful distance between herself and the children's greasy hands.

'Well, if you're sure?' Jinny put a plate down in front of Agnes, her expression reluctant. 'But Mrs Bannister wouldn't like it. '

'Then we'd best not tell her that either, had we?' Agnes reached for the dripping pot, smiling at the children who watched her in awestruck silence.

'And you're sure tha don't mind about the bairns? I'm taking 'em back home soon. Ma just told me to keep an eye on 'em while Mrs Arkwright came round.'

Agnes looked up. 'Arkwright? Would that be Hannah Arkwright?'

'Aye, miss. That's her.'

'I'm sick and tired of hearing that woman's name.'

'You'll hear it a lot round here.' Jinny wiped the mouth of one of the children. 'She and her mother have been nursing people in the village for years.'

Agnes stopped in the middle of spreading dripping on her bread. 'I'd hardly call it nursing, from what I can see,' she said. 'Real nurses don't go round concocting potions. My nursing is based on real medical knowledge. I don't suppose Hannah Arkwright and her mother have any formal nursing training.'

'I don't s'pose they have,' Jinny agreed cheerfully. 'But everyone swears by them, all the same.'

'Really?' Agnes went back to her spreading. 'Then I think I shall have to have a word with this Hannah Arkwright.'

'Rather you than me, miss!'

'Why's that?'

Jinny glanced at the children and lowered her voice. 'Because she's a witch. Her and her mother.'

Agnes laughed. 'Is that what people think?'

'It's the truth,' Jinny insisted. 'Her mother used to frighten us all when we were bairns – no one went up to their farm if they could help it. Mind, some of the older lads used to do it for a dare, but not me.' Her thin shoulders shuddered. 'No, there was summat not quite right about that place. There was talk that Hannah's father was a bad 'un, and her mother cast a spell to kill him and then got Hannah to bury him in the woods. I dunno if it

50

were true or not, but there were some as reckoned they'd seen his ghost, wandering through the woods in t'dead of night.'

'It all sounds like superstitious nonsense to me,' Agnes dismissed.

'Happen it is, but you won't find many round here willing to fall out with the Arkwrights.'

'So why is she visiting your mother? Is she ill?' Agnes asked.

'Oh, no, miss. It's our Ernest. The baby . . . '

Jinny stopped talking suddenly, her mouth closing like a trap. Her hair hung in a limp curtain over her face, but Agnes could still see the bright crimson tinge in her cheeks.

'Is he ill?' she asked. 'Because I could always pay your mother a visit . . . '

'Oh, no, miss,' Jinny said quickly. 'Ma wouldn't want that. She don't like strangers poking their nose into our business.' She stopped short, biting her lip as she realised what she had said. 'Sorry,' she mumbled.

'It's quite all right, Jinny,' Agnes sighed, helping herself to another slice of bread. 'It's no worse than I've been hearing all morning, I assure you.'

'Give me the bairn,' Hannah Arkwright said.

Ruth Chadwick looked into the other woman's coal-black eyes and without thinking tightened her arms around her baby, holding him close to her bosom.

Hannah must have noticed the gesture. She smiled, but there was no warmth in it. 'You want me to make him better, don't you, my duck?'

Hannah's voice was soft and lisping, like a child's. Even after knowing her for so many years, it still surprised Ruth to hear a little girl's voice coming from such a tall, strapping woman.

Ruth handed over the bundle. But as soon as little Ernest was in Hannah's arms he started screaming.

Ruth watched Hannah jiggling the baby roughly to shush him, biting her lip until she could stand it no more.

'Don't let his head loll like that,' she blurted out.

Anger flared in Hannah's eyes. 'Do you think I don't know how to hold a bairn?' she snapped. 'How many babies have I brought into the world over the years?'

But you've never been a mother yourself. Ruth couldn't say the words. Instead she scratched at her arms, the way she always did it when she was nervous. Her skin was red raw under her long sleeves.

Hannah seemed to read her thoughts. 'I don't have to help him, if you don't want me to?' She went to hand the baby back, but Ruth shook her head.

'No,' she said. 'No, I want you to help him. Make him better, Hannah, please.'

Hannah's wide mouth curved in a smile of satisfaction. 'Of course I will, duck.'

Ruth watched her examining Ernest and tried to remind herself what a good friend Hannah had been to her over the years. She had delivered all the Chadwick babies, and nursed them through childhood illnesses. Hadn't she cured little Maggie of whooping cough, after Dr Rutherford had sworn it would be the death of her? And she had nursed Ruth's mother and father through their various illnesses, and laid them out when they finally died. There was no reason to believe that she would harm little Ernest now.

Ruth felt the prickle of blood seeping through the sleeves of her blouse.

Finally Hannah handed the baby back. Ruth hadn't realised she had been holding her breath until Ernest was in her arms again.

'Well?' she said.

Hannah's face was solemn. They were the same age, but unlike Ruth, there wasn't a single line on Hannah's broad face, or a thread of grey in the swathe of flaming red hair she kept twisted up in an untidy knot at the back of her head.

It was what came of not having a husband or children to worry about, Ruth thought. Although she was sure Hannah must have troubles of her own, living with old Mother Arkwright.

'You did right to call me,' she said.

Ruth's mouth dried. 'What is it? Do you know?'

'His muscles are deformed, shorter on one side than the other. I daresay there's a fancy long medical name for it, but that's the up and down of it.'

Ruth looked down at the newborn in her arms. Ernest had calmed down and was looking up at her with bright, inquisitive eyes. Bless him, the poor little mite had no idea . . .

'Can you do anything for him?' she asked.

'Of course. I promised you I'd make him better, didn't I? I'll gather some herbs and make up a muslin bag to hang round his neck. Mind, he'll have to wear it all the time, until his muscles have grown stronger.'

'How long will that be?'

'I don't know, do I?' There was a touch of irritation in Hannah's voice. 'It could be weeks, or months. These things take time, lass.'

Ruth stroked the baby's downy cheek with her fingertip. 'I'm not sure I like the idea of a string round his neck. What if it gets caught on summat and chokes him?'

'And what if he grows up with a twisted neck because you didn't help him?' Hannah shook her head pityingly. 'Oh, Ruthie, you always were such a worrier. For as long

53

as I've known you you've been fretting about summat or other.'

Once again, Ruth pressed her lips together to stop herself from coming out with a sharp retort. She had seven children to feed and a husband who earned a pittance down the mine. Tom was a good man and provided for his family as best he could, but she lived in fear of him being taken ill or having an accident and not being able to work again.

And it wouldn't be long before her eldest, Archie, got himself engaged. He had been courting Nancy Morris for ages, and Ruth knew her son was working himself up to proposing. She was pleased for him, but once they were wed and had set up home together it would be one less wage coming in. Something else for her to fret about in the early hours of the morning, when the rest of the household was asleep . . .

But she knew she wasn't the only one. There wasn't a woman in the village who didn't have the same sleepless nights as she did, wondering how to make ends meet. The only difference was they didn't make such a fuss about it.

Hannah was right, Ruth Chadwick was a born worrier.

'I'll make us a nice pot of tea, shall I?' Hannah offered.

'I'll make it.'

'No, you sit thysen down. Take the weight off your feet a minute.' Hannah was up and at the stove before Ruth could reply.

Ruth sat on the wooden settle at the table and watched as Hannah busied herself in her kitchen. She didn't like it but there was never any point in arguing with her.

They had known each other for years, had started at the village school on the same day. The other children had quickly made friends with each other, but no one seemed to want to pal up with shy, nervous little Ruth or the sullen, red-haired girl with the staring black eyes, who stood a head taller than everyone else and whose mother was supposed to be a witch. So they had somehow latched on to each other. Or rather, Hannah had latched on to her, and Ruth went along with it because she was terrified that Hannah might cast a spell on her if she didn't.

Even now, after thirty years of friendship, she still lived with that uneasy feeling.

Hannah poured water from the kettle into an ancient teapot, clattered it around with a spoon, then carried it over to where Ruth sat at the kitchen table.

'You look worn out, love,' she said sympathetically.

'I am,' Ruth said. 'I hardly had a wink of sleep last night, after what happened at the pit.'

'You'll have slept better than Harry Kettle's mother and widow, I'm sure.'

'Aye,' Ruth sighed. 'Poor Harry.'

'He was in a terrible state when I saw him,' Hannah said matter-of-factly as she poured out the tea. 'I barely recognised the lad.'

'Don't.' Ruth suppressed a shudder. 'I can't think about it.'

'I stayed with his wife all night, after I finished laying him out. She were beside herself.' Hannah shook her head in sorrow.

'I'm sure.' Ruth picked up the cup, feeling its warmth through her chilly fingers. She felt for young Ellen Kettle and for Harry's mother. But at the same time she was deeply grateful it was not her own husband or sons who had come home on that cart.

They finished their tea as Jinny came in, ushering the children in front of her. All three of the little ones stopped in their tracks when they saw Hannah, like galloping horses shying at a fence.

'And who's this?' Hannah put down her cup and turned to face them. 'Freddie and Jane and little Maggie? Not so

55

little any more, eh? You've shot up like weeds. Come and say hello to your auntie Hannah.'

She reached out her long arms. The children backed away, but her grasping fingers caught Freddie's shirt and she dragged him into her rough embrace. Ruth saw her son flinch and prayed he would have the good sense not to pull away.

'He's shy,' she said quickly. She turned to Jinny, who was hanging up her coat. 'Mrs Bannister didn't catch you with the bairns, did she?'

'No, but Miss Sheridan came home. She was all right about it, though.'

'Miss Sheridan?' Hannah loosened her grip on Freddie, who darted away to safety under the table with his sisters. 'You've met the new nurse, then?'

'Aye.' Jinny put her hand to the teapot on the table, testing its warmth, then went and fetched herself a cup from the dresser.

'What's she like?' The question was carefully casual, but Ruth saw the sharp look on Hannah's face.

'She seems nice enough,' Ruth answered for her daughter, without thinking. It was only when Hannah turned her black gaze on her that she realised she should have kept her mouth shut.

'You've met her too? You never said.'

Ruth felt herself blushing. 'She was at the pit gates last night. We didn't have much of a conversation, though. I were too worried about Tom and the boys.'

'Was she indeed?' Hannah looked thoughtful. 'And what was she doing there, I wonder?'

'She came to help,' Jinny said, pouring herself a cup of tea. 'But no one needed her.'

Hannah gave a little smile. 'I should think not,' she muttered.

'She was asking about you,' Jinny said.

'Oh, aye?'

'She keeps hearing your name around the village. I think she's a bit put out that people are wanting your help and not hers.'

Hannah's smile widened. 'That's how it's always been, in't it? She'll soon find out she in't welcome here. Then with any luck she'll go back where she came from.'

'Aye,' Ruth said. But all she could think about was the previous night, and how that slip of a girl had stood at the pit gates, arguing with the overman to be let in so she could help.

Hannah looked at her sharply. 'You don't sound so sure about that?' she accused. 'Happen you want her to stay? Happen you think it's about time Bowden had a proper nurse?'

Ruth scratched at her arms. 'I'm sure I'm not thinking any such thing,' she muttered.

Hannah stared at her for a moment longer, and Ruth squirmed under her searching gaze. Then Hannah put down her cup and stood up. 'Well, I'd best be on my way,' she said. 'I've got a few more people to see.'

'Wait a minute.' Ruth fetched her purse from the dresser and rummaged in it for a couple of coins. 'Here, this is for you. For our Ernest.'

'Oh, no, you don't have to . . . ' Hannah started to protest, but Ruth pressed the money into her palm. Hannah's hand was icy cold, her palm rough and callused.

'Nay, you've got to take summat for your trouble,' she said. 'I don't like owing.' Especially not you, she thought.

'I don't like taking money from friends, either,' Hannah said, but she dropped the coins in the pocket of her apron all the same. 'I'll come round with those herbs later on. Remember what I told you. Keep them on a string round his neck.'

'Thank you, Hannah. I'm much obliged.'

'It's no trouble.' Hannah picked up the battered old carpet bag she had left by the door, then turned to Jinny. 'And you tell that new nurse that if she wants to know owt about me then she can come and ask me hersen. Happen she could come up to the farm for tea with Mother and me.'

She was smiling when she said it, but there was a glitter in her dark eyes that made Ruth afraid for Agnes Sheridan.

She only hoped the girl had the good sense to stay out of Hannah Arkwright's way.

Chapter Seven

On a damp Sunday afternoon, exactly a week after she arrived in Bowden, Agnes was invited – or rather, summoned – for tea with the Haverstocks.

'It's a great honour for you,' Dr Rutherford informed her as he drove them up to Haverstock Hall in his Austin 7. 'Sir Edward is not known for being sociable. Apart from with close friends such as myself, of course,' he added. 'But otherwise he tends to keep himself to himself. I daresay it was Miss Eleanor who invited you. She takes such an interest in the welfare of the village.'

'Then I look forward to meeting her,' Agnes said, staring out of the car window as they climbed the steep lane. 'I daresay we will have a lot to talk about.'

Dr Rutherford shot her a wary sideways look. 'I do hope you're not going to cause any trouble, Miss Sheridan,' he said.

'Trouble? What on earth do you mean, Doctor?'

'We have been invited for a pleasant afternoon tea. Sir Edward and Miss Eleanor won't want to be bothered with trivial matters that don't concern them.'

'But I thought you said Miss Haverstock was interested in the welfare of the village?'

'You know what I mean!' Dr Rutherford's face coloured.

'I'm sure I don't, Doctor.' Agnes blinked at him, feigning innocence.

Dr Rutherford's mouth tightened. 'That business with Jack Farnley. You're still fretting over it, I can tell.'

Agnes was silent. The truth was, she was still smarting over Dr Rutherford's refusal to sign Jack Farnley off work for another week. Agnes had reasoned and argued and even pleaded with him, but the doctor had ignored all her objections. Two days after she had visited him, Jack Farnley had returned to the pit, still nursing his badly injured hand.

Of course, Dr Rutherford had taken it as a sign that he had made the right decision. 'You see?' he'd told Agnes triumphantly. 'If he wasn't fit he wouldn't have turned up for work, would he?'

He might if he was worried about his family going hungry, Agnes thought. She had tried not to think the worst of Dr Rutherford, but Mrs Farnley's comment still stayed with her.

I've known that fool Rutherford send men back down that pit on their last legs, just to save the Haverstocks a few bob in sick pay.

'As I said, this is supposed to be a pleasant social occasion,' Dr Rutherford said. 'It would be considered very ill mannered to bring up such matters. Sir Edward wouldn't like it at all.' He shot her another sideways glance. 'I'm only thinking of you, Miss Sheridan. I would hate you to embarrass yourself.'

'I can assure you, Doctor, I do know how to behave,' Agnes replied tightly.

'I'm glad to hear it.' Dr Rutherford smiled, his shoulders relaxing against the leather seat. 'I'm sure you'll like Sir Edward. He can be a bit of an old curmudgeon at times, but he's very good company if you can get on his right side. And Miss Eleanor is quite charming.'

Agnes said nothing as she watched the scenery go by. Unlike Dr Rutherford, she had no interest in trying to get on Sir Edward's good side. One way or another, she'd already heard about as much as she needed to about the Haverstocks.

From the doctor, she had learned that Sir Edward's two sons had both been killed in the Great War and his wife had died shortly afterwards. Only his daughter Eleanor, twenty-eight years old and unmarried, remained with him. According to Dr Rutherford, Sir Edward was a man of great energy and enterprise, whose grandfather had built Bowden and several other local pit villages down the length of the valley.

But the people of Bowden had a very different story to tell, of a greedy, heartless man who worked his miners to their last breath and begrudged every penny he paid them.

'Well, here we are – Haverstock Hall.'

Dr Rutherford slowed the car as he drove in through the tall wrought-iron gates, clearly waiting for Agnes to be impressed.

Haverstock Hall had obviously been built to dominate its surroundings. It perched on a ridge above the village, large enough to be seen all over Bowden.

But on closer inspection, the featureless, red-brick building was gauche and ugly. It squatted at the end of a long, tree-lined drive, which spliced the ornamental gardens in front of the house. The gardens were beautifully kept, but too regimented for Agnes' liking, with their hard, angular flowerbeds and rigidly trimmed topiary hedges.

But she kept her opinion to herself, since Dr Rutherford seemed enraptured by it all.

Inside the house was just as imposing, with its grand sweeping staircase, marble floors and plaster cherubs on the ceilings. But to Agnes, it all seemed more like a vulgar display of wealth than of good taste and breeding

The butler showed them into the drawing room, where the Haverstocks were waiting for them.

Eleanor Haverstock rose to greet them.

'Oh, Dr Rutherford, how good of you to come. And on such a dismal day, too. And this must be Miss Sheridan?' She turned to smile at Agnes. She was an insipid-looking young woman, tall and thin in a faded silk dress. Her straight brown hair was cut short, which did nothing to flatter her long, pale face.

'Do come and meet my father, Sir Edward.' She turned to the old man who sat by the fire, still staring into the flames. 'Father, this is our new district nurse, Miss Sheridan.'

'Good evening, Sir Edward,' Agnes greeted him politely. 'Thank you for inviting me.'

'I didn't invite anyone. This is all Eleanor's doing,' Sir Edward grunted, not looking at her.

Agnes caught Dr Rutherford's eye. *What did I tell you?* his look said.

Eleanor seemed quite unfazed by her father's rudeness. 'Pay no attention to him, Miss Sheridan,' she said. 'If it were left to Father we would live here in splendid isolation, like a pair of hermits.' Even though she was smiling, the downcast droop of her grey eyes gave the impression of sadness.

'How are you, Sir Edward?' Dr Rutherford greeted him jovially.

'Famished.' Sir Edward turned to face them at last. He had a thin, hawk-like face, with hooded eyes and a prominent blade of a nose. His sparse grey hair was brushed back from a high, domed forehead. He reminded Agnes of a spider, with his long, thin limbs.

'Can we have tea now?' He addressed his daughter, his cold gaze skimming over Agnes without interest.

'Not yet, Father. We must wait for James.'

'We've been waiting long enough! Comes to something

when a man can't eat in his own house,' Sir Edward grumbled.

Eleanor ignored him, turning back to face Agnes. 'Do come and sit down, Miss Sheridan. You must tell me all about yourself.'

Agnes felt herself flushing. 'There's really nothing to tell . . . '

'But Dr Rutherford tells us you come from London? How thrilling. I did the Season there, and it was all most exciting.' Eleanor smiled, but once again her grey eyes told a different story. 'I suppose you must find Bowden rather dull by comparison?'

'Actually, I—'

'I don't think Miss Sheridan has had quite the warm welcome she was hoping for in the village,' Dr Rutherford put in before she could answer. Agnes glared at him.

'Really? In what way?' Eleanor asked.

Once again, Dr Rutherford answered for her. 'Oh, you know what they're like in Bowden.' He smirked. 'They're a suspicious lot. Don't like outsiders.'

Agnes forced a smile, but inside she was fuming. She wished she hadn't confided in Dr Rutherford about how difficult her first week in Bowden had been.

'I'm sure they just need time to get used to me,' she said.

'I wouldn't bet on it. They're an ungrateful bunch of swine,' Sir Edward muttered. He turned to look at Agnes at last, and she knew immediately that the people of Bowden had not been wrong about him. There was not a shred of kindness in his narrow, cunning face. His eyes were as cold and unblinking as a reptile's. Agnes felt a prickle of revulsion, and it was all she could do to remind herself that she was a guest in his house.

'Father!' Eleanor protested mildly.

63

'Well, they are. The more you do for 'em, the less they appreciate it.' He looked around, very impatient. 'Where is Shepherd? It's not like him to keep us waiting. He's usually a stickler for time-keeping.'

'I'm sure he'll be here in a minute, Father.' Agnes saw the flicker of anxiety on Eleanor's face.

'I daresay it's that wife of his to blame,' Sir Edward grumbled.

'Father!'

'I'm only speaking the truth, Eleanor. He did himself no favours when he married her.'

'Mr Shepherd is the pit manager at Bowden Main,' Dr Rutherford explained in an undertone to Agnes. 'Very clever young man.'

'Not clever enough to escape being caught by a common pit girl,' Sir Edward said.

Before Agnes could ask any more, the door opened and the butler announced that Mr and Mrs Shepherd had arrived.

'Show them in, please,' Eleanor said, then turned to Sir Edward. 'Father, do try to be civil,' she pleaded.

Chapter Eight

James Shepherd was not what Agnes had expected. She had imagined the pit manager would be a much older man, but he was in his mid-twenties, of medium height with a wiry build and neatly cut light brown hair with a hint of a curl over his ears.

Mrs Shepherd, by contrast, was extraordinarily pretty, with glossy black hair, a heart-shaped face and a pert nose. She was even younger than her husband, barely more than a girl. But there was a hint of defiance in her blue eyes as she gazed around her. She looked to Agnes as if she was readying herself for battle, not a pleasant afternoon tea.

Eleanor jumped to her feet to greet them.

'Oh, James, there you are. We were worried about you.'

'I'm sorry, Eleanor ... Sir Edward.' James Shepherd nodded in the old man's direction. Sir Edward turned to look into the fire again, deliberately ignoring them. Sulking, Agnes thought.

'We were beginning to think you weren't coming,' Eleanor said.

James glanced sideways at his wife. 'We were delayed. Carrie didn't feel well.'

'What did I tell you?' Sir Edward muttered under his breath.

'Oh, dear,' Eleanor said quickly. 'I hope you're feeling better now?'

'I'm very well, thank you.' Agnes caught the narrow-eyed

look Carrie Shepherd shot back at her husband. Her broad Yorkshire accent was a complete contrast to James Shepherd's quiet, cultured tones.

'Well, if you do take a turn for the worse you're in the right place, with the medical profession in attendance!' Eleanor's laughter sounded forced. 'Have you met Miss Sheridan, our new district nurse?'

James reached out to shake Agnes' hand. His thin face was all angles, a sharp chin and high cheekbones under deep-set, intelligent brown eyes. He looked as if he would be far more at home with his nose in a book than running a coal mine. 'Welcome to Bowden, Miss Sheridan. May I introduce my wife Carrie?'

'How do you do?' The young woman nodded a stilted greeting.

'Now everyone's here, perhaps we can have our tea at last?' Sir Edward said with exaggerated patience.

'Of course, Father.' Eleanor rang the bell to summon the butler as Sir Edward beckoned James to his side. Once again he ignored Carrie, and Agnes felt for the poor girl, left on her own.

'I thought I told them not to discuss pit business!' Eleanor sighed, as she returned to the women. 'Here, come and sit by me, Mrs Shepherd.' She patted the couch beside her. 'Tell me, how is your baby?'

'He's very well, thank you.'

'He really is the most delightful little creature, Miss Sheridan,' Eleanor said. 'How old is he now?'

'Nearly ten months.' For the first time since she had come into the room, the corners of Carrie Shepherd's mouth turned up a fraction.

'He'll be trying to talk now, I expect?' Agnes said.

'Oh, aye, he chatters all the time.' The young woman forgot her reserve for a moment, her eyes lighting up.

'That is to say, he's making all sorts of noises, but I don't think you'd call them words as such.' She suddenly seemed to remember where she was and her mouth closed like a trap.

'I shouldn't think it will be long now before he's speaking,' Agnes coaxed.

'Nay.' The word escaped from between obstinately closed lips.

'He's an absolute angel,' Eleanor enthused. 'Such a delight. I really must come and visit him soon. Or perhaps you could bring him up to the hall?'

'Aye.' Carrie Shepherd couldn't have looked more wretched about the idea if she had tried.

Just then the butler arrived to announce afternoon tea was served, and they all took their places around the lace-covered table. Agnes found herself seated opposite Mrs Shepherd at the far end, while Eleanor took a seat at the other end, between her father and James Shepherd.

Agnes noticed how animated Eleanor had become since James arrived. She was positively girlish as she poured tea for everyone. And when she passed James his cup and their hands brushed, two bright spots of colour lit up her cheeks.

Agnes glanced at Carrie Shepherd. She was watching Eleanor and James too, but her expression gave nothing away.

There was something about her that Agnes found highly intriguing. 'Are you from Bowden, Mrs Shepherd?' she asked.

'Aye, I've lived here all my life.' Carrie Shepherd kept her gaze fixed on the far end of the table. 'I were brought up on Coalpit Row.' There was a touch of defiance in her voice as she said it.

Eleanor gave a squawk of laughter from the other end

of the table and batted James playfully on the arm. Mrs Shepherd flinched and looked away.

'So your father works down the mine?' Agnes said.

Carrie nodded. 'He's a deputy,' she said proudly. 'He were a ripper, until he got TB in his spine ... ' Her voice faded.

TB of the spine ... Pott's disease. Agnes suddenly remembered the last time she had looked into a bright blue gaze just like Mrs Shepherd's. 'Your father wouldn't be Mr Wardle, by any chance?' she asked.

'That's right.' Carrie Shepherd looked up sharply. 'How do you know him?'

'I met him last week, when I first arrived in Bowden. He interviewed me with the rest of the Miners' Welfare Committee.'

Carrie Shepherd smiled. 'Aye, that'll be him. He's a good man, my father. You can ask anyone in the village and they'll tell you. He's done a lot of good for the people here, since he took over t'Miners' Welfare.'

'Miners' Welfare!' Agnes hadn't realised Sir Edward had been listening to their conversation until his voice suddenly boomed out from the other end of the table. 'As if collecting a few pennies off the men's wages every week makes a difference, compared to what I've done for the village.'

Agnes caught the quick look that passed between James Shepherd and his wife. It was the briefest of glances, but it carried a weight of meaning.

'You think the Miners' Welfare built the school, or the reading room, or the recreation ground?' Sir Edward blustered on. 'No, it all came out of my pocket.'

'Aye, but they're the reason we have books in the reading room, and slates and pencils for the children,' Carrie Shepherd murmured, so quietly only Agnes heard her.

'I certainly wouldn't be here if it weren't for them,' Agnes replied.

'In my opinion, it was a sorry day the men started organising themselves into these wretched committees and unions,' Sir Edward went on, as if she hadn't spoken. 'It wouldn't have happened in my father's day, that's for sure. He would have had them all horse-whipped if they'd started talking about their rights!'

Agnes looked across the table at Mrs Shepherd. She was staring down at the crumbled remains of a scone on her plate, her face crimson.

Agnes decided to change the subject. 'Actually, Sir Edward, I wanted to ask you if it would be possible for me to visit the colliery?' she asked.

The table went silent. Eleanor's brows shot up to her hairline, while Dr Rutherford's lowered into a warning frown.

Sir Edward sat back in his seat. 'Visit the colliery? Why ever would you want to visit Bowden Main?'

'A very good question, Sir Edward,' Dr Rutherford murmured, fiddling with his linen napkin.

'I feel it would help me gain a greater understanding of the miners' lives,' Agnes said. 'I've already seen how they live. Now I would like to understand more about their working conditions.'

She caught Mrs Shepherd's eye across the table. She was looking at Agnes with new interest.

'Working conditions?' Sir Edward looked suspicious. 'I do hope you're not going to start telling me what I should and shouldn't be doing in my own mine, Miss Sheridan? I have enough trouble with the union about that, thank you very much!'

'No, indeed, Sir Edward. I wouldn't dream of it.'

'I'm glad to hear it.' He turned to his pit manager. 'Well, Shepherd? What do you say about it? Should we let our new nurse visit the pit?'

James Shepherd looked thoughtful. 'I'm not against the idea, Sir Edward, but I'm not sure if it's the right time. Not with the situation as – unsettled – as it currently is.'

'Listen to him!' Sir Edward shook his head. 'That's typical of you, Shepherd, always so cautious. How many times do I have to tell you, this is all nothing more than a storm in a teacup?'

'I'm not so sure, sir,' James Shepherd said quietly. 'The unions are quite adamant they won't accept the new terms.'

'The unions can go to hell!' Sir Edward roared, so loudly that everyone around the table flinched and Eleanor dropped her cake fork with a clatter.

Agnes looked at the dismayed faces around her. She had read about the dispute in the newspaper. The government wanted mine owners to impose new working conditions on their workers, to make the pits more profitable. The Miners' Federation had until 1 May to accept the terms, or face being locked out of the pits. From the little gossip Agnes had picked up in the village whilst doing her rounds, it seemed as if the miners of Bowden were ready for a fight.

'Anyway, it will all come to nothing,' Sir Edward carried on. 'Of course the miners will accept the new terms. They won't want another crippling strike like the one we had five years ago. They just need time to come to their senses.'

'And what if they don't?' Agnes asked, curious.

Sir Edward frowned. 'Then we'll lock them out, of course. They'll soon change their tune when they don't have any wages coming in.' He pushed his teacup across the table for his daughter to refill. 'Of course, it doesn't help that their leaders are making so much noise about it. Rabble-rousers and trouble-makers the lot of them, whipping up the men and making them think they can win.'

'They can win.'

Agnes looked up sharply at the sound of Carrie Shepherd's voice. She sat across the table, her face calm. Only the bright spots of colour on her cheeks gave away her true feelings.

Sir Edward's cold, reptilian gaze sought her out down the length of the table. 'I beg your pardon?' he said icily. 'Did you say something, Mrs Shepherd?'

Carrie turned to face him, her chin lifting.

'Mr Churchill and Lady Astor might think they can push the miners about, but they are the engine room of this country and they always have been,' she said. 'And if they decide to down tools then the government and the mine owners will have to listen to them.'

Sir Edward looked as if he was about to combust.

'More tea?' Eleanor offered desperately, picking up the pot. Sir Edward waved it away, his eyes still fixed on Carrie.

'You think they can hold us all to ransom?' he snapped.

'I'm sure they don't want to hold anyone to ransom,' Carrie Shepherd replied. 'All the miners are asking for is a decent wage for what they do. Most of them are barely getting by as it is, especially when they're put on piecework. If you try to cut their wages any more, of course they'll want to do something about it.'

Agnes looked at James Shepherd, staring silently down at his plate.

Sir Edward's lip curled. 'You see what I mean?' he addressed the rest of the table. 'This is the kind of nonsense the rabble-rousers are spreading. And the men are stupid enough to listen to them.' He turned back to Mrs Shepherd. 'If the local men don't want to work down our mine then I'm sure we can find many others who do,' he said. 'Either way, I can tell you, Mrs Shepherd, the miners won't bring us to our knees.'

'And you won't bring us to our knees either.'

71

Sir Edward gave a triumphant sneer. 'Us? Did you hear that, Shepherd? It sounds as if your wife has already decided whose side she's on!'

James said nothing. He looked as if he hoped the ground might open up and swallow him.

'Let's stop all this talk, shall we?' Eleanor's voice was over-bright in the heavy silence that followed. 'It's quite spoiling a lovely afternoon.'

Perfect hostess that she was, she had soon steered the conversation round to the more neutral topic of Dr Rutherford's garden. But the mood around the table had already sunk too low, and it almost came as a relief when James Shepherd announced he and his wife had to go home.

'Oh, must you?' Eleanor did a good job of sounding disappointed.

'I'm afraid so. Carrie doesn't like to leave the baby for too long.' He didn't look at his wife as he said it.

'Of course not. Well, you must come and visit again soon, Mrs Shepherd.'

'Thank you, I will.' Mrs Shepherd smiled politely. But it was clear from both women's faces that neither of them meant it.

The butler had barely shown them out before Sir Edward said, 'You see? What did I tell you? I don't know what the boy was thinking, marrying a girl like that. She scarcely knows how to behave in polite company.'

'She was only offering her opinion,' Agnes said quietly, but Sir Edward wasn't listening.

'I warned him,' he went on. 'I told him, a man in his position should be careful about whom he marries. He needs a wife who will support him, not drag him down.'

'We can't help who we fall in love with, Father,' Eleanor sighed.

'Love, indeed!' Sir Edward scoffed. 'Well, now he's

paying the price for his foolishness.' He shook his head. 'She'll be the ruin of him, you mark my words.'

James said nothing as they made their way back down the hill towards the village in the darkness, but Carrie could feel the weight of his disappointment pressing down on her.

She cursed herself silently. Why did she have to open her mouth? She had promised herself she would be on her best behaviour today, for James' sake. But Sir Edward riled her so much, it was impossible for her to stay silent.

It was a cloudy, moonless night, and she stumbled over the uneven path, but James did not put out a hand to help her. Instead he walked on ahead, his hands thrust deep in his pockets.

Finally, Carrie couldn't bear the silence any longer.

'If you've got something to say to me, I'd rather you just came out and said it.' Guilt and shame made her snap.

'I think you've said more than enough for both of us, don't you?' His voice sounded weary in the darkness.

'What was I supposed to do? Just sit there and listen to that old goat going on, spouting his nonsense?'

'I thought you might at least try, for my sake.'

The sadness in his voice piqued her.

'I did try,' Carrie protested. 'I said nothing when he was going on about the Miners' Welfare, boasting about everything he'd done for the village. But when he started insulting the people I've grown up with, well – I couldn't just sit there and say nowt.'

'Obviously,' James said.

Carrie turned on him. 'I never wanted to go in the first place,' she reminded him. 'I told you it wasn't a good idea. But you would insist.'

She been brought up to hate the Haverstocks and

everything they stood for. Growing up in the rows, Carrie had lived in the shadow of the big house, as they all called it. She had never dreamed a day would ever come when she would be invited there.

But now she was married to James, and the Haverstocks were part of his life. She should have made more effort. She should have tried harder.

Carrie turned to him in the darkness. 'I'm sorry,' she said. 'I didn't mean to make things difficult for you, honestly.'

He sighed. 'I'm sure Sir Edward will get over it. It might do him good to have someone disagreeing with him for a change.'

Carrie looked at her husband, trying to make out his angular features. James would never be foolish enough to argue with the pit owner, that was for sure.

'He doesn't like me, does he?' she said.

'I rather got the impression the feeling was mutual?'

'Aye, it is. The pompous old windbag!' She shot him a sideways look. 'He thinks you could have done better for thysen.'

'Well, I don't. And that's all that matters.'

They trudged on in silence for a few moments. 'You could, though,' she said. 'If you'd married Miss Eleanor like you were supposed to.'

He sighed. 'Not this again!'

'I mean it, James. She's more your kind. She'd never let you down or embarrass you, like I do.'

It was what everyone had expected. Everyone knew Sir Edward looked on James as his son after his own boys were killed in the war. He might even have inherited the Haverstock mining fortune, if he had had the good sense to marry into the family as he was supposed to.

But instead he had chosen Carrie Wardle.

'You could have been rich, if you'd played your cards right,' she said.

'I'd rather have you and Henry.'

'Yes, but . . . '

James stopped in his tracks. 'How many more times do I have to say it?' He sighed. 'I would never want to marry Eleanor Haverstock, any more than she would want to marry me. She's like my sister.'

Carrie smiled. 'Oh, James! You know, for a clever man, you can be very dense sometimes. Anyone can see Eleanor Haverstock's besotted with you.'

Carrie didn't mind, because she felt sorry for her. For all her wealth, she knew poor Eleanor must have a lonely life, stuck in that miserable house with her monstrous father. Who was Carrie to begrudge her a little harmless flirting, if it made her feel better?

James looked startled. 'Do you think so?' He pretended to consider it. 'I had no idea. Oh, but this changes everything! Goodness, what an idiot I've been. I must go straight back to Haverstock Hall and start wooing her immediately.'

He made to turn round, but Carrie reached for his arm.

'Too late!' she laughed. 'You're mine now.'

'So I am.' He paused, then said, 'You don't regret ending up with me, do you?'

She looked up at him, making out the sharp planes and angles of his face in the darkness. She couldn't see the expression in his eyes, but she could hear the uncertainty in his voice.

He was thinking about Rob. Neither of them ever mentioned him by name, but he was always there, lingering between them.

If Rob hadn't gone, then perhaps both their lives would have been very different.

A chill breeze whispered over Carrie's skin, making her shiver. James immediately took off his jacket and draped it around her shoulders.

The tender gesture made her think of the day when he had found her outside the pit gates, crying in the rain after Rob had gone. He hadn't said a word, but he had taken off his jacket and put it round her shoulders then. She remembered looking up at him, the rain soaking through his shirt and plastering his hair to his face, and truly seeing him for the first time. Not the shy, awkward pit manager, but a kind, loving man who wanted to take care of her.

That was the day Carrie began to fall in love with him.

She smiled up at him. 'Of course I don't regret it.'

'Then that makes two of us.' She heard the relief in his voice as he put his arm around her.

Chapter Nine

'Pay attention please, children. This is Miss Sheridan, the school nurse. She has come to inspect you all.'

Fifty small, round faces gawped up at Agnes as she stood at the front of the high-ceilinged classroom beside the teacher, Miss Warren. It was not a promising sight. Even from where she stood, she could make out rows of reddened, runny noses, sore eyes and scabbed mouths. A couple were scratching their heads. Even so, Agnes tried to smile at them in what she hoped was an encouraging manner. They all stared blankly back.

It was her first visit to Bowden Main School, although she had passed the grey-stone building with its squat bell tower and gabled roof many times since she had arrived in the village three weeks earlier. She often heard the sound of the children's voices ringing out from within, singing a hymn or reciting their times tables, and she had seen them running around the playground, playing their lively games as she had gone about her rounds.

The headmaster, Mr Hackett, had reacted with some dismay when Agnes presented herself in his office at ten-thirty that morning.

'Oh, is it today you're supposed to be coming? I'm sure I had it written in my diary for next week.' He searched his untidy desk, shifting papers aside. He was a slightly built, nervous-looking man, bespectacled, with thinning, ashy brown hair.

Agnes watched him shuffling papers around for a

77

moment, fighting to keep her patience. 'I definitely have it in my diary for this morning,' she said.

'Have you? Oh, well, I daresay you're right. I can never keep track of these things.' He squinted at her through his thick spectacles. 'So, how do these things work, do you know? We've never had a nurse come round before.' Then, before Agnes could reply, he went on, 'I'll tell you what, why don't you speak to Miss Warren? I expect she'll know what to do with you.'

Miss Warren was one of the two teachers at the school, in charge of the senior class. Before she had even reached the classroom Agnes heard her voice ringing out from the other side of the door.

'No!' she boomed. 'That simply will not do. Start again, if you please.'

Beside Agnes, Mr Hackett's shoulders twitched nervously. 'I'll leave you here,' he said, pushing open the door and ushering her inside. 'Miss Warren will know what to do.'

'But—'

Agnes looked round to protest but he was already scuttling back down the passageway. A moment later she heard the door to his office closing firmly.

She found herself at the back of a large, lofty room, smelling of chalk, old boots and damp wool, with rows of wooden desks lined up facing away from her. A map of the world adorned one wall, the countries of the British Empire proudly shaded in red. From the opposite wall, light streamed in through two tall windows, illuminating the tall, ramrod-straight figure of Miss Warren.

Agnes could see straight away she was a formidable character. Middle-aged, stern and unsmiling, her plain grey dress and her drawn-back hair did nothing to soften the severity of her features. Her hands were clasped around a slender cane, which she twitched as she listened to a child reciting a poem in a faltering voice.

The child fell silent when Agnes entered the room, and every pair of eyes turned in her direction, including the steely gaze of Miss Warren herself.

For a moment, no one spoke. Then, suddenly, the teacher brought the cane down with a loud crack that made Agnes and all the children jump.

'Turn around, class,' she barked. 'Did I give you permission to gawp at our visitor?' In a slightly quieter voice, she added, 'Daisy Carter, carry on reciting the poem while I am occupied. And don't think I won't be listening,' she warned, pointing her cane at the child, who quailed in her seat. 'Because I will hear every word.'

As the hapless Daisy stumbled to her feet and resumed reciting, Miss Warren made her way to where Agnes was standing.

'You must be the new nurse,' she said crisply, still unsmiling. 'We've been expecting you.'

'Have you?' Agnes said. 'I wasn't sure. Mr Hackett seemed to think I wasn't due until next week.'

Miss Warren sighed. 'Fortunately, not all of us have to rely on the headmaster's memory.' She gave Agnes an appraising look. 'I understand you are here to inspect the children's general health?' Without waiting for the nurse to reply, she went on, 'Well, I must say, it's about time something was done about them. Although I think you will have more to deal with than you bargained for.'

Agnes soon understood what the teacher had meant as she examined the children. They stood before her in a neat crocodile, stripped to their vests, each child stepping up in turn before taking a place at the back of the classroom, as orderly as soldiers under Miss Warren's commanding gaze. They had been joined by the infants' class, led by the other teacher, Miss Colley. She was the exact opposite of Miss Warren, a pleasant young woman with soft curves, a round, smiling face and gentle, whispering voice.

Agnes examined each child carefully, looking at their hair, their teeth, into their eyes and down their throats. She also checked their bones, and the way they were standing. As Miss Warren had predicted, there was barely a child who did not have something wrong with them, whether it was nits, a cold or cough, flat feet or the bowed legs of rickets.

Meanwhile, Miss Warren stood behind her, watching each child with a flinty expression and occasionally barking out an order.

'No talking!'

'Take your hands out of your pockets!'

'Stop fidgeting. You there, I'm talking to you!'

The small boy in question paid no attention as he bent double, scratching behind his knees, which were bare under his short trousers.

'Who is that?' Agnes whispered to Miss Colley.

'Billy Stanhope,' she replied.

Agnes noted the name down, then beckoned him forward. 'Let's have a look at you, Billy.' He stood quite straight, and his eyes were bright. His neck and nails were spotless, for a five-year-old boy, at least. But when Agnes inspected his hands, she immediately saw the problem. The soft skin between his fingers was a mass of raised spots and pinprick marks.

'Have you been very itchy lately, Billy?' she asked. The boy stared mutely back at her with wide, grey eyes.

The girl behind him poked him hard in the back. She had the same grey eyes and mop of black hair as the small boy, and wore the worried expression of an older sister.

The boy shrugged her off and remained silent.

'Please, miss, he never stops scratching,' the girl finally burst out. 'Our aunt's been putting sulphur ointment on him. Stinks the house out, it does, but it in't doing no good.'

'Did anyone ask you to speak, Elsie Stanhope?' Miss Warren snapped. The girl instantly fell silent. 'Well?' The teacher turned to Agnes. 'Is there something wrong with the child, Miss Sheridan?'

'I believe he has scabies,' Agnes said.

'Oh, dear, that sounds rather serious.' Miss Warren looked accusingly at Miss Colley, as if it were somehow her fault.

'It can be cured, but it is very infectious.' Agnes made a note next to Billy's name.

'Infectious?' Miss Warren stiffened, her gaze hardening on the junior teacher. The younger woman bit her lip and looked close to tears. 'Just what we need. You should have noticed this before, Miss Colley.'

'I haven't seen it in any of the other children, so you should be all right,' Agnes said. 'Where do you live, Billy?' she asked the boy, who stared mutely back at her.

'Well?' Miss Warren snapped. 'Speak up, lad. And take your hands out of your pockets!'

Behind him, his sister cleared her throat.

'Please, miss, we live on Railway Row,' she said, earning herself another stern look from Miss Warren.

'Tell your mother I will be round to talk to her,' Agnes said to the girl.

'We in't got a mother.' Elsie spoke up again.

'She's dead.' Billy found his voice helpfully.

'Oh. I see. Well, who takes care of you?'

'Our dad and our aunt, miss,' Elsie said.

'In that case, tell your aunt I will be visiting her,' Agnes said.

Behind her, Miss Warren stifled what might have been

a cough but sounded suspiciously like laughter. By the time Agnes glanced over her shoulder, the teacher was straight-faced again.

It took over an hour for Agnes to finish her inspection.

'What did I tell you?' Miss Warren said with grim satisfaction, as she watched Agnes making her notes against each child's name. 'Their parents do their best, but the children are in very poor health. May I ask, Miss Sheridan, what you intend to do with all this information now you have collected it?'

Agnes considered the list. 'I will be calling on the parents to offer treatment and advice, if I can.'

'Including Billy Stanhope's family?' Agnes glanced at Miss Warren. There it was again, the slightest suspicion of a twitch at the corners of her mouth. It was the first time she had seen the older woman smile all day.

'Is there something I should know about this family, Miss Warren?' she asked.

The teacher shook her head. Her face was as straight as a poker but unmistakable mirth lit up her eyes. 'Oh, no, Miss Sheridan. I have always found Mr Stanhope to be very civil, in his own way.' She paused, then said, 'But the aunt . . . Well, let's just say you may have some trouble convincing her of your good intentions!'

Agnes had visited some poor places during the three weeks she had been in Bowden Main village, but her rounds had never before brought her to Railway Row.

She hadn't even realised there were cottages so close to the pit, until she found the narrow lane nestling up against the goods yard, so close the ground shook under her feet with the rattle of the trains on the track. The air felt oily against her skin. It was a thoroughly unpleasant place.

Agnes quickly found the Stanhopes' cottage in the middle of the row. She knocked, but there was no answer. She cautiously pushed at the door and it yielded, opening slowly.

'Hello?' she called out. 'Is anyone at home? It's the nurse.'

She had stepped into the room before she spotted the man taking a bath in a galvanised tub in front of the fire.

Agnes stopped dead at the sight of him. She wanted to run away but for a moment she could only stand and stare, transfixed by the sight of the rivulets of water that ran over his broad shoulders, making tracks in his gleaming, blackened skin. An ugly scar ran down the length of his back, parallel to his spine. As Agnes stared, he reached out one thickly muscled arm to run the soap along it, the muscles and tendons like ropes under his skin, flexing and contracting.

As he moved, he glanced over his shoulder and saw her. The soap fell into the water with a splash.

'What the . . . '

She recognised him as she found herself staring into those flinty grey eyes. Of course. Stanhope . . . The name suddenly came back to her. How could she have forgotten?

Seth Stanhope recognised her at the same moment.

'Oh, it's you.' His mouth hardened. 'Do you always barge into folks' houses without knocking?'

'I – I did knock, but . . . ' As he twisted around, Agnes caught a glimpse of his broad chest, smattered with dark hair. She quickly averted her eyes, just as the door opened behind her.

'What's going on?'

Agnes swung round. A woman stood in the doorway, carrying a large stew pot in her hands. She was at least a head taller than Agnes, and as broad-shouldered and muscular as a man.

83

'What are you doing here?' Her voice shocked Agnes. It was soft and girlish, and completely at odds with her appearance.

'I called to see Mr Stanhope.' Agnes straightened her shoulders and forced herself to regain her composure. 'I'm Miss Sheridan, the new—'

'Oh, I know who you are, all right.' The woman stared at her with unblinking dark eyes.

Agnes cleared her throat. 'You must be Billy's aunt?'

'That's right.' The woman sneered. 'Happen you've heard of me, too? I'm Hannah Arkwright.'

Chapter Ten

Agnes wasn't surprised everyone was afraid of Hannah Arkwright. She was an intimidating presence, tall and solid, with a square, strong-featured face framed by a thick curtain of flaming red hair. She dressed like a man, in old work boots and a heavy overcoat.

Agnes looked up at her. 'You're Billy Stanhope's aunt?'

'That's right.' The reply came back, fiercely defiant. 'What about him?'

From the bathtub behind them came an exaggerated sigh. 'For pity's sake! Can't a working man have a bath in peace?'

'I'll sort this out, Seth, don't worry.' Hannah's voice sounded ominous as she set the stew pot down on the table and ushered Agnes out of the cottage, half closing the door behind her.

She stood in the doorway, arms folded across her chest. 'What's all this about?' she wanted to know. 'What's our Billy done now?'

'Nothing,' Agnes said. 'I'm concerned about him, that's all. I went up to the school to carry out a health inspection earlier – ' she ignored the roll of Hannah's eyes '– and I noticed Billy was suffering from scabies.'

'Oh, that. Aye, I know,' Hannah muttered. 'I'm taking care of it.'

'Your niece mentioned you were using sulphur ointment. May I suggest benyl benzoate emulsion might be more effective? I've brought some with me.'

Agnes opened her bag and took out the brown glass bottle. 'It needs to be painted on after a bath. From head to foot, not just the affected—'

But Hannah was already shaking her head. 'We don't need your medicine,' she cut Agnes off.

'It isn't medicine. It's—'

'I'm not bothered what it is. I told you, I don't need it. I'm taking care of Billy in my own way.'

'Well, whatever you're doing, it's obviously not working!' Agnes snapped back.

Hannah stared at her. 'Now you listen to me, Miss Sheridan. My mother and I have been tending to the people of this village for years. You ask anyone and they'll tell you. So we don't need the likes of you coming along with your fancy bottles, laying down the law and telling everyone what to do!'

'Well, now I'm here they can start receiving proper care,' Agnes replied primly.

Hannah's eyes widened in shock, as if Agnes had slapped her. 'Proper care, is it? Well, from what I hear, no one's interested in your proper care, are they, Miss High and Mighty!'

Agnes looked past Hannah's shoulder towards the cottage. 'Perhaps I should have a word with the boy's father.'

'You heard him. He in't interested in talking to you,' Hannah said. 'I look after the bairns and their ailments. Their father trusts me.'

Then perhaps you should take better care of them. Agnes pressed her lips together to stop the words coming out. Antagonising Hannah Arkwright would get her nowhere.

'I really think this would help.' She proffered the bottle again, but Hannah pushed it away.

'I told you, we don't need your help,' she said. 'So I'd

be obliged if you didn't come round here again, sticking your nose in where it in't wanted.'

Agnes straightened her shoulders, determined not to be intimidated. 'I'll certainly call round again if I feel I—' she started to say.

But Hannah had already gone inside, slamming the door in her face.

Seth Stanhope was out of the bathtub, dried and half dressed, when Hannah went back inside.

'What did she want?' he asked, buckling his belt.

'Nothing to trouble thysen about.' Hannah moved past him to put the pot down on the stove.

'I heard her mention our Billy. What's wrong with him?'

'Nowt. She were just poking her nose in where it wasn't wanted.'

'She'd best not come poking it in my house.'

'Oh, she won't, don't worry about that. I sent her packing.'

As Seth turned away from her, buttoning up his shirt, Hannah paused, allowing herself the luxury of watching him for a moment, then remembered herself and averted her eyes.

'I'm sorry I wasn't here when you got home from your shift,' she said. 'I meant to be here to do your bath, but I had to see to Mrs Wilmslow's bad back.'

'It's good of you to come at all,' Seth said. 'I don't know how we would have managed without you these past few months.'

'It's no trouble.' Hannah turned away so Seth wouldn't see her blushing face. The truth was, she enjoyed it. Bustling about in the kitchen, she could almost pretend it was her own cottage, and that she was preparing a meal for her family. 'I'm taking care of my sister's bairns. It's what she would have wanted.'

She saw Seth's face cloud over, and wished she hadn't said it. Six months after Sarah had died, and he could still hardly bear to hear her name mentioned.

Hannah changed the subject quickly. 'I've made you some stew for your tea. I'll just put it on to heat, shall I?'

'Aye. Thank you.'

'As I said, it's no trouble.'

She busied herself at the stove, wondering if now was the right time to say what was on her mind. 'You know, I was thinking ... ' she said slowly ' ... I could always stop here, if that would help you?'

He frowned. 'Move in, d'you mean?'

'If it would help?' She kept her voice deliberately casual. 'I could cook and clean and keep house for you. You wouldn't have to worry about the children or owt like that.' She risked a glance over her shoulder at him. 'What d'you think?'

Seth shook his head. 'Nay,' he said. 'You've already put thysen out more than enough for us. I couldn't ask you to do more.'

'But you're not asking me. I'm offering.' She heard the desperation in her voice, but she couldn't help herself. 'I don't mind.'

'You might not mind, but I would,' he said. 'Besides, I reckon your mother would have something to say about it!'

'She won't,' Hannah said. 'Mother likes you.'

Seth's mouth twisted in a rare smile. 'Now we both know that's not true.'

'Well, I could look after you both. You need help, Seth.'

More than he cared to admit, Hannah thought, seeing his desolate face. Seth was used to being the man of the house, the breadwinner. But then Sarah had died and he had suddenly found himself having to be mother and father to his children. He was out of his depth, anyone could see that.

'We'll be all right,' he muttered.

'Will you?'

He looked at her. Before he could reply, the door opened and Elsie came in, ushering Billy ahead of her. She had a book tucked under her arm as usual.

'Dad! Guess what? We played football in the playground today, and . . . ' Billy started to run to his father, but Elsie grabbed him by the hand and drew him back.

'Get your hands washed, Billy,' she said, her wary gaze on her father. 'You're filthy.'

'But I wanted to tell—'

'You heard your sister, Billy.' Seth turned his shoulder to his son as he pulled on his boots.

'Come here, lad, I'll help you.' Hannah drew off some water from the jug on the windowsill and helped the little boy wash his hands. Billy looked bewildered as he kept glancing over at his father. Hannah guessed what was going through his mind. There was a time when Seth might have welcomed his son with open arms, but now he could barely bring himself to look at his children.

At least Elsie seemed to understand. The girl retreated quickly to a corner of the settle to read her book without a word to her father.

'And you can put that down, my girl,' Hannah told her, 'I need you to set the table. And where's our Christopher?' she asked, as Elsie laid aside her book with a sigh.

Elsie shrugged. 'Off in the woods with the other lads, I expect. He didn't come to school,' she added, with another quick look at her father.

'Did you hear that, Seth?' Your son's not gone to school again. You're going to have to have a word with that lad before he gets himself in serious trouble.'

'Aye,' Seth said.

'He's running wild. It won't be long before we have the police knocking on our door. Seth, are you listening?'

'I heard you, woman! And I said I'd have a word with him, didn't I?' Seth finished putting on his boots and stood up.

'Where are you going?' Hannah asked, as he took his jacket down from the peg behind the door.

'There's a meeting at t'Welfare Institute.'

'Another one?'

'It's union business. There's a lot going on.' He didn't look at her as he shrugged his jacket on.

'But what about your tea?'

'Leave some in the oven, I'll have it when I get back.'

Hannah bit back her disappointment. 'I can't stop and look after the bairns. I promised Mother I'd be back.'

'Elsie can keep an eye on Billy.' He threw them a glance. 'They'll be all right by themselves for an hour.'

Hannah looked at the children's resigned faces. They knew as well as she did that their father would stay out until long after they had put themselves to bed.

And as for Christopher . . . Hannah shuddered to think what trouble that boy was getting up to, only twelve years old and already hanging around with the older lads.

Not that Seth cared. His only thought was to escape from the house and its memories as quickly as he could.

The door closed behind him. Billy ran to the window and clambered up on to the settle so he could watch his father walking down the lane. Hannah turned away to stir the pot. She couldn't bear to see the little boy with his nose pressed against the glass, pining. The poor bairn had already lost his mother and now he was losing his father, too.

'Where have you been?' her mother wanted to know as soon as Hannah let herself back into their cottage later.

The place was almost in darkness. As her mother was nearly blind, she did not bother with lamps.

'You know where I've been.' Hannah set her bag down on the table.

'Aye, I know all right.' Her mother's voice was croaky in the shadowy darkness. 'You've been gone so long the fire's gone out.'

'I'll see to it.' Hannah set about lighting the gas lamp, fumbling with the mantle.

'I could have frozen to death, not that you'd care!' her mother pecked at her. 'You're too busy making eyes at Seth Stanhope.'

'I was looking after the bairns.'

'Aye,' her mother cackled. 'You might fool him, but you can't fool me. I know what you're after my girl!'

Hannah ignored her as she finished lighting the lamp. The dim light reflected off her mother's wizened, dissatisfied face. Age had shrunken Nella Arkwright, carving deep lines in her papery skin. Her eyes were so deep-set, they were lost in pools of shadow.

'The wood basket's empty,' Hannah said. 'I'll go out and chop some more before it gets too dark.'

'Pity we don't get free coal like the rest of the village,' her mother said. 'Tha should ask your friend Seth. Heaven knows, he owes thee summat, all the time tha spends round there.' She paused, then said, 'But happen tha's got tha sights set on more than a free basket of coal, eh?'

'I don't know what you're talking about,' Hannah muttered.

'I may be all but blind, but I can still see into your heart, lass. Tha's allus had a soft spot for that man. Pity for thee he preferred your sister!'

Hannah picked up the empty log basket, her cheeks burning. 'I'll fetch that wood,' she murmured.

91

The night was growing dark and cold as she set about chopping the logs. Hannah didn't need light to see what she was doing. She had been chopping firewood since she was a child, and even in the gloom she managed to swing the axe down in just the right place, splitting the logs cleanly. She was as strong and capable as a man, much to her shame. Sometimes she wished she was dainty and fragile, like her sister Sarah.

Perhaps that was what Seth had seen in her, she thought. Sarah was always such a delicate little thing, always needing looking after. But her delicacy had been her downfall, in the end. If she had been stronger, she might never have succumbed to that sudden fever.

Hannah hauled the logs into the cottage and set them on the fire. She soon had a good blaze going.

'That's better.' Her mother turned her face to the flames, firelight catching her opaque, unseeing eyes. Suddenly she said, 'Tha's seen her, then?'

'Who?'

'T'new nurse.'

Hannah looked up sharply. She was about to ask how her mother had known, then stopped herself. Nella Arkwright knew everything.

She turned back to the fire, adding another log to the flames. 'Aye, she brought round something for Billy's itching.'

Her mother twitched with outrage. 'She had no business calling on Seth Stanhope or his bairns. They're family!'

'That's what I told her,' Hannah said.

Her mother fidgeted in her armchair, a sure sign she was put out. 'No business,' she kept muttering. 'She wants to keep her nose out.' Finally, her impatience seemed to burst out of her and she reached a bony, clawed hand out to Hannah. 'Fetch me t'mirror.'

Hannah was instantly wary. 'Why? What does tha want it for?'

'Don't ask questions. Just fetch it for me.'

Hannah reluctantly went off to do as she was asked, fetching the old mirror from the corner of her mother's room. It was an ancient, shabby old thing, with the gilt peeling off the cracked wooden frame. The glass was so spotted with age, it was nearly impossible to see anything through it. Only Hannah and her mother knew the power it bestowed, in the right hands.

'You in't going to do anything, are you?' Hannah asked as she handed it over.

'Niver you mind what I'm going to do!' The old lady grasped the mirror, snatching it from her. 'Now sit down and be quiet. And mind not to stand over me, I don't want thee putting me off!'

Hannah watched as her mother dusted off the mirror with her sleeve, then peered into it. In spite of her mother's instructions, she tried to look over her shoulder, but she couldn't see anything in the grimy glass.

Her mother stared into the mirror for a long time, breathing hard. Then, finally, she gave a sigh of satisfaction.

'Ah, there she is,' she said. 'I can see her on her bicycle, going round all the houses in that fancy uniform of hers. Bloody busybody!' She shook her head. 'She'll take over, given half the chance.'

'She won't,' Hannah said. 'She can't. No one in the village likes her.'

'I daresay they don't. But she'll not be one to give up easily. She's already fought too many battles in her life . . .' Nella was quiet for a moment, her unseeing eyes peering into the grimy glass, as if she was watching a story unfold. 'Aye, she's got some spirit, I'll say that for her. She'll keep on going until she's found a way to win, you see if she doesn't.' If Hannah had not known better, she could have sworn there was a hint of admiration in her mother's voice. 'She'll make a fool of thee, my girl, if tha lets her.'

'What do you mean?'

'Exactly what I said!' Her mother's voice was sharp. She went back to peering in the mirror. 'She's got a strong will, this lass.'

'So have I,' Hannah said defensively.

'I don't know about that. I don't think tha can stand up to this one.'

'I can!' Hannah protested, her voice rising.

'She'll take away everything if tha's not careful.'

'She won't,' Hannah declared fiercely. 'I won't let her.'

Her mother gave her a withering look. 'Oh, aye? And what can tha do about it?'

Hannah looked into the age-spotted glass, but she could see nothing but her own distorted reflection.

She didn't need a mirror to tell her what she already knew: that she was second best. She had been second best to her sister all her life, and now she was second best to her mother, too. She knew there were already those in the village who whispered that her remedies were not as good, although they didn't dare say anything to her.

But she had fought hard for her place in Bowden Main, and she wasn't about to give it up. Especially not to the likes of Agnes Sheridan.

Chapter Eleven

Agnes had passed the pit gates of Bowden Main often enough over the month she had been in the village, but nothing had prepared her for the sheer brutality of what lay inside: a bleak landscape of coal heaps, outbuildings, workshops and rail tracks, all set against the relentless noise of the coal wagons and the winding engine.

The men were changing shifts as she arrived at two o'clock in the afternoon. Agnes could smell the rank tang of sweat as the miners emerged from the lift cage, bent with weariness and so caked with coal grime that they looked like grotesque shadows. They blinked in the sunshine as they emerged, their eyes white in gleaming black faces.

'Quite a sight, isn't it?' James Shepherd spoke aloud the thought that ran through her head. 'Can you imagine what it must be like, spending your whole life working underground?'

'Indeed I can't,' Agnes said.

'I can. I've been down to the bottom of the pit shaft, Miss Sheridan, and it's not a pleasant place, believe me. It's as hot and as dark as hell down there, and the noise is unbearable. Sometimes, before the rippers manage to open up the rest of the face, the hewers have to work in seams no higher than here.' He put his hand to his hip. 'They're there for seven hours, crouched low, up to their ankles in water with rats running over their boots.' He shook his head. 'You can't help but admire the courage of a man who can do that.'

'Do you have to spend much time underground, Mr Shepherd?'

He looked away, his expression darkening. 'I rarely go down the pit if I can help it. I have a fear of dark, enclosed spaces, you see.'

'I wonder that you sought a job in a coal mine, in that case!'

'Yes, I suppose it must seem strange.' He gave her a wistful little smile. 'Now, perhaps we should proceed with our tour. We'll start in the lamp room, I think.'

He led her towards one of the outbuildings closest to the pit opening.

'Each of the men is given one of these before his shift.' He reached into his pocket and took out a tarnished brass coin with a small hole in it. 'It's called a check. You see it has a number on it? Each number corresponds with the number on their lamp. They put their check in their boot, and hand it back in at the end of their shift. That way if an accident happens below ground, we can look on the board to see whose check is missing.'

It must make it easier to identify a body, too, Agnes thought, but she held her tongue.

They had almost reached the lamp room and James Shepherd was just reaching for the door when suddenly it swung open and Seth Stanhope stood there.

'Where d'you think you're going?' He blocked Agnes' path, his arms folded across his chest.

'Miss Sheridan has asked for a tour of the pit,' James Shepherd said. 'I was about to show her the lamp room.'

Seth threw a chilly glance her way. 'She'll have to wait. The men are still lining up to collect their checks.'

Agnes stiffened at his tone. 'I beg your pardon?'

'You'll have trouble on your hands if you take her in

now.' Seth ignored her and went on speaking to James. 'Unless you want half the shift turning tail and heading home?'

Agnes waited for James to argue, but he turned to her and said, 'I'm sorry, Miss Sheridan, but Stanhope's right. I'd forgotten how many of the older men consider it bad luck to meet a woman on their way down the pit.'

'I've known men go home and miss a day's pay rather than take the risk,' Seth said.

Agnes looked from one to the other. 'But that's absurd!' she said. 'Nothing but superstitious nonsense.'

Seth drew himself up to his full height. 'Whatever you think about it, it's our way,' he said tightly.

James took Agnes' arm. 'Perhaps we should go to the winding room, instead?' he suggested.

As they walked away, Agnes looked back over her shoulder at Seth. He stood in the doorway, watching them with narrowed eyes.

'What a thoroughly rude man,' she said.

'I agree, his manners do leave a lot to be desired.' James smiled. 'But he's the best hewer at Bowden Main.'

'A hewer? So he cuts the coal?'

'That's right. The rippers open up the face and take out the rock, then the hewers get to the coal. But there's more to it than that. It's a skilled job. A good hewer can sense when a seam will give a good yield. And he can also read the conditions below ground, know when and where to cut, and where to leave well alone. They develop a sort of sixth sense for it. And Stanhope is one of the best. Right, here are the stairs up to the winding room. Watch your step, Miss Sheridan.'

Agnes only half listened as James explained the mechanism of the winding room, how the lift was operated by the banksman, the onsetter and the winding engineman, and what the various signals denoted. She was still thinking about Seth Stanhope.

He didn't like her, she could tell. She wasn't sure quite what she had done to offend him. But whatever it was, as far as Agnes was concerned, the feeling was entirely mutual.

Once the men were all safely underground, James showed her the rest of the outbuildings and explained about the other jobs at the mine, the men who filled the hewers' tubs below ground, and the drivers who guided the ponies bringing the tubs up to the surface. These jobs were usually given to the boys just starting down the mine, or the older men reaching the end of their working days. Each tub would then be sorted and checked by more men in the screening sheds, and the hewers would be paid according to the number of tubs they had managed to fill, and how they were graded.

'We don't want hewers filling their tubs with stones just to make up the weight,' James explained. 'If they do, then their pay gets docked at the end of the shift.'

After the tour they returned to the pit manager's office. 'I hope you've seen all you wanted?' James said.

'Thank you, it's been very helpful.' She looked up at the framed photograph on the wall. It showed two men, shaking hands. Agnes immediately recognised the narrow, sly features of Sir Edward Haverstock. The other man was a stranger, tall and distinguished-looking. But there was something familiar about his sharp, angular face and those deep-set eyes . . .

'Your father?' she said.

James nodded. 'He was the pit manager here until he died four years ago.'

'And you took over from him?'

James Shepherd gazed up at the portrait. 'It's what he wanted.'

But not what you wanted? Suddenly it made sense to Agnes why a man with a fear of enclosed spaces should become a pit manager.

'I'm sure he would be very proud you'd followed in his footsteps,' she said.

There was sadness in James Shepherd's smile. 'I don't know about that,' he said.

Agnes was still thinking about James Shepherd as she cycled through the pit gates later. She liked him, far more than she had thought she would when they first met at Haverstock Hall. That evening, she had been left with the impression of a rather insipid character. But now she saw he was a kind-hearted, sensitive man who truly cared about the work he was doing. She pitied him, working for someone as boorish as Sir Edward Haverstock.

She was so lost in her own thoughts, she didn't see the black figure until it stepped out into the lane in front of her. Agnes swerved to avoid it, and cycled straight into a hawthorn hedge.

The man rushed to help her as she fought to untangle herself from the thorny branches.

'Sorry, Nurse. I didn't mean to startle you.'

Agnes looked up sharply. She didn't recognise the face caked with coal dust, but she remembered the voice. 'Mr Chadwick?'

He grinned, displaying a wide red mouth. 'That's right, Nurse.' He took Agnes' bicycle from her and set it straight on the path. 'Beg your pardon for jumping out on you like that. Only I've been meaning to call on you up at the surgery, but I didn't like to, not with that Mrs Bannister there. I know what she's like, wanting to know everyone's business . . . ' He grimaced. 'Then I saw you coming in through the gates this morning and I thought I'd wait for you.'

Agnes stopped picking hawthorns out of her coat. 'You mean to say you've been waiting for me all this time?'

'It's no matter, Nurse. As I said, I've been waiting for the chance to have a word with you in private.'

'Whatever is the matter, Mr Chadwick? Are you unwell?'

Even through his coal-caked mask, she could read Tom Chadwick's uncomfortable expression. 'Not me, Nurse.' His gaze dropped. 'It's about our bairn . . . '

Chapter Twelve

The coal wagon had visited the rows and most of the women were out of their houses, shovelling coal from the heaps that had been deposited at the end of each lane to fill their own cellars. As she rounded the corner beside Tom Chadwick, Agnes could see his wife's thin figure at the far end of the row, tipping coal into the small wooden hatch.

'Your mester's here at last, Ruth,' one of the women called out to her.

'About time, too.' Ruth straightened, putting up her hand to mop her brow. 'I were beginning to worry.' She saw Agnes and her face fell.

'Hello, Mrs Chadwick,' Agnes greeted her cheerfully.

Mrs Chadwick ignored her, setting down her shovel. 'What's she doing here?' she said to her husband.

'I've asked her to come and look at our Ernest.'

Ruth Chadwick looked around sharply at the other women, who were all staring their way. Then she hurried into the cottage. Agnes and Tom Chadwick followed.

'Your husband told me the baby has a problem with his neck, Mrs Chadwick?' Agnes said.

'Nay.' Ruth closed the cottage door firmly and stood against it. 'There's nowt wrong with the bairn.'

Agnes glanced at Tom. 'Oh, but Mr Chadwick said . . . '

'As I said, there's no need to trouble thysen. Sorry you had a wasted journey.' Mrs Chadwick glared at her husband.

'Let her see the bairn, Ruth,' Tom Chadwick said.

'I told you, there's no need.'

'All the same, it won't do any harm for her to have a look since she's here, eh?'

For a moment none of them spoke. Agnes felt herself caught in the middle of a tense, silent battle between husband and wife. Then Mrs Chadwick released her grip on Agnes and crossed the room to the baby's makeshift cot, a wooden box propped on crude rockers.

She took a long time to gather the infant into her arms before she brought him back to Agnes, bundled in several layers of shawl. Agnes could feel the other woman's reluctance in every tense muscle of her body as she handed the baby over.

'That's it.' Tom Chadwick exhaled with relief. 'The nurse will soon tell us what's what. In't that right, Nurse?'

'I'll do my best, Mr Chadwick.'

Agnes set the baby down on the rug in front of the fire and set about peeling off the woollen layers. Out of the corner of her eye, she could see the accusing look Mrs Chadwick was giving her husband.

She knew straight away what was wrong, even before she had taken off the final layer of shawl.

'Torticollis,' she said. 'Wry neck, it's sometimes called. The muscles on this side of the neck are contracted, do you see? It happens quite often, especially after a difficult birth.'

'You did have a hard time with him, didn't you?' Tom turned to his wife. Ruth Chadwick said nothing, her mutinous gaze still fixed on the baby.

'Can it be put right?' Tom asked. 'He won't need an operation, will he?'

'I shouldn't think so,' Agnes said. 'If you catch it early enough, it's possible to – what's this?' She smelled the pungent herbs before she found the small muslin pouch fastened around the baby's neck and tucked inside his vest.

'It's to treat the bairn.' Ruth finally spoke up.

Agnes did not need telling. She recognised Hannah Arkwright's handiwork straight away.

'Yes, well, it's very dangerous,' Agnes gently unhooked it from the baby's neck. 'Ernest could have strangled himself in his sleep.'

'Hannah said it wouldn't do any harm,' Ruth muttered.

'It won't do a lot of good, either,' Agnes said. 'The only way to correct this condition is with regular massage to stretch the shortened muscle.'

Tom looked at his wife, his coal-caked face breaking into a smile. 'You hear that, Ruth? The nurse can make him better.'

Mrs Chadwick said nothing. Her gaze was fixed on the pouch of herbs in Agnes' hand. She hugged herself, her thin fingers clawing away at her arms through the long sleeves of her dress.

'I could show you how to do it, too?' Agnes offered. 'Then you can treat him yourself.'

'That's very good news, Nurse. Isn't it, Ruth?' Tom Chadwick looked encouragingly at his wife.

Pent-up emotion seemed to burst out of Mrs Chadwick. She lunged forward and made a grab for the baby. 'I'd rather do what Hannah says, if you don't mind,' she muttered, bundling him back in his layers of shawl, as if she couldn't cover him quick enough.

'But Mrs Chadwick—'

'Ruth!'

Tom and Agnes spoke together. But Ruth Chadwick shook her head.

'I've made up my mind. And I'll take that, if you please?' She held out her hand for the bag of herbs. As Agnes handed them over, she noticed the other woman's fingers were trembling.

She watched helplessly as Ruth Chadwick looped the string back over the baby's neck. 'He really would do better if I could treat him, you know,' Agnes said gently.

'No, thank you.'

'Ruth, please.'

'I said no!' Ruth Chadwick raised her voice, startling her husband. 'I know what I'm doing,' she said, more quietly.

Agnes got to her feet. 'In that case, I'd best go,' she said.

Tom Chadwick saw her to the door. 'I'm sorry for your trouble, Nurse,' he said.

'It's quite all right, Mr Chadwick.' Agnes looked past his shoulder to where Ruth rocked her baby, pressing him close into her shoulder. 'You know where to find me if your wife changes her mind.'

'Aye, I do.' Tom Chadwick glanced over his shoulder. 'But I doubt she will,' he said regretfully.

Ruth Chadwick turned on her husband as soon as he had closed the door.

'What did you have to bring her here for, in front of everyone? They'll all be talking now.'

'They'll know soon enough. You can't hide him forever, Ruth.'

Hot colour flooded her face. 'He'll be all right soon. Hannah said—'

'And you heard what the nurse said. The bag of herbs won't do him any good. It's all superstitious nonsense.'

'You're not to talk like that! What if Hannah was to hear you?'

Ruth hurried to the window and looked out, half expecting to see her marching down the path.

'I don't care if she does. I'd say it to her face if she was here.' Tom shook his head. 'I don't know why you're so scared of her, Ruth.'

'I in't scared.' But Ruth could see her own blanched face in the mirror, giving her away.

'That's the way it looks to me. I've seen the two of you together, the way she orders you about. And you don't dare say a word back to her. Is it because you believe all this nonsense about her being a witch? Is that why you're so afraid?'

'You've got it wrong,' Ruth insisted. 'Hannah's my friend, that's all. '

'Friend!' Tom mocked.

'And she promised to take care of our Ernest, and I think it's only fair we give her a chance.'

'She's done no good for the bairn so far, with all her herbs and her spells.'

'We have to be patient.' Ruth looked down at the baby in her arms. She tried to tell herself that Ernest was getting better, but deep down she knew she was imagining it. His poor little head still sat at an awkward angle, his right ear nearly touching his shoulder.

'You're as worried as I am,' Tom said. 'You know Hannah's treatment in't doing him any good. The bairn needs proper nursing care. And the longer we leave it, I reckon the harder it'll be to put right.' He moved to stand behind her. 'Why don't you let the nurse treat him?' he coaxed.

Ernest opened his eyes and stared back up at her, his gaze innocent and trusting. 'Hannah will make it better,' she insisted stubbornly.

'For heaven's sake!' Tom lost patience, turning away from her. 'I'm beginning to think you'd rather the bairn stayed the way he is, for the rest of his life, than upset Hannah Arkwright!'

'That's not true!' Ruth put the baby back in his cot, pulling the covers up to his chin. 'We've got to trust Hannah,' she said quietly. 'She knows what's best.'

She only hoped her friend never found out that Agnes Sheridan had been to visit.

Chapter Thirteen

Carrie Shepherd's mother was waiting outside the Co-op with Carrie's younger sister Eliza, who was shivering dramatically, in spite of her thick coat and the mild April day.

'Here she comes at last!' Eliza said as Carrie approached, pushing Henry in his pram. 'D'you know how long we've been waiting out here? I'm nithered.'

'You could have gone in without me,' Carrie said.

'You know Mother won't do that. She likes to see the manager bow and scrape, and he only does that when you're with us.'

'Now, Eliza Wardle, that's not true!' her mother denied furiously, but her blushing face gave her away.

'It's all right, Mother.' Carrie smiled, parking the pram outside the shop. 'I must say, I quite enjoy it, too!'

Before she married James, Carrie had worked at the Co-op and the manager, Mr Fensom, had been a monstrous bully to her and the other girls. It did give her a tiny twinge of satisfaction to see him rush to open the door for them as they walked in.

'Good morning, Mrs Shepherd ... Mrs Wardle. What can we do for you today?' He greeted them in a warm, treacly voice, his smile stretched over his large teeth. Carrie could only guess how much it hurt him to have to be pleasant to her. But she was the pit manager's wife, and he couldn't afford to be anything else.

Out of the corner of her eye she could see aprons being smoothed and caps being straightened, the salesgirls standing to attention behind their counters. She had been just the same herself when an important customer approached the drapery counter where she had worked with her pal Nancy Morris.

'Good morning, Mr Fensom,' Mrs Wardle greeted him politely. Carrie glanced sideways at her mother as she handed the manager her shopping list. She could remember the times when her father had been too ill to work, and her mother had scrimped and scratched around to put food on the table. She deserved to be treated with some respect now.

'She'll have a fit when she finds out you're putting everything on your account,' Eliza whispered, as they watched their mother walking off with Mr Fensom bobbing obsequiously behind. 'You know she don't like charity.'

'It in't charity if it's from family.' That was what Carrie had told her mother a few weeks earlier. It had been too much to hope Kathleen Wardle wouldn't notice that Carrie was settling her bills for her – after all, she was used to counting every penny. Eliza was right, her mother was furious. But Carrie had insisted and finally Kathleen had given in on the understanding that no one else knew anything about it, including her other daughters.

'I don't reckon Mother will see it like that. I, on t'other hand, don't mind accepting your charity, sister dear.' Eliza linked her arm through Carrie's. 'I need to buy some buttons for the new dress I'm making, and I'm happy to put 'em on your account!'

'I'm sure you are!' Carrie laughed. 'But happen I don't mind, because it means I can have a chat with Nancy while you're choosing them.'

Eliza sent her a curious look. 'I didn't know you two were still friendly?'

'Of course we are. Nancy's my best friend.'

'Oh, aye? When was the last time you spoke?'

Carrie thought about it for a moment. 'I can't remember,' she admitted. 'But that doesn't mean anything. She's still my friend.' She and Nancy Morris had been thick as thieves ever since they were babies. Their fathers worked together at the pit, their mothers were friends, and Carrie and Nancy had sat next to each other at school and plaited each other's hair and played with dolls for as long as she could remember.

'So you'll have heard her news, then?'

'What news is that?'

Eliza smiled slyly. 'I'd best let her tell you herself.'

There was a new girl behind the drapery counter with Nancy. Carrie frowned when she saw who it was.

'Iris Maskell! I didn't know she'd started working in drapery?' When Carrie worked there, Iris had been one of the grocery girls, cutting cheese and weighing out tea and sugar into twists of brown paper.

'There's a lot you don't know, I reckon.'

'What's that supposed to mean?'

Eliza gave her an infuriating smile. 'You'll see.'

Carrie ignored her, turning back to Iris. 'Nancy won't like that.'

Iris had been at school with her and Nancy, but they had never liked her. She had been full of airs and graces just because her father worked as an overman at the pit.

'They look friendly enough to me.'

Carrie watched them for a moment, giggling as they arranged gloves in a glass case. Her sister was right, they did seem very thick together.

Iris spotted them as they approached the counter. She left Nancy arranging the gloves and came over.

'Yes?' she said. 'Can I help you?'

She was just as sharp as she had been at school, Carrie

109

thought. Everything about her was small and mean, from her spiteful, foxy face to her pinched mouth and beady eyes.

Eliza stepped forward. 'I'm looking for some buttons,' she announced.

'Certainly,' Iris said. She had a funny way of speaking, not like the rest of the girls in the village. Once Sam Maskell was promoted to overman, his wife had sent all their children for special lessons in Leeds on how to speak correctly. 'What kind are you looking for?'

'Oh, I don't know ... ' Eliza looked beyond Iris, scanning the shelves. 'I think you'd best show me everything, so I can make up my mind.'

Iris blinked at her. 'Everything? You mean you want to see them all?'

'That's right.' Eliza smiled back innocently.

Iris' tiny mouth pursed even more, as if to hold back a retort. She opened the glass cabinet and started bringing out the boxes of buttons, dumping them ungraciously on the counter top.

Carrie left Eliza enjoying herself with Iris and went over to where Nancy was putting away the gloves. She was as pretty as Iris Maskell was plain, with a rounded figure, rosy cheeks and hair the colour of honey.

'Hello, Nance,' Carrie said.

'Ribbon, Madam?' Nancy replied, glancing past her shoulder. 'Yes, I'm sure we have something to suit.'

'Oh, but I don't want ... ' Carrie started to say, then she followed Nancy's gaze over her shoulder to where Mr Fensom was watching them from the doorway that led to the grocery department. 'Thank you,' she said.

She waited while Nancy went off to fetch the ribbons from the cabinet behind her. At the far end of the counter, Eliza was carefully picking her way through several boxes of buttons while Iris Maskell glared at her.

Nancy finally returned. 'As you see, we have quite a selection for you to choose from . . . ' She carefully arranged the skeins of ribbon on the glass-topped counter. Her cheeks dimpled with the smile she tried to hold in. 'Sorry about that,' she murmured under her breath. 'Old Fensom's already warned me about chatting twice today, and it in't even dinnertime.'

'He in't changed, then?' Carrie said as she pretended to peruse the ribbons.

'No such luck.' Nancy rolled her green eyes. 'So what's brought you in here? I didn't think you did your own shopping these days?'

Carrie blushed. Nancy made her sound so grand. It hadn't been her idea to have their groceries delivered, but James seemed to think it was the right thing to do, and she had gone along with it. But she did miss shopping at the Co-op every week and going to the markets in Leeds on a Saturday with her mother and sisters.

'I'm helping Mother,' she said.

'Where's the bairn? Has tha brought him wi' thee?'

Carrie nodded. 'He's outside, in his pram.'

Nancy's mouth turned down. 'That's a shame. I would have liked to see him. He must be getting big by now.'

'Aye, he is. You'll have to come and visit.'

'Aye.' Nancy kept her head down, straightening the ribbons on the counter. 'I will, soon.'

'I hope so. It seems like ages since we've had a proper chat.' Carrie looked around her with a sigh. 'Y'know, I miss working here sometimes.'

Nancy grinned. 'What? Being on tha feet all day and having to put up wi' old Fensom?'

'Happen not that, so much. But I miss us having a laugh together.'

'Me too.' Nancy grinned. 'We had some times, didn't we?'

'That we did. But I see you've got someone else to have a laugh with now.' Carrie glanced down to the end of the counter, where Iris Maskell was watching them out of the corner of her eye. 'Poor you,' she said in an undertone.

'She in't that bad,' Nancy muttered, glancing in Iris' direction. 'She's all right once tha gets to know her.'

'If you say so.' Carrie turned back to Nancy. 'So what's been going on since I last saw you? Eliza said you've got some news?'

Nancy's gaze slid away, back towards Iris. Carrie felt a warning tingle on the back of her neck. 'Nancy Morris, is there something you're not telling me?' she teased.

Before Nancy could reply, Iris spoke up from the other end of the counter. 'You mean to say you in't told her, Nance?'

'I – I in't had a chance.'

Carrie looked from Iris to Nancy. 'Told me what?'

'Nancy's engaged,' Iris answered for her.

Carrie stared at Nancy. 'Is this true?' Nancy nodded. 'Since when?'

'Archie asked me two weeks ago.' Nancy kept her gaze fixed on straightening the ribbon skeins. As she did, Carrie suddenly noticed the engagement ring on her finger. How had she not seen it before?

'Two weeks?'

'I was going to tell you, next time I saw you,' Nancy said quietly.

Carrie looked at her friend's glum face and pulled herself together. This was supposed to be a happy occasion, she had no right to make Nancy feel bad about it. And she certainly wouldn't give Iris Maskell the satisfaction of seeing her fall out with her friend.

'So Archie Chadwick finally proposed?' She forced a bright smile. 'I never thought I'd see the day.'

'Nor did I!' Nancy finally looked up at her, a smile of relief on her face. 'But I reckon he only did it because I told him if he didn't make an honest woman of me, I'd start courting someone else!'

'Oh, Nance, you didn't!'

'Well, I had to do something, didn't I? If I'd waited for him to make his mind up I would have ended up an old maid!'

They laughed. At the far end of the counter, Carrie could see Iris quietly fuming.

'Have you made up your mind yet?' she snapped at Eliza.

'That's no way to speak to a customer, is it?' Eliza replied loftily. 'I'll have a look at those ones, up there.' She pointed to one of the topmost shelves.

'But you've already seen them!'

'Then I'll have another look.'

As Iris stomped off to fetch a ladder, Eliza winked at Carrie.

'Old Fensom's looking again,' Nancy hissed. 'Best choose summat quick, before he comes over.'

'I'll have that one.' Carrie pointed to a skein of ribbon without even looking at it. 'I'll take two yards, please.'

As she watched Nancy deftly measuring the ribbon against the metal rule set into the counter, she said, 'Have you set a date?'

'We're seeing the minister tomorrow, but we were thinking early June.'

'You'll have to start on your dress soon, then?'

'I already have. I've found a nice pattern, but I haven't begun to look for any material yet.'

'I could help you, if you like? We could go into Leeds, next time you have a day off?'

'That would be nice.' Nancy kept her head down as she

snipped off the length of ribbon. 'But I'm not sure when that might be.'

'Oh, it don't matter. Just let me know. And happen we could go and have tea at the Queen's Hotel afterwards, to celebrate?'

'Steady on!' Nancy smiled weakly. 'I've got a bottom drawer to save for, remember? I in't made of money.'

'It'll be my treat,' Carrie said, looking sideways at Iris. For all her posh voice and put-on manners, she would never be able to treat anyone to tea at the Queen's Hotel.

'That's very nice of you, I'm sure,' Nancy mumbled.

As they left the Co-op with her mother, Eliza whispered, 'I hope you don't mind, but I bought the most expensive buttons I could find, just to see that cat Iris' face.'

'Of course I don't mind,' Carrie said absently, her thoughts elsewhere.

Eliza looked sideways at her. 'Are you still fretting about this wedding business?'

'I don't know why Nancy didn't tell me,' Carrie said. 'After all, I am supposed to be her best friend.'

'I don't think Nancy sees it like that.'

'What's that supposed to mean?'

'Well, she hardly rushed to tell you her news, did she?'

'I wish you'd told me, instead of letting me stand there looking a fool!'

'I didn't have the chance, did I? And anyway, I didn't think *you'd* be interested. You've hardly seen her since you got married.'

'That in't true!'

'When was the last time she visited you?'

'I—' Carrie started to reply, then shut up. Nancy hadn't been to her house once since she had married James.

'You see?' Eliza said. 'If you ask me, she in't as good a friend as you think. Not since you went up in the world.'

'I haven't gone up in the world! I mean, I'm still the same person I was,' Carrie protested.

'Your sister's right,' Kathleen Wardle put in. 'Whether you like it or not, you and Nancy Morris mix in different circles now, lass.'

'That's not true!'

Eliza laughed. 'Don't look so fed up about it. I wouldn't mind going up in the world, if it meant I could look down my nose at the likes of Iris Maskell all the time.'

'Now, Eliza, you mustn't speak like that,' her mother warned. 'Pride comes before a fall, as they say.'

'Oh, Mother!' Eliza mocked. 'I'll tell Mr Fensom not to bow and scrape to you next time you go into the Co-op, shall I? Then we'll see who's proud and who isn't!'

Chapter Fourteen

Carrie had hoped to see her father once she had helped her mother home with the shopping, but the cottage was empty.

'He'll be up on his allotment, I daresay,' Kathleen Wardle said. 'He'd be up there all day, if he could. I reckon he'd even sleep in that shed if I'd let him!'

'The fresh air does him good,' Carrie reminded her.

'Fresh air in Bowden?' her mother scoffed. 'That'll be the day. Which reminds me, best leave the bairn here, if you're thinking of going up to the allotments to see him. We don't want the little lad getting coal dust on his lungs, do we?'

Carrie knew her mother really wanted an excuse to have her grandchild to herself. But as she left the cottage, she knew Kathleen Wardle's judgement had been right. The April sun had disappeared behind a pall of filthy fog. Carrie pulled her coat collar up to stop herself breathing in the acrid air, thick with smoke and coal dust. Less than two years after leaving Coalpit Row, it was hard to believe that this had all once seemed normal to her, the dirt and dust, the cramped lanes, and the low thrumming of the winding tower.

This was where she grew up, in the shadow of the coal heaps. She had measured her days by the drone of the pit hooter marking the miners' shifts, and the sound of the trains pulling in and out of the goods yard. Her father always said they had coal dust in their veins, and he was right.

But she felt like a stranger now as she made her way down the narrow row, past the middens and the water pump, and headed up the lane towards the patchwork of allotments.

James had wanted to come with her to visit her family, but as usual she had made an excuse. Even though he was always quietly charming to her mother and sisters, and very respectful to her father, seeing him in her family's cottage always made her feel uneasy. He didn't seem to fit in, with his smart suit and well-polished shoes. And that made Carrie feel as if she didn't belong there any more, either.

But it was more than that. When she was back in Coalpit Row, Carrie could pretend for a while that she was a pitman's daughter again. She didn't feel she had to behave like the manager's wife, watching what she said and what she did all the time.

Her father was a distant, solitary figure on his allotment, body bent over a spade. Carrie watched him for a while, digging over the soil. Eric Wardle looked like an old man, moving gingerly, badly stooped. Her younger sisters could barely remember a time when he hadn't been ill. But Carrie had been eight years old when he went off to war, and she could clearly recall the fit, strong man in uniform who had swept her up on to his shoulders and carried her, laughing, along the platform as he boarded the train that took him off to France.

And she remembered the broken man who had returned. Eric Wardle's spirit was as strong as ever, but the spinal tuberculosis he had contracted in the trenches had weakened him physically. In the eight years since the war ended, he had been bedridden in hospital several times, sometimes for months on end, and each time Carrie feared it would be the last they would ever see of him.

But Eric Wardle went on fighting, digging his allotment

and turning up at the pit gates for his shifts, his body encased in a painful brace, to provide for his family as best he could. He was one of the deputies at the pit, responsible for the miners' safety. He tested for gas, measured the seams and supervised the detonations when the rippers were blasting the rock. Carrie was fiercely proud of him, but like her mother she would have preferred him not to be working down the pit, breathing in the hot, dusty, poisonous air.

Once she had married James, Carrie had hoped her father might be content to give up work. But not Eric Wardle.

'Nay, lass, I'm not one to be sitting idle,' he had said. 'What would I do wi' mysen all day? Besides, I'd miss the other lads.'

As if he knew he was being watched, he suddenly straightened up and turned to face her. Eric Wardle was never a man to show his feelings, but Carrie caught the brief flare of delight in his eyes before he concealed it in the briefest of nods.

'Now then, lass,' he grunted.

'Hello, Father.' Carrie leaned on the fence and looked at the bare earth. The rich, sour smell of manure assailed her nostrils. 'Been muck spreading, I see?'

'Aye. I've got to get the compost dug in or we'll get nowt grown otherwise.'

'Tha'll be putting the onions in soon, I s'pose?'

He shook his head. 'Not just yet, lass. Ground's too wet.' He squinted up at the sky and she noticed how pale and thin he looked, his skin almost translucent in the greyish light. 'We're in for another lot of rain soon, I reckon.'

'Can I lend a hand digging it over?'

Her father looked her up and down, and for a moment

Carrie thought he was going to refuse her help. But then he nodded towards a second spade propped up against the tumbledown shed.

'Go on, then,' he said. 'But mind those nice clothes of yours. I'll not hear the last of it from your mother if tha spoils 'em.'

They worked side by side in companionable silence, just as they always had when Carrie was younger. While she was happy to help her mother in the house with her younger sisters, if she had the chance she would always prefer to be out with her father, digging and planting and weeding the soil. It seemed like a little miracle to her, watching the plants grow.

And it was a chance for her to escape, too. Inside the house, there was always a noisy hubbub, with Eliza, Hattie and Gertie bickering amongst themselves and her mother scolding them all. Much as she loved them, Carrie liked to have time and space to think.

She knew her father felt the same. Eric Wardle was a thoughtful, intelligent man who had educated himself despite his humble beginnings. He was keen to pass on his hard-won knowledge, and Carrie had learned a lot from him during the time they spent together. He discussed politics and history and the events of the world with her, almost as if she were a son.

But they didn't speak much now as they worked together, turning over the soil and digging in the manure. Carrie sensed it was taking all her father's strength to keep working.

'We can have a rest, if you like?' she ventured, as she watched him fighting for breath.

He shook his head. 'I need to get all this sorted out.' He winked at her. 'What's the matter, lass? All that fine living made tha soft, has it?'

Carrie gritted her teeth. 'I'll show thee who's soft!'

She heard her father chuckling as she attacked the soil with her spade. She knew he was only teasing, but his words rankled with her. They made her think of what Eliza and her mother had said, about her going up in the world and mixing in different circles.

She was so busy digging, she didn't notice for a moment that her father had stopped and was leaning on his spade, watching her from the other side of the allotment.

She straightened up, pushing her hair out of her eyes. 'What is it?' she asked. 'What's wrong?'

'You tell me, lass.' He nodded towards the ground she had been digging. 'Anyone would think tha's digging the Haverstocks another pit shaft the way tha's going about it.' He smiled. 'There's summat on tha mind, I can tell. So tha'd best spit it out afore tha ends up in Australia!'

'It's nothing—' Carrie started to say, but then she saw her father's face and knew she couldn't lie to him. 'Do you think I've changed since I got married, Father?'

Eric Wardle blinked at her. 'What's brought this on?'

'It's daft, really,' she sighed, putting down her spade. 'Just summat that happened today . . . '

She told him about the shopping trip, and finding out that Nancy Morris was engaged, and how upset she was that she had been the last to know about it. Her father listened carefully, his gaze fixed on hers. Carrie didn't know any other man who would have listened to their daughter the way he did.

'Eliza said I didn't belong with Nancy's sort any more, and I should consider mysen lucky about it,' she finished miserably.

'Happen she's right,' Eric Wardle agreed.

Carrie's gaze flew to his in dismay. That wasn't what she wanted to hear. She wanted her father to tell her that

120

everything would be all right, that she hadn't changed and she didn't have to, either.

'So I have changed? Is that what you're saying?'

'I'm not saying that, lass. I'm just saying that happen things are different now.'

'But I don't want things to be different!'

'We all want a lot of things we can't have. But that's not the way the world works, is it? Besides, as Eliza said, there's plenty as would be glad of what tha's got in life.'

'I know,' Carrie sighed miserably. 'I'm being ungrateful.'

Eric Wardle sighed. 'It in't easy for thee, lass. Tha's caught between two worlds. Tha's the pit manager's wife but in your heart tha'll always be a pitman's daughter. But tha can't be both. Tha's got to let go of one or tha'll niver enjoy the other.'

Panic pierced her. 'But I don't want to let go!'

Suddenly all she wanted was to be back at the cottage, helping her mother with the washing and the baking, working at the Co-op with Nancy and gossiping about the lads they liked.

Her father shook his head. 'As I said before, that in't the way the world works, lass.'

Carrie was silent for a moment, taking in his words. As usual, Eric Wardle spoke a lot of sense.

But at the same time, her mind shrank from the idea. She wasn't ready to embrace the life of a pit manager's wife, not if it meant turning her back on her old friends and family.

'If anyone expects me to start hobnobbing with the Haverstocks, then they've got another think coming,' she declared fiercely. 'I tried that before, and it didn't work out well for any of us. Not that I suppose Miss Eleanor would ever invite me again, after the way I spoke to her father the last time—' She stopped talking, seeing her father's face. 'What's funny?' she demanded.

'Oh, Carrie!' Eric Wardle took out his handkerchief and dabbed at his eyes. 'And to think tha was worried about changing. I don't reckon tha could change if tha wanted to, lass. Not while tha's got that quick tongue in your head!'

Chapter Fifteen

Agnes was in a good mood as she left the Tollers' cottage on Middle Row.

She visited them every morning to give their eldest son Laurie his insulin injection. For the first month or so, Susan Toller had barely tolerated her presence like most of the other women. Then, two weeks ago, her middle child had developed a nasty rash, which Agnes had cured with gentian violet.

This morning, Susan Toller had smiled and thanked her. It wasn't much, in the great scheme of things. But Agnes couldn't stop smiling as she left the cottage. She was making progress, at last.

Added to which, it was a glorious late April morning. It was barely nine o'clock, but already the sun was wonderfully warm in the cloudless blue sky. Even Bowden looked quite pretty in the clear spring light.

Agnes was so pleased with herself and life in general, she didn't notice the skinny boy who ran out into her path until he was almost under the front wheel of her bicycle.

She jammed on the brakes, putting her feet down to stop herself hurtling over the handlebars.

'Please, miss.' He looked up at her, his face pleading. He was no more than twelve years old, his hands thrust into the pockets of his ill-fitting trousers. An oversized cap sat on the back of his fair curly head.

'It's our Ellen. The baby's on its way. They need you to come.'

'Me?' Agnes couldn't keep the surprise out of her voice. 'But surely it's Hannah Arkwright you should be sending for?'

Stephen Kettle snatched his cap off his head and wrung it between his hands. 'Miss Arkwright's off delivering another baby so Ma sent me to fetch you instead.'

All kinds of smart replies flew into Agnes' mind. But then she looked down at his anxious face. 'I'll need to go back to the surgery to fetch my bag,' she said. 'You go on ahead and tell your mother I'll be there shortly.'

The boy sprinted off, and Agnes cycled quickly back to Dr Rutherford's house to fetch the metal maternity case she kept packed in her room, in case of emergencies. Back in Steeple Street, Bess Bradshaw had been adamant that they must be prepared at all times, but after nearly six weeks, Agnes had given up expecting that she would ever need to use it.

Her case strapped firmly to the back of her bicycle, she pedalled furiously down to the rows where Ellen Kettle lived.

The back door was thrown open, and some of the neighbouring women had gathered to see what was going on. They watched her as she dumped her bicycle against the back wall and unstrapped her bag, then parted to let her enter the cottage.

The boy who had summoned Agnes was sitting at the kitchen table, while a young girl busied herself at the range, heating up water. They both looked up with relief as Agnes entered.

'Ma says to go through.' The girl at the range nodded towards the other room.

'Thank you. Is that water for me?' Agnes nodded towards the range. 'Could you bring in two bowls, please? And some newspaper, towels and clean sheets, if you have them.'

Having issued her orders, Agnes went into the other room, where Ellen Kettle lay still on the high wooden bed, her pale face slick with sweat.

Her mother-in-law was with her, perched on the side of the bed, clutching her hand. She shot to her feet when Agnes walked in.

'Oh, Nurse, thank the Lord!' She left Ellen's side and went over to speak to Agnes, her voice low. 'Her waters broke in the early hours, and she started with her labour pains, but there in't been nowt since. Not to speak of anyway.' She cast a worried glance back at the girl in the bed. 'I don't like it,' she murmured. 'She should be well on the way by now, don't you think?'

'Sometimes these things take time, Mrs Kettle.' Agnes set down her bag and took off her coat. She smiled bracingly at Ellen, who let out a low moan and turned her face away to the wall.

The girl brought the bowls of water and newspaper, and Agnes washed her hands, set out her instruments and changed into a clean apron, then set about examining Ellen. Mrs Kettle was right; the girl's contractions did seem to be very weak.

And when Agnes examined her, she realised why.

'Is everything all right, Nurse?' Agnes hadn't realised Mrs Kettle was watching her closely until she turned round and found herself staring into the other woman's eyes.

She took a deep breath, trying to quell her rising panic. Whatever she did, she must not cause any alarm.

'I think we should send for the doctor,' she said.

Mrs Kettle looked dismayed. 'The doctor? But why? She in't in any danger, is she?'

Agnes took the woman's arm, steering her away from the bed and out of Ellen's earshot. 'I'm afraid the baby is facing the wrong way,' she said. 'Its back is against the mother's back, and the head is not flexed, which would explain the weak contractions.'

Mrs Kettle's eyes widened. 'Can't tha do summat?' she whispered.

I might if I'd been allowed to visit her earlier, Agnes thought. But this was no time for bitterness or recriminations.

'Not on my own. I need to call the doctor,' she repeated firmly.

'Ma?' Ellen whimpered from the bed. 'What's going on, Ma? What's t'nurse saying? Is my baby all right?'

'Everything's fine, pet,' Mrs Kettle called back. Then she turned to Agnes. 'Just do what tha must,' she hissed. 'We don't want another death in this house.'

Agnes found young Stephen in the kitchen, and was just passing on the message to give to Dr Rutherford when the door opened and Hannah Arkwright came in. She wore a shawl over her shabby man's overcoat in spite of the warm day, a carpet bag hooked over her arm.

'Now then.' She set her bag down on the stone-flagged floor and pulled her shawl off her head to reveal her thick red hair. 'Sorry I'm late, I—' She stopped dead when she saw Agnes. 'What are you doing here?'

Before Agnes could reply, Mrs Kettle appeared in the room. 'Oh, Hannah! Thank the Lord you've come. It's our Ellen. She's in a terrible way.'

'She's started, has she? I'll go and have a look at her.' She picked up her basket, but Agnes stepped in.

'I'm sending for the doctor,' she said, fighting to regain control of the situation. 'The baby is in the occipito-posterior presentation, and Mrs Kettle needs medical help.'

'Aye, well, let's have a look at her first.' Hannah went to move past her, but Agnes barred in her way.

'I don't think that's wise,' she said. 'You've just come from another delivery, there may be a risk of cross-infection.'

'I know what I'm doing.' Hannah laid her large hands on Agnes' arms and moved her out of the way, as easily as she might lift a child.

'But I must insist . . . ' Agnes gave a squeak of protest, but Hannah and Mrs Kettle were already making their way through to the bedroom, and all she could do was follow.

The sight of Hannah Arkwright seemed to have a miraculously calming effect on Ellen Kettle. The tension left her body and she relaxed against the pillows.

'Hello, love.' Hannah set her bag on the table, ignoring the instruments Agnes had so carefully set out. 'How are you? Worn out, I expect.'

'A bit.' Ellen smiled up at her, her round eyes as trusting as a child's.

'Well now, let's have a look at you and see if we can't get this bairn born, eh?'

Her presence seemed to have a remarkable effect on everyone. Even Mrs Kettle was smiling as Hannah carried out her examination.

Meanwhile, Agnes twitched with irritation. This was all wrong. Hannah did not have the first idea what she was dealing with. And she had barely even washed her hands. Agnes shuddered to think what terrible germs she might be spreading . . .

Finally, Hannah straightened up and said, 'Yes, the bairn is a bit twisted round. But it's nothing we can't sort out.' She smiled reassuringly at Ellen.

Agnes stared at her. Was she quite mad? 'She needs a doctor,' she hissed.

'Then you go off and fetch him, if tha wants,' Hannah replied mildly. 'I'll just stay here and deliver this baby.'

She turned to Mrs Kettle. 'Right now, we're going to need some thick towels. And summat to use as a binding.'

'I could tear up an old sheet?' Mrs Kettle suggested.

'Aye, that'll do nicely.'

All the while, Agnes stared from one to the other. 'You're not going to try to turn it yourself?'

Hannah didn't glance her way as she busied herself taking items out of her basket. 'Nay, I'm going to let nature take its course.'

'And how do you plan to do that?'

Hannah sighed. 'Honestly, didn't they teach you owt in that fancy nursing school of yours?' She said it with such exaggerated patience, even Ellen managed to laugh. 'If you bind a thick pad around the back, it'll push the bairn round to the front.'

'What?' Agnes was horrified. 'But – you can't. It will never work. It's just an old wives' tale.'

'We'll see, won't we?'

'But an occipito-posterior presentation—'

Hannah turned on her impatiently. 'You just keep on using them fancy words of yours, but stay out of my way if tha can't make thysen useful.' Once again, her large hands clamped down on Agnes' shoulders, shifting her into a corner of the room.

Agnes watched in stunned fascination as Mrs Kettle returned with the towel and the strips of sheet, and Hannah started to bind the pad around Ellen's slender flanks. It would never work. It couldn't. The baby would die, and poor Ellen too, if she didn't do something . . .

'I'm going to fetch Dr Rutherford,' she said. But no one paid any attention to her.

At the doctor's surgery, she threw her bicycle down on the front step and jumped over it, dashing into the house.

Once again, Mrs Bannister was in the hall. If she hadn't

128

known better, Agnes could have sworn the housekeeper was lying in wait for her.

'Rushing about again, Miss Sheridan?' She lifted a disapproving eyebrow. 'And is that your bicycle abandoned on the step? You can't leave it there, you know.'

'Where is the doctor?' Agnes cut across her.

Mrs Bannister's lips thinned, furious at the interruption. 'He's in morning surgery, of course – where are you going?' she said, as Agnes rushed past her. 'You can't just barge into—'

Fortunately the doctor was alone in his office, writing up his notes from the last patient. He peered over his spectacles as Agnes rushed in.

'Miss Sheridan? Good heavens, what is it? You seem in rather a fluster.'

'You have to come with me!' Agnes fought to get the words out, her chest rising and falling.

'I'm sorry, Doctor. I told her you weren't to be interrupted.' Mrs Bannister appeared behind Agnes.

'It's quite all right, Mrs B.' Dr Rutherford turned back to Agnes. 'What is going on?'

'Mrs Kettle . . . Ellen . . . she's in labour and it's in the wrong position.' Even as she gasped out the words Agnes was aware that she was being far less professional than she should in her report. 'You need to come!' she finished.

'Oh, for goodness' sake!' Mrs Bannister exclaimed. 'You can't expect the doctor to drop everything in the middle of morning surgery, just because you decide—'

'No, Mrs Bannister, the nurse is quite right. This is an emergency.' Dr Rutherford rose, picking up his bag. 'Send everyone else home, if you please. Take their names and tell them I'll call on them later.'

As Dr Rutherford drove them down to the rows, Agnes was able to explain more clearly about poor Ellen Kettle and her prolonged labour, and the appearance of Hannah Arkwright.

'You should have seen her. What she was doing was quite monstrous.' Agnes' hands shook in her lap. She was almost too afraid to return to Ellen Kettle's cottage, she was so worried about what they might find.

But what she didn't expect was to find Hannah Arkwright calmly sipping a cup of tea in the kitchen.

'Morning, Doctor,' she greeted him with a nod, her black eyes giving nothing away.

'Good morning, Miss Arkwright. I understand Mrs Kettle is in labour?'

'Was, Doctor. It's all over now.' Hannah glanced past him to Agnes, and once again her face was implacable.

'What's happened? What have you done to her?' Agnes demanded.

Hannah shrugged. 'Go and see for thysen.'

Ellen Kettle was sitting up in bed, nursing her baby, her mother-in-law at her side.

Ellen looked up at them, her face shining. 'It's a boy,' she said proudly. 'I'm naming him Harry, after his dad.'

Agnes looked from mother to baby and back again. 'But I don't understand. How did you—'

'Nature took its course, the way I said it would,' Hannah said smugly.

'Hmm, so it has.' Dr Rutherford looked grim. 'Well, it seems as if you called me away from my morning surgery for nothing, Miss Sheridan.'

Agnes stared down at the colourful proddy rug on the bedroom floor, unable to meet anyone's eye. 'Yes, Doctor.'

'In future perhaps you should think before you act.' Dr Rutherford turned to the young woman sitting up in bed, her baby clamped to her breast. 'Your son appears to be thriving, Mrs Kettle. I wish you both well.'

'Thank you, Doctor.'

He turned back to Agnes. 'I'll give you a lift back to the surgery, Miss Sheridan. It doesn't appear as if either of us is needed here.'

'No, Doctor.' Agnes couldn't look at Hannah's face as she followed him. She could only imagine the expression of triumph she would see written there.

'You should have seen her,' Hannah told her mother later. 'She kept looking at me and then the bairn and back again, like she couldn't believe her eyes! And the way the doctor spoke to her . . . Well, I hardly knew where to put myself!' She laughed at the memory of it. This morning couldn't have gone better if she had planned it.

Her mother's face was unsmiling as she rocked back and forth in her chair. 'I daresay you're very pleased with thysen?' she said.

Hannah's own smile faltered. She had been looking forward to telling her mother all about it, certain that Nella would enjoy the moment as much as she had.

'Why wouldn't I be?' she answered defiantly. 'It was one in the eye for Nurse Sheridan. And she thought she was so clever, with all her shiny instruments laid out like soldiers in a line! I soon showed her what was what.'

'So tha reckons tha've got the best of her, do you? You think she'll just pack up and go home?'

Hannah stared at her mother, trying to fathom out what was going on behind those narrowed, almost blind eyes of hers. 'Why not? I spoke to Mrs Kettle this morning, and she says she's going to let everyone know what happened with her Ellen. I shouldn't think Miss Sheridan will be asked to deliver any more babies in Bowden. She'll soon get the message that no one wants her here. '

'That won't do it!' her mother snapped. 'I told you, she's

got some spirit. The more you try and push her away, the more she'll fight back.'

'She didn't look like she was fighting back this morning,' Hannah said. 'Slunk away with her tail between her legs, she did.'

'But she'll be back. And it won't be long before she finds a way to win people over. There are already folk in the village who think she should be given a fair chance. People who you might consider loyal to you.'

Hannah's head went up. 'What people? Who are you talking about?'

'I in't saying.' Nella's mouth clammed up. 'Now fetch me a cup of willow bark tea, will you? My arthritis is playing up.' She stretched her thin arms, wincing.

Hannah went to put the kettle on, feeling defeated. She had felt so elated this morning, when she had managed to deliver Ellen Kettle's baby safely. Two bairns born one after the other had more than made up for her missing a night's sleep. She had come home jubilant, brimming with triumph, but as usual her mother had crushed her happiness and ruined her moment.

She stared at her reflection in the spotted fragment of mirror over the sink as she washed her mother's cup. A plain, tired face stared back at her, the spark gone from her dark eyes.

But she knew her mother was not right. Not this time. She had seen Agnes' face that morning. She was utterly humiliated. It wouldn't be long before the nurse left Bowden, and never came back.

Chapter Sixteen

As soon as Carrie woke up, she knew something wasn't right.

Dawn was breaking, a crack of pale light through the gap in the curtains. She lay for a moment, trying to work out what had woken her. Then she saw James, sitting at the foot of the bed, with Henry in his arms.

Instantly she had snapped fully awake, sitting bolt upright, pushing her tangled hair off her face. 'What is it? What's wrong? I didn't hear him cry. '

'He didn't. I woke him. I wanted to see him before I left.'

Her dazed mind registered that he was dressed for work in his suit and tie. 'What time is it?'

'Just after five.'

'But why are you up so early on a Saturday morning—' she started to say, then remembered. 'You're going to the pit.'

He nodded.

'So you're really going to lock the men out?'

It was 1 May, the deadline for the miners to accept the government's ultimatum. But the Miners' Federation had stood firm, and now it was the mine owners' turn to carry out their threat.

'I don't have much choice.' James kept his gaze fixed on the baby, studying his tiny features with such intensity it made Carrie feel uneasy.

'Here, let me take him.' She stretched out her arms, but James held the baby closer to him.

'In a minute. I just want to spend a bit more time with Henry.'

Her husband looked so wretched, Carrie's heart went out to him. Poor James. She knew he had been worrying about this day coming. He had barely slept at all the past few nights. She could feel him tossing and turning beside her, and twice she had woken up to find the bed beside her empty.

Carrie felt for him, but she felt even more for the men who would be turning up for their shift at six o'clock that morning, only to be met by locked pit gates.

'Well, I hope you know what you're doing,' she said. 'Those men will have to go home to their wives and tell them there'll be no money coming in today.' She knew how that felt. She had witnessed the fear on her own mother's face when she saw her husband trudging back up the lane on the days there was no work for him at the pit.

'They should have thought of that and accepted the terms they were offered, shouldn't they? Then we wouldn't all be in this mess.'

Carrie stared at her husband, shocked by his tone. James had never spoken to her so sharply before. 'You really expected them to work longer hours for less pay?'

'I expected everyone to see sense!' He stood up and passed the baby to her. Suddenly he seemed like a stranger, towering over her in his smart suit. 'Anyway, I suppose I have to go and face the consequences.' He grimaced.

What consequences? Carrie wanted to ask. James wasn't the one who would be coming home to an unlit fire and no dinner on the table. She bit her tongue to stop the words coming out. Her husband was already tense enough.

As soon as he'd gone, Henry started to wriggle in her arms, his little arms held out imploringly to the closed door.

'Da!' he cried, his round brown eyes brimming with tears.

It had been his first proper word, uttered a week ago, and he had been saying it ever since. Carrie kissed Henry's head, with its fuzzy covering of pale wispy hair. She could smell James' shaving soap on him. It gave her a pang.

'Daddy's gone, my love,' she murmured.

The house always felt too large and empty without James there. There was usually little to do after Carrie had bathed and dressed and fed the baby. She would have liked to busy herself around the house, but the maid took offence if she tried to help. As it was, Carrie knew she could have done a better job. The girl was very lackadaisical when it came to dusting and polishing, and Carrie had never seen her beat a rug properly.

She had said as much to James, but all he'd said was that if she wasn't happy they could get rid of the maid and engage someone else.

'I'd be better off doing it mysen,' Carrie had said, but James wouldn't hear of it.

'You have better things to do with your time than scrub floors, my love,' he had said.

What sort of things? Carrie wondered as she stood at the window, staring out at the street. What did fine ladies do to fill their hours? If she didn't have an excuse to visit her mother, all she did was drift around the house, playing with the baby, getting in the maid's way and counting the hours until James came home.

She smiled to think how she and her sisters used to complain about the chores they had to do. Who would have imagined she would ever miss kneading bread dough or hanging out a line of washing on a blowy day?

At least today she had something to look forward to. All through the morning, Carrie kept hurrying to the window to look for the Goodman's van to arrive.

It finally pulled up just as she was giving Henry his

lunch. She dropped the spoon and jumped to her feet before she remembered it was unseemly for the lady of the house to open her own front door. Instead she had to wait impatiently, listening to the maid passing the time of day with the delivery man. It seemed a very long time before she tapped on the door and entered with a large, brown paper parcel in her arms.

'This arrived for you, madam.'

'Thank you. Put it over there, will you?' Carrie forced down her excitement. It wasn't seemly for a lady to show too much of that, either.

After lunch, she settled Henry for his afternoon nap and then finally she could unwrap her package.

It was even better than she could have hoped. Ten yards of white silk brocade, enough to make the most beautiful wedding dress.

She hadn't heard from Nancy about going shopping, so after waiting nearly two weeks had decided to surprise her friend by ordering some fabric herself. From one of the finest shops in Leeds, no less. Carrie ran her hands over the silky fabric, letting it slide through her fingers. It made her smile to think how thrilled her friend would be when she saw it. It was far nicer than anything Nancy would ever buy for herself.

Carrie was so excited she couldn't wait for Nancy to see it. So once Henry had woken up from his nap, she dressed him in his woolly coat and hat and set off to the Co-op, the parcel tucked underneath the pram.

The store wasn't nearly as busy as it usually was on a Saturday. Carrie was aware of the other women turning their heads to look at her as she dodged Mr Fensom's greeting and hurried to the drapery counter.

There was another girl, Betty Willis, behind the counter. They had been friends when Carrie worked there.

'Hello, love – oops, I mean, Mrs Shepherd,' Betty corrected herself, smiling. 'What can I do for you today?'

Carrie glanced over her shoulder, but Mr Fensom was busy with another customer on the other side of the store.

'I was looking for Nancy. Is she here?'

Betty shook her head. 'It's her day off today. She's gone shopping in Leeds with Iris Maskell.' She pulled a face. 'All right for some, in't it? They should never have been allowed the same day off by rights, but Nancy managed to sweet-talk Mr Fensom. I reckon he's got a bit of a soft spot for her mysen, dirty old goat! Anyway, I've been left to look after drapery and haberdashery all by myself. Lucky it's not too busy.' She looked around. 'I suppose no one feels like shopping, with all this business going on at the pit. Have you heard they've locked—?'

But Carrie's mind was racing so fast she hardly heard the girl's chatter. 'Are you sure Nancy's gone to Leeds?' she interrupted her.

'Oh, yes, I heard them talking about it. Very excited they were, off to buy the material for her wedding dress. Been going on about it for days . . . Oh, where are you going? Are you sure I can't sell you anything? We've just had a new delivery of silk stockings, if you're interested . . .'

Her words followed Carrie as she walked away.

She stomped home, pushing the pram before her like a battering ram, so fired up with anger she scarcely noticed the people who scattered on the pavement before her.

How could Nancy do it? Carrie searched her mind, trying to come up with reasons why her friend would be so unkind. Had Nancy forgotten to invite her? But that didn't make sense. The trip to Leeds had been Carrie's idea, so Nancy would hardly leave her out.

Perhaps it was all Iris Maskell's doing? She had always been a jealous cat. She probably wanted Nancy all to herself, so she had worked out a way to come between the friends. But if that was true, why hadn't Nancy stood up for Carrie?

There was only one way to find out, Carrie decided, and that was to ask her outright.

The last bus back from Leeds that afternoon was due in soon. Carrie pushed the pram up to the stop at the top of the lane. As she walked, her mind simmered with rage, planning what she might do. She would throw the package at Nancy and then stalk off, her head in the air. She would slap Iris around her smug face. She would . . .

But when the bus finally trundled into view down the lane and came to a halt in front of her, it was all Carrie could do to stop her heart beating right out of her chest.

The girls stepped off the bus, laughing together. Nancy was clutching a brown paper parcel similar to the one that had arrived that morning from Goodman's.

The air was cold against Carrie's scalding face, and she felt the sudden urge to run, but there was nowhere to hide.

Nancy saw her first. She stopped laughing, and grabbed Iris' arm. Then Iris looked round, her smile widening into something more malicious.

'Did you have a nice time in Leeds?' Carrie greeted them, her bitterness spilling over.

'Yes, thank you,' Iris replied.

'We were going to ask you.' Nancy's words tumbled out in a rush. 'But we only found out at the last minute that we both had the day off, so there wasn't time.'

'That's not what Betty Willis told me. She said you've been talking about it for ages.'

Nancy blushed. 'I—'

'It's all right,' Carrie said. 'You can spare me more lies. You were never going to invite me, were you?'

'That's not—' Nancy started to say, but Iris interrupted her.

'You're right, we didn't want you to come,' she said bluntly.

'Iris!' Nancy hissed, but Iris was defiant.

'Why shouldn't I speak the truth? It's about time someone put her straight.' She turned to Carrie, her eyes narrowed in spite. 'You would have only spoiled Nancy's day, showing off and looking down your nose at her.'

Carrie looked at Nancy. She was biting her lip, close to tears. 'Is that true?'

'She'll not say anything because she doesn't want to hurt your feelings,' Iris spoke for her again. 'But Nancy doesn't want to know you, not any more.' She linked her arm through the other girl's possessively.

Carrie stared from one to the other of them. Nancy was staring down at her shoes, while Iris looked like the cat that got the cream.

'In that case, I'll not bother you again.' She fought to keep her dignity, hating the treacherous wobble in her voice.

'Carrie, please!' Nancy found her voice at last, but Carrie didn't stop to hear what she had to say. She moved past them, pushing the pram.

'And you needn't think you're going to be matron of honour, either!' Iris called after her.

Carrie had turned the corner and was halfway down the street when Nancy caught up with her. Carrie heard her friend's footsteps running after her, but was too hurt and upset to stop.

'Carrie! Wait!' Nancy cried after her.

'What for?' She carried on walking, her head down.

Nancy grabbed her by the arm, swinging her round to face her. Her round face was pink and shiny from running. 'Don't be like that. I'm sorry about what Iris said. Don't take any notice of her. She's just jealous of you because we used to be such good friends.'

Used to be. The words stung. Carriee swallowed hard. 'So are you saying it was her idea not to invite me to go to Leeds with you?'

Nancy hesitated for a moment. 'No, it was mine.' She stared down at the ground. 'But it in't because I don't like you – I do,' she added in a rush. 'I was just worried you'd insist on paying for everything. You were talking about going for tea in a posh hotel . . . '

'I just wanted to do summat nice for you, that's all.' Carrie kept her eyes fixed on the top of Henry's head, encased in a woolly bonnet. 'We always used to talk about going somewhere posh for tea one day, don't you remember? I thought you'd enjoy it.'

'I would have enjoyed it more if I could pay my share,' Nancy said.

'But you didn't have to. It was my treat.'

'It would have felt more like charity to me.'

Carrie stared at her friend, shocked. 'I – I just wanted to make it special for you.'

'But I don't want you to do anything special!' Nancy cried. 'Don't you understand, Carrie? It doesn't feel right any more, you and me.'

Her mother's words came back to her. *Like it or not, you mix in different circles now.*

'So we can't be friends any more because my husband is the pit manager, is that it?' Carrie said miserably.

'I didn't say that.' Nancy laid a hand on hers. Even her fingers, red and callused from helping her mother with the housework, looked different from Carrie's soft white hands. 'But surely you must be able to see it can never be like it was before? I'm going to be a pitman's wife, Carrie. You'll never understand that life.'

'How can you say that? I was brought up in that life, same as you. Our fathers worked down the mine together. We used to dash their clothes for them, and get all the beetles out of the pockets.' She saw Nancy's grimace. She always hated touching the little black bugs, it was Carrie who'd had to get them out for her. 'Anyway, I might have been a pitman's wife too, if only Rob hadn't—' She stopped herself, pressing her lips together.

She hadn't asked him to break her heart. Rob Chadwick and his cousin Archie had been Carrie and Nancy's child-hood sweethearts. The two girls had planned their futures around their weddings. They had already made up their mind that once they were married they would live in cottages next door to each other. Rob and Archie would work down the pit together, and Carrie and Nancy would have babies, and look after their houses, and be closer to each other than their own sisters.

But then Rob's father had been killed in a pit accident three years earlier, and his mother had decided to move back to her own family in Durham. And Rob had gone with her and his younger brothers and sisters, even though he was turned twenty-one and could just as easily have stayed in Bowden and married Carrie as they had always planned.

'I know,' Nancy said quietly. 'Perhaps things might have been different then.'

Carrie smiled wistfully. 'Remember how we used to plan our weddings?' she said. 'We used to sit on the wall at the bottom of the lane and talk about what we would wear, and what flowers we would have.'

'And how handsome Archie and Rob would look in their suits,' Nancy added.

'We were even going to have a double wedding, until we realised we couldn't be each other's bridesmaid if we got married at the same time.'

Nancy turned to face her. 'I still want you to be my matron of honour,' she said.

A lump rose in Carrie's throat. 'That's not what Iris said.'

'Oh, take no notice of her. I told you, she's just jealous. But it's my choice, not hers.' Nancy squeezed Carrie's hand. 'Besides, we promised each other, didn't we?'

Carrie felt her smile tremble. Was Nancy just trying to be nice? It was hard to tell, but at that moment she was too happy they were still friends to question it too deeply.

'I'd love to,' she said.

They said their goodbyes. As they parted, Carrie suddenly remembered the gift she had bought.

'Nancy?' she called out to her.

Nancy turned. 'Yes? What is it?'

Carrie thought about the brown paper parcel Nancy had carried so proudly off the bus, the fabric she had chosen to make her wedding dress. Carrie hadn't seen inside the parcel, but she was willing to bet it was nowhere near as beautiful or as expensive as the silk brocade she had ordered.

Then she saw the wary look in Nancy's green eyes.

'Nothing,' she said. 'It doesn't matter.'

She could send the fabric back to Goodman's first thing on Monday morning.

Chapter Seventeen

By Wednesday, the miners' dispute had spread like a virus throughout the country. Agnes woke up that morning to the news that the whole country had gone on strike.

'There are no buses running, no gas or electricity. And I don't know what Dr Rutherford is going to do without his morning newspaper.' Mrs Bannister made a rare appearance in the kitchen to fret about the situation.

'I'm sure the doctor will be able to make do, like the rest of us,' Agnes said mildly as she chewed on the slice of bread and jam Jinny had put in front of her.

'Yes, well, he shouldn't have to make do, should he? He works hard, he's entitled to his home comforts.'

Agnes glanced at Jinny Chadwick, over by the sink. The girl said nothing, but Agnes could tell by the hunch of her thin shoulders that she was struggling not to speak out.

'The miners are entitled to their home comforts, too,' Agnes spoke up for her.

'Oh, don't talk to me about them!' Mrs Bannister pursed her lips. 'It's their fault this country is going to the dogs. If only they'd put a stop to this – what's that?'

Mrs Bannister gave a squawk of dismay, threw open the back door and shouted outside, 'Who's there? What's the meaning of this?'

Agnes caught Jinny's eye and they both hurried to look out of the window. There, in the kitchen garden, happily munching their way through Dr Rutherford's prize spring cabbages, were a pair of stocky little brown ponies.

'Pit ponies,' Jinny whispered. 'They had to bring 'em up when they locked the mine.'

'But how did they get here?' Agnes asked.

As if in answer to her question, there was a rustle in the shrubbery. Agnes caught a glimpse of a boy's tousled dark head coming out from behind the potting shed before quickly disappearing again.

'I see you, Christopher Stanhope!' Mrs Bannister called out to him. 'Come out here and show yourself!'

The boy broke cover and sprinted off down the path, vaulting the back gate easily until all that was left was the echo of his laughter and the two ponies, cabbage leaves hanging from their chewing mouths, wondering what all the fuss was about.

'I know where you live!' Mrs Bannister shouted down the garden, even though the boy was long gone. 'And you can be sure the doctor will have something to say to your father when he sees all this mess!' She stared at the ponies. They gazed back at her calmly from under long blond fringes. It was all Agnes could do not to laugh at the sight. Next to her, Jinny had clapped her hand over her mouth, trying to stifle her own laughter.

But her grin disappeared when Mrs Bannister swung round to face them. 'Well, don't just stand there, girl! Do something!' she screeched at Jinny.

The maid looked blank. 'What am I supposed to do, ma'am?'

'I don't know, do I?' Mrs Bannister waved her hand towards the ponies. 'Round them up and take them back where they belong before they do any more damage. Poor Dr Rutherford, as if this nasty strike business wasn't difficult enough for him.'

Agnes glanced at Jinny. Once again, the girl said nothing, but her look spoke volumes.

By the Thursday morning, much to Mrs Bannister's relief, volunteers had managed to get the electricity working again, so at least Dr Rutherford wasn't inconvenienced for too long. The government had even managed to produce a newspaper, *The British Gazette*, for him to read over his cooked breakfast. Agnes caught Jinny just before she used it to light the fire.

On the Friday morning, Agnes returned to Steeple Street for the first time to report back to Miss Gale, the Superintendent.

It had been three months since she left, and she hadn't realised how much she had missed it until she was cycling back through the city. Seeing the familiar busy streets bustling with people, cars and carts cheered her. She felt her heart lifting as she cycled up Steeple Street, towards the tall, gabled district nurses' house. And when Dottie the maid answered the door it was all Agnes could do not to hug her.

Everything in the Steeple Street house was still the same. The long hallway, with its airy high ceiling, black-and-white-tiled floor, the telephone on the wall and the noticeboard covered with rotas. The pigeonholes where Agnes had searched so patiently for a letter from her mother . . .

It was odd to see so many new names there, written on the labels. Her own pigeonhole was now taken by someone with the rather grand name of Deborah Banks-Hulme.

Agnes couldn't help smiling to herself, wondering what Bess Bradshaw would be making of that particular girl. The Assistant Superintendent delighted in taking posh girls down a peg or two. Hadn't she done just that to Agnes when she first arrived? Or at least had tried. As it turned out, they had ended up learning a lesson from each other.

But even though the district nurses' house was still

familiar to Agnes, at the same time it felt strangely distant, as if it was no longer her home. Agnes had moved on, but life in Steeple Street had continued just as it always did and the hole she had left had quickly been filled in and forgotten.

It gave her a pang. How she longed to be back there, surrounded by her friends in the safety of Steeple Street rather than isolated in Bowden.

Even Dottie seemed puzzled by her presence. 'Have you come back? Only there's someone else in your room now,' she said bluntly. 'There's no room for you any more,' she added, just in case Agnes had missed her point.

Agnes smiled patiently. 'No, Dottie, I've come back to see Miss Gale.'

The maid looked blank. 'Well, she in't here. She's gone off for one of her meetings.'

'A meeting?' Agnes tried to suppress her annoyance. 'But she knew I was coming.'

'Perhaps she forgot?' Dottie shrugged her narrow shoulders.

Agnes frowned. It wasn't surprising. The Nursing Superintendent spent much of her time in various meetings, rushing from one to the next with barely time to think in between.

'Do you know when she's expected back?' she asked. Dottie shrugged again. 'Then I'll wait for her.' Agnes started towards the Common Room, but Dottie blocked her path.

'You can't,' she said. 'That's the nurses' room.'

'I am a nurse—' Agnes started to say, but Dottie stood firm, her skinny arms folded.

'You can wait there.' She nodded to the solitary chair outside the Superintendent's office. 'That's where visitors sit.'

'But I'm not a visitor,' Agnes started to explain again. But Dottie would not be budged, so in the end Agnes gave up and waited where she was put.

She took her place on the chair in the hall, remembering how she had sat there on her very first day. She had been so different then, so convinced that she knew it all. She had come up from London, where she had trained as a nurse in one of the best hospitals in the country. As far as she was concerned, there was nothing anyone could teach her.

How wrong she had been.

'No!' A voice boomed out from the porch outside, making her jump. 'I've said how it should be done, and I want no more arguments. And if you look at that watch of yours again, I'll take it off you and chuck it in the canal! It'll take as long as I say it'll take.'

Agnes smiled. She would have known that forthright manner anywhere! She turned towards the front door as it opened and Bess Bradshaw entered, a weary-looking student nurse trailing behind her. Agnes recognised at once the look of nervous exasperation on the poor girl's face. She had felt the same way many times while out on her rounds with Bess.

Bess Bradshaw stopped short when she saw Agnes.

'Well, now. Who have we here? I thought we'd got rid of you, Miss Sheridan.' She greeted her in her usual gruff way, but Agnes could see the gleam in Bess' blue eyes. The Assistant Superintendent took off her cap, revealing short brown curls threaded with grey. She was in her late forties, a stout, uncompromising figure in her nurse's navy blue coat.

'You see this one, Deborah?' She turned to the girl in the doorway. 'This is Agnes Sheridan, one of my former students. She was like you when she arrived, thought she knew everything. But I soon showed her what was what, didn't I, Miss Sheridan?'

'Take no notice,' Agnes told the frightened-looking girl, 'her bark is far worse than her bite.'

'Now, don't you go telling her that!' Bess did her best to look outraged. 'You don't take any notice of what she says,' she warned the girl. 'I can blooming well bite when I have a mind to.' She nodded towards the District Room. 'Go and write up your notes from this morning. And be sure to sort out that district bag, too,' she called after her. 'You must have packed it in a dream this morning.'

The girl hurried off. Bess turned to Agnes, shaking her head. 'I ask you. What self-respecting Queen's Nurse goes on her rounds without boracic ointment?'

'Is that Miss Banks-Hulme?' Agnes asked.

'Miss Banks-Hulme, indeed!' Bess rolled her eyes. 'I call her Deborah. She doesn't like it, but it's her own fault for having such a daft name. And she's even worse than you are for asking questions,' Bess added. 'And always looking at that watch of hers, just like you used to.'

'That's because you're always late,' Agnes said.

Bess' eyes widened. 'Just because you've got your badge now, you needn't think you can give me any cheek, Miss Sheridan,' she warned. 'I'm still the Assistant Superintendent, you know.' She shrugged off her coat and hung it up on the peg. 'Anyway, it's about time you showed your face. We all thought you'd abandoned us!'

Agnes blushed. 'I know I should have come earlier, but I wanted to get myself settled in Bowden first,' she mumbled.

'And have you?'

Agnes couldn't meet her eye. 'Yes, thank you.'

'And the patients have taken to you?'

'Yes.' Once again, Agnes couldn't meet her eye. But she should have known that Bess' shrewd gaze missed nothing.

'I thought as much,' she said grimly. 'I told Miss Gale that's why we hadn't seen you. You're having trouble, in't you?'

'No ... ' Agnes started to protest, but the words died in her throat. 'It's not going as well as I'd hoped,' she admitted reluctantly.

It was an understatement. Even with her determinedly optimistic nature, she had to admit her progress had been slow. What little confidence she had gained had quickly been lost after all the business with Ellen Kettle's baby.

News had quickly spread of how Hannah Arkwright had managed to deliver the baby safely while Agnes ran off to fetch the doctor in a complete panic.

She was angry with herself every time she thought about it. She should have stayed calm, tried to manage the situation herself. She knew she had done the right thing, but her reputation in the village had suffered because of it.

'Well, I can't say as I'm surprised,' Bess said. 'Those pit villages don't take kindly to outsiders. And if I know you, you'll be rushing in like a bull in a china shop, thinking you know best, trying to tell everyone how to run their lives.'

'I haven't!' Agnes protested. 'I'm doing my best to fit in, honestly. But no one seems to like me very much,' she added glumly.

Bess stared at her for a long time. Then, finally, she said, 'Tell you what, why don't you stop and have a bit of dinner with us?'

'I can't.' Agnes sent a quick look towards the door of the Superintendent's office. 'I'm supposed to be meeting Miss Gale.'

'Oh, she's off with the District Association Committee, and you know what they're like. Could go on for hours. And you don't want to be sat on that chair all day, waiting for her, do you? It's nearly midday. The other nurses will be coming back from their rounds soon. I'm sure they'd like to see you.'

Agnes hesitated. She didn't want to admit she had timed her meeting so she might catch them between their morning and afternoon rounds. She was longing to see them all again, too.

'I should go back to Bowden . . . ' she started to say, but dread settled like a heavy stone in her stomach at the thought of it.

'I'm sure they can spare you for another couple of hours,' Bess said. Then she added, 'Besides, from what you say they probably won't even notice you've gone!'

Agnes ignored the crushing comment. It was just Bess' way. She might be blunt to the point of rudeness, but she could also be a wise and understanding friend.

A few of the other nurses – Miss Jarvis, Miss Goode, Miss Hook and Miss Templeton – returned from their rounds shortly afterwards, and just after midday they all sat down for their lunch. The others were curious about her, wanting to know how she had been getting on. Proud as she was, Agnes would have preferred to keep her difficulties to herself and present a more positive picture of her time in Bowden, but of course Bess Bradshaw had other ideas. She insisted on telling everyone the true story. And in the end Agnes was glad she had, as the other nurses were all surprisingly sympathetic and full of advice.

They were especially understanding when she told them about Hannah Arkwright.

'Oh, we've all met women like her in our time,' Miss Hook said. 'Nearly every village has one. They call themselves healers and witches and everyone is afraid of them.'

'Superstitious nonsense!' Bess muttered.

'Superstitious or not, the people of Bowden certainly

seem to believe in her,' Agnes said sadly. 'I don't know what to do.'

'Just carry on. It's all you can do,' Bess said, helping herself to another slice of bread. 'You'll see, one day you'll be able to prove yourself.'

'She's right,' Miss Jarvis agreed. 'It's all you can do.'

'Actually, there is something else I could do,' Agnes said slowly. 'I was thinking of asking Miss Gale if I could come back to Steeple Street. Perhaps transfer to another area?'

She looked up from her plate to see a circle of shocked faces staring back at her.

'You can't do that!' Miss Jarvis spoke for them.

'But they really don't need me in Bowden.'

'Of course they need you,' Bess said. 'Besides,' she added practically, 'it's where you've been assigned. Miss Gale won't like the paperwork if she has to move you somewhere else.'

It didn't seem a good enough reason to Agnes. She still meant to discuss the matter with the Superintendent at their meeting. But Miss Gale had had not returned by the time lunch had finished, so Bess suggested that Agnes might like to accompany her on her round instead of sitting waiting.

'We're off to the new mother and baby clinic we've just opened in Quarry Hill,' she said. 'I think you might find it quite interesting. Besides, we're a bit short-handed. We could do with an extra pair of hands. And you might as well make yourself useful while you're here.'

Chapter Eighteen

Quarry Hill had not changed in the three months Agnes had been away. The narrow little alleys and courtyards still teemed with life, ripe with the smell of middens and the fish market.

She commented as much to Bess, who sent her a sharp look as she wobbled along on her bicycle beside Agnes', her bulk spilling over the tiny saddle.

'What did you think? You've only been away five minutes. Did you think we'd fall apart without you, Miss Sheridan?' She looked around her. 'I doubt if this place will ever change,' she said.

The clinic was being held in the local church hall. Agnes was thrilled to see her old room mate Polly Mallone emerging from behind the canvas screens, carrying a set of baby weighing scales, under the watchful eye of the Senior District Midwife, Miss Hawksley.

Polly looked just as delighted as Agnes felt to see her. She set the scales down on the table and hurried over.

'Agnes! What are you doing here?'

'She's come to visit us,' Bess answered for her. 'I thought she might like to see the new clinic, since she's here.'

Polly looked around, pride written all over her face. 'Well, this is only our fourth week, but we've been busy the last two. The local mothers certainly seem to appreciate us.'

'I'm surprised,' Agnes remarked. 'I wouldn't have expected it to be so popular in a place like this?'

Too late she realised what she had said. Bess pounced on her.

'Why not? The women here care about their children, same as anywhere else,' she retorted.

Polly and Agnes exchanged knowing looks. They had both suffered from Bess' sharp tongue during their training. Polly had suffered most of all because she had the added misfortune of being Bess' daughter.

Agnes watched now as Bess turned her critical attention to the room.

'You don't want to put those scales there,' she said. 'The bairns will catch the draught from the door while they're being weighed.'

'I was just about to move them,' Polly replied, tight-lipped. 'Besides, I've lit the fire, so it will be warm enough.'

'Even so—'

'It will be warm enough,' Polly said firmly.

Agnes waited tensely for Bess to argue, but to her amazement the Assistant Nursing Superintendent backed down like a lamb. 'Come on,' she said to Agnes. 'You can help me set the chairs out.'

Agnes followed her, sending a brief backward glance at Polly as she went. The young midwife's smile told her everything she needed to know. Bess had singled her daughter out for some harsh attention when they were training, and for a long time the rift between them had been bitter. But in the end they had learned to love and respect each other, and now their arguments had mellowed into nothing more than good-natured bickering.

At two o'clock, Polly opened the doors and a steady stream of mothers began to arrive, pushing prams and trailing more young children behind them. Agnes was pleased and surprised to see several faces she knew. As she took her place beside Polly, taking patients' names, weighing the babies and writing down their notes, she found herself relaxing, even enjoying herself.

'So are you coming back to Quarry Hill, Nurse?' one of the mothers asked her.

'I'm afraid not.' Agnes smiled back at her, genuinely regretful. How could it be that these women accepted her so easily, compared to the suspicious faces she met in Bowden?

And then, just as she had finished advising one worried young mother on her baby's nappy rash, Bess nudged her and whispered, 'Have you seen who's just walked in, Miss Sheridan? An old friend of yours.'

Agnes looked up to see Lil Fairbrass pushing an enormous pram through the double doors. She entered like a galleon in full sail, parting the tide of waiting mothers to take her place in the front row.

Agnes smiled uneasily. Once upon a time, Lil Fairbrass had been her biggest enemy in Quarry Hill. The first time they had met she had knocked Agnes flat with a flying fist. It had been an accident, but it had set the tone for further bruising encounters.

Things had only got worse when Agnes dared to suggest that Lil's schoolgirl daughter Christine might be pregnant. But as it turned out she was right, and Agnes had been the one to find Christine after she ran away, and to deliver her baby. She had earned Lil's respect and gratitude ever since.

'Look at the size of that pram,' Bess said. 'She in't one to do things by halves, is she?' She looked approving. 'That bairn wants for nowt.'

Agnes felt a pang. Having children out of wedlock was nothing unusual in Quarry Hill, but when it happened it was usually hushed up. But not by Lil. She paraded her illegitimate grandchild as if she was the proudest woman in the world. And with her being a Fairbrass, no one dared argue.

It made Agnes think of her own mother, hurrying her off to that dismal maternity home and leaving her there, frightened and alone, to face her fate alone. Even now, over a year later, Elizabeth Sheridan still couldn't bring herself to forgive Agnes for the shame she might have brought on her family. The last time Agnes had tried to visit, her mother had made it clear she was no longer welcome at home.

Lil saw her and roared out a greeting. 'Well, look who it is! Nurse Aggie!'

Agnes winced. The other residents of Quarry Hill might have called her by that name in private, but only Lil used it to her face.

'This is the nurse who delivered our Christine's,' Lil announced to everyone. 'Saved her, she did. Dunno what would have happened if she hadn't been there with her quick thinking.'

'I don't know about that ... ' Agnes blushed as she looked into the pram. 'How is little Lilian?'

'Lilian Agnes,' Lil corrected her. 'Oh, she's just grand.' She beamed with pride as she took the baby out of the pram. Agnes caught a flash of bright red hair, covered up with layers of shawls. 'Putting on weight nicely. Proper little spoiled princess, she is.'

'She looks very bonny,' Agnes said. 'And how is Christine?' she asked, lowering her voice.

'She's doing well too. Going back to school in September. She'll matriculate and then she's going to be a teacher.' She said it loud enough for everyone in the room to hear.

'How will she manage, with school and the baby?'

'We've thought about all that, Nurse. I'm going to take on the bairn as my own, for the time being.' Lil beamed down at the infant. 'She'll want for nothing, what with me and my lads to help take care of her. And Christine needs to think about her future,' she added firmly.

'That's very good of you, Mrs Fairbrass,' Agnes said.

Lil Fairbrass frowned at her. 'In't nowt to do wi' being good,' she said. 'It's what families do.'

Agnes looked down at the baby, sleeping so peacefully in the safety of her grandmother's arms, and thought again about her own family. Elizabeth Sheridan would no doubt look down her nose at Lil and her unruly brood, but the Fairbrass family could teach her a lot about loyalty and love.

When the clinic was over, Agnes helped Polly and Bess pack away the equipment and tidy up the chairs.

'Well?' Bess said. 'Did you enjoy yourself, Miss Sheridan?'

'Yes, I did. Very much,' Agnes said.

'I could see that. You seemed to be getting on well with the mothers, too.'

'It was lovely to see them again,' Agnes said.

Bess sent her a shrewd look. 'Bet you never thought you'd be saying that when you first arrived here to start your training?'

Agnes laughed. 'I should say not! I thought it was a dreadful place.'

'Remember when Nettie Willis chased you out of her house with a broom?' Bess chuckled. 'And that time you nearly got a chamber pot emptied over your head?'

'Don't remind me!' Agnes shuddered.

'But you won them over in the end, didn't you? Even Lil Fairbrass sings your praises now.' Bess paused and added, 'All they needed was time to get used to you, so you could show them what you're capable of doing. That's all anyone needs, Miss Sheridan. Time.'

The next minute Bess had turned away to talk to Miss

Hawksley, leaving Agnes to stare at her broad back. And then it dawned on her. The Assistant Superintendent hadn't brought her here because they needed an extra pair of hands at the clinic. She had brought her here because she wanted to remind Agnes how far she had come.

And if she had done it once, here in Quarry Hill, then surely she could do it again in Bowden.

Chapter Nineteen

'What do you mean, you're not coming?'

Carrie looked at her husband's reflection in the mirror as she sat at the dressing table, pinning up her hair.

James sighed. 'Think about it, my love. How can I possibly go to a wedding with the situation as it is? I pass Tom and Archie Chadwick and Ron Morris and his brothers at the locked pit gates every morning. I hear the names they call me, I know what they think of me. Last week I had to call in the special constables because I caught one of the Morris boys trying to get over the fence into the coal yard. I can't see how I'd be very welcome at this wedding, do you?' He shook his head. 'If I go, it will only make things difficult for everyone.'

He was right, Carrie realised. Deep down she had always known it wasn't a good idea for James to come to Nancy's wedding. It would have been difficult at the best of times, having the pit manager there, but the wretched lockout made the situation impossible.

It had been going on for more than a month now. At first, the whole country had been united, with riots on the streets and clashes with the police in several big cities. But behind the scenes, the Trade Union Congress was busy making a deal with the government. Within a week everyone had gone back to work, leaving the miners to struggle on alone.

'They've stabbed us in the back,' her father had said. He was so bitter and angry it had made him ill, and Carrie and her mother and sisters had feared it might bring on a relapse in his TB.

The lockout had taken its toll on James, too. Carrie had barely seen him since all the trouble began. He spent long hours in his office at the pit or up at the big house with the Haverstocks. And on the rare occasions he did come home he might as well have not been there, he was so distracted.

Carrie could see the lockout weighed heavily on her husband, even though he tried to put on a brave face for her sake.

But in spite of everything, she had a selfish reason for wanting James with her at the wedding.

Because today was the day she would see Rob Chadwick again.

'Sorry Carrie, but he is Archie's cousin,' Nancy had said when she had broken the news to Carrie the week before. 'It would be strange not to invite him when the rest of the family is coming.' She paused and then said hopefully, 'But you know what Rob's like. He probably won't even turn up.'

He certainly hadn't bothered much with his relatives in Bowden over the past three years. The only time he had returned to the village was when he paid a surprise visit to the Miners' Gala a year after he'd left. By then Carrie had been engaged to James but still nursing her newly patched-up heart, and Rob's visit had caught her completely unawares. This time she wanted to be prepared for him. More than anything, she desperately wanted to walk in to the wedding on her husband's arm, defiant and proud with her head held high.

But now James was not coming, she could feel her confidence sinking.

'Perhaps I shouldn't go either,' she said.

'Of course you must go, you're matron of honour,' James

said. 'You can't let your friend down. Besides, you've been looking forward to it.'

'I know, but—'

'Carrie, you must go.' James rested his hands on her shoulders and looked down at her lovingly. 'I'm only sorry I can't come with you. But you do understand why, don't you?'

'Of course.' She pressed her hand over his, smiling at his reflection. Poor James. He looked so tired.

'Are you going to work today?' she asked, and saw the brief look of pain that flitted across his face before he shook his head.

'I shouldn't think there'll be any trouble at the pit, with everyone at this wedding.' He paused, then added, 'Actually, I thought I might stay at home and look after Henry.'

'There's no need for that,' Carrie said. 'I can leave him with my mother. She's stopping at home since Father's taken poorly, so she won't be going to the wedding.'

'Please, Carrie, I'd like to look after him. He is my son, after all. And I've been like a stranger to him lately.'

Carrie looked at James in the mirror. She couldn't think of another man who would willingly look after his children while his wife went off to a wedding. Even her own father, much as he loved his daughters, regarded looking after bairns as 'women's work'.

But James was different. He was special, like no other men she had ever met.

She smiled at her husband. 'I'm sure he'd like that very much.'

The sun had come out for Nancy's wedding. Even Bowden Main looked beautiful, basking in the warm June sunshine.

Inside the doors of the tiny, crowded chapel, Nancy was fretting. 'Do I look all right? What about my hair? And my dress? Oh, I wish I wasn't so nervous!' She picked at a wilted petal on the posy she gripped in her fist. Her pretty face was pale under her rouged cheeks.

'You look beautiful,' Carrie reassured her.

'Do I? Are you sure?' Nancy reached out and grasped her hand. 'I'm so glad you're here,' she whispered. 'I don't know what I would have done without you.'

They both glanced towards Iris, who was looking sour and fiddling with the sash of her dress. She had spent more time fussing with her own appearance than helping calm Nancy's raging nerves.

'I'm glad to be here.' Carrie squeezed Nancy's hand in return, but all the time her own heart was fluttering against her ribs.

Somewhere in that tiny chapel, Rob Chadwick would be waiting.

She tried to look for him from the corner of her eye as they made their way down the aisle. She could see her three sisters, Eliza, Hattie and Gertie, sitting in a row. But there was no sign of Rob.

Perhaps he had decided not to come after all? Carrie knew she should feel relieved, but after a week of working herself up into a state of worry, she could only feel deflated. As the ceremony went on, she held herself rigid, expecting at any moment to hear the chapel door creak open behind her. But still Rob did not come.

There was no sign of him at the Welfare Institute afterwards, either, and Carrie began to relax.

The long trestle table in the centre of the large function room groaned with food – sandwiches, sausage rolls, cakes and an enormous pie in the centre of it all.

'I heard Nancy's mother had to pawn her wedding ring to pay for it,' Eliza said.

'And her brother went poaching on the Haverstocks' land to catch a rabbit for that pie,' Hattie put in.

Carrie stared at them. 'Nancy never said?'

'No, well, they wouldn't,' Eliza replied. 'No one tells you anything.' She sighed. 'Poor Nancy. It's nothing like your wedding, is it, Carrie?'

'I'll say,' Hattie put in proudly. 'We had a proper shop-bought cake.'

'You shouldn't say that. My wedding was – different, that's all,' Carrie mumbled. But she was suddenly aware that neither of her sisters was listening to her. They were both staring over her shoulder towards the door, their expressions aghast.

Carrie didn't need to turn around to know who had just walked in. She felt his presence as a cold prickle up the back of her neck.

'What's Rob Chadwick doing here?' Eliza hissed.

'He was invited. He's Archie's cousin, remember?' Carrie did her best to sound casual, even though all the muscles in her shoulders were rigid.

'He's got a nerve, showing his face.' Eliza's glance was worried. 'Are you all right, Carrie?'

'Of course. Why shouldn't I be?' She forced a smile.

'Don't worry, we'll stay with you all night,' Hattie promised, linking her arm through Carrie's.

'That's right,' Eliza said. 'We won't leave your side. And he'd better not dare speak a word to you, or he'll have us to answer to!' she added, her face screwed up in a fierce scowl.

But by the time everyone had finished eating, the chairs were pulled back around the edge of the room and Nancy's uncle struck up on his accordion, her sisters forgot their promise. Gertie went off to gossip with her friends, and Eliza and Hattie were quickly claimed by a couple of local lads.

So much for not leaving my side, Carrie thought as she

watched them spinning around the dance floor in the boys' arms, laughing. But she couldn't blame them for wanting to have a good time. Once upon a time she would have been joining in, dancing with the rest of them.

But now, she was too conscious of Rob Chadwick on the other side of the room to move. Typical Rob, to turn up and catch her unawares again, just as she had started to let her defences down.

She tried not to look at him, but he drew her gaze, like a flower turning towards the sun. Even when they were courting, she often found herself staring at him, drinking in his good looks. He was easily the most handsome lad in the village, with his burnished gold hair and his laughing hazel eyes.

But while she couldn't stop stealing glances at him, he barely seemed to be aware of her as he stood on the far side of the room, laughing and joking with his friends.

It was just as well, Carrie thought. The less she had to do with him, the better. But that didn't stop a little worm of disappointment burrowing into her heart.

She looked around the room. And to think, once upon a time, she had expected they would end up like this, celebrating their wedding in the Welfare Institute with their friends and family ...

'What's this I hear about your husband bringing in scab labour?'

Carrie turned around, startled at the sound of the voice behind her. Nancy's uncle stood there, his arms folded across his burly chest.

She could see straight away he was drunk. He swayed on his feet like a tree in the wind.

'I don't know what you're talking about,' she said.

The man sneered, his face mottled red with drink and anger. 'You would say that, wouldn't you? I heard he's sent word out asking for men willing to work down t'pit in our place.'

Carrie shook her head. 'You heard wrong,' she said. 'James would never do that.'

'Tom Chadwick's seen a copy of the letter that's gone out to Durham and Nottingham, and even as far up as Scotland. Begging 'em to come and take our jobs! And he reckons it had your husband's name on it.'

Carrie stared at him, trying to take in what she was hearing. James always refused to discuss pit business with her, but she couldn't imagine him doing such a thing willingly. 'Then the Haverstocks must have forced him to do it,' she said.

She tried to turn away from him but Mr Morris grabbed her arm, swinging her back round to face him. 'That'd be right,' he sneered. 'Sir Edward's bloody lapdog, that's all he is.'

Carrie knew she should walk away, but anger bristled inside her. 'You leave my husband alone!'

'I'll say what I like!' Flecks of spittle flew from his slack, wet mouth. 'Licking Sir Edward's boots is all he's fit for. He reckons he can crush us like his father did five years ago, but we all know your mester in't half the man his father was.' His voice was slurred. 'He didn't ought to have that job. Whoever heard of a pit manager who's too frightened to go underground?'

'That's not true!' Carrie protested, but Alec Morris was in no mood to listen.

'You in't seen him,' he sneered. 'Last time he had to come down, he were like a lass, clinging to that cage, his eyes shut, his face as white as a sheet . . . It would have been funny if it weren't so bloody pathetic!' He shook his head. 'Nay, by rights that job should have gone to a proper miner, a man with experience. Your mester has no business being

164

there. At least his father had summat about him, for all he was a hard man. At least he was worthy of some respect.'

Carrie stared at him, balling her hands into fists at her sides. Alec Morris was at least twice her size, but she was angry enough to knock him flat.

'Now then, what's all this?'

The sound of Rob's voice behind her ran right through Carrie like a jolt of electricity. She went rigid, not daring to turn round.

Mr Morris kept his watery gaze fixed on her. 'I'm telling this one what we reckon to her husband.'

'Come on, Alec, leave the lass alone. She's only come to celebrate the wedding, just like the rest of us.'

'She ought to know . . . '

'Then tell her another time. You don't want to spoil your Nancy's day with bad feeling, surely?' Rob stepped forward and clapped Mr Morris on the shoulder. 'Why don't we have a drink? They've just opened another barrel, and I can't abide seeing a man with an empty glass in his hand.'

For a moment Mr Morris didn't respond. Then he said grudgingly, 'I hope you're paying?'

'When have you known me not to stand my round?' Rob laughed. 'Come on, before they empty that barrel too. You know how we Chadwicks like to drink!'

The next minute they were going off together, Rob with his arm firmly around Alec Morris' shoulders, half holding him up. As they walked away, Rob said something to the other man, who roared with laughter.

Carrie watched them go, silently marvelling at the way Rob could work his charm on people, bending them to his will with nothing more than a smile and a joke. It was like magic.

And still he hadn't so much as looked at her.

165

Her argument with Mr Morris had left her feeling unsettled, so after a while she decided to go home. She desperately wanted to be there with James and Henry.

It was still light outside, and the evening air was so warm Carrie didn't need her shawl around her shoulders as she slipped out of the Welfare Institute and started to make her way home.

She had barely gone a few yards down the lane before she heard that familiar voice behind her.

'What's this? You're leaving without saying goodbye?'

Carrie swung round, dismayed. Rob was leaning against the wall, smoking a cigarette. For the first time that evening their eyes met, and suddenly she was sixteen years old again, running down the lane into his arms.

'It in't like you to leave a party, Carrie Wardle,' he said. 'You used to be the last one on the dance floor, as I recall.'

'Yes, well, happen I've got a home and a husband to go home to,' she snapped.

'Ah, yes.' Rob took a long drag on his cigarette, squinting at her through the smoke. 'You ended up marrying him, then?'

Carrie felt her cheeks burning. 'Why shouldn't I?'

'Why indeed?'

His words hung in the still evening air like the smoke from his cigarette.

'Stay a bit longer,' he said. 'I've hardly had a chance to speak to you yet.'

Carrie forced herself to look back at him. 'I don't think we've got much to say to each other, do you?'

He smiled again. That maddening smile that melted her heart and made her want to hit him at the same time. 'You still haven't forgiven me then?'

'I'm sure I haven't even thought about you,' Carrie said haughtily.

'Not once?' His brows rose.

Carrie turned away. 'I have to go,' she muttered.

'You shouldn't let them chase you away, you know,' Rob said.

'I'm not. And I didn't need you to rescue me from Alec Morris, either,' she said.

'Oh, I wasn't. I saw how angry you looked and I was afraid you were going to knock him out!'

'I nearly did!' Carrie smiled, then remembered herself. 'Anyway, I have to go.'

She turned to walk away from him, but his voice followed her up the lane.

'It was nice to see you, Carrie. Happen we'll see each other again soon.'

Carrie pulled her shawl around her shoulders, suddenly feeling a chill in spite of the warm evening.

'Not if I can help it,' she muttered under her breath.

Chapter Twenty

'You'll never guess what t'new nurse is doing now.'

Ida Willis spoke up over the clatter of pots and pans. Some of the village women had assembled in the back kitchen of the Miners' Welfare Institute to make soup for the children for when they came out of school. They stood in rows, chopping vegetables, peeling potatoes and sawing up loaves of bread, talking and laughing over the sound of clattering knives and bubbling pans.

Ruth Chadwick stopped stirring the onions she was frying. She knew what was coming next, because Jinny had told her about it the previous week.

'What's that?' Mrs Farnley asked, her knife moving swiftly through the pile of carrots she was chopping.

'A baby clinic,' Ida Willis said. 'She's asked the committee if she can have this place for two hours every week.'

'Did they say yes?'

'Well, my Reg reckons they weren't too keen on the idea of the place being filled with screaming bairns, but t'nurse talked 'em round to her way of thinking.'

'That don't surprise me,' Edie Farnley said ruefully. 'You'd have trouble saying no to that lass. I told her enough times not to bother coming round to visit my Jack, but she would insist.'

Ruth glanced sideways at Hannah Arkwright, who was busy cutting up ham bones for stock. Her face gave nothing away, but Ruth could see from the tight line of her mouth that she was listening to every word.

'What's a baby clinic, anyway?' Mrs Kettle asked.

'Blessed if I know.' Ida Morris shrugged.

'It's somewhere new mothers can bring their bairns to have them weighed and make sure they're getting on all right. And they can come when they're expecting, too, so t'nurse can make sure everything's as it should be.'

The words were out before Ruth knew what she was doing. She looked over her shoulder to see the other women staring at her. And no wonder, she was usually the quiet one of the group.

'You seem to know a lot about it?' Hannah said in a low voice.

Ruth went back to stirring the onions, her face flaming. 'T'nurse was telling our Jinny about it.' She didn't meet Hannah's eye, but she could feel the other woman staring at her accusingly.

'What I don't understand is, why she's bothering?' Susan Toller said. 'Surely we don't need a nurse telling us how to look after our bairns, do we? Women have been having babies for a long time in this village without her sticking her nose in.'

There was a mutter of agreement from the other women.

'Aye,' Edie Farnley said. 'And if they need to know owt, they go to their mother or their sister to help out.'

'Or to Hannah,' Ida Willis put in loyally.

'That's true,' Mrs Kettle agreed. 'I don't know what would have happened to our Ellen and little Harry if it hadn't been for her.'

Ruth glanced at Hannah, hacking away at the bones and looking pleased with herself.

'Happen if your Ellen had gone to the clinic, the nurse might have seen the bairn was in the wrong position a bit earlier?' Susan Toller spoke up, saying the words that Ruth didn't dare.

Mrs Kettle shook her head. 'Nay, it was the shock of losing our Harry that caused the baby to turn round. In't that right, Hannah?'

'Aye, that's right,' she muttered.

'And t'nurse were no good then, I can tell you,' Mrs Kettle went on. 'You should have seen her. She had no idea what to do with herself, for all her fancy instruments. Running about that bedroom like a chicken with its head cut off, she was . . .'

She stopped speaking abruptly. Ruth turned round to see what had shut her up, and saw Agnes Sheridan standing in the kitchen doorway.

She must have heard every word Mrs Kettle had said, although her mask of composure gave nothing away. Even so, Ruth was embarrassed for her.

Ida Willis stepped forward, wiping her hands on a tea towel. 'Can I help you, miss?'

'I've brought some money for the welfare fund.' Miss Sheridan stepped forward and held out an envelope. From across the kitchen, Ruth could see it was heavy with coins. 'I asked all the other nurses at Steeple Street to do a collection in their districts, and this is what they came up with. I hope it will help.'

Mrs Willis took the envelope from her. 'Much obliged, I'm sure,' she said stiffly.

Ruth willed her to leave. But Agnes Sheridan lingered, looking around her. 'What are you cooking?'

None of the other women seemed inclined to answer, so Ruth spoke up.

'It's a soup kitchen, miss. For them as can't afford to feed their bairns. We all put in what we can from our allotments and such, and try to cook a meal of sorts, so no one has to go without.'

'I see.' Miss Sheridan nodded, taking it all in. 'Can I help out at all?'

Ruth heard Hannah's muffled snort of derision behind her. 'You, miss?' she said.

'Why not? I've got some spare time before I'm due back on my rounds. I can't say I've had much experience of cooking, but I'm sure I could peel a few potatoes.'

Ruth looked at the young woman's face, bright with hope, and her heart went out to her.

Then Edie Farnley spoke up. 'I reckon we've got all the help we need, thank you.'

Ruth glanced at Hannah's smirking expression, half hidden by her curtain of red hair. She was enjoying every moment of this.

Agnes Sheridan's smile faltered. 'Oh. Well, if you're sure?' She paused, then said, 'I hope I'll see some of you at my first baby clinic next Friday?' A row of blank faces stared back at her. Ruth turned away back to her cooking, unable to look at the poor girl's mortified face.

Why did she have to come? She must know she was not welcome, so why would she put herself in this position?

Because she cared, Ruth realised. Her desire to help meant she was willing to risk humiliation and rejection. It was what made her turn up on people's doorsteps when they were sick, even though she knew they would probably turn her away.

Ruth felt a stab of shame and guilt that she had done exactly the same when Agnes Sheridan came to see little Ernest.

How she had begun to regret turning her away! The baby was getting no better, in spite of Hannah's efforts. And Jinny spoke so highly of the nurse, too. What if Ruth had robbed her baby of his only chance to recover, just because she was afraid of Hannah Arkwright?

Finally, Agnes left. The moment the door closed behind her, the women fell to talking about her.

'I didn't know where to put myself when she walked in!' Mrs Kettle said. 'I wonder if she heard me talking about her?'

'Don't matter if she did,' Hannah muttered. 'It's about time she realised where she's not wanted.'

'Did you hear her?' Mrs Morris said. '"Can I help out, at all?"' She mimicked Miss Sheridan's cultured voice. 'I don't suppose those soft hands of hers have ever peeled a potato in her life!'

'She was only trying to be helpful,' Ruth murmured, ignoring the dark look Hannah shot in her direction

'She's been helpful, all right,' Ida Willis said, still rifling through the envelope Miss Sheridan had handed her. 'You ought to see how much she's collected.'

'Let's have a look.' Mrs Kettle put down her knife. She and the other women gathered round, apart from Hannah, who went on working. Only Ruth noticed the tautness of her jaw as she swung the cleaver downwards, smashing the bones.

Mrs Morris let out a low whistle. 'There must be at least ten pounds here. That'll keep the wolves from the door for a while.'

'God bless her,' Edie Farnley said. 'Y'know, perhaps she in't so bad after all.'

'I told you she means well,' Ruth said.

'She in't that bad, really,' Susan Toller said. 'My Laurie looks forward to her coming every morning to give him his injection. He used to scream the place down when the doctor did it.'

'Aye,' Edie Farnley agreed. 'I must say, she really looked

after my Jack. And she tried to get Dr Rutherford to give him extra sick leave.'

'Didn't manage it, though, did she?' Hannah muttered.

'Well, no.'

'And don't forget it were my ointment that made your husband's hand better,' Hannah reminded her sourly. 'It were already on the mend before t'nurse stuck her nose in.'

Ruth saw Mrs Farnley's face fall, and quickly joined in the conversation.

'I happen to know she's been visiting Eric Wardle, even though Dr Rutherford told her she shouldn't treat any men or their families while they're locked out.'

Ida Willis looked shocked. 'Did he say that? I didn't know.'

'He did,' Ruth said. Our Jinny reckons they've had some right old rows over it, too.'

'You've got a lot to say for yourself, Ruth Chadwick,' Hannah muttered. 'I didn't know t'nurse was such a good friend of yours?'

'She in't,' Ruth defended herself. 'But our Jinny reckons she's a nice lass, once you get to know her. And she seems to care . . . '

'You didn't welcome her when she came to see your Ernest,' she said in a low voice.

Ruth stared at her, shocked. 'How did you – ?'

'You don't think I know what goes on in this village?' Hannah smirked. 'You did the right thing, sending her away. I'm helping the bairn, not her.'

Ruth glanced around, anxious that the other women might have heard.

'Don't worry, they'll not hear owt about it from me,' Hannah said. 'I know how to keep a secret. Not like our new nurse.'

'What do you mean?' Ruth frowned.

'I mean she's a trouble-maker.' Hannah raised her voice, loud enough for the other women to hear. 'And you've all been taken in by her.'

'Oh, aye? And how do you work that out, then?' Ida Willis wanted to know.

'Well, look at you. She hands over a few pounds, and suddenly you're acting as if she's one of us. In't anyone bothered to ask themselves why she's set up this clinic of hers?'

Edie Farnley's eyes narrowed. 'Ruth said, it's to see the bairns are looked after.'

'Aye, and why do you think she wants to do that?' Hannah's dark gaze skimmed the room. 'Because she don't think you can look after 'em thysen, that's why.'

The women looked at each other. 'And what's that supposed to mean?' Mrs Farnley asked.

'It means I have it on good authority that your precious Miss Sheridan has been talking to Miss Warren up at the school, saying what a terrible state the children are in.'

Ruth stared at Hannah, shocked by her words.

'She never!' Mrs Morris gasped in outrage.

'She did,' Hannah nodded. 'She said they were all dirty and crawling with lice. Said she'd never seen bairns like it, not even in the slums of Leeds.'

'The cheek of her!' Edie Farnley looked shocked. 'I'd better not hear her saying owt like that to me. My bairns might have holes in their boots and patches on their clothes, but no one can say I don't send 'em to school clean.'

'We do our best,' Susan Toller agreed. 'She should try being in our shoes, see what it's like.'

'She even had something to say about Seth Stanhope's children,' Hannah went on. 'Came round to his cottage she did, shouting the odds about the way he looks after 'em. I tried to tell her my poor sister hadn't been long

174

dead, but she reckoned they'd be better off in an orphanage than being looked after by their father and me.'

'No!' Mrs Kettle looked scandalised. 'Those poor bairns. Can you imagine anyone saying owt so cruel?'

'It were heartbreaking,' Hannah sniffed. 'I mean, I know I in't the children's mother, but I've done my best . . . '

'Of course you have, ducks. No one can say you in't done your sister proud.' Ida Willis patted Hannah's broad shoulder.

'Well, she needn't think I'll be going to her clinic!' Mrs Farnley declared.

'And I'll be telling our Ellen not to go, neither,' Mrs Kettle said. 'I don't care how much that Miss Sheridan puts in the welfare fund, she'll never be able to buy her way in to Bowden!'

'No one's going to take my bairns away from me, either!' Susan Toller said.

Ruth glanced at Hannah, still dabbing away at her imaginary tears. Under her apron, she could see the other woman's sly smile.

That smile troubled Ruth for the rest of the afternoon. It wasn't until all the children had been fed and the dishes washed up and cleared away that she finally plucked up the courage to speak to Hannah.

'It wasn't true, was it?' she ventured, as she dried up the battered metal soup pan.

'What's that?' Hannah had her back to her, putting a dish up on the top shelf that only she could reach.

'What you said about Miss Sheridan. She hasn't been complaining to Miss Warren about our children, has she? And she don't want to take 'em away from us, neither.' Hannah was silent, as if she hadn't heard Ruth. 'Why would you say such a thing, trying to cause trouble and setting everyone against her?'

175

'Because she deserves it!' Hannah swung round, so fiercely that Ruth flinched away. Her mouth was a tight line of anger. 'She should never have come here. She doesn't belong in Bowden!'

Ruth stared at her. Under all that blazing anger, she suddenly realised that Hannah was afraid.

She might come across to the world like a strong, powerful woman, but underneath it all Hannah Arkwright was still an awkward, lonely girl, desperate to find her place in the world.

And now Agnes Sheridan was threatening to come along and take it away from her. No wonder Hannah was afraid.

'You don't have to worry, you know,' Ruth tried to reassure her. 'We all think a lot of you.'

Hannah stiffened. 'What are you talking about?'

'I'm saying surely there's room for you and Miss Sheridan in Bowden.' She saw Hannah's dark eyes narrow, but paid no need to the warning sign. 'I know you think you might be pushed out, but—'

'Me? Pushed out?' Hannah laughed harshly. ''I'm not thinking any such thing! And I'll thank you to spare me your pity, Ruth Chadwick. It'll be a sad day indeed when I need someone like *you* feeling sorry for me!'

Ruth stared at her, bewildered. 'What's that supposed to mean?'

'Look at you!' Hannah looked her up and down, her mouth curling in contempt. 'You're a laughing stock, Ruth Chadwick, you and that useless husband of yours. Having all those bairns, one after the other, when you can barely afford to feed them all! You're the one who should be pitied, not me! All those children going to school with their backsides hanging out of their trousers. And as for that baby of yours . . . '

Ruth gasped, and her body seemed to collapse in on itself as if Hannah had punched her in the stomach with one of those big fists of hers.

At the same moment, Hannah seemed to realise what she had said. She stopped suddenly.

'Oh, Ruth, I didn't mean it,' she cried. 'You riled me up, I was only lashing out.' She reached for her, but Ruth shifted away, out of reach. 'Ruth, please. You know what I'm like when I get in a temper. I've always been hot-headed, in't I? But I didn't mean it, honestly.'

She reached for her again. Ruth stared down at Hannah's fingers, curled around her arm. She wanted to step away, to shake her off, but she was too numb with shock to move.

'You know how much I dote on all your bairns, especially little Ernest,' Hannah was saying, her voice girlish and lisping. 'I'd do owt for that little lad. And I'm going to make him better for you, I promise.' She smiled, fixing Ruth with her dark eyes. 'Take no notice of me, ducks. We're still friends, in't we? You forgive me, don't you?'

Ruth stared into Hannah's face. Her smile was stretched, her eyes staring at Ruth, compelling her.

'Yes.' The words came out automatically, just as they always did when Hannah had been cruel to her. 'Yes, I forgive you.'

But this time I won't forget, Ruth added to herself silently.

Chapter Twenty-One

'My dear, you can't be serious?'

Carrie could feel James' appalled gaze on her over the top of his newspaper, but she kept her eyes fixed on the piece of toast she was buttering.

'Why not?' she said.

'I don't know how you could even ask such a thing.' He folded up his newspaper and put it down on the table beside him. 'Surely you must realise how it would look? What if the Haverstocks were to find out you were helping out at a soup kitchen for the striking miners? What would they think?'

'The soup kitchen is for the miners' families,' Carrie pointed out. 'And besides, they're not on strike. They'd be working if they hadn't been locked out of the mine.'

'They've been locked out because they won't accept the new employment terms. What else are the Haverstocks supposed to do?'

'To hell with the Haverstocks!' Carrie threw down her knife with a clatter. 'I'm sick and tired of hearing their name mentioned. Why should I care what they think?'

'Because they pay my wages,' James said.

'You might be paid to do their bidding, but I'm not.'

Carrie saw her husband's face darken and realised she had gone too far.

It wasn't James' fault, she knew that. But she was so desperately angry and upset by what was happening in the village, she needed to vent her frustration on someone.

She had heard stories from her mother and sisters of families going hungry, mothers pawning their belongings, selling everything they had to feed their children. Some of the men had managed to find casual work on the local farms, but others were having to leave Bowden and their families to look for work.

Carrie longed to do something. These were her friends and neighbours, the people she had grown up with. She couldn't bear to sit in her big house and do nothing while they were struggling to survive.

'I only want to help,' she said.

'I know,' James sighed. 'But the miners aren't the only ones who need your help.'

Carrie felt a twinge of guilt as she watched him across the breakfast table. Poor James. The responsibility of trying to keep the mine open was beginning to show in the lines of strain around his eyes and mouth. He had lost weight, and the jacket of his suit seemed to hang from his shoulders.

He was right, she thought. He was her husband, and he deserved her support. He was the one she should be worried about.

'James—' She'd started to speak when they were interrupted by a knock on the door.

He looked up, frowning. 'I wonder who that could be, calling at this hour?'

Carrie tensed, feeling her ribs tighten around her heart as she listened to the maid scuttling to answer the door. She was always afraid of an early or late knock on the door, fearing it might be one of her sisters coming to say their father had taken another turn for the worse.

The door opened and the maid appeared, and Carrie shot out of her seat. 'Who is it?' she said.

The maid sent her a level look, then turned to James. 'Sergeant Cray to see you, sir,' she said.

James laid down his newspaper. 'Show him into the parlour,' he instructed the girl.

He didn't seem too surprised by this visit, Carrie thought as she followed him to the parlour.

Sergeant Cray was standing at the window, looking out. He was a big man, and his burly frame blocked out the June sunshine. He turned when James and Carrie came into the room.

'Good morning, Mr Shepherd. Mrs Shepherd.' He gave Carrie a brief nod. In spite of her nerves, she couldn't help smiling. When she was a child and Sergeant Cray was a fresh-faced young constable, he had often chased her and her friends for scrumping apples from the Haverstocks' orchard, and playing 'knock down ginger' on the neighbours' doors.

And now look at them both. She could tell from the policeman's frowning expression that the same thought was going through his mind.

'Good morning, Sergeant Cray,' James said. 'You have some news for me?'

The sergeant nodded. 'I thought you'd want to know, sir. We arrested two men last night.'

'Arrested?' Carrie interrupted in dismay. 'Who's been arrested?'

James said nothing. Sergeant Cray cleared his throat. 'Mr Shepherd informed us there has been a spate of thefts from the pit yard,' he said. 'Men breaking in at night, stealing coal. But I reckon it should stop, now two of them are behind bars.'

His smug little smile made Carrie itch to slap him. 'What are their names?' she asked.

'Does it matter?' James said.

'It does to me,' Carrie said firmly. She turned to Sergeant Cray. 'Who are these men?'

The policeman looked uneasily at James, then back at Carrie. 'Johnny Horsfall and Matthew Toller,' he said.

'But Mr Horsfall's old mother is bedridden. He's all she's got. She needs him!'

Sergeant Cray's broad face flushed. 'He should have thought about that before he went stealing, shouldn't he?'

'Thank you for coming to let me know, Sergeant,' James said quietly.

'Aye, well, I'll be on my way,' Sergeant Cray said. 'Those men will be up before the magistrate this morning. And a good thing too,' he added, with a sideways glance at Carrie.

She waited until the maid had shown him out, then turned to James.

'You have to do something,' she said.

'What do you suggest?'

'I don't know!' Carrie shrugged helplessly. 'But they don't deserve to go to prison. You know them. They work at Bowden Main. They're hard-working, trustworthy men.'

'You heard the sergeant. They were caught stealing.'

'Yes, but they wouldn't have done it if they hadn't been driven to it!' Carrie seized James' hand. 'You must go to court, plead for them.'

He stared at her. 'I can't do that.'

'Why not? I'm sure if you spoke up for them, the judge wouldn't lock them up. Please, James? Those men shouldn't go to prison for what they did. You know that as well as I do.'

James looked down at her hand in his for a moment, then slowly withdrew from her grasp. 'The law must take its course,' he said stiffly.

'You mean you won't help?'

'I can't, my love. Surely you must understand that?'

181

Carrie turned away from him. Behind her, she heard James sigh. 'It's getting late,' he said. 'I must go to the pit office.'

'Of course,' Carrie said bitterly. 'You mustn't keep the Haverstocks waiting.'

'Carrie . . . '

'Just go,' she snapped, turning away from him.

She stood at the window, staring out at the trees across the street. She heard James go to the door, then stop.

'I'm not the enemy, you know,' he said quietly.

'You could have fooled me,' Carrie muttered.

She stayed at the window for a long time after he had gone. All she could think about was poor Susan Toller. She must be worried sick, wondering what was to become of her husband. And old Mrs Horsfall, too. Who was going to take care of her, with her son gone?

She made up her mind. James might not be willing to do anything to help, but she would. Whether her husband and the Haverstocks liked it or not.

Carrie crept carefully around the side of the doctor's house, keeping close to the wall in case Mrs Bannister happened to look out of the front windows and saw her.

She had no wish to meet the housekeeper. Mrs Bannister was always conspicuously nice to Carrie now she had come up in the world, but she would never forget when she was younger and her mother would send her to fetch the doctor because her father was poorly, and Mrs Bannister would send her away because she knew they didn't have the money to pay.

Mrs Bannister might want to brush all that under the carpet now Carrie was the pit manager's wife, but Carrie's memory was too long, and too bitter.

It was a warm June morning, and the smell of frying

bacon drifted through the open kitchen door. As Carrie approached, she could hear Jinny humming to herself as she went about her work. Through the open door, she could see the girl at the stove, while Miss Sheridan was sitting at the kitchen table, drinking a cup of tea. She was reading the newspaper, turning the pages carefully with her fingertips. Carrie guessed it must be Dr Rutherford's, and that Miss Sheridan was not supposed to touch it.

Jinny jumped as Carrie sneaked in quietly.

'Carrie – I mean, Mrs Shepherd.' Jinny put her hand to the chest of her oversized apron. 'What are you doing here? I didn't hear the doorbell.' Her panic-stricken gaze flew towards the door leading to the hall.

'It's all right, I didn't ring.' Carrie nodded towards Miss Sheridan. 'I wanted to catch t'nurse before she went on her rounds.'

'Me?' Agnes blinked in surprise. She looked cool and efficient in her smart blue uniform, her chestnut hair gathered in a smooth knot at the nape of her neck. Carrie had seen her cycling around the village on that battered old bicycle of hers, and it always struck her how calm the young woman seemed, as if nothing in the world could disturb her composure. 'I've come to ask a favour.'

Agnes put down her teacup, her expression wary. 'What sort of favour?'

'There's someone I want you to go and visit … Mrs Horsfall, lives down on Middle Row. She's bedridden with arthritis.'

'I know her,' Agnes Sheridan said. 'I've been to see her a couple of times, but her son told me he takes care of her.'

'Aye, well, he can't take care of her now. He's been arrested.'

'Arrested?' The colour drained from Jinny's pale face.

'He were caught stealing coal from the pit yard with

Matthew Toller.' Carrie turned back to Miss Sheridan. 'His mother's all on her own. Will you go and see her, Nurse?'

'Of course.'

'T'doctor won't like it,' Jinny mumbled.

'The doctor won't like his bacon burned to a crisp, either,' Miss Sheridan said, nodding towards the smoking frying pan. 'Besides, I don't take my orders from Dr Rutherford,' she added, picking up her teacup.

'Thank you, I appreciate it. And I'm sure her son will, too.' Carrie paused for a moment, then said, 'I wonder if you'd give her this while you're there?'

She placed the wicker basket on the table in front of her. Miss Sheridan looked at it. 'What is it?'

'Just a few bits and pieces from our larder. I wasn't sure if she'd have owt to eat.'

'That's very kind of you. But why don't you give it to her yourself?'

Carrie could feel herself blushing. 'It's difficult. I shouldn't really be seen to be helping . . . And you'd best not say owt, either,' she warned Jinny.

'As if I would,' the girl mumbled, scraping furiously at a rasher of burned bacon stuck to the bottom of the pan.

Miss Sheridan nodded. 'Of course. I understand you're in a difficult position.' She nodded towards the basket. 'I'll certainly make sure Mrs Horsfall gets this.'

'Thank you. Well, I'd best be on my way.'

The visitor started back towards the back door. 'Will I see you on Friday?' Miss Sheridan said.

Carrie frowned, blankly. 'Friday?'

'My first baby clinic. At the Welfare Institute?'

'Ah.' Carrie had forgotten all about it. She certainly hadn't intended to bother going, but then she looked at Miss Sheridan's face, so bright with hope. 'I'll try to be there,' she promised.

'Thank you. I'd appreciate it. And I'm sure you'll find it useful.'

Carrie wasn't sure how she would find out anything she couldn't learn from her mother, but she nodded and smiled anyway. Miss Sheridan was doing her a favour, the least she could do was to return it.

She turned to Jinny. 'And you'd best warn your Archie there'll be extra police and specials guarding the pit yard,' she said. 'If they've caught two of the men, they're bound to be looking out for more.'

'I don't know what you're talking about, I'm sure,' Jinny mumbled, but her crimson face gave her away.

Chapter Twenty-Two

'Are you deliberately trying to provoke me, Miss Sheridan?' Dr Rutherford asked.

Agnes sat back in her seat, surprised by the doctor's accusation. 'No, Doctor. Why would I do that?'

'Why indeed? But I'm afraid that's the conclusion I've come to, after the way you've behaved lately.' He leaned across the desk, looking at her over the rim of his spectacles. His kindly, avuncular smile had disappeared some time ago. 'First you insist on attending patients whom I have specifically asked you not to visit. Now I learn that you've been to see the mother of a man who is not only on strike, but has been apprehended by the police for stealing from the Haverstocks' coal yard!'

'It isn't a strike, it's a lockout.'

Dr Rutherford made an exasperated sound. 'Now you're beginning to sound just like them! Lockout, indeed! It makes it sounds as if the Haverstocks are at fault.'

'So they are.'

Dr Rutherford stared at her, scandalised. 'I wouldn't go around saying that, if I were you. Not if you know what's good for you.'

Agnes stared at him across the desk. If only he lavished as much consideration on his patients as he did on his friends the Haverstocks, the people of Bowden might be a lot better for it, she thought.

'I'm not afraid of the Haverstocks, I assure you,' she said. 'Besides, that really isn't the point. The point is Mrs

Horsfall is a poor, elderly woman who is bedridden and in pain. What was I supposed to do? Let her suffer?'

'You were supposed to do as you're told!' Dr Rutherford burst out. 'You know as well I do that my instructions were not to give medical attention to any miners or their families.'

'I didn't give her any medical attention. I made her a cup of tea and something to eat, and I organised for one of her neighbours to look in on her until her son came home. I don't think that counts as—'

'Don't try to split hairs with me, Miss Sheridan!' A tiny vein pulsed in Dr Rutherford's temple. Agnes didn't think she had ever seen him so angry.

But she was angry too. His lack of feeling disgusted her. He was supposed to be in a compassionate profession. And yet all he seemed to care about was keeping his precious friend Sir Edward happy.

Agnes wondered if Dr Rutherford really understood what the lockout was doing to the families in Bowden. She had seen so much hardship, with women desperately struggling to feed their children. She had seen the empty spaces on the mantelpiece where cherished possessions had been pawned, witnessed families lining up outside the makeshift soup kitchen at the school. On her last visit to Steeple Street she had even seen Reg Willis' wife on the corner of Briggate, selling handkerchiefs she had made. Agnes had crossed the street, averting her eyes to save the poor woman's pride.

Dr Rutherford took off his spectacles and made a show of polishing them on the corner of his tweed jacket, to give himself time to calm down.

'You have to remember we are in a very delicate position here, Miss Sheridan,' he said, more calmly. 'We have a duty to the owners of the pit.'

'You might have a duty to Sir Edward, but I don't,' Agnes pointed out. 'May I remind you, I'm funded by the Miners' Welfare, not the Haverstocks. So really, neither of you is in any position to tell me who I can and can't visit, or what treatment I can give them.'

Dr Rutherford stared at her, his eyes glacial behind his spectacles. 'I don't like your tone, Miss Sheridan.'

'And I don't like your attitude, Dr Rutherford.'

They glared at each other for a moment. Then Dr Rutherford sat back in his chair and said, 'Well, we may not have to put up with each other for much longer.'

Agnes sat up straighter. 'What do you mean?'

'As you've just pointed out, your position here is funded by the Miners' Welfare Fund. But with no one paying in any more, and all the money going towards the strike, I wonder how long your employment can continue?'

Agnes stared at him, shaken. She hadn't thought of that.

Dr Rutherford smiled nastily. 'So you see, Miss Sheridan, if you want to go on working in the village, it might pay to be a little more – pragmatic?' he suggested.

'We'll see, shall we?' Agnes rose to her feet. 'Now, if you'll excuse me, I have to go and prepare for my clinic.'

'Oh, yes. Your clinic.' Dr Rutherford's smile widened, but there was no warmth in it. 'Another waste of the miners' money. You do realise no one will come, don't you?'

Agnes' chin lifted. 'You don't know that.'

'Oh, I do. You see, I know these people, Miss Sheridan. Unlike you, I've lived here for twenty years. I understand them. And I have to tell you, they bear no loyalty to anyone but themselves and each other.' He leaned forward, steepling his fingers. 'I know you think you're winning them over, tending to them and supporting their strike—'

'It's not a strike, it's a—'

'—but if you think they'll support you in return then

188

you're quite wrong,' Dr Rutherford went on, as if she had not spoken. 'You're putting yourself out on a limb for nothing.' He shook his head. 'You really should think more carefully about where your loyalties lie, Miss Sheridan. For your own sake.'

His warning stayed with Agnes as she sheltered in the doorway of the Miners' Welfare Institute later, her coat collar turned up against the drizzling rain, waiting for Phil to arrive with the equipment Agnes had arranged to borrow from Steeple Street.

She was late. The clinic was supposed to start at one o'clock, and it was already nearly noon.

She saw Ruth Chadwick at the bottom of the lane, struggling to push her pram up the hill. She caught Agnes' eye and hurried to cross the street, but Agnes called out to her.

'Good afternoon, Mrs Chadwick.' She walked down the hill to meet her. 'Here, let me help you.'

Agnes went to take the handle of the pram, but Ruth held on fast. 'I can manage, Nurse,' she insisted.

'At least let me push it up to the top of the hill for you.'

'It's heavy,' Ruth warned.

'Oh, I'm sure I can manage. I'm stronger than I look.' Agnes started to push, but the pram wouldn't budge. 'Goodness, you're right,' she gasped. 'Is the brake on?'

Ruth Chadwick smiled reluctantly. 'Nay, Nurse. It's just a bit overloaded, that's all. I've been down to t'allotment to pick some veg for the soup kitchen.'

Agnes peered into the pram, where she could just glimpse little Ernest Chadwick sleeping peacefully amid two sacks of potatoes and carrots. His woollen shawl was still wrapped tightly around him to conceal his twisted neck.

'The soup kitchen? So we're going the same way,' Agnes

said. 'I'm holding my first clinic at the Institute this afternoon.'

'Aye, Jinny said you were going ahead with it.'

'Of course. Why shouldn't I?'

Agnes threw her shoulders forward, and the wheels began to move slowly. 'I'm looking forward to seeing little Ernest there. You will be bringing him, won't you?'

A dull flush spread over Ruth's pale face. 'Thank you, Nurse, but I'll not bother,' she muttered. 'There's nowt wrong with my bairn.'

'Mrs Arkwright's remedy is working, then?'

Ruth looked away sharply.

She seized the pram, shouldering Agnes aside in her eagerness to wrestle control of it.

'I could help him, you know,' Agnes said, but Ruth was already pushing the pram away from her, as if she couldn't escape fast enough.

Agnes watched her, hurrying away up the street, her narrow shoulders hunched as she struggled with the pram's weight. She reached the top of the lane and crossed the street, narrowly avoiding Phil's car as it swung around the corner and came to a halt outside the doors to the Institute.

Agnes caught up just as her friend was getting out of the car. 'Sorry I'm late,' Phil said. 'Veronica gets a bit out of breath on hills, so I have to go slowly.'

Agnes wondered if Phil even knew the meaning of the word, after the speed with which she had come round the corner, nearing running down poor Ruth and her pram of potatoes.

'It doesn't matter,' she said. 'I'm just grateful you could come at all. Did you manage to borrow all the equipment I asked for?'

Phil nodded. 'And I brought something else too, that I thought you might find useful ... '

'Oh, yes? What's that?'

Agnes looked round as the passenger door opened and a blonde-haired figure stepped out.

'Polly!' Agnes cried. 'What are you doing here?'

'My mother sent me. She thought you might be in need of some moral support.'

'She's right, as usual.' Agnes sent up a silent prayer of gratitude to Bess Bradshaw for her wisdom.

'Don't tell her that, will you?' Polly smiled. 'She'll be even more insufferable.'

'Come on, let's get this equipment unloaded before we get soaked,' Phil interrupted them, looking up at the grey sky.

The three of them busied themselves, carrying in the equipment, moving tables and chairs and setting up screens. All the while, Ruth and the other local women went to and from the back of the building where they were setting up the daily soup kitchen, but none of them looked Agnes' way.

'I expect we'll be seeing some of them later?' Polly said.

'I expect so,' Agnes agreed, thinking about Ruth Chadwick's look of dismay.

Once again, Dr Rutherford's words came into her mind. *If you think they'll support you in return then you're quite wrong.*

They finished setting up the rows of chairs and screens on the stroke of one o'clock. Then Phil and Polly took their places behind the tables while Agnes walked down the length of the hall to open the doors.

She hadn't really expected there to be a long queue waiting to come in, but the sight of the empty passageway still came as a shock to her. The only sign of life was a scrawny dog sniffing around the doorway.

She turned back to the others and shook her head.

191

'Oh, well.' Polly smiled bracingly. 'It's still early. I'm sure things will pick up soon.'

But they didn't. Agnes sat between Phil and Agnes at the long trestle table, painfully conscious of the minutes ticking ponderously away on the clock behind them. Meanwhile, she could hear the cheerful, chattering voices of the women in the soup kitchen at the other end of the passageway.

'You did put the right date on the notices, didn't you?' Phil asked.

'Of course.'

'And the right time?'

'For heaven's sake, Phil, I'm not an idiot!' Agnes snapped, then instantly regretted it when she saw the frown on her friend's face. 'I'm sorry,' she said. 'I shouldn't take it out on you. I'm just disappointed, that's all.'

'Don't take it to heart,' Polly said. 'It might just be the weather keeping them away. I know in Quarry Hill we always have far fewer mothers turning up when it rains. They don't want to risk their babies catching a cold.'

'Hardly!' Phil mocked. 'Can't you hear them, larking about in the kitchen? I'm going to go and have a word with them.' She started to her feet, but Agnes put out a hand to stop her.

'Please don't,' she said.

'But—'

'If they're not here then it's because they've decided they don't want to come,' Agnes said quietly.

Another half an hour ticked by in agonising silence. Agnes was painfully conscious of Phil discreetly checking her watch beside her.

'You can go, if you like?' she offered. 'I'm sure you must both have better things to do with your time than sitting here in an empty clinic with me?'

'Well—' Phil started to say, but Polly cut her off.

'Oh, no, we're happy to stay, aren't we, Phil?'

'Are we?' she said, earning herself a sharp look from kind-hearted Polly. 'Oh, I suppose so,' she sighed. 'I mean, if I weren't here I'd only be in a muddy farmyard somewhere, getting soaked to the skin and chased by pigs. At least I'm dry in here!'

'Honestly,' Agnes said. 'It's been an hour and no one has walked through those doors. I doubt they'll come now.'

'You never know. '

Agnes shook her head. 'You don't have to spare my feelings. This clinic has been a dismal failure.' She looked around. 'We might as well get this lot put away, then you two can get back to Leeds.'

Chapter Twenty-Three

They packed away the equipment in silence. Agnes was too heavy-hearted with disappointment to speak.

Polly did her best to comfort her. 'Try not to take it to heart,' she said. 'It's early days yet. I'm sure once word gets round they'll come.'

'I'm sure you're right.' Agnes tried to smile bravely. But she couldn't help thinking the doctor was right. The truth was, no matter how hard she tried, the people of Bowden simply didn't like or trust her. And she had started to think they never would.

Agnes waved her friends off, standing in the rain until Phil's car disappeared around the corner at the top of the hill. Then she went back into the hall to put away the chairs. Seeing all the rows set out made her feel utterly foolish. How had she dared to imagine she would fill the hall with mothers and babies? Everyone had tried to warn her the idea was doomed to failure, and as usual she had insisted that she knew best.

Would she ever learn her lesson? she wondered.

'Am I too late?'

She swung round. Carrie Shepherd stood in the doorway, her baby in her arms.

'I meant to come earlier, but I had to go and visit my father.' The baby started to grizzle and she jiggled him in her arms to quieten him.

The sight of her standing there was too much for Agnes.

The pent-up emotion she had been holding in all day finally burst out and tears sprang to her eyes.

'Now then, Nurse. What's all this about?' Carrie looked dismayed.

'Oh, nothing. Just me being foolish, that's all.' Agnes brushed away her tears and summoned a smile. 'Thank you for coming, Mrs Shepherd.'

'Aye, well, I said I would, didn't I? You did me a favour, visiting old Mrs Horsfall, and now I'm repaying it.' Carrie looked around. 'But I see I've missed it, so I'll be on my way.'

'Don't go,' Agnes begged. She pulled herself together, smoothing down her apron. 'Since you're here, we might as well make sure all's well with the baby, shall we? I'll start by weighing him. Will you undress him down to his nappy, please?'

She left Carrie undressing the baby and went to fetch the scales out of the cupboard.

'Have you been busy?' Carrie asked.

'Not as busy as I would have liked.' Agnes set the scales down on the table. 'In fact, you're my first and last mother!' She made a brave attempt at a smile.

Carrie stared at her, appalled. 'You mean no one else turned up?'

'I'm afraid not. Right, let's put Henry on the scale, shall we?'

The sound of women's laughter rang out from beyond the hall. Carrie lifted her head.

'The soup kitchen,' Agnes explained, as she made a note of the baby's weight. 'They've been there since noon.'

'And yet no one could be bothered to come to your clinic?' Carrie's mouth tightened.

'I daresay they were busy.' Agnes looked down at the

baby, who gurgled back at her. She didn't need to check Henry over to see he was in perfect health.

Carrie frowned. 'It's a crying shame folk won't give you a chance,' she said.

'I expect they just need time to get used to me.'

'Aye,' Carrie said. But there was something about her expression that made Agnes wonder.

'Is there something you're not telling me, Mrs Shepherd?' she asked.

Carrie kept her head down, concentrating on dressing her baby. 'It's just summat my mother told me, that's all. She reckons . . . ' Carrie paused, and Agnes could see her weighing her words carefully. 'She reckons there are rumours going round about you,' she said finally.

Agnes was shocked. 'What kind of rumours?'

Carrie was silent for a long time, carefully buttoning her son's knitted matinee jacket. Finally, she said, 'Someone's putting it around that you don't think the mothers in the village look after their children properly. They reckon that you're after taking their bairns away from them.'

Agnes gasped. 'But that's not true!'

'That's what I said, but you know what gossip is like once it starts to spread.'

'But I don't understand . . . Who would say such a thing?'

Carrie looked away. 'I couldn't say,' she muttered, but her expression told a different story.

Agnes knew there was no point in pressing her on it. The people of Bowden were very close-mouthed when they wanted to be.

She remembered what Dr Rutherford had said.

Their only loyalty is to themselves and each other.

'Well, thank you for telling me what you've heard,' she said.

There was an awkward silence while Carrie finished dressing Henry.

'You mustn't take it to heart, you know,' she said. 'I know the folk here seem to be unfriendly, but they're all right once you get to know them.'

'Yes, but how do I get to do that?' Agnes asked.

Carrie looked thoughtful for a moment. 'I'm not sure,' she admitted at last. 'I s'pose these things take time.'

Bess Bradshaw's wise words came back to Agnes.

All they needed was time to get used to you, so you could show them what you're capable of doing. That's all anyone needs, Miss Sheridan. Time.

But how much time? Agnes wondered. She had already been in the village for more than four months. Even the hard-bitten residents of Quarry Hill had started to warm to her after that long.

Carrie had parked the baby's pram in the passageway outside the hall, propped between the glass trophy cases. It filled the space where Agnes had left her bicycle a couple of hours previously.

'Have you lost summat?' Carrie looked over her shoulder at Agnes as she placed Henry carefully back in his pram.

'My bicycle.' Agnes looked around blankly. 'I could have sworn I left it here.'

Carrie thought for a moment. 'I noticed a bicycle here when I arrived. Happen someone's moved it outside, out of the way? It'll be round the side, I'm sure.'

'I hope you're right.'

Agnes helped Carrie with her pram down the stone steps of the Miners' Welfare Institute. The murky grey day had given way to watery sunshine, making the cobbles gleam like polished stones. But there was no sign of her bicycle.

Then Agnes heard a shout behind her. She swung round in time to see her bicycle freewheeling past her down the hill, a dark-haired boy clinging to the handlebars as it bumped over the cobbles, his legs stuck out in front of him, laughing wildly.

It all happened so suddenly, Agnes couldn't react at first. By the time she had found her voice to shout after him he was nearly out of sight at the bottom of the hill.

'Come back! Stop, thief!'

Without thinking, she gave chase down the hill, her stout shoes slipping and sliding on the wet cobbles.

'Give up,' she heard Carrie calling out behind her. 'You'll never catch him.'

She was right. By the time Agnes reached the bottom of the hill the boy was long gone. She stared down the empty lane, fighting for breath.

She was still nursing a stitch in her side when Carrie caught up with her a minute later, pushing the pram.

'Any sign?' she asked. Agnes shook her head. 'I daresay it was just a lad, messing about. He'll bring it back when he gets fed up.'

'I'm sure I recognised him from somewhere . . . ' Agnes thought for a moment, trying to remember where she had heard that wild laughter before. Then it came to her. 'I know, he let some pit ponies loose in Dr Rutherford's garden. Now, what did Mrs Bannister call him . . . Christopher! Yes, that's it. Christopher Stanhope.' The name hadn't meant anything to her at the time, but now she realised he must be Seth's son. It didn't surprise her. 'You saw him, didn't you? Was it him?'

'I – I really couldn't say. It all happened so fast . . . ' Carrie's gaze dropped. 'As I say, I expect he'll bring it back soon enough.'

'I hope so.' Agnes bit her lip, determined not to give in

to the humiliation and frustration that welled up inside her. 'That bicycle might not be a thing of beauty, but it means a great deal to me. It was a present from my former patients in Quarry Hill.'

She remembered the pride in their faces when they presented it to her. She knew how much hard work and effort had gone into fixing the old bicycle up. Old and battered it might be, but it meant the world to her.

Once again, she felt the sting of hot tears at the back of her eyes, and blinked them away.

'Look.' Carrie nodded past her in the direction the boy had gone. 'What did I tell you?'

Agnes looked round sharply, to see a distant figure pushing her bicycle back up the lane. She rushed down to meet him, Carrie following slowly behind.

'I take it this is yours, miss?'

The young man pushing the bike grinned at her. He was big and well built, with coppery fair hair and a handsome, smiling face.

'Yes, it is. Thank you.' Agnes looked it over. 'Did you see the boy who took it?'

'Nay, miss. I found it in a ditch.'

'Are you sure? He must have cycled right past you.'

'As I said, I found it in a ditch, miss.'

There it was again, that shuttered look she had recently seen on Carrie Shepherd's face. The people of Bowden knew how to close ranks when they needed to.

'Hello, Carrie,' the handsome young man said.

Agnes looked round. She had been so preoccupied with her bicycle she had almost forgotten Carrie Shepherd standing behind her.

'You two know each other?' she said.

'Oh, aye, we're old friends. In't that right, Carrie?'

She looked dazed.

'I thought you'd gone home to Durham?' she said.

'I did. But I decided to come back, stay here for a while.' The young man's smile broadened. 'You don't mind, do you?'

Carrie didn't reply. Her mouth was held in a tight line, and Agnes had the feeling there was a torrent of words she was trying to hold in.

'We haven't been introduced, miss.' The young man held out his hand. 'I'm Rob Chadwick.'

'Agnes Sheridan.'

'So you're t'new nurse?' His appraising glance travelled slowly from her feet to the top of her head. Agnes felt a treacherous blush spreading up from the starched collar of her dress.

'Are you related to Tom and Ruth Chadwick?' she asked, for something to say.

'He's my uncle by marriage. His wife's my dad's sister, though he's now departed. That's where I'm lodging presently.'

'How long are you planning to stay?' Carrie blurted out.

The young man shrugged his broad shoulders. 'We'll have to see how things turn out, won't we? Happen I might decide to stay on permanently.'

'I'm sure the Chadwicks will welcome an extra mouth to feed,' Carrie said bitterly.

'As a matter of fact they're glad to have me, since their Archie got wed and moved out. I'm making mysen useful, bringing in some money where I can.'

'And where do you earn that?' Carrie asked.

He tapped the side of his nose. 'That would be telling, wouldn't it?'

Agnes looked from one to the other, aware of a strange tension between them that she couldn't quite understand.

Rob turned his attention to the baby. 'Who's this, then? I heard you'd had a bairn, Carrie. Let's have a look at him.'

He made a move towards the pram, but Carrie seized the handle, wheeling it round and away from him. 'I'd best go,' she said.

'I'll walk back up the hill with you,' Agnes offered, but Carrie was already on her way, pushing the pram rapidly towards the Welfare Institute.

Rob watched her go, a knowing little smile on his lips. 'Someone's in a hurry,' he said.

'Yes, she is.'

It suddenly occurred to Agnes that Carrie was going in entirely the wrong direction to reach her house, but she seemed intent on putting as much distance as she could between herself and the handsome stranger.

Chapter Twenty-Four

It was a late Friday afternoon, and for once Seth was at home. Although he might as well not have been, for all the notice he was taking of anyone around him as he sat in his chair by the empty fireside, mending the children's boots.

Hannah watched him as she stood at the kitchen table, skinning the rabbit Seth had trapped that morning for the pot. Now and then she would think of something to say to him, a passing comment on a piece of news she had heard. But apart from the odd nod or grunt of acknowledgement, Seth kept his head down, stitching away at the worn, patched leather.

Hannah smiled to herself. For all his silence, she would still rather have been here than anywhere else in the world. This was where she could once again indulge in her favourite fantasy: that she was Seth's wife and this was her home.

Much as she enjoyed pretending she had a family and children of her own, she preferred the fantasy where it was just the two of them. Then she could imagine him sweeping her up in his arms and carrying her off to his bedroom in the front parlour, and laying her down gently on the big feather bed . . .

Heat rose in her face and she looked up sharply to make sure no one was watching her. But Seth was still busy with his mending, both boys were out – Billy playing a noisy game in the lane, while Christopher was long gone, up to heaven knows what. Only Elsie sat at the other end of the kitchen table, laboriously copying neat rows of letters on to an old scrap of newspaper she had found.

For some reason the sight of the girl, her tongue poking out in concentration as she carefully inscribed the letters with the stub of a pencil, irked Hannah.

'If you've nowt better to do, you can help me with this stew,' she said.

Elsie looked up at her with those serious grey eyes so like her father's. 'But Miss Warren said we were to practise.'

'Miss Warren in't got a family to feed, has she? Come on, lass, I've only got one pair of hands.'

'But—'

'Help your aunt, Elsie,' Seth spoke up, his deep voice filling the room.

Elsie knew better than to argue with her father. Setting down her pencil with a sigh, she came round to the other side of the table, next to where Hannah stood.

'What do you want me to do?'

'You can start by peeling those potatoes. If it in't too much trouble?' Hannah added with heavy sarcasm.

Elsie fetched a battered old knife from the dresser drawer and set about doing as she was told, although the longing looks she kept casting towards her writing made Hannah realise she was doing it with very bad grace.

'Honestly!' Hannah mocked her. 'I don't know why you're so set on learning your letters. It in't as if you know anyone outside the village to write to, is it?'

'That in't the point. Miss Warren says it's important to know how to read and write.'

'Is that so?' Hannah glanced at Seth, who didn't respond. 'Well, you can tell your Miss Warren that I in't never learned to read nor write, and it in't done me any harm.'

'Yes, but I want to get on in the world,' Elsie said.

Hannah stood back, her hands planted on her hips.

'What a little madam you are! I reckon you could do with learning some manners, never mind reading and writing!'

She stared hard at the girl, until finally Elsie's gaze slid away. 'I'm sorry, Aunt,' she mumbled.

'I should think so, too. And mind how you're peeling those potatoes. You're throwing half of them away with the peel.'

'Sorry.'

Hannah finished skinning the rabbit and started to hack it into joints. Once she'd chopped through the muscle and sinew, the little bones snapped easily in her strong hands. And all the while she kept her stern gaze fixed on Elsie.

She had never warmed to the little girl the way she had to the boys. Billy and Christopher could be wild when they wanted to be, but they were simple lads who wore their hearts on their sleeve.

But Elsie was different: more thoughtful, more secretive. She had hidden depths, like her mother.

Hannah had never been able to understand Sarah, either. She was always too quick for her. Hannah had certainly never noticed how her sister was moving in on Seth, not until she had stolen him right away from under Hannah's nose.

As if he was ever yours, a voice inside her head mocked her. It was just another fantasy, like the ones she spun now to cheer up her miserable life.

The knock on the door startled them all. Seth looked up, frowning.

'Who's that?'

'I'll go and see.' Hannah laid down her knife and went to the door, wiping her bloody hands on her apron.

She had thought it might be someone from the village needing her help. The last person she expected to see was Agnes Sheridan.

'Yes?' Hannah folded her arms and looked the nurse up and down. She seemed so proper in her navy blue coat, in spite of the warm June day, her little cap perched at a perfect angle on her shiny chestnut hair. 'What do you want?'

'I'm looking for Mr Stanhope. Is he in?'

Before Hannah could reply, Seth called out from inside, 'Who is it, Hannah?'

'It's t'nurse.' She kept her dark gaze fixed on Miss Sheridan. 'Wants to have a word with you.'

A moment later Seth came to the door, and Hannah was gratified to see the frown on his face. 'Oh, aye?' he addressed the nurse. 'What do you want now?'

To her credit, Agnes didn't seem fazed by Seth's surliness. 'It's about your son,' she said.

Hannah rolled her eyes. 'If this is about our Billy's rash—'

'No, not Billy.' Miss Sheridan kept her cool gaze fixed on Seth. 'Your eldest – Christopher, is it?'

Seth's eyes narrowed. 'What about him?' he said.

'He stole my bicycle.'

Seth looked past the nurse's shoulder to the bicycle propped against the wall. 'It don't look stolen to me. Are you sure you in't imagining things?'

Hannah smiled to herself. An angry flush rose in Miss Sheridan's face.

'Someone got it back for me,' she said. 'After your son abandoned it.'

'Then there's no harm done, is there?'

Seth went to turn away, but Miss Sheridan said, 'That's not the point. He's a menace, and he should be punished.'

Hannah held her breath as Seth turned slowly to face her again. 'And have you got a witness to all this?' he asked.

Miss Sheridan dropped her gaze. 'Well, no, but . . . '

'In that case, happen you should go away and stop bothering people.'

205

He started to close the door in her face but Miss Sheridan stood her ground.

'And that's how you bring your children up, is it?'

It was the wrong thing to say. Hannah could see in Seth's face that Agnes Sheridan had hit a raw nerve.

'What do you know about the way I bring up my children?' he growled.

Anyone in their right mind might have fled from the blazing anger in his eyes, but not Agnes Sheridan. The girl was either very brave or utterly foolish, Hannah decided.

'I know you don't seem to be making a very good job of it, if that's the way they behave.'

Once again, Hannah found herself holding her breath as she saw Seth's jaw pulsing angrily. Had Miss Sheridan been a man, he would have been flat on the ground before he'd had the chance to finish his sentence. As it was, the nurse had no idea what kind of dangerous ground she had strayed on to. But she didn't seem to care, either. It was there in her defiant gaze as she stared back at him, standing so straight and sure of herself.

Hannah was more attuned to Seth's moods, and she saw the anger that darkened his grey eyes.

Finally, he managed to speak. 'Go away,' he bit out. 'And don't come back here, either.'

He turned on his heel and walked away.

Hannah might have been able to judge his mood, but Agnes Sheridan obviously couldn't. She opened her mouth to call out to him, but Hannah blocked her way.

'You heard him,' she said, before Agnes could get a word out. 'You in't wanted here. So stop sticking your nose in where it don't belong!'

'But I—' Hannah didn't wait to hear any more before she slammed the door in Agnes' face.

She glanced uneasily at Seth. He had gone back to

mending the boots, but Hannah could see the rage in him still simmering close to the surface. He looked as if he might rip the worn leather apart with his bare hands, such was his anger.

She wondered about speaking to him, then thought better of it. The fire would die down quicker if she didn't poke it, she decided.

Elsie seemed to sense his mood, too. She went about her chores with her head down, moving stealthily around the room so as not to antagonise her father further.

For an hour none of them spoke, and after a while Hannah allowed herself to relax. The silence had become less oppressive, and glancing out of the corner of her eye, she could see some of the tension had left Seth's body. The storm had passed.

But then Christopher swaggered in, and all hell broke loose. Hannah and Elsie swung round, and Hannah cried out, but Seth had got there first. Throwing down the boot he was mending, he crossed the room in a couple of strides and grabbed his son by the collar, slamming him back against the wall.

'What's all this about you pinching bicycles?' he growled, shoving his face close to Christopher's.

Hannah saw the shock on the boy's white face. 'I – I didn't,' he stammered.

'Don't give me that, it's written all over your face!' Seth shook his son like a terrier with a rat, lifting him until the boy's toes scraped the stone-flagged floor. Elsie let out a little cry of dismay.

'For pity's sake, Seth, let the lad go before you throttle him,' Hannah pleaded.

Her words galvanised Seth out of his stupor of fury. He let go of the boy's collar and Christopher dropped to the floor, slumping against the wall.

Hannah prayed that the lad would be wise enough to hold his tongue, but she should have known better. As soon as he had regained his composure and was safely out of reach of his father, Christopher said, 'It were only a bit of fun anyway.'

'I'll not have my children lying and stealing,' Seth muttered.

'You steal coal from the pit yard.'

Hannah flinched as Seth swung round again, but this time Christopher had the good sense to dodge out of his way.

'I do what I need to do to keep my family together!' Seth's voice rose, filling the small cottage with a roar of rage. 'And I in't having no one turning up on my doorstep, telling me I in't bringing up my children properly, just because you're a light-fingered little sod! I won't have it, d'you hear?'

'And what are you going to do about it?'

Hannah stared at Christopher, shocked. He was goading his father, she could see it.

'Teach you a bloody lesson, that's what!' Seth started to fumble for his belt buckle. Elsie whimpered and ducked behind Hannah. Even Christopher's face lost its insolent expression.

Hannah stepped in quickly. 'Seth, what are you doing?'

'Summat I should have done a long time ago. He won't be stealing after I've finished with him!'

His aunt stood in front of Christopher. 'There's no need for that,' she said. 'I'm sure he's already learned his lesson. He won't be stealing again. Will you, lad?'

She turned to Christopher, who remained resentfully silent, his gaze fixed on the belt in his father's hand. He was proud and stubborn, just like Seth. He would rather take a beating than admit he was sorry.

'Out of the way, Hannah,' Seth said in a low voice.

'But Seth—'

'I said, out of the way!' He turned his furious grey gaze on her. 'This in't your concern.'

'But you've never laid a finger on the lad before.'

'Happen that's why he thinks he can get away with owt!' He took a step towards Christopher, but Hannah stood her ground.

'D'you think this is what Sarah would have wanted?'

That halted him for a moment, long enough for Christopher to seize his chance and make a dash for the door, slamming it shut behind him.

Seth started to follow, but Hannah stopped him.

'Leave it, Seth, please.'

'But he's defied me!'

'I know, and you've every right to be angry. But in't it better to talk to the lad when you've had a chance to calm down?'

Seth stood still, his broad chest rising and falling, his resentful gaze still fixed on the door. 'He can't get away with this,' he muttered.

'I know, Seth. And he won't. He'll come back and take his punishment, just like he knows he must.' But by then with any luck his father would have calmed down and regained his senses, Hannah thought silently.

Seth looked down at the belt dangling from his hand, as if seeing it for the first time. He would not have thought about using it if Sarah had been alive. Unlike some of the other men in the village, he had never laid a finger on his children.

But these days he was a changed man. It was there in the defeated slump of his broad shoulders.

'Give the boy a chance, Seth,' Hannah tried to reason with him. 'It's just high spirits, that's all. All lads get into mischief.'

Seth shook his head. 'I don't like strangers turning up on my doorstep, making out I can't look after my family properly . . . '

He glowered back at the door, and Hannah knew he was picturing Agnes Sheridan standing there. She paused for a moment, wondering if she should dare to say what was on her mind.

'Happen you should spend a bit more time with the bairns, instead of punishing them when they do wrong?' she suggested gently.

Seth flashed her a quick, narrow-eyed look. 'What do you mean?'

'Well, you've not spent much time with them lately, have you? You're always out on the picket line, or discussing union business – not that I'm criticising you or owt,' she added hastily, seeing his expression darken. 'I just think the bairns need their father. Especially since they've not long lost their mother.'

'I'm here now, in't I?' Seth snapped.

Are you? Hannah wanted to say. Even when he was in the cottage, Seth's thoughts seemed to be constantly else-where. 'Yes, but—'

'Anyway, I've got union business to attend to. Some-one's got to keep the men going, stop them giving in. And we've got to raise money for their families, too. And man the picket lines. We've had word that they're bringing in more blacklegs from Scotland, and we've got to be ready for 'em.'

'And that's more important than your children, is it?'

The words were out before Hannah knew what she was saying. Seth turned on her, his eyes like flint.

'So now you're telling me how to bring up my children too?'

'No, of course not. I just—'

'You sound like that nurse. I reckon you two make a good pair, both full of ideas about how I should be going about things.'

Hannah flinched at the harshness of his words, but Seth didn't seem to notice. He put his belt back on and reached for his jacket.

'You're not going out?' she said.

'Aye.' He jammed his cap on his head.

'But what about your tea?' She glanced at the rabbit stew bubbling on the stove.

'I'll have it when I get in.'

'And what time will that be?'

'When I'm ready!'

The door slammed, and Hannah exchanged a look with Elsie. They both knew it would be a long time before Seth came home.

A couple of hours later, Hannah went out to find Christopher. He was skulking down by the allotments, as she knew he would be, sitting on the low wall, swinging his legs back and forth.

He looked up as she approached, and Hannah caught a glimpse of his sad, tearful face before his defiant mask slipped back into place. He might put on a front but deep down he was still a hurt little boy.

'Your tea's on the table,' she said. 'It's all right, your father's gone out,' she added, seeing his wary expression.

'I don't care anyway,' Christopher shrugged, but Hannah saw his shoulders relax a little.

'I'm sorry about what happened earlier.' She paused, wondering how to put into words what she had to say. 'You won't tell him?'

'That it was you who told me to steal the bicycle?' He shook his head. 'I won't say owt. He probably wouldn't listen anyway.'

A twinge of guilt went through Hannah. It was only meant to be a bit of fun, to bring Agnes Sheridan down a peg or two. She had never thought Seth would find out. Or that he would be so angry with Christopher.

'You mustn't mind your father,' she said. 'He's under a lot of strain, what with the lockout and trying to keep the family together.'

Christopher sneered. 'He don't care about us! And I don't care about him, either. I hate him.'

'Don't say that.'

'I do! I wish it had been him who died instead of Mother!'

Hannah stared at him, shocked. He didn't mean it, she could see it in his face. Christopher adored his father, he always had. Before Sarah had died, he and Seth had done everything together. They had gone fishing and hunting for rabbits. Seth had taught him how to play cricket and football, and how to box. Which was why it was so difficult for the boy that his father had apparently abandoned him when he needed him most.

Poor Christopher had not only lost his mother, he had lost his father too. But he was twelve years old, the eldest, and he already thought of himself as a man. He couldn't allow himself to cry like his brother and sister. So instead he reacted against his father, defying him and causing trouble.

That was why he had tried to goad Seth, Hannah realised. Because even a beating was better than being ignored.

Chapter Twenty-Five

It was turned seven o'clock and still light on a fine July evening when Carrie arrived at her parents' cottage.

She paused for a moment to watch them through the window before she let herself in. Her father dozed to one side of the fireplace, the family Bible in his lap, while her mother and three sisters were busy brodding a new rug. Eliza and Gertie sat around the table, cutting up strips of cloth and adding them to the pile, while her mother worked at her frame, poking the strips into the hessian cloth. Meanwhile Hattie sat at her father's feet, unravelling an old jumper and winding the wool around her fingers ready to be knitted up again.

Carrie felt a pang, watching them. Not so long ago she would have been sitting there with them, laughing with her sisters. But these days she always seemed to be on the outside looking in.

Her mother looked up in surprise as Carrie came through the door hauling a heavy sack behind her.

'Carrie! What are you doing here?' Her face grew anxious. 'Where's the bairn? Is everything all right?'

'Everything's fine, Ma. I've left Henry with James.' Carrie dropped the sack she was carrying at her feet and examined her hands. The rough hessian cloth had cut into her fingers where she had hauled it all the way through the village.

Kathleen Wardle pushed her brodding frame aside. 'What's all this, then?'

'Just some bits and pieces I've sorted out. I thought they'd do for Susan Toller.'

'Let's have a look.' Eliza dropped her scissors and jumped to her feet.

'They're not for you . . . ' Carrie started to say, but her sister was already delving into the sack.

Her mother frowned. 'But I don't understand, why have you brought it all here? Why not take it straight down to t'Institute?'

'I wasn't sure if they'd take it.'

'What are you talking about? They're always glad of donations.'

'Not from me.' She couldn't imagine what Mrs Morris and the other wives would say if the pit manager's wife turned up with a sack of cast-offs.

'You're never going to give away this hat?' Eliza pulled out a felt cloche and tried it on. 'I swear you promised it to me if you ever got tired of it.'

'Put it back.' Carrie snatched it off her sister's head. 'It's for charity.'

'It's too good for Susan Toller,' Eliza mumbled. 'It won't suit her anyway. She hasn't got the right face for hats.' She stuck her arm in the bag again, pulling out a skirt and a pair of shoes.

'And what does James think of all this?' Her mother wanted to know.

Carrie dropped her gaze. 'He doesn't know. And he doesn't need to know, either,' she added.

She had already had enough arguments with him over it. He was most insistent he didn't want her to be seen helping the striking miners in case the Haverstocks found out. Which was why Carrie had decided to go about things in this way.

Her mother frowned. 'I'm not sure it's right, you having

secrets from your husband. What do you say about it, Father?' She had turned to Eric Wardle, sitting in his chair at the fireside.

'I think we should leave the lass alone. I daresay she knows what she's doing.'

Carrie smiled gratefully at her father, but Eric Wardle wasn't looking at her. He stared into the empty grate, his attention a million miles away. For the first time Carrie noticed how pale and listless he seemed, the dim lamplight casting deep shadows on his hollowed cheeks.

'Are you all right, Father?' she asked.

He turned to face her then, summoning up a wan smile that didn't reach his eyes. 'Aye, lass. Just a bit tired, that's all.'

'It's the lockout,' her mother had said. 'It's draining the life out of all of us.' But Carrie noticed the worried way she looked at her husband when she said it. A feeling of dread started to gnaw away at her.

Her mother changed the subject, looking back at the sack her daughter had brought. 'So what are you going to do with all this?' she asked.

'I thought I'd leave it on the Tollers' doorstep once it got dark.'

'Sneak out in the dead of night, you mean? That sounds exciting,' Hattie said.

'Can we come?' Gertie joined in.

Carrie shook her head. 'You'll only start giggling and playing about and wake everyone up.'

'There's food in here,' Eliza announced, pulling out a loaf of bread. 'Look, Ma.'

'I told you to put it all back!' Carrie seized the bread from her sister and stuffed it back in the sack. 'Mrs Toller won't want it once your mucky hands have been all over it.'

'I'm sure she'll appreciate it,' her mother said. Then

she added, 'You know they've given her husband three months?'

Carrie nodded. 'I heard.'

'It's a terrible business. I know stealing's wrong, but the poor man must have been at his wits' end.'

'The village is full of special constables now,' Eliza put in. 'We can hear them all day and all night, walking up and down the fence by the pit yard.'

'That's a point.' Kathleen Wardle looked worried. 'Perhaps you shouldn't be sneaking about after dark, Carrie love. You don't want to get thysen arrested.'

Carrie laughed. 'How can they arrest me for giving away what's mine? Besides, who would dare suspect the pit manager's wife?'

It was past ten o'clock when darkness fell. She said goodbye to her family and set off towards Middle Row, hauling her heavy sack behind her.

There was a light on in the Tollers' cottage, but the curtains were drawn. Carrie hid in the darkness on the other side of the yard and peered across at the row of low houses, checking that no one was about. From somewhere high above her came the unearthly hoot of an owl, breaking the silence.

Finally, she chose her moment and hurried across the yard. But in her haste her foot caught a tin bucket someone had left near the door, sending it skittering across the cobbles. Carrie barely had time to dive back into the shadows before a curtain twitched and Susan Toller's anxious face appeared, looking out into the darkness.

Carrie held her breath, certain she would be seen. But a moment later the curtain was lowered again, blocking out the light.

She paused to gather her nerve, then moved quickly forward and dumped the sack down on the Tollers' doorstep, then scurried away, back into the shadows. When she was safely on the other side of the yard she risked a glance back, but no more curtains twitched, and the row of houses slumbered in silence.

Carrie smiled to herself, wondering how Susan would react when she found the things on her doorstep. If nothing else, she could always pawn the clothes to make some money. And the food would come in useful, too. Carrie had been careful not to take too much, in case the maid noticed and started asking awkward questions in front of James.

It was nearly eleven o'clock and there was no moon over Bowden Main, but the late hour and the deep darkness held no fears for Carrie as she made her way home. She knew the village rows too well to be afraid. Besides, she could hear the murmuring voices of the special constables patrolling the pit yard, and see the occasional flash of their lamps in the darkness.

As she skirted the pit yard, heading towards the gates, she heard a scuffle, and caught a flash of movement out of the corner of her eye as a dark shape slipped into the shadows to one side of her.

She froze, looking around her. She had passed the specials in the pit yard, so she knew it couldn't be them.

Her legs twitched, ready to run, but she made herself stand her ground.

'Who's there?' she whispered, her voice trembling in the still night air.

There was a scuffling sound, this time behind her. Carrie swung round to face it, her hands balling into fists, ready to defend herself.

'Keep your voice down, for pity's sake,' a voice hissed in the darkness. 'Do you want to bring the specials running?'

Carrie's heart did a somersault in her chest at the sound of that voice.

'Rob?' She squinted into the shadows. 'Is that you?'

The next moment a dark shape detached itself from the shadows. Carrie couldn't make out his features, but she would have known him anywhere.

'Carrie Wardle,' he said. 'Now what are you doing, wandering the streets at this time of night?'

'I might ask you the same question!' she retorted. Then the answer occurred to her. 'You're not – surely you're not intending to steal coal?'

'As if I would!' Rob's tone was mocking. 'I'm out here taking the fresh air, just like you.'

'Liar.' Carrie glanced over her shoulder, into the darkness. 'You ought to be careful,' she said. 'You don't want Sergeant Cray to catch you.'

'Sergeant Cray couldn't catch a cold! Remember how he used to chase us for scrumping apples? The big windbag used to be out of breath before he got to the end of the road!'

'All the same, you ought to watch thysen,' Carrie said. 'You don't want to end up in jail like Matthew Toller, do you?'

'Why, Carrie Wardle, I didn't know you cared!'

'I don't,' Carrie snapped. 'And it's Mrs Shepherd to you,' she added.

'How could I forget?' His voice was soft in the darkness. 'Does your husband know you're out so late?'

Carrie lifted her chin. 'It's no concern of yours if he does or he doesn't.'

'I'd take better care of you if you were my wife.' Before Carrie had a chance to react, someone whistled in the darkness. 'That's Archie,' Rob said. 'He must have found a way in through the fence. I'd best go.'

'Be—' Be careful, Carrie started to say, then stopped herself. 'Don't blame me if you get locked up,' she muttered instead.

She stood rooted to the spot long after Rob had disappeared into the darkness. She knew she had to get used to seeing him around the village, but it still gave her a shock.

She started back up the lane, but had not gone very far before the harsh blast of a police whistle stopped her in her tracks. It was followed a few seconds later by the sound of shouting and footsteps behind her, running down the lane in the direction Rob had taken only a few moments before . . .

'Help!' she screamed out without thinking. She heard the footsteps change direction, there was a flash of light and then two young constables appeared out of the darkness, barrelling down the lane towards her.

'Mrs Shepherd?' One of them stopped in front of her, fighting for breath. 'What the—?'

'I've just seen two men, running out of the pit gates,' Carrie interrupted him. 'They pushed past me and went down that way.' She pointed back towards the lower rows.

'Two men, you say?' One of the constables held up his lamp, peering into the shadows.

'Yes, and they went that way.' Carrie pointed in the opposite direction from the one Rob had taken.

'Did you get a look at their faces?'

Carrie shook her head. 'It was too dark, and it all happened too fast,' she said. 'But they were definitely going towards the pit cottages.'

'Are you sure? Only Constable Lloyd thought he heard someone getting through the fence up there—'

'I'm telling you, they pushed past me!' Carrie cut him off. 'If you run, you might be able to catch up with them.'

The constables looked at each other for a moment, and Carrie held her breath. Then they both ran off in the direction of the cottages.

Carrie watched them until they had disappeared out of

sight. When she was satisfied they had gone far enough in the wrong direction, she headed home.

The following morning, they had just finished breakfast when Sergeant Cray arrived.

'Hello, Sergeant,' James greeted him, with a weary smile. 'Are you here with another report for me?'

'Actually, sir, it's your wife I've come to see.'

'Me?' Carrie's heart lurched into her throat.

'My specials told me you saw two men breaking in to the pit yard last night?'

She was guiltily aware of James looking at her. 'Is this true, Carrie? You didn't say anything about it last night?'

'There was nothing to tell.' She shrugged. 'I didn't really see anything.'

'But Constable Lloyd reckons you saw them running away, out of the pit gates?'

'That's right.'

'Yet when my men went to look, they couldn't find anyone.'

'Then they must already have got away.'

'They couldn't have got away that fast, carrying sacks of coal. And the pit gates were locked.'

Now they were both staring at her. Carrie forced herself to meet the policeman's sceptical gaze.

'Then I must have been mistaken,' she said.

'But while my men were sent on a wild goose chase, the real thieves managed to get in and out through a hole in the fence on the other side of the yard. Strange, don't you think?'

'What exactly are you trying to say, Sergeant?' James' voice was cordial, but with an underlying note of steel Carrie had rarely heard in it before.

Sergeant Cray obviously hadn't heard it before either. He looked taken aback. 'Nothing, sir.'

'Really? Because it sounds as if you're accusing my wife of something.'

Sergeant Cray cleared his throat. 'Not at all, sir.'

'I'm glad to hear it. If you intend to take anyone to task, I suggest you start with the two constables who allowed these thieves to steal from under their noses.'

A dull flush spread over Sergeant Cray's face. 'Yes, sir,' he said gruffly.

Henry started to cry and Carrie hurried to attend to him, relieved for the chance to escape. She was too overcome with guilt to look at either the sergeant or James at that moment.

She was changing the baby's nappy in the nursery when James came in. Carrie kept her attention focused on Henry, conscious all the time of her husband watching her.

'Why didn't you tell me what happened last night?' he said.

Carrie stiffened. 'What do you mean?'

'Running into those men. It must have been utterly terrifying for you.'

Relief flooded through her. 'I didn't want to worry you. Anyway, it all happened so fast, I hardly knew about it until it was all over.'

She felt his hands press lightly on her shoulders. 'All the same, I wish you'd allowed me to come and meet you. I don't like to think of you being out on your own after dark, especially with all this business going on.'

I'd take better care of you if you were my wife. Carrie closed her eyes, trying to push Rob's words out of her head.

'There's no need to worry about me, honestly. I grew up here, I have nothing to fear from a couple of local lads—'

She closed her mouth like a trap, but she felt James' hands tighten on her shoulders.

'How do you know they were local?' he said. 'I thought you told Sergeant Cray you didn't see their faces?'

Carrie went back to pinning Henry's nappy, hoping her husband wouldn't notice her hands shaking. 'I just thought they must be from round here,' she said lightly. 'I mean, who else would come to Bowden, looking to steal coal?'

It was a long time before James spoke. 'Who indeed?' he said finally.

Chapter Twenty-Six

Agnes had grown to dread Friday afternoons.

Sitting alone in the hall at the Miners' Welfare Institute, surveying the rows of empty chairs in front of her – not so many now, she had learned her lesson after that first week – she would listen to the ponderous ticking of the clock, willing the hands to inch around to half-past three, when she could pack everything away again and the agony would be over for another week.

She knew she should give up. It was her fourth clinic, and not a soul had come in all those weeks. Apart from Carrie Shepherd, who turned up in a show of loyalty that somehow made Agnes feel even more of a failure.

Dr Rutherford had hardly been able to disguise his satisfaction.

'What did I tell you?' he had said. 'These people will never appreciate you, no matter what you do. Might as well give it up, my dear.'

It was his words, as well as her own stubborn streak, that kept Agnes turning up at the Welfare Institute every week, setting up the chairs and putting out her screens and scales.

At the end of the passage, she could hear the women laughing as they went about their work in the soup kitchen. It was three o'clock and the children would be coming out of school now, making their way up the lane for their only meal of the day.

The rich scent of frying onions drifted through the open double doors, making her stomach groan. She hoped Jinny had remembered to leave her something to eat before she started on the afternoon rounds.

The sudden sound of a shower of gravel rattling against the window shook Agnes out of her reverie. She started to her feet in surprise, just as another missile came sailing through the open window, landing inches from where she had been sitting.

Agnes stared down at the jagged rock at her feet, too shocked to move for a moment, until a shout of laughter from outside galvanised her. She rushed outside, squinting in the bright sunshine, just in time to see a group of boys running up the road.

'Come back!' Agnes called after them. 'You could have hurt someone—'

'Oi, miss!'

Before she had time to react, a hand reached up and snatched the cap from her head, wrenching it free of its pins and making her yelp in pain.

Agnes swung round and found herself staring into the insolent, smirking face of a dark-haired boy. Christopher Stanhope. He and his tearaway friends always seemed to be hanging around the village these days, jeering at her as she cycled past.

He twirled her cap in his grubby fingers, just out of her reach.

'Give me that back,' Agnes said, trying to keep the anger out of her voice.

'Shan't.'

'It doesn't belong to you.'

'It does now.' He took off his cap and put hers on instead, striking a comical pose. 'Don't you think it suits me?'

'Give it back!' Agnes made a grab for it but Christopher was too quick for her. His skinny body ducked out of reach.

'How much will you give me for it?' he demanded.

Agnes stared at him. 'I'm not giving you anything. You're lucky I don't go and fetch a policeman.'

'Give me sixpence or I'll set fire to it.'

Agnes gasped. 'You little—'

'Give it back to her, Chris.'

Over his shoulder Agnes saw little Elsie Stanhope standing in the middle of the lane, dressed in her school pinafore. She was regarding her brother with weary resignation, as if she was used to his silly games.

Christopher glared at his sister mutinously. 'Go away, Elsie,' he growled, but the little girl stood her ground.

'You don't want to upset Dad again, do you?'

Her words caught him off guard for a moment. Agnes seized her chance and made another lunge for the cap, but Christopher quickly recovered himself, jerking it out of her grasp.

'You want it, you fetch it!'

He flung the cap into the air, sending it spinning skywards. For a moment the three of them stood still, watching it sailing up into the clear blue sky before it came down on the edge of the Institute roof.

Christopher's face broke into a grin of delight, and a moment later he sprinted off up the lane after his friends, laughing wildly.

Agnes stood looking up at her cap, which was hanging from the guttering.

'How on earth am I supposed to get that down?'

'I'll help you, miss.'

She hadn't realised she had spoken her thoughts aloud until she looked down and saw Elsie standing beside her, gazing up at her with a sweet, honest face that was very different from her brother's.

'Please, miss,' she said. 'I'm sorry for what our Chris did, and I'd like to help if I can?'

'There's no need,' Agnes started to say, but Elsie was already walking away from her, wiping her hands on her pinafore.

'Look, I can easily get up this drainpipe . . . ' She pulled on it to test if it would hold her weight. A moment later, she was shinning up the pipe like a little monkey, her patched-up boots scrabbling for a foothold in the brickwork.

'Really, I don't think it's safe.' Agnes stood below, wringing her hands. 'Please come down, before you—'

A shower of red dust and fragments of mortar came down, filling her eyes and mouth and making her cough. There was an ominous creaking sound as the drainpipe came away from the crumbling brickwork. Elsie let out a scream, and the next moment she had landed on the cobbles at Agnes' feet.

She had only fallen a short distance, but she had landed heavily. For a second Agnes held her breath, unable to move until the girl finally stirred, groaning with pain.

'Oh, thank God!' Agnes rushed over to her. 'Are you all right? No, don't try to move. I need to check if you've broken any bones.'

'I – I think I'm all right. Just winded, that's all.'

'All the same, I'd better check. Lie still for me, ducks.'

Elsie remained motionless while Agnes checked her limbs. The girl stared up at her with wide, trusting eyes. She looked as if she was doing her best not to cry.

'Well, there doesn't seem to be anything broken, which is good news. Did you hit your head?'

'I don't know . . . I don't think so.' Elsie looked mournfully at her dress. 'I've ripped my pinafore. Aunt Hannah's going to thrash me.'

'Dresses can soon be sewn up,' Agnes said briskly. 'Besides, I'm sure your aunt will just be glad you weren't badly hurt. Now, can you tell me how many fingers I'm holding up?'

Finally, Agnes had satisfied herself that Elsie was suffering from nothing more than skinned hands and knees.

'Come inside with me and I'll clean you up and put a dressing on.'

Elsie looked reluctant. 'I dunno . . . Aunt Hannah won't like it.'

'Aunt Hannah doesn't have to know, does she?' Agnes thought for a moment. 'I'll just clean the dirt out of those cuts. And I think I might have some sewing thread and a needle in my bag. We could sew up the tear in your dress?'

Finally she managed to coax Elsie into the hall. She sat quietly at Agnes' table at the front of the room, looking around her at the rows of empty chairs as Agnes set about collecting a bowl of boiled water, swabs and antiseptic dressings.

'How will you get your hat down?' the child asked finally, looking worried.

'Oh, I'm sure I'll think of something. I daresay one of the men will put up a ladder and get it down for me later.'

Elsie paused, taking it in. 'I'm sorry . . . about what Christopher did.'

'You're not the one who should be apologising.'

'Christopher never says sorry for owt.' Elsie bit her lip. 'I'll have a word with him. Tell him to stop making a nuisance of himself.'

Much good that will do you, Agnes thought. But she knew Elsie was trying to help, so she smiled and said, 'Thank you, I'd be very grateful.'

'You won't tell our dad, will you?'

Agnes looked over at Elsie's round, earnest face. A pair of anxious grey eyes met hers.

'No,' she said. It wouldn't do any good, anyway. And the last thing she needed was to face Seth Stanhope again. Really, he was as ignorant as his son in his own way. No wonder Christopher had turned out the way he had.

Elsie's shoulders slumped. 'Thank you.' She paused, then said, 'Christopher don't mean any harm really. He's just run a bit wild since our mother died.'

Agnes glanced at her again, feeling a pang of pity. Elsie was ten years old, but she had a wise old head on her young shoulders. She pitied the poor motherless girl, living in such a family. The closest thing she had to a mother was Hannah Arkwright, God help her.

'Right, that's you patched up. Now I'll find that needle and thread.'

As Agnes set about sewing up the rip in Elsie's dress, the girl sat idly swinging her legs and looking around her.

'What are all the chairs for?' she asked.

'I've been holding a mother and baby clinic.'

Elsie nodded her head. 'I heard Aunt Hannah talking about it. She reckons it's a waste of time,' she said matter-of-factly.

'She might be right,' Agnes sighed.

'Why do you do it, then?'

Why indeed? 'You never know, someone might want to come one day.'

Elsie picked up a stethoscope from the table. 'What's this for?'

'You use it to listen for a heartbeat.'

'How does it work?'

'You put these two bits in your ears, and this other end goes on the patient's chest.' Agnes put down her needle. 'Would you like me to show you?'

Elsie nodded eagerly. 'Yes, please.'

Agnes demonstrated the stethoscope, and Elsie grew

wide-eyed with amazement as she heard her own heartbeat.

'But why do you need to listen to it?' she wanted to know. 'Surely you must know it's there, or you wouldn't be alive?'

'That's true,' Agnes said. 'But you can tell a lot about what's wrong with someone from the way their heart is beating. If it's fast, or too slow, or faint or irregular, for instance, that can help you work out what illness they might be suffering from.'

'Aunt Hannah reckons she can tell what's wrong with someone just by looking at them.'

Agnes tightened her lips. 'Yes, well, that's not the way real doctors and nurses go about things. We use instruments and take careful notes.'

'What kind of instruments?' Elsie asked, looking around.

'Well . . . we use a thermometer to check temperatures. That way we can tell if a patient has a fever. Would you like me to show you?'

Agnes ended up demonstrating most of her equipment, as well as going through her bag and showing Elsie what the various dressings and ointments were for. It took a while, but the girl seemed so rapt, listening to everything and asking lots of questions, that Agnes barely noticed the time passing.

'I want to look after sick people when I'm older,' Elsie declared, as she helped Agnes pack up her bag.

'Like your aunt?'

'No, like you. I want to be a real nurse.'

Agnes smiled to herself.

'Then you'll have to carry on at school, and pass all your exams,' she said.

'That's what I want to do.' Elsie nodded wisely. 'And then what?'

'Well, you'll have to go and train at a hospital.'

The girl's face clouded. 'I don't think I'd be allowed to do that. Aunt Hannah says too much learning is a bad thing for a lass.'

Agnes pursed her lips to stop herself from speaking out. 'But what about your father? Surely he'd want you to better yourself?'

Elsie looked away. 'He in't interested in us. He only cares about what goes on at the pit.'

'I'm sure that's not true . . . ' Agnes started to say, then remembered Seth Stanhope's surly indifference when she had tried to talk to him about his son.

The girl slid off her chair. 'Anyway, I'd best be going,' she said. 'Aunt Hannah will be wondering why I in't come home from school.'

'Here's your pinafore, as good as new.' Agnes handed it to her.

'Thank you.' Elsie slipped it on. 'And I won't forget to tell our Chris not to bother you any more.'

'I'd appreciate that.' Agnes watched her fumbling with the ties on her pinafore. 'Perhaps you'd like to come back to the clinic sometime? I could teach you how to tie different types of bandages, if we're not too busy.'

Elsie smiled shyly. 'I'd like that.'

She left, and Agnes finished putting away the rest of the equipment with a much lighter heart than when she'd started. Her conversation with Elsie had cheered her up no end. At last, there was someone in Bowden who actually seemed to like her!

She was closing up the cupboard when she heard the double doors creak open behind her. Thinking it was Reg Willis come to collect the key from her as usual, she called out, 'I won't be a minute, Mr Willis.'

Someone cleared their throat behind her. A woman.

Agnes looked over her shoulder to see Ruth Chadwick standing in the doorway, her baby boy in her arms. He was swaddled up as usual in spite of the warm July day, layers of shawl concealing his crooked neck from view.

Agnes smiled at her. 'Oh, good afternoon, Mrs Chadwick. Did you want to see me?'

'I—' Ruth hesitated on the threshold, looking nervously about her, as if she might turn and flee at any moment.

'How is little Ernest?' Agnes prompted her.

Mrs Chadwick clutched her son tighter to her shoulder. She stared at Agnes, her pale eyes looking huge in her white face.

'You said you could help him.' The words seemed to burst from between her tight lips. 'Is it right what you said, that you could do exercises to make him better?'

'Well, I'd have to examine him properly first.' Agnes saw the look of dismay on Ruth's face. 'But, yes, I think it's possible.' She paused. 'I thought you wanted Hannah Arkwright to tend to him?'

'I changed my mind,' Ruth cut her off. 'I've got to do what's best for our Ernest, never mind anything else.'

She flinched slightly as she said it, almost as if she expected to be punished just for uttering the words. Hannah Arkwright really had people in the grip of fear, Agnes thought.

'Why don't I have a look at Ernest, and we'll see what's to be done?' she suggested gently.

'What? You mean – now?' Ruth looked panic-stricken. 'But you're just shutting up shop. I don't want to put you to any trouble . . . '

'It's no trouble, really. And the sooner we get started on Ernest's treatment, the better. Bring him over here and lay him down on this table, and I'll examine him.'

For a moment Ruth stayed rooted to the spot, her baby clutched tightly to her shoulder.

'I don't want anyone thinking I don't take care of him,' she said, the words tumbling out in a fearful rush. 'I look after my bairns as best I can.'

'I know that, Mrs Chadwick. Anyone can see what a good mother you are.' Agnes held out her arms. 'May I?'

Slowly, reluctantly, Ruth eased her baby from her shoulder and placed him in Agnes' arms.

She laid him down on the table and carefully unwrapped the woollen layers that swaddled him, conscious all the time of his mother standing at her shoulder, watching her. She could feel the waves of tension coming off Ruth Chadwick, her whole body poised, ready to snatch her baby away at any moment.

Finally Agnes had unpeeled all the layers of shawls and clothing, until Ernest was down to nothing but a nappy and a woollen vest – and the charm on a tatty old piece of string around his neck.

'We'll start by getting rid of this, I think . . . '

Behind her, Ruth let out a hiss as Agnes unfastened the string, but she didn't try to stop her.

Agnes smiled to herself. She had broken Hannah Arkwright's spell in more ways than one, it seemed.

And this was only the beginning.

Chapter Twenty-Seven

The congregation rose to their feet as the organ ponderously sounded the opening bars of 'Onward Christian Soldiers'. The music swelled and voices joined in, filling the church to its towering rafters.

Carrie gazed around, lips moving, mouthing the words. She had been coming to St Matthew's ever since she and James were married, but she wasn't sure she would ever get used to the vast building, with all its rich embroidered hangings and tall stained-glass windows casting coloured diamonds of light on to the pages of her hymn book.

It was so different from the simple little village chapel she had attended with her family. She had gone to Sunday School there every week with her sisters, and her father sometimes read the lesson there when he was well enough. The chapel was nowhere near as impressive as St Matthew's, only a simple place with whitewashed walls and wooden benches, but Carrie felt at home there, surrounded by her family and friends.

But James and his family had always worshipped at this church, so this was where they had come.

She glanced sideways and caught the eye of Eleanor Haverstock, sitting in the family's box pew across the wide, stone-flagged aisle. She towered over the people around her, an unbecoming cloche hat pulled low on her head.

Eleanor beamed back at her, still singing enthusiastically, while her father stood at her side, frowning down at his hymn book, his mouth not moving, as if he was somehow affronted by the words written there.

Carrie's gaze darted guiltily back to her hymn book. She could feel her face starting to flush with embarrassment at being caught out staring like a bored child. And by Miss Eleanor, too.

That was another reason St Matthew's always made her feel so uncomfortable. All the grand people worshipped there, travelling from their big houses to the pleasant country church.

The hymn ended, and everyone sat down again as the vicar climbed the steps to his place in the carved stone pulpit.

'The sermon today is taken from *Genesis*, chapter two, verse twenty-four,' he announced. '"Therefore shall a man leave his father and his mother, and shall cleave unto his wife, and they shall be one flesh . . ."' He looked up, gaze skimming the congregation over the rim of his spectacles. 'In other words, the blessed sanctity of marriage,' he intoned gravely. He seemed to seek out Carrie directly, his eyes meeting hers. 'I see many married couples before me this morning. But how many of us have forgotten the vows we made before God?'

His words went like a dart straight to Carrie's heart, piercing her with guilt. She thought about the many secret donations she had made to the Miners' Welfare Fund over the past few weeks. Old baby clothes Henry had outgrown, food from their larder, even money from the housekeeping allowance James gave her. All delivered in secret via her mother or sisters, so no one ever knew the gifts came from her.

Even so, she knew James would never approve. She also knew that if the Haverstocks were ever to find out, he would be in terrible trouble.

'The Bible teaches us that the bond between husband and wife is sacred, and that we must place our spouse first,' the vicar went on, his deep voice echoing into the high rafters. 'As it says in the marriage vows, "Forsaking all others . . . "'

Carrie thought about the morning Sergeant Cray had arrived, the way she had stood there and lied to him, and to her husband. Even now, she still wondered what had made her do it. One word from her could have helped James, and yet she had lied to them both because her loyalty to her friends was stronger than her loyalty to her own husband.

She glanced sideways towards the Haverstocks' pew. Sir Edward was now dozing in his seat, his head nodding towards his chest. Eleanor gazed up at the vicar, her face rapt, taking in every word.

Carrie felt a twinge of pity for her. Poor Eleanor. She didn't have much of a life, stuck in that miserable big old house with her grumpy father.

Perhaps Carrie ought to put more effort into making friends with her? Miss Eleanor had always been very kind and welcoming to her, after all. And she couldn't help being a Haverstock.

And James would certainly like it. Carrie knew she owed it to him to make more of an effort to become part of his world instead of clinging so grimly to her old life.

Forsaking all others, as the vicar had said.

With that in mind, she didn't rush out of the church the minute the service was over, but allowed Eleanor to catch up with them.

She immediately rushed to admire baby Henry, asleep in his pram.

'Look at him, what a little duck he is! And how he's

grown! He's such a handsome chap. He looks just like you, James, don't you think?'

'I was rather hoping he might take after his mother,' James said, glancing at Carrie.

'Oh, James, you've made your wife blush! Anyway, I think you're being far too modest,' Eleanor gushed. 'He definitely has your nose, at any rate. Although his hair is really quite dark . . . '

'As I said, he takes after his mother.'

'He's delightful anyway,' Eleanor went on. 'Don't you think so, Father?' She turned to Sir Edward, who had just joined them.

'What?'

'Little Henry. Don't you think he's the most delightful child?'

Sir Edward gave the pram a cursory glance. 'All babies look the same to me,' he dismissed. Then, turning to James, he said, 'I want a word with you, Shepherd. Have you seen to that business we discussed?'

'Yes, Sir Edward. It's all in hand.'

'When?'

'Tomorrow morning. First thing.'

James spoke in a low voice, his back half turned. Carrie wondered what it was she was not supposed to hear.

'You know, you really should come and visit again soon.' Eleanor's cheerful chatter drowned out the rest of the men's conversation. 'I'm sure little Henry would love to explore the grounds of the Hall. We could have a picnic by the pond . . . '

'That sounds very nice,' Carrie replied absently, her attention still fixed on the hushed conversation between her husband and Sir Edward. They had both turned their backs now, heads close together.

'Do you mean it? Oh, that's wonderful!' Miss Eleanor

clasped her hands together in delight. 'We'll arrange a date, shall we? Oh, it will be such fun!'

Finally they said their goodbyes, and Carrie and James left the Haverstocks and started to make their way back down the lane towards the village.

'What did Sir Edward want to talk to you about?' Carrie asked him.

He shrugged. 'Just some pit business.'

'What kind of business?'

'Nothing to concern you.' He was being deliberately evasive, she could tell. 'Did I hear you making arrangements with Eleanor to go up to the Hall?'

'Yes, I think I did.' Carrie's heart sank at the prospect.

'Thank you.' James reached for her hand and squeezed it. 'I know it's difficult for you, but I do appreciate it.'

The vicar's words drifted back into her mind. It felt good to be doing the right thing for once, rather than deceiving her husband.

'It must have been urgent pit business, for Sir Edward to seek you out on a Sunday?' she remarked.

James' mouth twisted. 'Oh, you know Sir Edward. Everything is urgent if it concerns him and his business.'

'What did he want this time?' Carrie asked again, but just at that moment Henry woke up, and James took him out of his pram to carry him.

Carrie watched him with his son in his arms, showing him the wild flowers growing in the long grass along the side of the lane. There was something about the sight that made her uneasy.

After church, she went down to the rows to visit her father. He had rallied slightly after his recent bout of illness, enough to insist on going up to the allotment with her to lift some carrots. But Carrie had ended up doing most of the work while her father sat on an upturned bucket, fighting for breath. He maintained he was quite well, but his white, sunken face told a different story.

So when the hammering on the door woke her up at dawn the following morning, Carrie shot out of bed, convinced it must be one of her sisters come to tell her Eric Wardle had been taken ill in the night.

Her feet had barely touched the floorboards when she heard a man's voice, shouting up angrily from below.

'Come out here, Shepherd!' he roared. 'Come out and face us like a man!'

Carrie turned to James in dismay, but he was already out of bed and heading for the door.

'Wait here,' he ordered grimly.

'But who—' The bedroom door closed on her, cutting her off. Carrie sat on the edge of the bed and listened to James' footsteps hurrying down the stairs. Then she pulled on her robe and crept after him.

As she reached the top of the staircase, she could see James standing on the doorstep, his back to her.

'Go home,' he was saying. 'Go before I set the law on you.'

'Aye, that'd be right! Have me put in jail, so you can throw my family out on the streets, just like you have t'others. I don't know how tha can live with thysen after what tha's done.'

Carrie recognised the voice. It was her friend Nancy's father, Ron Morris. As she reached the foot of the stairs, she could see his stocky figure squaring up to James, the miner's blazing anger a contrast to her husband's icy calm.

'What's happened?' she asked.

James glanced over his shoulder at her. 'I told you to stay upstairs.'

Carrie ignored him, turning to Mr Morris. 'What's going on?'

'You mean he in't told you what he's done?' Mr Morris sent James a filthy glance. 'Aye, I daresay he was too ashamed.'

Carrie turned to her husband. 'What's he talking about?'

James shook his head, tight-lipped. 'It's nothing—'

'Nothing! You call it nothing to turn innocent women and children out on the streets?'

Ron Morris looked at Carrie. 'I'll tell thee, shall I, since he's too cowardly to tell you himself? He's turned Susan Toller and Mrs Horsfall out of their cottages.'

'No!' Carrie stared at James' stony profile. 'Is this true?'

'Carrie . . . '

'Is it true, James?'

He let out an angry sigh. 'Mr Toller and Mr Horsfall are in prison, and therefore no longer employed by Bowden Main Colliery,' he recited stiffly. 'Since the cottages are supplied to miners' families, the women have been issued with an eviction notice.'

'Eviction notice!' Ron Morris retorted. 'The bailiffs are there now, tossing their furniture out on t'street!'

Carrie ignored him, her attention still fixed on her husband. 'But you can't do that! Where will they go? What will they do?'

He didn't reply. Nor did he meet her pleading eyes.

'I wouldn't waste tha breath, missus,' Mr Morris said scornfully. 'You only have to look at him to see he couldn't care less.' He shook his head. 'And you, a pitman's daughter. I dunno how you can live with him, lass, I really—'

He didn't get to the end of his sentence before James slammed the door in his face, so hard it shook in its frame.

Carrie stared at him, still struggling to take in what she had heard.

'How could you?' she whispered.

Ron Morris' fist crashed against the other side of the door, making them both jump.

'You might reckon you can shut the door on me, but you'll have to face what you've done in the end, Shepherd!' he shouted.

Upstairs, Henry started to wail. James headed for the stairs, Carrie at his heels.

'You haven't answered my question!'

'I had no choice,' he said, his footsteps heavy on the stairs ahead of her. 'The cottages are for the miners and their families.'

'But Mrs Horsfall is an old lady! And Susan Toller has five children. Where are they supposed to go?'

Once again, James was silent. Carrie stared at him. His face was so cold and implacable, she barely recognised him any more.

'What happened to you, James?' she murmured.

'I don't know what you mean.'

'You never used to be like this. I remember when you used to have a heart.'

For a moment she thought she saw the slightest flicker of emotion in his eyes. Then it was gone.

'I'm only carrying out Sir Edward's orders.'

'He pays you to manage his pit, not to put innocent families out on the street!'

'Nevertheless, I – where are you going?' he asked, as Carrie turned away from him, heading for the bedroom.

'I'm getting dressed. Then I'm going down to the rows to see what's going on.'

'You can't! You saw how Ron Morris was. I don't want them turning on you like that.'

'They won't,' Carrie said.

'How do you know that?'

'Because I'm one of them.'

The words were out before she had time to think about them. She saw the flare of hurt in James' eyes a second before he turned away from her.

Chapter Twenty-Eight

Susan Toller's cottage was empty, the door locked and the shutters closed over the windows. An old iron bedstead stood on its end against the wall, next to a worn-out armchair, a table and settle, and a pair of stained horsehair mattresses. The rest of Susan's belongings – odds and ends of china, pots and pans and a clock – were piled up by the door where they had been dumped by the bailiffs.

A lump rose in Carrie's throat at the pathetic sight. She felt humiliated for poor Susan, having all her bits and pieces, everything she had carefully gathered together over ten years of marriage, strewn about for everyone to see.

'Shameful, in't it?'

Carrie turned to see Rob Chadwick standing behind her. He nodded towards the cottage, grim-faced. 'They didn't even give her time to pack. Just picked it all up and threw it in the street.'

'You were here when it happened?'

He nodded. 'We heard the commotion two rows away. Everyone came to see if they could help, but there was nowt to be done.' His jaw tightened. 'I would have taken a swing at those bailiffs mysen, but we all knew it weren't their fault. They were just following the orders they'd been given.'

Carrie looked away sharply, heat rising in her face.

'What about Mrs Horsfall? Have you heard anything about her?'

'Luckily she's gone off to stay with family in Leeds, so

she weren't at home when it happened. But all her furniture's been turned out on the street, just like this.'

'Thank the Lord she wasn't there.' Carrie couldn't imagine how terrified the poor old lady would have been if she'd been woken up by strangers crashing in through her door. 'What will happen to their furniture? It can't stay here, surely?'

'Old Mother Arkwright has said they can store it in one of her barns. I've just been down to Barratt's Farm to borrow the cart so I can shift it.' Rob jerked his head towards a cart waiting at the other end of the lane, the old carthorse nodding peacefully between the shafts.

'That's very good of you,' Carrie said quietly.

'I wish I could do more.' A muscle flickered in his cheek. 'If I could get hold of the swine who ordered this . . . '

Carrie looked away. She wanted to defend James, but the words wouldn't come. 'Where are Susan and the bairns?'

'Mrs Morris has taken them in for now.'

'Does she know what she's going to do?'

'You'd best ask Susan that, not me.'

'I'll go and see her.'

'I in't sure she'll want to see you.'

'Why not?'

'You have to ask that?' Rob nodded towards the shuttered cottage. 'In case you hadn't noticed, your mester's the reason she's been put out on the streets.'

Carrie didn't even try to deny it. 'That's nowt to do with me. She's still my friend.'

'If you say so.' He shrugged. 'But don't blame me if she don't fall into your arms,' he called out as Carrie walked away.

Carrie didn't look back until she had reached the end of the row, where the cart stood. She paused for a moment to pat the horse's broad, velvety muzzle, and glanced back towards Susan Toller's cottage. Rob was trudging up the cobbled lane towards her, his head down, the wooden settle slung easily across his broad shoulders.

Carrie hurried away before he could look up and see her watching him.

Susan Toller's children were playing outside the Morrises' cottage. Thankfully they seemed none the worse for their ordeal, judging by the way they chased each other up and down the row, shrieking with laughter.

But their mother was a different story. Susan Toller looked like a wraith, drained of life, as she sat at the kitchen table, her hands wrapped tightly around an untouched cup of tea. She was wearing one of the blouses Carrie had left on her doorstep. It hung from her thin shoulders.

Mrs Morris sat across the table from her. She barely glanced at Carrie as she let herself in through the back door, her attention fixed on poor Susan.

'Are you sure you won't eat summat, ducks?' she coaxed. 'You need to keep your strength up.'

'Nay, I couldn't.' Susan looked up and saw Carrie, and her manner changed. 'What are you doing here? Come to gloat, have you? Or has your mester sent you to make sure I've gone?' Anger flashed in her eyes.

'No, I just came to see how you are.'

'How do you think I am? Me and my bairns are homeless, thanks to your husband. I hope he's pleased with himself!'

Carrie opened her mouth to defend herself, then closed it again. She couldn't blame Susan for wanting to vent her rage on someone. The poor woman was humiliated and scared, terrified of what the future might hold for her and her children.

And Carrie had no right to defend herself. All she could do was brace herself against the torrent of anger.

'Nay, lass, don't be too hard on her. It in't her fault.' Mrs Morris spoke up for Carrie. 'Sit thysen down, lass,' she told her. 'There's tea in't pot, if you want one? It'll be stewed, but it's warm and wet.'

'Nay, thank you.' Carrie lowered herself on to the settle beside Susan, who promptly burst into tears. Carrie and Mrs Morris both stared at her, shocked. Women in Bowden didn't cry, not in front of each other at any rate.

'I'm sorry,' she faltered. 'I don't know what I'm saying. I'm beside mysen, I really am.'

'You've every right to be upset.' Carrie reached for Susan's hand. It was thin and cold as ice in spite of the warm day. 'I'm the one who should be sorry. If only there was summat I could do . . . ' She paused, feeling helpless. 'Have you thought about where you might go?'

'I've no idea.' Susan shook her head. 'This has all happened so sudden, I in't had a chance to think.'

'You know I'd have you all, but we're already bursting at the seams, what with Nancy and Archie stopping here.' Mrs Morris looked apologetic.

Susan managed a watery smile. 'I know, love. And I'm very grateful. But I wouldn't want to impose on you.'

'Have you got any family?' Carrie asked her.

'Only an aunt in Barnsley – my mother's sister. She might have us.'

'It's such a long way to go though, in't it?' Mrs Morris said.

'That's true,' Susan agreed with a sigh. 'It'll be hard for the bairns, leaving Bowden. They've lived here all their lives, they don't know any different. And after everything they've been through lately, what with their dad being put away . . . ' She shook her head. 'Anyway, there's no use moping about it. We've just got to make the best of things. It won't be too long before Matthew's out, and then we'll be able to get back on our feet.'

But there was sadness behind her brave smile. They all knew it was unlikely the Tollers would ever return to Bowden. Just like all the other families who had been driven from the village by this wretched lockout. Carrie could feel life changing around her, her past and everything she had known slipping away from her.

Unless . . .

She looked from Susan to Mrs Morris and back again. 'I've got an idea,' she said.

The clock on the wall chimed five times, and James Shepherd leaned back in his chair, massaging the stiff, knotted muscles in his neck.

It had been a long, hard day. The business with the Tollers and Mrs Horsfall had blackened the men's mood and shortened their tempers. They roared at the pit gates all day, chanting James' name, cursing him for what he had done. He had closed the window to shut out the sound, but their words still echoed in his head as he tried to go about his work.

Then, as the shift was changing at two, some of the blacklegs started provoking the Bowden men and a scuffle broke out. Insults were hurled, fists flew, and three local men had been taken away by the specials.

James had told the constable in charge to give them time to cool down in the cells, then release them. He only hoped Sir Edward didn't get to hear of it. He would expect them to go straight before the magistrates. He wouldn't be satisfied until they were behind bars, their cottages seized and their families turned out on to the street.

James' gaze strayed up to the portrait of his father on

the wall. Henry Shepherd dominated the room, looking down on his son, just as he had when he was alive.

His father had done his best to make a man of James. He taught him to fight, pitting him against the hefty local boys like dogs in a ring, berating his son for his weakness when he emerged battered and bruised, with black eyes and a swollen lip.

Once he had even ended up in hospital after one of the bigger lads set about him while he lay on the ground, kicking him and cracking two of his ribs. But all his father said was, 'Perhaps this will teach you to hit first, and hit hard. You're too soft, that's your trouble. You need to toughen up, boy.'

When he was eight years old, Henry Shepherd had sent him down the mine. James still remembered his terror as his father shoved him into the cage alone, the metallic clang of the gate shutting, followed by the rush of cold air on his face as it plummeted downwards.

He could also recall his shame as he stumbled out of the cage at the pit bottom and was sick with fear, emptying his guts in the hot, noisy darkness, while the men laughed at him.

But his father hadn't laughed when James returned to the surface, his clothes stained and stinking of vomit. He had taken his riding crop to him, furious at being humiliated.

'I want you to make me proud!' he had roared as the crop snapped painfully against James' thin legs.

And James had done his best. But every day he was painfully aware of how badly he failed.

He was even more aware of it now, with the lockout heading into its third month and no sign of surrender on either side. He had no doubt his father would have had the Bowden miners back to work by now. He would have crushed them into submission without mercy, just as he had during the last strike five years ago.

Henry Shepherd had earned the Haverstocks' admiration then, and now Sir Edward expected James to do the same. A couple of pits down in Nottingham had already gone back to work, and Sir Edward could not understand why Bowden had not given in too.

'You need to get tougher, Shepherd,' he warned James. 'Do what needs to be done.'

You need to toughen up, boy.

James looked up at the portrait. Everyone who saw it commented on the resemblance between them. But James knew he was only a pale imitation of his father.

Henry would have relished this battle. He certainly wouldn't have balked over evicting families from their homes. He would not have needed to wait for orders from Sir Edward, either. He would have been down there on the rows that morning, watching the bailiffs throwing women and children out on to the street and enjoying every moment.

Instead, James had stayed at home like a coward, trying to pretend none of it was happening, unable to look his own wife in the eye.

He felt wretched when he remembered the look of reproach on her face that morning. He longed to tell her that he cared, more than he could allow himself to let on. But then she would think he was a failure for not standing up to Sir Edward. Either way, he couldn't win.

He returned home, weary and steeling himself for another fight. He only hoped that Carrie had had time to calm down, but he knew she would not get over this easily, and he didn't blame her.

His key was in the door when he heard the crash of china coming from inside the house, followed by a clamour of women's voices.

He let himself in, and found the maid on her hands and knees, picking up fragments of what had been a Wedgwood vase, a fine piece that had been in the family for generations. An anxious-looking woman stood over her, holding firmly on to a child with each hand.

'It was an accident, I swear.' He didn't recognise Susan Toller until he heard her voice. He was shocked by her changed appearance. She used to be an attractive woman, but worry had turned her face gaunt, stretching the skin over the bones.

James looked from one to the other of them. 'What's going on here?'

The maid sent him a look that spoke volumes. 'It's Mrs Shepherd, sir. She—'

Just at that moment Carrie came down the stairs, smoothing her hands over her skirt. 'Right, I've been through the cupboards and there is more than enough linen,' she addressed herself to the maid. 'So perhaps now you will make up the beds as I asked you?'

'Yes, ma'am.' The girl shot James a quick, resentful look then hurried off, carrying the broken pieces of china in the ash pan.

James looked from Carrie to Susan Toller and back again. Since the moment he had stepped into his home, he had felt as if he was caught up in the strangest of dreams.

'Would someone mind telling me what's happening?' he said.

'I've invited Mrs Toller and her children to stay with us.'

James stared at his wife. 'You did what?'

Carrie lifted her chin. 'I've invited them to stay,' she repeated. 'They had nowhere else to go since they've been turned out of their cottage.'

He read the unspoken challenge in her eyes. She

expected him to yield, to give in to her plans. She expected him to be as weak as everyone knew him to be.

You need to toughen up, boy.

He turned to Susan. 'I'm afraid there's been a mistake,' he said bluntly. 'You can't stay here.'

Carrie gasped. Susan Toller looked panic-stricken. 'But Carrie . . . Mrs Shepherd said . . .'

'Yes, well, she shouldn't have made any promises without consulting me first.' James shot Carrie a quick glance. She was staring back at him as if she had been slapped. 'I'm sorry, Mrs Toller, but it's quite out of the question for you to stay here.'

He walked away before Carrie had a chance to say anything. As he closed the door to his study, he could hear Susan Toller sobbing quietly.

He sat down behind his desk and buried his face in his hands, only to spring up again when the door flew open and Carrie stood there, her eyes blazing.

'Why?' she demanded. 'Why can't they stay?'

'Because I don't want them here. If Sir Edward were to find out—'

Carrie gave a contemptuous laugh. 'I might have known he'd be the reason! Mustn't do anything to upset your precious Haverstocks, must we? Never mind that there's a woman and her children out on the streets tonight because of him!' Her chest rose and fell as she drew in deep, angry breaths. 'Well, unlike you I don't care what Sir Edward thinks. I wanted to help out someone in need, and I had hoped you'd want to help them, too.'

He read the appeal in her eyes and felt himself weaken. He had almost opened his mouth to say they could stay when he heard his father mocking him.

You're too soft. That's your trouble.

'They're not our problem, Carrie,' he repeated firmly.

'But they're my friends.'

'And I'm your husband! Doesn't that count for anything?'

Carrie took a step back, her eyes widening. Before she had a chance to reply, Susan Toller crept up behind her.

'It's all right, Carrie love. We can go to Barnsley. I'm sure my aunt won't turn me away.'

'You see?' James said to Carrie. 'I'm sure you'll be much happier there, Mrs Toller. And if I can help you with expenses . . . ' He started to take out his wallet, but Susan Toller shook her head.

'Thank you, Mr Shepherd, but I don't want anything from you,' she said, stiff with dignity.

'Are you sure? If it would help you . . . '

'You heard her. She doesn't want your help.' Carrie turned away. 'Come on, Susan. I'll get you something to eat before you go.' She ushered her out of the door, shooting James a look of pure disgust as she closed it behind her.

He stayed in his study until the Tollers had gone. He heard the clip-clop of hooves and looked out of the window to see Rob Chadwick sitting up on top of a cart, the horse's reins in his hands.

James felt a shot of dislike. Why was he still in the village? He had taken to hanging around the pit gates with the other miners, shouting the odds at the blacklegs even though it had been more than three years since he himself had worked at Bowden Main.

As James watched, Carrie came out of the house and spoke to Rob for a few minutes. Then Susan came out with all her children, and Rob climbed down and picked them up tenderly one by one, swinging them high up into the back of the cart before gallantly helping Susan on to the seat beside him. He leaned over and said something to her, and James saw the woman's sad face slowly transformed as she laughed.

Bitterness rose in his throat, nearly choking him. Rob Chadwick, hero of the hour.

Carrie remained standing by the gate, watching the horse and cart until it disappeared out of sight. As she turned away, James thought he saw a look of longing on her face.

Chapter Twenty-Nine

Everyone agreed it was the hottest day of the summer so far.

Even first thing in the morning, Agnes could feel the warmth of the sun on the glass as she drew back her curtains. In the kitchen, Jinny had thrown open the back door to let in some cool air, only to have Mrs Bannister close it again on account of the flies coming in.

'If she reckons I'm going to stay shut in here on a baking day, she's got another think coming!' Jinny grumbled as she lit the range. 'I'll melt into a puddle by dinnertime!'

By mid-morning, the sun was high in the cloudless blue sky, bouncing off the cobbled streets and scorching the scrubby patches of grass verge. Dogs lolled in the shade of shop awnings, for once too weary to try to chase Agnes' bicycle as she cycled through the village. Even the children in the school playground seemed more languid than usual. There were no cries of excitement and laughter, no running about. They moved slowly, flopping down here and there, too hot for play.

Agnes hopped off her bicycle and parked it in the shed. She was sweltering inside her thick blue cotton dress, hair damp with perspiration under her cap.

In the senior classroom, she found Miss Warren and Miss Colley sitting side by side at the senior teacher's desk, a pile of books in front of them. Miss Colley was pasting book plates into the front of each book, then passing them to Miss Warren, who inscribed them. Miss

Warren looked as cool and collected as ever, unlike Miss Colley, who had damp strands of hair sticking to her round, pink face.

'You'll have to do this one again, Miss Colley. It's not quite straight, do you see?' Miss Warren handed her back one of the books.

Miss Colley held it up, squinting at it. 'It looks perfectly all right to me.'

'I'm telling you, it isn't.' Miss Warren looked up as Agnes came in. 'Ah, Miss Sheridan. We weren't expecting you until eleven o'clock. It's barely ten to.' She glanced at the clock on the wall accusingly.

'I finished my rounds early, so I thought I'd come straight here.'

'I see.' Miss Warren was tight-lipped. 'There are some who would say being too early is almost as impolite as being too late.'

Agnes glanced at Miss Colley, who rolled her eyes. *You see what I have to put up with?* her long-suffering expression said.

'I'm sorry,' Agnes said, setting down her bag. She had already learned that where Miss Warren was concerned, it was always better to apologise. Trying to argue got her nowhere. 'What's all this?' She nodded towards the books on the table.

'School prize-giving,' Miss Warren explained. 'Miss Colley and I are putting in the children's names ready for the prizes to be handed out. Although I daresay we would get through them all a great deal faster if Miss Colley here were to pay more attention to what she is doing,' she added, thrusting another book back at the hapless junior teacher.

'Sorry, Miss Warren,' Miss Colley muttered between clenched teeth.

'When is the prize-giving?' Agnes asked.

'Next week, at the Miners' Welfare Institute. Perhaps you would like to come?' Miss Warren said.

'I would, thank you.'

'Excuse me, Miss Warren?' Miss Colley interrupted, holding up one of the books. 'What shall we do about Elsie Stanhope?'

Miss Warren paused, her fountain pen poised. She looked at the book in Miss Colley's hands, then let out a sigh. 'Better not, I suppose.'

Agnes' ears pricked up at the mention of Elsie's name. 'Why won't you give Elsie a prize?'

'Oh, believe me, I'd like nothing more. Elsie is one of the brightest and most able pupils in this school, and by rights she should be collecting a prize with the other children. But her father has forbidden it.'

'Forbidden it? But why?'

'The prizes have been donated by the Haverstock family. Miss Eleanor is going to be handing them out at the ceremony. And I'm afraid Mr Stanhope won't allow Elsie to take anything from them.'

Agnes stared at her, shocked. 'Surely not?'

'He feels very strongly about it,' Miss Warren said. 'I've tried to talk to him, but he won't hear of it. Mr Stanhope is very – uncompromising – in his views.' She chose her words carefully.

Pig-headed, you mean, Agnes thought.

She had got to know Elsie Stanhope better recently. The little girl had been turning up regularly at Agnes' clinics, loitering around the doors until it was time to close up, then helping her to put away the chairs. Agnes thought she might grow bored eventually, but for now she was keen to learn, asking her all kinds of questions about nursing, and the equipment used. Agnes was continually surprised by how bright the girl was, soaking up all the information like a sponge, desperately keen to learn.

Elsie had told her a little about her own life, too. She was careful about what she gave away, but Agnes had built up a picture of a lonely little girl, desperately grieving for her mother, and missing the father who had shut himself off from his children just when they needed him most.

Agnes pictured the child, carefully putting away chairs in the Welfare Institute after the clinic, in her ragged dress and patched boots, and her heart lurched in her chest. Poor Elsie. She spent her life being ignored, and now she was to be deprived of her one moment to shine.

Eleven o'clock struck, and Miss Warren put down her pen. 'Time to get the children in,' she said to Miss Colley. 'The bell, Miss Colley, if you please. Miss Sheridan, perhaps you would like to carry out your inspection in the other classroom, while I finish writing out these? You can assist her, can't you, Miss Colley?'

'Of course, Miss Warren.'

As Miss Colley followed Agnes outside, she said, 'What a relief to escape! Honestly, she was starting to drive me mad. As if I'm not capable of pasting in a book plate! I'm tired of her continually finding fault with me. I've a good mind to walk out one of these days, you see if I don't.' Her words came out in a torrent, like a dam bursting its banks. 'And did you notice how cool she was? It was so hot and airless in that room, I thought I would melt. But not her ... I wouldn't be at all surprised if she had ice water running through her veins – are you all right, Miss Sheridan? You're very quiet this morning?'

Only because I haven't had the chance to say a word! Agnes thought, and smiled to herself. 'I was still thinking of Elsie Stanhope,' she said.

'Ah, yes. Poor little Elsie.' Miss Colley sighed. 'Such a pity. Even Miss Warren can't find a bad word to say about her, which means she must be some kind of child prodigy.' She shook her head. 'But I suppose if her father has made up his mind then there's nothing to be done, is there?'

'I suppose not,' Agnes agreed. But her mind was already busily working.

'Blackleg scum!'

'Bloody traitors!'

'Tha should be ashamed of thysen!'

Seth Stanhope and the other men vented their fury on the bars of the locked pit gates, rattling the chains that bound them. On the far side of the yard, the newly recruited men barely looked their way as they emerged from the cage, squinting in the bright sunshine, then headed towards the lamp room. After nearly three months they had grown used to the chants and the curses and the name-calling from the striking miners.

'Look at them. At least they used to have the grace to look ashamed. Now they're brazen about it.' Tom Chadwick spat on the ground in disgust,

'Aye, you're right,' his son Archie agreed. 'One of 'em even waved at me this morning as the bus went in.'

'I'd like to see him waving if I got hold of him in a dark alley!' Alec Morris muttered.

'It makes you wonder what's the point of being here, if no one's going to take any notice of us?' Reg Willis said quietly.

Seth turned on him, narrowing his eyes. 'What are you saying?'

Reg took a step back, pulling himself up to his full height. He still barely came up to Seth's earlobe. 'We've all just said, no one pays us any attention any more. And it's not as if we've been able to stop the blacklegs coming in, is it? Production's going on, same as it always did. Management don't seem to care if we're here or not, so why are we bothering?'

'Then what are we supposed to do? Sit at home twiddling our thumbs and waiting for the Haverstocks to unlock the gates so we can go back to work?' Seth said.

He looked around at the other men, who shuffled their feet. He could tell they all agreed with Reg Willis, even if they didn't want to speak up in front of Seth. He could scent the air of defeat coming from them.

'We can't give in now,' he urged them. 'We've got to keep coming here, to show 'em we're still strong, still united. We've got to keep fighting.'

'Do we?' Tom Chadwick spoke up. 'I wonder sometimes.'

Archie looked dismayed. 'You don't mean that, Dad. You'd never break the lockout, surely?'

'I didn't say that.' Tom shot a quick, cautious glance at Seth. 'All I'm saying is that it's getting harder to keep going. My Ruth pawned her wedding ring last week.' His voice was choked. 'I see how hard she struggles to keep the family together, and I wonder if it's worth it, since we'll have to accept the Haverstocks' terms sooner or later.'

'Who says we'll have to accept them?' Seth flared back. 'We're going to win this lockout. If we stick together, they'll have to listen to us.'

'Yes, but we in't sticking together, are we? The TUC stabbed us in't back within a week. And even the other miners are turning on us. Like that lot.' Tom nodded towards the pit yard. 'There are more men going back to work every day. Why should we be the ones to stick it out when we could be back down the pit, earning a wage again?'

'You mean you want to join the rest of the blackleg scum?' Seth cut him off angrily. 'Then don't let us stop you.' He stood aside. 'Go on, have a word with Mr Shepherd, I daresay he'll welcome you back wi' open arms. But you won't be able to look thysen or the rest of us in't face if you do,' he warned.

Tom was mutinously silent, his face turned towards the pit yard. 'I'm only saying, it's hard to keep going,' he murmured.

Seth laid a hand on his shoulder. 'I know, Tom. It's hard for the rest of us, too. But we're like a house of cards. If one falls, then the whole lot will come down. You owe it to your mates to stand with us.'

'I owe it to my family to keep them fed, too,' Tom muttered.

Before Seth could reply, Reg Willis called out, 'Hello, what's she doing here?'

They all turned round. Seth's heart sank at the sight of Agnes Sheridan cycling towards them, her battered old bicycle bumping over the rutted track that led to the pit gates.

He turned away, but the other men went on staring.

'Happen she's come to join the picket line?' Archie Chadwick grinned.

'I wouldn't mind that,' Reg Willis said. 'At least it'd give us summat pretty to look at while we're wasting our time here.' Seth ignored the sideways glance Reg gave him.

'I dunno about that.' Tom Chadwick nodded towards Miss Sheridan. 'I've seen that look in your mother's eye, Archie. It generally means they've got it in for someone!'

Seth kept his attention fixed on the pit yard. The bus would be leaving soon, taking the men home. He wanted to be ready for when the gates opened.

The next thing he knew, someone was speaking his

name. He turned around to see the nurse standing at his shoulder, looking up at him.

'May I have a word with you, Mr Stanhope?' she said in that ever-so-polite, cut-glass accent of hers.

He caught the eyes of the other men standing behind her, watching him with amusement. 'Not now, I'm busy,' he dismissed.

'So I see.' She looked around her, and he could hear the sarcasm in her voice. 'But I promise I won't take up too much of your valuable time.'

She wasn't going to go away, he could tell. Determination was written all over her face.

Seth sighed. 'If this is about our Christopher, I've already told you—'

'It's not about your son. It's about Elsie.'

That caught his attention. 'Elsie? Why, what's she done? She in't ailing?'

'No, she isn't.' Agnes paused. 'Are you aware your daughter has won a prize at school, Mr Stanhope?'

Seth blinked at her, not sure if he had heard her correctly. 'You mean to tell me you've come all this way to talk about a school prize?' He shook his head. The girl obviously had more time on her hands than she had sense. 'Aye, Hannah mentioned it. What of it?'

'I hear you've forbidden her to collect it?'

Seth's mouth tightened. 'And what business is it of yours if I have?'

'Don't you think you're being rather unfair?'

'You wouldn't understand.' Seth turned away, looking through the gates again. The blacklegs were filing out, climbing on to the bus. Any minute now, the overman would be crossing the yard to unlock the gates.

'Oh, I understand perfectly. You're prepared to sacrifice your daughter's happiness for the sake of your own pride.'

One of the listening men laughed nervously. Seth turned to glare at whoever it was, but they were all busily looking down at the ground, taking a sudden interest in their boots.

Only Agnes Sheridan went on meeting his eye, her expression perfectly composed. She really did have the nerve of the devil, he decided.

'And how come you know so much about my family all of a sudden?' he asked.

'I've got to know Elsie recently. She's been coming down to the clinic every week. I've been teaching her about nursing. She's a very bright little girl, Mr Stanhope.'

'You don't need to tell me that.' Seth had a sudden picture of his daughter, tucked beside her mother on the settle, learning how to read. Sarah always said Elsie took more interest than the boys.

'It seems such a shame she won't be collecting her prize.' Agnes Sheridan's voice brought him back to the present.

'She doesn't mind,' he muttered, wondering all the time why he was even giving her the time of day. Didn't she ever keep her nose out of other people's business?

'How do you know that? Have you spoken to her properly about it?'

Seth opened his mouth, then closed it again. It was Hannah who had told him. He couldn't remember the last time he had listened to a word his daughter said to him.

The revelation stopped him in his tracks for a moment. But at that moment he was distracted by the overman. He was crossing the yard, his keys jingling.

'I've heard enough,' Seth said shortly. 'Time you went.'

Agnes stood her ground, squaring her slim shoulders. 'You can't tell me what to do!'

'And you can't tell me how to bring up my family!'

The overman reached the gate and glared at them

through the bars. 'We don't want any trouble from you lot,' he warned.

Seth joined the other men, poised around the entrance as the bus slowly rumbled across the yard towards it. The special constables began to gather around, forming a protective guard.

So you're not going to change your mind?' Seth heard Agnes Sheridan's voice saying behind him. 'Mr Stanhope? Are you listening to me?'

'Not now!' He muscled his way to the front of the crowd, his body tensed. The bus was close enough now that he could make out the blackened faces of the men through the windows.

'Perhaps if you paid as much attention to your children as you do to this pit, your family wouldn't be in such a woeful state!'

Seth turned around slowly. The other men had stopped speaking and jostling each other. They froze where they stood, watching him warily, waiting for him to explode.

'You know nowt about my family,' he growled.

'Neither do you, it seems. But at least I take an interest in them, which is more than can be said for you!'

He stared at Agnes, too stunned to speak. She stared back at him, her bright brown eyes devoid of fear.

Behind him, the overman started to unlock the gates.

'Tha'd best go, lass,' Tom Chadwick spoke up. 'Before t'bus comes out.'

She opened her mouth to argue, then closed it again. 'Very well,' she said, her gaze still fixed on Seth. 'Think about what I've said, won't you, Mr Stanhope?'

'Stay out of my business!' But his words were lost on her as she cycled down the track.

He turned to the other men. A row of faces stared back at him silently. No one dared speak.

The gates creaked open and the bus came through. Straight away the miners surged forward, tussling with the specials so they could reach up and bang the windows with their fists.

'Blackleg filth!'

'Go back where you came from, you in't wanted here!'

But for once, Seth Stanhope didn't join them. He was too busy staring at the nurse as she freewheeled away down the lane.

Chapter Thirty

Hannah could tell Seth was in a bad mood as soon as she saw him striding down the row. She was beating a rug on the washing line. Billy ran around her, ducking back and forth under the line, flying an aeroplane he had made out of old newspaper.

He saw his father first and started towards him. 'Dad, look what I've got! '

Seth barely glanced at his son as he pulled off his boots and dumped them on the stone step.

'It's a Sopwith Camel,' Billy went on, undaunted. 'Look, I can make it fly . . . '

Hannah caught him by the shoulder. 'Why don't you go and knock for one of your pals?' she said. 'I bet they'd like to see your aeroplane.'

'But I want to show Dad.' Billy's face fell as Seth disappeared inside the house, slamming the door behind him.

'He can look at it later. Go on, off with you.'

Hannah watched the boy go, his little shoulders slumped with disappointment. Then she went into the cottage.

Seth was standing by the range, peering into the teapot.

'What's happened?' asked Hannah.

'Who says owt's happened?'

'I know you, Seth Stanhope. What's wrong?' She went over and took the teapot from his hands and set it down, then put the kettle on. 'Has there been more trouble on the picket line?' Seth generally returned from picket duty in a sour mood.

'Nay.' He was silent for a moment, then said tightly, 'Unless you call that bloody interfering nurse trouble!'

Hannah looked over her shoulder at him as she set the kettle to boil. 'Miss Sheridan? What's she done this time?'

'I'll tell you, shall I? Turned up at the pit gates, shouting the odds and making a fool of me.'

'She never did?'

'Oh, aye. Telling everyone my business, she was. Making out I don't care about my bairns.' His face darkened at the memory.

'No! And she said it in front of the other men?' Hannah could scarcely believe it. Even she would never have imagined Agnes Sheridan to be that foolish. 'But she had no right to do that, Seth. No right at all.'

'You think I don't know that?' He looked furious. 'That woman don't know when to keep her nose out, that's her problem.'

'You're right there.' Hannah was still seething over Ruth Chadwick. She could scarcely believe how her friend had turned against her, telling her the nurse would be treating her wretched baby from now on. Hannah knew Ruth would never have found the courage to defy her if it hadn't been for Agnes Sheridan. 'What did she want anyway? Our Christopher hasn't been playing up again, surely?'

He shook his head. 'It's Elsie. According to the nurse, she's got hersen upset over that prize-giving business.'

Hannah frowned. 'How did t'nurse know about that?'

'Elsie told her. By all accounts, they've been getting quite thick together.'

'Have they now?' Hannah was thoughtful as she spooned tea into the pot.

'Aye. She reckons our lass has been turning up at that clinic of hers, learning all about nursing.'

Hannah stiffened with annoyance. What a treacherous

little sneak Elsie was! Hannah had always suspected the child didn't like her. And after she had worked so hard, trying to be a mother to them all!

'The nurse reckons I put my principles before my bairns' happiness,' Seth went on. His expression was still dark, but Hannah heard the note of doubt creeping into his voice.

'She had no right to say such things! Everyone knows what a good father you are, Seth. Take no notice of her.'

He didn't reply. Hannah watched him out of the corner of her eye as she made the tea.

'The lass does work hard at her lessons,' he said.

Hannah was silent. She was still furious that Elsie had been sneaking off to see Agnes Sheridan. She might have known that stuck-up madam would take a fancy to the girl. They were two of a kind, a pair of know-alls.

Elsie took after her mother, too. Hannah knew Sarah had looked down on her, just because she had never learned to read or write properly. As the eldest, Hannah had been the one to shoulder the responsibilities of looking after the farm and helping their mother carry out her healing duties in the village. Sarah had been the cosseted little pet, allowed to go to school and do as she pleased.

Not that her sister had ever thanked Hannah for the sacrifices she had made. Sarah had taken them all as her due, just as she had taken Seth Stanhope . . .

A wave of bitterness washed over Hannah. 'I've always said too much book learning in't good for a girl. It'll give her ideas.'

'That's what Sarah would have wanted,' Seth said. 'She was always very keen that the bairns should get on and do better than us.'

Hannah looked round at him in surprise. It was the first time in months she had heard him willingly say that name.

266

'They're your children, and you must do as you think fit,' she said, setting his teacup down in front of him. 'But they'll never learn any respect if they think they can get round you whenever they want summat,' she warned.

Elsie sloped in an hour later, just as Hannah was putting the food on the table. She prickled with irritation at the sight of the little girl, a book tucked under her arm as usual.

'Where have you been? There were errands to be done,' Hannah scolded her.

'Sorry, Aunt. What do you want me to do?' Elsie didn't look in the least bit repentant, staring back at her with those clear grey eyes. Hannah could feel irritation rising in her. If the girl had wanted to know about nursing, why couldn't she come to her aunt?

'You can fetch some more water from t'pump, for a start.' Hannah snatched the big earthenware jug from the windowsill and thrust it into her hands. Even Elsie's politeness got under her skin.

She told herself she shouldn't feel spiteful towards a little girl, but she couldn't help it. She hoped Seth wouldn't give in and let Elsie collect that prize.

She noticed him watching his daughter thoughtfully down the length of the table as they settled for their meal. It was the first time Hannah could recall him paying his children any attention since Sarah died. Usually he kept his head down, shovelling in his food as quickly as he could, an island of solitude while the children argued and laughed and teased each other around him.

Hannah felt a stab of resentment. How many times had she tried to get him to show an interest in them? And yet that wretched nurse had turned up and suddenly he was sitting up and taking notice.

Finally he spoke. 'I've been thinking,' he said, 'about this prize-giving of yours, Elsie.'

She kept her gaze fixed on her plate. 'Yes, Father.' She sounded resigned.

'If it's that important to you, then I reckon you should go.'

Elsie's head shot up, disbelief written all over her face. 'You mean it? I can have my prize?'

'Aye, if that's what tha want.'

'Oh, thank you!' The little girl's face was suddenly radiant with happiness. She clung to the edge of the table, as if to stop herself from jumping up and throwing her arms around him.

Hannah glanced down the table at Seth. There was the faintest shadow of a smile on his face, too.

'And will you come and watch me collect it?' Elsie asked.

Seth's smile disappeared like the sun vanishing behind cloud. 'Nay,' he said. 'Don't ask me to do that, lass. I couldn't sit in the same room as them Haverstocks.'

Elsie's shoulders slumped. Hannah stepped in quickly.

'There's no need to look like that,' she said sharply. 'You've already had more than you deserve. Don't you dare pull a face because you can't get things all your own way!'

'No, Aunt. Sorry, Father,' Elsie sighed.

Later on, Hannah managed to get Elsie alone while she was helping to clear the table.

'What's all this I hear about you sneaking off to see that nurse?'

Elsie looked startled. 'I – I didn't think I was doing any harm.'

'Then why did you keep it a secret?'

'I didn't—'

'Don't lie to me, child!' Hannah grabbed her arm, her fingers tightening. 'You've been creeping off to that clinic behind my back, having cosy chats with *that woman*.'

Elsie found her voice. 'I want to be a nurse when I'm older,' she said. 'Miss Sheridan has been teaching me.

'And what do you think she can teach you that I can't?'

Elsie stared back at her aunt defiantly. 'I want to be a real nurse,' she said. 'I want to work in a hospital.'

Her insolence enraged Hannah, and it was all she could do not to shake her. 'Do you really think someone like you could be a nurse?'

'Miss Sheridan said—'

'Never mind what Miss Sheridan said!' Hannah cut her off. 'She didn't ought to be putting ideas in your head. Lasses like you don't go to work in hospitals.' She stood looking Elsie up and down scornfully. 'Marrying a pitman is all you're good for.'

'That in't true!'

'Not good enough for you, eh? Think you're meant for better things?' Hannah curled her lip. 'Let me tell you summat, lass. You can win all the school prizes you like, but you'll still end up in a place like this, dashing your mester's pit clothes and filling his bath when he comes home from a shift.'

Tears sprang to Elsie's eyes. 'You're hurting me!'

Hannah looked down at the child's arm. She hadn't realised how tightly her fingers were biting into the flesh. She released her abruptly, and Elsie darted for the door.

'I don't want you hanging around that woman any more, d'you hear me? And no telling anyone our business, either!' Hannah called after her, as the door slammed.

Chapter Thirty-One

It was a wet Wednesday afternoon, and Carrie had missed the last bus from Leeds.

She stood outside the draper's shop on Wade Lane, watching the bus trundling away around the corner as the rain dripped off the brim of her hat and down her face. It was her own stupid fault for getting lost in the back streets. Now she was stuck with no other way of getting home, except to walk the eight miles back to Bowden.

Her mother would be worried about her. Carrie could imagine her standing at the window of her cottage, Henry in her arms, peering out into the driving rain and wondering where she was.

James probably wouldn't even notice she was gone, since he spent all his waking hours at the pit these days.

Carrie set off determinedly up the road out of the city, head down against the pelting rain, cursing herself for not bringing her umbrella. She had been too preoccupied to pay attention to the threatening grey sky as she had left the village that morning. But by the time the bus pulled in to the city the heavens had opened and the downpour began. Now she shivered in her wet clothes, her calfskin shoes squelching with every step. They were almost new but Carrie knew they would be ruined by the time she got home.

As she left the busy centre of the city and took the road west, the shops gave way to straggling streets of houses, which in turn gave way to factories and then, finally, to open fields. There were fewer people this way too, so it was easy to spot the horse and cart lurching along ahead of her, going in the same direction she was heading.

Even from a couple of hundred yards away, she could make out Rob Chadwick in the driver's seat, his burly shoulders hunched against the rain. Carrie's heart sank. She hadn't seen him in Bowden recently, but she'd heard he'd started working up at Barratt's Farm just outside the village.

Anyone else and she might have run to catch them up and beg a lift to Bowden. But this time she hung back, deliberately slowing her steps.

The cart rounded a bend in the lane ahead of her and disappeared from view. Carrie was relieved, until she turned the corner herself a few minutes later and found the cart standing at the roadside, waiting for her.

Carrie stopped, wiping the rain from her wet face. She could only imagine what she looked like, in her mud-splashed stockings, her hair plastered to her face under her sodden, shapeless hat. She might not have been interested in catching Rob Chadwick's eye any more, but she still had her pride, and she didn't want him to see her looking like a drowned rat.

But the cart did not move, and finally Carrie had no choice but to catch it up. She walked on with as much dignity as she could muster, conscious of Rob looking down at her from his high perch.

'Missed the bus, did you?' he called out.

'No,' Carrie shot back. 'It was such a pleasant day I thought I'd walk.'

He grinned. 'If you give me cheek like that, I won't give you a lift home.'

'What makes you think I want one?'

'So you'd rather walk back to Bowden in the pouring rain?'

Carrie hesitated, looking from the cart to her shoes and back again. The truth was, she would rather have walked all the way to York and back, than have to ride beside Rob Chadwick in awkward silence.

'Come on, I promise I won't bite,' he said. 'Although I can't answer for old Jeremiah here.' He nodded towards the horse. 'Unless you don't trust yourself alone with me?' He sent her a taunting look from under the brim of his cap.

Carrie felt herself blushing furiously.

'Don't flatter thysen, Rob Chadwick!' She hauled herself up on to the wooden slat beside him, ignoring the helping hand he offered her.

Rob laughed. 'That's just like you, Carrie Wardle. Always so independent.' He jingled the reins and the horse lurched off, throwing her sideways so she collided awkwardly with Rob's solid bulk.

She pulled herself upright, carefully straightening her damp hat.

They travelled in silence for a while, except for the sound of the rain and the steady clopping of the horse's heavy hooves on the track.

'So how come you missed the bus?' Rob asked at last. 'Forgot the time, did you?'

'Summat like that,' Carrie replied evasively. 'How about you?' she changed the subject. 'What were you doing in Leeds? I didn't think it was market day?' She half turned to glance back at the empty cart. It gave off a faint whiff of pigs.

He shook his head. 'It in't. But it's my day off, so old Barratt let me borrow the cart to go and visit Susan Toller.'

Carrie twisted in her seat to look at him. 'You went all the way to Barnsley to see Susan? Why?'

'I wanted to make sure she'd settled in all right. I were worried about her.' Rob sent her an embarrassed glance. 'I know, I must be going soft in my old age!'

Carrie looked at him for a moment. She certainly couldn't imagine the brash young man she used to know sparing a thought for anyone else.

'How is she?'

'Seems to be doing all right, from what I could tell. Her aunt don't seem a bad old stick, and she loves the bairns. Susan reckons they miss Bowden, but at least they've got a roof over their heads.'

'I'm glad.'

'I expect you'll want to pass the good news on to your mester. I daresay he in't been sleeping at night for worrying,' Rob said dryly.

Carrie turned away to stare at the road ahead of them. 'James does care,' she said quietly.

'Didn't stop him turning 'em out on the street, did it?'

'That wasn't his fault.'

'It's all right, Carrie, you don't have to defend him just because you're his wife. I know you don't agree with what he's done.'

Carrie pressed her lips together to stop herself speaking. The truth was, she couldn't defend James. She had tried to understand all the things he had done since the lock-out began. But the business over the Tollers and Mrs Horsfall had driven a wedge between them. They had barely spoken since, and James had taken to sleeping in his study every night. She was in no mood to forgive him, and he hadn't even tried to apologise, either.

'I mean, what kind of a man could do that to a helpless mother with children?' Rob went on. 'And as for poor old Mrs Horsfall . . . '

'I don't want to talk about it,' Carrie said.

'He's his father's son, all right. Haverstock's man through and through.'

'I said, I don't want to talk about it!' She turned on him.

273

'And if you carry on like this then you can let me down off this cart right now, Rob Chadwick!'

'All right, I didn't mean owt by it.'

They carried on in silence for a while. The lane ahead of them started to rise, following the line of the hill, but the horse plodded on easily.

'So what were you really doing in Leeds?' Rob's voice broke the silence, startling her.

Carrie hesitated. 'I went shopping.'

'And yet you've come home empty-handed?' His brows rose. 'Come on, Carrie, you can't fool me. You were up to summat, weren't you?' He nudged her. 'Here, you in't got a fancy man, have you?'

'Certainly not!' Carrie edged away from him.

'But you've got a secret, though. I can tell.'

She was silent for a moment, weighing up her words. 'If you must know . . . I went to the pawn shop.'

'You? At the pop shop?' Rob threw back his head and laughed. 'Your old man keeping you short, is he?'

'No! I wanted to sell some things for the Miners' Welfare Fund.'

She had already given away as many of her old clothes as she could spare, but the nosy maid was beginning to ask questions about her empty wardrobe, and all the items missing from the pantry. The only thing Carrie had left to sell had been her jewellery.

'Did you make anything?'

'Enough.' She had twenty pounds in her purse, enough to bolster the Miners' Fund for a few more weeks at least.

'Well, well.' A smile played on Rob's lips. 'And I suppose Mr Shepherd knows nowt about it?'

Carrie was silent for a moment. 'No,' she admitted reluctantly.

Rob smirked. 'Keeping secrets from your mester, eh? That don't sound right to me.'

'Shut up, Rob!'

'Keep your hair on, I were only joking.' He sent her a sideways look. 'What's up wi' you, lass? I've never known you to be like this.'

'Yes, well, you don't know me any more, do you?' she snapped back.

'I know you in't happy.'

Carrie looked away, out across the fields. 'You know nothing about it.'

Another silence fell. 'We're a right pair, in't we?' Rob said at last.

'How do you make that out, then?'

'Well, look at us. Both doing our good deeds in secret. And getting soaked into the bargain!' He gave her a rueful look. His crooked, comical smile under the dripping brim of his cap made her smile in spite of herself.

'That's better,' he said. 'It's good to see you smile, Carrie.'

She looked away sharply. It was another three miles to Bowden at least, and the road ahead of them seemed to stretch on forever.

'How do you like working on the farm?' she asked, changing the subject.

'It in't too bad. All the fresh air beats being down the pit. And some of the other lads are working there, so we can have a laugh.'

'I'm surprised you haven't gone back to Durham?'

He shrugged his broad shoulders. 'Happen I prefer it here.'

'Why's that?'

She knew she had said the wrong thing as soon as she saw the glint in his eye. 'Wouldn't you like to know?'

'It's nowt to do with me, I'm sure.' She paused, then

said, 'Anyway, I heard you were stopping here because you'd got in trouble with a girl in Durham.'

The shock on his face made her smile.

'Who told you that?' he spluttered.

'It's all round the village. You should know you can't keep a secret in Bowden!'

'Oh, aye, I know that all right!'

The look on his face made her laugh. It felt strange, as if she hadn't laughed in a long time.

'They also say you're courting Ellen Kettle now.'

He looked sharply at her. 'Tongues have been wagging, in't they?'

'Is it true?'

'Would you mind if I was?'

'Certainly not!' Carrie said, tossing her head. 'Why should I care who you're courting?'

'Why indeed?' Rob smiled. 'I remember when you used to get jealous if I so much as looked at another girl.'

Carrie glanced away. 'That's all in the past. I'm a married woman now.' She touched the third finger of her left hand, reassured by the ridge of her wedding ring under her glove.

'So you are.' Rob sounded thoughtful. 'Anyway, it in't true. Harry Kettle were a mate of mine, we started down t'pit together. I'm looking out for his widow, nowt more than that.'

'Another good deed?' Carrie said.

'If you want to put it like that.' Rob gave her another crooked smile. 'Don't look at me like that, Carrie Wardle. I have got a heart, y'know. Even if I don't care to show it very often!'

The cart bumped over the track and she slid towards him, into the solid warmth of his body. She jerked away from him, pulling herself together.

They travelled on in silence, cresting the hill. Carrie was

relieved to see the winding tower and coal heaps of Bowden Main coming into view in the valley below.

'You can let me down here, before we get to the village,' she said.

'Are you sure? I can take you a bit further if you'd like? Save you getting wetter.'

'Here will be fine, thank you.'

He seemed to read her thoughts because he pulled on the reins, slowing the cart. As it drew to a standstill, Carrie gathered up her belongings, ready to scramble down. But Rob had already jumped to the ground and come round to her side, and was there, with arms outstretched, waiting to help her. Carrie hesitated, then reluctantly put out her hand. The next moment, Rob's hands had closed around her waist, lifting her down easily.

He set her on the ground but didn't release his hold on her. For a moment their eyes locked and Carrie felt a sudden, unexpected flare of attraction. She knew he was going to kiss her, and she didn't want to stop him.

But the next moment he had released her and was climbing back up to the seat of the cart. Carrie stood, horrified by her reaction to him, her legs trembling like a newborn foal's, scarcely able to hold her up.

'I'll be seeing you, Carrie Wardle,' he shouted back over his shoulder.

'I'm Carrie Shepherd now,' she called after him. But Rob only lifted his hand in an insolent wave.

Rob smiled all the way back to Bowden.

Carrie had wanted to kiss him. He could see it in her parted lips and the way the pupils of her eyes had widened, half in desire, half in terror.

He had done the right thing in not responding, although it had taken all his will-power not to do so. But it would have been a mistake. She was too vulnerable, and he would have frightened her off for sure.

As it was, he had left her wanting more. She might be horrified with herself, but she would be intrigued. He had wakened something inside her, a memory of what they had once had.

He hadn't meant to do it. He had come to Bowden intending to make a fresh start, without any complications. He had had enough of them in Durham.

What a mess that had turned out to be! The lass he'd been dallying with was only meant to be a bit of fun . . . until her husband found out. Rob didn't care enough to want to stay around and fight for her, so he'd flitted back to Bowden.

His stepfather had been glad to see the back of him, and his mother didn't care. She didn't need him any more since she had remarried. Her new husband had made it clear he was the man of the house now. He and Rob had clashed heads so many times, his mother was probably relieved when he packed his bags.

But he certainly hadn't meant to pick up where he had left off with Carrie. Until he'd found out she had married James Shepherd.

Rob had always hated James, and knew the feeling was mutual. Everyone knew he had no right to be pit manager. It was a job that usually went to an experienced miner, not a posh lad who liked poetry and was frightened of going underground. He'd only got the job because of his father.

Rob had had his fair share of run-ins with James Shepherd when he'd worked down the pit at Bowden Main. Rob resented being told what to do by someone so wet behind the ears. James, for his part, had decided Rob was lazy and careless. He was always docking his pay, and once or twice had sent him home with nothing because Rob had dared to answer him back.

Rob knew the real reason James picked on him was because he was secretly pining for Carrie Wardle. The daft sap was in love with her, anyone could see that.

Rob used to tease Carrie about it all the time, although she always used to deny it.

'Stop talking nonsense,' she would say. But Rob knew the poor girl was embarrassed.

He knew Carrie would never look twice at the pit manager. She was far too spirited for someone as docile as James.

So when he had come home after a year away to find that they were engaged to be married two weeks later, Rob had scarcely been able to believe it.

Of course, he understood why she had done it. He had broken her heart, and so she had turned to the first man to show her any kindness. He couldn't blame her for that. But the thought of her wasting her life on James Shepherd had been almost too much for him to bear.

So he had set about claiming her back. And, of course, he had succeeded. That day at the gala had proved to Rob that no matter how hard she tried to hide it, Carrie's heart still belonged to him.

He had not believed her wedding would go ahead after that. So it was an unpleasant shock to return to Bowden and find out Carrie, his Carrie, was now Mrs Shepherd.

Mrs Shepherd . . . He couldn't even bring himself to use the name. It was all wrong.

But whatever she called herself now, he knew Carrie still belonged to him. He had seen it in her face when he had put his hands around her waist and pulled her close to him. She was lonely and unhappy, and she was his for the taking.

Perhaps it might be fun to show James Shepherd who had the upper hand now, Rob thought. It would be something to pass the time while he was here. God knows, there weren't many other girls who had caught his eye. Ellen Kettle was throwing herself at him, but he had no interest in his friend's widow. Not when he could have the pit manager's wife.

Rob laughed to himself at the thought. He would show James Shepherd who was the better man. James might have the money, the big house and the power, but he would never have Carrie Wardle's heart.

Chapter Thirty-Two

Agnes knew something was happening when the fair arrived on the recreation ground.

She had seen the brightly coloured trail of caravans coming down the hill into Bowden the day before. Now, as she cycled past after her rounds, she watched them setting up their stalls, the red-and-white-striped awnings fluttering in the warm summer breeze.

'It's the Miners' Gala on Saturday,' Jinny explained later as she made the tea. 'Every year miners come to Bowden from all the other pit villages. There's a parade, and competitions and races, and we play games.'

'If you ask me, it's just an excuse for the men to get drunk all day. It's a disgrace,' Mrs Bannister put in. She had made one of her rare appearances in the kitchen to inspect the cutlery. She claimed she was looking for signs of tarnish, but Jinny told Agnes that she really wanted to make sure the maid hadn't stolen anything.

'My dad says it's a chance for the miners to get together and show their pride,' Jinny went on, aiming a scowl at Mrs Bannister's back.

'I can't think why they should be proud of themselves, since none of them have done a day's work in months!' the housekeeper snapped back.

Agnes saw Jinny open her mouth to reply and quickly intervened.

'I shall have to walk up to the recreation ground and have a look for myself,' she said.

'Oh, no, I don't think Dr Rutherford would approve of that,' Mrs Bannister said. 'Besides, I don't suppose anyone would welcome you, Miss Sheridan. You're hardly part of the village, are you? In spite of all your efforts,' she sneered.

Agnes stared down into her empty cup, crestfallen. She believed she had started to win people's trust. She had even had a couple of new mothers coming to her clinic recently.

'Take no notice of her,' Jinny whispered, when Mrs Bannister had finally gone. 'You'll be very welcome at the gala, miss. You can go with us, if you like? We're taking a picnic.'

'Thank you, Jinny.' Agnes smiled at her gratefully. 'That's very kind of you. But perhaps Mrs Bannister is right. I don't want to antagonise Dr Rutherford any further.' They had already had too many disagreements recently. Agnes might not agree with the doctor, but she knew she still had to work with him.

But on Saturday morning Dr Rutherford decided to go on one of his fishing trips, and Mrs Bannister went to Leeds to do some shopping, so there was no one in the house to disapprove. It was a gloriously warm, sunny day, and since Agnes had nothing better to do she decided she would walk up to the recreation ground. She had always enjoyed the excitement of a fair, even though her mother thought they were vulgar and had refused to take her as a child.

The fair was in full swing when Agnes arrived. She could hear the jaunty sound of a barrel organ playing as she headed up the lane, and the mingled aromas of toffee apples and frying onions lured her on.

The recreation ground was a sea of people, all dressed in their Sunday best. Half the field was given over to the fair, with its brightly coloured stalls, rides and attractions.

The other was marked out for the races, which were due to take place later on.

Here the men were already mustering for the parade, dozens of colourful banners fluttering, headed up by a proud brass band. Seeing happy, smiling faces all around was a wonderful contrast to all the misery and worry that had hung over the village for so long.

Agnes found the Chadwicks, the children gathered in a ring around their mother, who was busy handing out jam sandwiches. Baby Ernest was perched on her knee, all dressed up in his best clothes like the other children.

Jinny spotted Agnes and waved her over.

'I'm glad you came,' she said, leaning over to wipe smears of jam from her little sister's mouth.

Ruth smiled shyly up at the nurse. 'Would you like to sit wi' us, Miss Sheridan?'

Agnes looked at the meagre picnic. There was barely enough to go round all the children as it was. 'That's very kind of you, Mrs Chadwick, but I won't, if you don't mind?' She looked around at them all. 'You look very smart, I must say. Especially little Ernest.' She smiled at the baby, who gave her a gummy grin back. 'He's looking particularly handsome. Is that a new bonnet?'

'It's just summat I made out of some old scraps.' Ruth's cheeks turned pink.

'Mum's going to enter him in the bonny baby competition,' Jinny said.

'Now, Jinny, I only said I might . . . '

'So you should,' Agnes said. 'I reckon he stands a very good chance of winning.'

Ruth beamed with pride. 'So do I, miss. And I reckon we've got you to thank for that,' she added quietly.

She cooed at her baby, chucking him under the chin. Pride and delight shone out of her as she looked at him.

A few weeks ago she would have had him hidden away under several shawls. But the exercises Agnes had shown her had soon corrected his wry neck.

'You put in most of the hard work, Mrs Chadwick.'

'All the same, we're very grateful. And if there's anything we can ever do for you . . . '

You already have, Agnes thought. She was sure part of the reason more women had started coming to the clinic was because Ruth had quietly put in a good word for her.

She left the Chadwicks and crossed the field just as the parade was starting. Carrie Shepherd was there, standing a short distance from the other women, one hand on the handle of a pram, the other shading her eyes from the sun. She was wearing a straw hat and a crimson dress that contrasted beautifully with her sleek raven-black hair and pale skin.

She jumped when Agnes greeted her. 'I'm sorry, Nurse, I was miles away.' She pressed one hand to her chest while she recovered. 'I was just watching the parade getting ready to start.'

Agnes gazed over towards the men. 'It's a fine sight, isn't it?'

'Aye, it is. This is the first year my father in't here to carry the banner for Bowden Main.' She glanced at Agnes. 'You know he's been taken bad again?'

Agnes nodded. 'I went to see him this morning.'

'How was he?'

'As well as can be expected.' Agnes chose her words carefully. 'He was disappointed to be missing the gala.'

'I bet he was.' Carrie looked back at the parade. 'But I daresay he'll be up and about again in time for the next one. There's no keeping my father down for long!'

Her smile trembled, and Agnes wondered if she was putting on a brave face, or if she really understood how poorly Eric Wardle was. But Agnes didn't want to be the one to tell her, especially not on a day like today. Better to let her enjoy herself while she could.

Instead she distracted Carrie by asking what the various banners represented.

'Let's see . . . That one's Allerton Silkstone.' She pointed over to the right. 'The one next to it's Glasshoughton, then there's Caphouse, South Elmsall . . .' She strained her eyes to see. 'But I'm not sure what the one on the far left is . . .'

'Denby Grange,' said a voice behind them.

Agnes turned round to see Rob Chadwick, the young man who had found her bicycle after Christopher Stanhope had made off with it.

'I would have thought you'd know that, Carrie Wardle. Time was when you knew all the colliery banners better than any of us.'

Agnes noted the dull flush that crept up Carrie's throat. 'That were a long time ago,' she muttered, her gaze fixed on the parade.

'True. But there are some things you never forget, eh?'

Agnes looked from one to the other of them. Carrie suddenly seemed very tense, her knuckles white where she gripped the pram. Rob, by contrast, seemed very relaxed.

'Your husband not with you?' he said, looking around.

'Of course he isn't!' Carrie snapped. 'I dunno why you'd even ask that.'

'But he's the pit manager. They generally come to the gala, don't they?'

It sounded like an innocent enough question, but Agnes saw the way his green eyes gleamed with intent.

'You know he wouldn't be welcome,' Carrie muttered.

'And there was me thinking you might have left him at home so you could have some fun?'

285

Agnes saw Carrie's uncomfortable expression and spoke up.

'Hello, Mr Chadwick,' she said to distract him. Rob turned slowly to face her, as if noticing her for the first time.

'Oh, hello, Nurse. I didn't recognise you out of your uniform.' His gaze travelled slowly from her feet to her face. 'You should dress up like that to see your patients. You'd be a sight for sore eyes at any man's bedside.'

Agnes smiled thinly at the well-worn remark. She had met Rob several times when she had visited the Chadwicks to nurse little Ernest, and he never missed a chance to flirt with her.

He was attractive, there was no doubt about that, with his burnished gold hair and handsome, laughing face. But he knew it too, and that took some of the edge off his appeal for her.

'I'm going to walk further down to watch the parade,' she said to Carrie. 'Would you like to come with me?'

'Or you could both come to the fair with me, if you like?' Rob offered. 'I could win you another coconut on the shy, Carrie. Like last time, remember?'

He winked at her, and Carrie's blush deepened until it almost matched her dress.

'I'd be glad to watch the parade with you,' she said to Agnes.

As they walked away, Rob called after them, 'I'm in the tug-of-war later. Be sure to come and watch me, won't you?'

'That young man seems very full of himself,' Agnes remarked, looking back over her shoulder. Rob Chadwick stood watching them, his arms folded across his burly chest.

'Aye, he is.' Carrie kept her gaze pointing resolutely forward, her lips tight.

'He's an old friend of yours, you say?'

Carrie paused for a moment. 'We were sweethearts once,' she said. 'We were supposed to be married. But then he left the village and broke my heart.'

Agnes stared at her. 'When was this?'

'Three years ago.'

Agnes looked back across the field. Rob had joined another group of men, his golden head bobbing above theirs.

'And now he's come back,' she said.

'Aye.'

There was something about the way Carrie said it that made Agnes glance sideways at her. Carrie looked desolate, as if there was a part of her heart that had still not healed.

Agnes understood that feeling all too well.

'I had a sweetheart too, once,' she said.

She didn't know why she had uttered the words. Daniel was a memory she had kept to herself for so long, it felt strange to talk about him.

Carrie's blue eyes widened. 'Who was he?'

'He was a junior doctor at the hospital where I did my training. We were supposed to be married, too.'

It was an old story, a student nurse falling in love with a young doctor. Most of the girls in her set had done the same, some several times over. Nearly all these attachments had ended up in tears or drama, with the poor heartbroken girl being consoled in the nurses' home when her doctor admirer moved on to someone else.

But it was different for Agnes and Daniel. Right from the start they had fitted together, like two halves of the same whole. Everyone knew they were one of the few couples who would end up living happily ever after.

And then . . .

'Did he break it off, like Rob did?' Carrie enquired.

'No, I did.'

'Why?'

Agnes had a sudden picture of her mother standing over her, the day she discovered Agnes was pregnant.

'Of course Daniel must marry you,' she had said briskly. 'We'll organise the wedding as soon as possible, then when the child is born we can say there was some confusion with the dates.'

'There isn't going to be a wedding.'

Her mother had stared at her, horror written all over her face. 'What on earth do you mean?'

'I don't want to marry him.'

'Don't be silly, of course you must be married,' her mother had dismissed Agnes' objection. 'Daniel is to blame for all this mess, and now he must do the right thing by you.'

But Agnes had never told him about the baby. Instead she had broken off the engagement and left the hospital, never to see him again. But even as she faced her mother's wrath, Agnes had known she had done the right thing. 'I made a mistake,' she said sadly.

Carrie looked as if she wanted to probe further, but Agnes was saved by the brass band striking up to mark the start of the parade.

Agnes felt her heart swell as she watched the ranks of men marching round the field, hundreds of them, heads held high, banners flying aloft. As the Bowden men went past, she was surprised by the hot tears of pride that sprang to her eyes. She knew the men's names, recognised their faces. She had witnessed the struggles they went through every day. Their weary determination was written all over their faces.

The people of Bowden might not have taken her to their hearts, but she had certainly taken them to hers.

The parade ended, and the men started to disperse, most of them going off to enjoy the beer that was being served in one of the tents.

'It's too hot to stand out here,' Agnes said to Carrie. 'I'm going to look for some shade.'

'Aren't you staying for the tug-of-war?'

Agnes looked at her. 'Are you?'

'I thought I might as well.' Carrie shrugged, turning her gaze away.

It's nothing to do with you, Agnes Sheridan, she told herself as she walked away. For all you know, it could be an innocent friendship. But she had the feeling there was nothing innocent in Rob Chadwick's intentions.

She only hoped Carrie Shepherd knew what she was doing.

Chapter Thirty-Three

Agnes made another slow circuit of the fairground, then bought herself an ice cream from the hokey-pokey man and sat under a tree to eat it, enjoying the warmth of the sun on her face.

Then she made her way slowly back to the field. The tug-of-war had finished and the next race was being set up. Agnes saw Carrie with her three sisters, laughing together on the other side of the field. They were a handsome family, the four girls all as radiantly pretty as one another.

They looked so happy together, Agnes decided to let them be. Instead she wandered over to the competition ring, where the contestants were preparing for a three-legged race. Elsie Stanhope, standing close to the start line, watching her two brothers tying their legs together.

'They won't let me join in,' she told Agnes sadly. 'I told Chris I'm a faster runner than our Billy, but he says I'll hold him back because I'm a girl.'

'Is that right?' Carrie glared across the field at Christopher Stanhope. 'You don't want to take any notice of him, Elsie. Girls are every bit as good at running as boys.'

'That's not what Chris says.'

'Then perhaps you should show him?'

'How can I, when I don't have a partner? Unless . . . ' Elsie looked up at her. 'Would you, miss?'

Agnes shook her head. 'Oh, no, I can't. I haven't run in a race since I was at school.'

'You could do it, miss. Please?'

'Really, I shouldn't—'

'Go on, Nurse.' Mrs Willis, who was standing close by, grinned at her. 'You can't disappoint the lass, surely?'

Agnes looked from one to the other. She was about to refuse when she saw the bright hope on Elsie's face.

'Oh, why not?' said Agnes 'But I'm warning you, I'll probably fall over.'

She began to regret her decision as she and Elsie hobbled to the starting line, arms around each other. Mrs Willis had spread the word, and quite a crowd had gathered to watch her.

'Go on, Nurse! You show 'em!' someone cried out.

'A halfpenny on t'nurse to win!' someone else said.

Soon the comments were flying thick and fast. Agnes gave an embarrassed smile, glad that Dr Rutherford and Mrs Bannister were not there to witness the scene. She couldn't think what Miss Gale would make of it, either. It was hardly dignified behaviour for a district nurse.

'On your marks, get set . . . go!' Suddenly it was chaos. Everyone else seemed to get off to a flying start, while Agnes and Elsie set off on the wrong foot and somehow managed to stumble over each other. Agnes could hear the cheers and jeers coming from the crowd as they picked themselves up and started again.

This time they managed to fall into pace with each other, and soon they were catching the other contestants up. They even managed to overtake a couple, including Elsie's brothers. She shrieked with delight as they ran past them, and Agnes couldn't resist a grin over her shoulder at Christopher's outraged face.

That'll teach you to steal my cap, she thought.

The finishing line was in sight. The winner had already broken through the rope, but Agnes and Elsie were heading for third place. Just another few yards, and then—Christopher Stanhope came sprinting out of nowhere, half carrying his squealing brother, whose little legs pumped to keep up with Christopher's long strides. As they passed, Christopher put a foot in Agnes' path, tripping her up. The next thing, the rope bonding her to Elsie had come untied, Agnes' feet had left the ground and she was flying headlong. She put out her hands to break her fall, but instead of hitting the ground she suddenly felt a pair of strong arms catch and hold her.

Agnes looked up in dismay to find herself staring into the face of Seth Stanhope.

He looked as shocked as she felt as he held her close to him. For an unguarded second they could only stare at each other, her hands resting against the muscular wall of his chest. His grey eyes were ringed with bright green, Agnes noticed.

Then they both seemed to recall themselves at the same moment, pushing away from each other and stepping apart self-consciously.

'Are you all right, miss?' Elsie came up to Agnes, her round face full of concern.

'I'm fine, thank you.'

'Nowt damaged then?' Seth said gruffly.

'Only my pride!' She smiled sheepishly. When she looked up, she was surprised to see he was smiling too.

'You've lost your hat,' Elsie pointed out.

'Have I?' Agnes put her hand up to her head. Her hair had come loose from its pins and flowed over her shoulders.

'It's over here.' Seth picked it up from the ground, dusted it off and handed it to her. As she took it, their hands brushed and she felt a sudden, alarming pull of attraction.

Seth must have felt it too. He snatched his hand away from hers as if he'd had an electric shock.

'Can I go and look at the gallopers, Dad?' Elsie interrupted them, breaking the tension.

'Aye,' Seth said, but he didn't move.

'Will you come?'

'Nay.' Seth seemed to pull himself together, shaking his head. 'I can't, lass. I've got to have a word with someone.'

He looked around vaguely. He was making excuses, Agnes could tell. Anything so he didn't have to spend time with his own children.

The thought was enough to vanquish any attraction she might have felt for him.

'Why don't I come with you?' she said to Elsie. 'I might even find a penny for you to have a ride, how about that?'

Elsie's face lit up. 'Could I?'

'I don't know about that,' Seth muttered. 'We don't want charity.'

'For heaven's sake!' Agnes snapped back at him. 'It's my money and I'm allowed to spend it how I choose. Or are you telling me I can't?'

Their eyes met again, but this time there was no warmth in Seth's stormy gaze.

'Tha can please thysen,' he muttered.

It was a relief once they started arguing again. Seth felt himself on safer ground, feeling anger towards the nurse, reminding himself what an outspoken busybody she was.

It was far more comfortable than the sensation he'd had when he had briefly held her in his arms.

It was the crowd that had drawn him over to the ring, wondering why so many had gathered to watch a children's three-legged race.

293

'It's t'nurse, racing with your Elsie,' Reg Willis had laughed, a glass of beer in his hand. 'She's a game lass, I'll say that for her.'

'Aye.' Even when Reg pointed her out, Seth still hadn't recognised Agnes. She looked so young and pretty in her flowery cotton dress, her chestnut hair flying loose about her shoulders, like one of the village girls.

And then his son had barged past and tripped her, and without thinking Seth had stepped into her path to catch her in his arms before she fell.

He felt the heat rising in him at the memory. It had been so long since he had held a woman close to him, he had forgotten what it was like. It was the only excuse he could give for the tug of attraction he had felt then, his hands on the curve of her hips, breathing in the scent of her skin.

He watched her walking away beside Elsie. She was pinning her hat back in place. He found himself thinking about the softness of her hair against his cheek.

'What's *she* doing with our Elsie?'

Seth started at the sound of Hannah's girlish voice behind him, pulling him out of his reverie. 'T'nurse is taking her on the gallopers.'

'Is she now? I would have taken Elsie, if she'd asked.' Hannah sounded offended. 'Nurse's got no business, sticking her nose in.'

'I daresay she means no harm.'

Hannah sent him an accusing look. 'You've changed your tune, Seth Stanhope. You didn't have a good word to say about her a few weeks since. Or have you forgotten how she turned up at the picket line, making a fool of you in front of the other men?'

Seth's mouth firmed at the memory. 'Nay, I haven't.'

'I'm glad to hear it,' Hannah said. 'If I were you, I'd

give that lass a wide berth. You don't need someone like her, bringing you trouble.'

'Aye,' Seth said, his gaze still fixed on the slender, chestnut-haired figure. 'Aye, I reckon you might be right.'

Chapter Thirty-Four

May Edcott was being crowned Gala Queen, and Eliza was furious about it.

'It in't fair,' she fumed, as they watched last year's queen place the crown of flowers on May's head. 'I'm much prettier than she is. And look at those fat ankles!' She turned on Carrie. 'This is all your fault.'

'Me?' Carrie was shocked. 'How do you work that out?'

'Well, it stands to reason, doesn't it? They're not going to make me Gala Queen because I'm related to the pit manager.'

'And there was I, thinking it was because you look like a heifer!' Hattie muttered.

'And you can shut up, too,' Eliza snapped, swinging round to face her.

'At least you can be one of her maids-in-waiting,' Carrie said, trying to placate them both.

Eliza lifted her chin. 'I've a good mind not to do it,' she said haughtily. 'The last thing I want to do is trail round after May Edcott all day, listening to her showing off!'

'She won't say no,' Hattie whispered, as Eliza stalked off. 'You watch, she'll be on that float next to May in a couple of minutes, trying to get her face in all the pictures.' She rolled her eyes. 'I suppose I'd better go and keep an eye on her, make sure she doesn't try to tear that crown off May's head!'

'Can I take Henry on the shuggy boats?' Gertie asked Carrie.

'If you like. But don't let him go too high, will you?'
Carrie called after her sister as she headed off with the
pram. 'And don't be too long, either. I'll need to take him
home soon. It's getting too hot for him to be out.'

She watched Gertie disappear into the sea of people,
clutching Henry by the hand, his plump little legs toddling
beside her. It was a scorching day, and Carrie could feel
rivulets of perspiration running down inside her dress.
She usually loved the sunshine, but this time its brightness
made her feel dizzy.

She sought out the cool shade of the tent, where the
mothers were gathering for the bonny baby competition.
Carrie sank down on a bale of hay at the back to watch
them preening their babies, adjusting bonnets and fastening
bows, and spitting on handkerchiefs to clean grubby faces.

It gave her a pang, thinking about the previous year,
when she and James had come to the gala together. He
had been welcome then, everyone nodding a greeting to
them as they walked around the fair, a happy young couple
with their newborn son.

James had insisted on holding Henry in his arms,
showing him all the sideshows, even though he was barely
four months old and couldn't take in anything but the
sounds and colours.

'You're wasting your time, you know,' Carrie had
laughed when James insisted on demonstrating how to
hook a duck on one of the stalls. 'He can't understand a
word you're saying.'

'How can you say that?' James had stared at her in
mock outrage. 'My son happens to think I'm very wise.
Look at that rapt expression on his face. Or, of course, it
might just be wind,' he added ruefully.

Then they had come to the tent where the bonny baby
competition was being judged, and Mrs Morris had smiled

and said, 'You'll have to enter your bairn next year, Mr Shepherd.'

'Indeed we will, Mrs Morris,' James had replied, so proud of his wife and son he looked fit to burst.

They had been so happy and in love then. It was hard to believe that a year later they were scarcely speaking to each other.

Now Carrie barely recognised her husband as that same smiling young man who had carried his baby around the fair and made her laugh. James moved like a ghost around the house these days, largely staying out of her way. On the rare occasions they did meet, he was tense and taciturn.

Carrie was so worried about him; she had long since forgotten her anger with him for the evictions he had ordered. The lockout weighed heavily on him, making him look haggard and older than his years. He barely seemed to eat or sleep these days. Carrie longed to comfort him, but there was such a chasm between them she didn't know how.

She saw Rob Chadwick enter the tent and sat back, trying to retreat into the shadows. But it was too much to hope that he wouldn't see her.

'Hello again.' He plonked himself down on the bale next to her.

'What are you doing here?' she asked. 'I didn't know you were interested in the bonny baby competition?'

He grinned. 'I just wanted to get out of the sun for a while. It's fair baking out there.' He took off his cap and wiped his brow with his shirtsleeve.

'And there was I, thinking you'd come to see Ellen Kettle?' Carrie nodded to where Ellen was primping the ruffles on her baby son's bonnet. She caught Rob's eye and gave him a sly smile.

Rob sighed. 'How many times do I have to tell you, I in't interested in Ellen Kettle?'

'She likes you.'

'That's her lookout, not mine.' He nodded towards the mothers gathered on the platform. 'Is your bairn in the competition?'

Carrie felt another pang, thinking about last year. She shook her head. 'Our Gertie's taken him to look round the fair.'

'Shame. With looks like yours he'd be bound to win. Unless he takes after his father?' he grinned.

'Shut up about his father!' Carrie turned on Rob. 'If you haven't got anything nice to say, you can go and bother someone else!'

He blinked at her in surprise. 'Keep your hair on, I were only having a laugh.'

'Well, don't.' Carrie put her hand to her throbbing temple as Rob's face swam briefly out of focus before her eyes. When she looked back at him, he was staring at her, frowning with concern.

'Are you all right?' he asked.

'I'm a bit dizzy, that's all,' she said. 'It must be the heat . . . '

'Do you want me to fetch t'nurse?'

'No, I don't want any fuss. I'll be fine if I just sit here for a minute.'

She buried her face in her hands, resting her eyes. She wasn't sure how long she stayed in that position, but the next thing she knew, Rob was holding out a cup towards her.

'Drink this,' he said gently. 'It'll make you feel better.'

'What is it?'

'Just water.' He smiled sheepishly. 'I in't trying to get you tipsy, if that's what you're wondering.'

Carrie felt herself blushing as she gulped down the water. It felt cool as it slid down her parched throat.

'Thank you,' she said, handing him back the empty cup. 'That was very kind of you.'

'I've told you, I have got a heart. ' He tilted his head. 'Are you feeling better now?'

'Much better, thank you.' The water had worked wonders, clearing her head. But it did nothing for her heart, which was fluttering against her ribs like a caged bird.

She had been dreading seeing Rob again after that day he'd brought her home from Leeds. Her reaction to him had shaken her. She'd thought that after two years she would be immune to his charms, but he had only had to take her in his arms and suddenly she felt herself weakening again.

She tried to tell herself it was because she was too vulnerable. Things weren't going well between her and James, and Rob had come along and made her smile, and reminded her of the old days, when she was a girl and everything had been so simple. That was the only reason she had reacted to him the way she had.

But then, she reminded herself, being vulnerable around Rob Chadwick was never a good idea.

'I saw Eliza, trailing after May Edcott,' Rob said, breaking into her reverie. 'She didn't look too happy, I must say.'

Carrie smiled. 'She reckons it should have been her crowned queen, not May.'

'Happen she's right. She's a good-looking girl, your Eliza. Takes after her sister.'

Rob paused then, and Carrie knew with a sinking dread what he was going to say when he finally spoke.

'Do you remember when you were crowned Gala Queen?' he asked in a soft, insinuating voice.

She said nothing, silenced by the old familiar rush of shame and fear.

'It was the year I came back to Bowden to visit,' Rob reminded her. 'I arrived back on gala day and there you were, wearing that pink dress with those flowers in your hair. I thought you were the most beautiful girl I'd ever seen. You remember that day, don't you, Carrie?'

She heard the challenge in his voice. Of course she remembered. She had tried to blank it from her memory but it was there, like a scar that would never heal.

'I don't like to think about it,' she murmured.

'Why not?'

She lifted her gaze to face him. Did he really have to ask that question? 'Because it was a mistake. It should never have happened.'

'So why did it happen?' Rob said softly.

Why indeed? That was a question she had asked herself endlessly, ever since. She had been weak and foolish that day. When he had taken her in his arms and kissed her, nothing else had mattered. Least of all that she was about to marry James Shepherd.

'I told you, I don't like to think about it,' she said. 'It's all in the past now.'

'Is it?' He shifted around to face her, lowering his voice so she could barely hear him. 'I thought it was in the past too. But the last time we saw each other . . . '

'Don't.'

'I felt something, Carrie. Something between us. And you felt it too. Don't try to deny it, you know what I mean.' He was so close, she could feel the warmth of his breath fanning her face. 'You still love me, don't you?'

'No!'

'Look me in the eyes and tell me that.'

Over his shoulder, Carrie spotted her sister Gertie at the entrance to the tent, holding a grizzling Henry in her arms.

301

Relieved, Carrie jumped to her feet, waving to her.

'There you are!' Gertie made her way over to them. 'I've been looking everywhere for you. He's been howling for ten minutes and I can't quieten him.'

'He's probably tired, poor lamb. Give him to me.'

'With pleasure.' Gertie dumped the baby into Carrie's arms. Henry immediately stopped crying and rested his head on her shoulder. 'I want to go and meet my friends now, anyway.'

'He's a bonny lad.' Rob stood at Carrie's shoulder. He put out a finger and Henry grasped it. 'Got a strong grip on him, too. How old is he?'

Carrie hesitated. 'He's just turned a year.'

Gertie laughed. 'Surely you in't forgotten your own son's birthday, Carrie Shepherd? He's sixteen months old,' she told Rob. 'His birthday was back in April.' She shook her head reproachfully at her sister.

'April?' Rob said.

'I'd best get him home,' Carrie muttered. 'It's too hot for him, and he needs a nap.'

'I'll walk with you,' Rob offered, but Carrie shook her head.

'I'd rather be on my own,' she said. The truth was, she couldn't put enough distance between herself and Rob Chadwick.

Chapter Thirty-Five

Carrie had expected James to be at the pit as usual, so she was surprised to hear voices coming from the parlour when she came home.

Her heart sank as she heard Eleanor Haverstock's nervous tittering laughter, followed by Sir Edward's gruff tones. Oh, Lord, why did they have to be here now?

She went upstairs to put Henry down for his nap, and to give herself time to gather her thoughts and tidy herself up. She gazed in despair at her reflection in the mirror, her hair limp with perspiration, her face sunburned. She applied powder, but her cheeks still glowed red.

Finally, she could put it off no longer. She walked into the parlour to find Sir Edward and Eleanor Haverstock having tea with James.

She caught her husband's quick, guarded look at her. Please don't let me down, he pleaded silently.

'Oh, I'm sorry,' Carrie said, smiling around at everyone. 'I didn't know we were expecting company.'

'It's entirely my fault,' Miss Eleanor said cheerfully. 'We were passing the village and I begged Father to let us drop in.'

'Complete waste of time,' Sir Edward grumbled.

'How was the gala?' Eleanor asked, ignoring him. 'Did you have a pleasant time, Mrs Shepherd?'

'Yes, thank you. I've had a lovely day.'

Carrie glanced at James. He was staring down at his hands, looking uncomfortable.

'You've caught the sun, at any rate. You look as flushed as a farm girl.'

Carrie put her hand to her cheek. As she had feared, the face powder had fooled no one. Miss Eleanor was far too well bred to allow the sun to touch her porcelain complexion.

'It was a hot day,' she said apologetically.

'A gala, indeed!' Sir Edward retorted. 'I don't understand it. These men complain their families are starving, yet they soon find the money to squander on beer and sideshows. And on my land, too! It's an absolute disgrace. I should have ordered the police to move them all on.'

I'd like to see you try. Carrie smiled to herself at the thought of Sergeant Cray squaring up to five hundred angry pitmen.

'Well, I'm jolly glad you didn't,' Eleanor said. 'Really, Father, it's a local tradition. And I must admit, it always looks rather fun, although I've never been myself.'

'I should think not!' Sir Edward dismissed. 'It's no place for a woman of breeding.'

'Father!' Eleanor sent Carrie a quick, embarrassed look.

'I must say, Shepherd, I'm surprised at you for allowing your wife to go to this – gathering,' Sir Edward said, turning to James.

He frowned. 'I'm not quite sure I understand, Sir Edward.'

'Well, it's hardly seemly for the pit manager's wife to be seen – cavorting – with the lower classes, is it? Especially with the way things are now. You really should keep better control of your wife.'

'Now just a minute—' Carrie opened her mouth to defend herself, but James got there first.

'My wife is not a chattel for me to control,' he said quietly. 'She makes up her own mind where she goes and what she does.'

Carrie stared at him. His words were softly spoken, but he could not have shocked her more if he had bellowed them at the top of his voice.

Sir Edward glared at him. 'Then more fool you,' he muttered.

James' expression didn't flicker. 'You think I'm a fool, Sir Edward?'

Eleanor jumped in quickly to smooth things over, as usual. 'I'm sure my father didn't mean to imply that.'

'For God's sake, Eleanor, I don't need you to explain what I mean!' Sir Edward rounded on his daughter angrily. 'You want to know the truth?' he said to James. 'Yes, I do think you're a fool. I thought you were a fool to marry the girl in the first place, but you went off and did it anyway.' He cast a bitter glance at Carrie. 'But allowing her to go off to this gala – it makes you look weak.'

Carrie looked at James. He was staring back at Sir Edward, his expression unreadable.

She thought guiltily of the food parcels she had stolen from the larder, of all the donations she had made in secret. She'd even brought the Tollers to the house unannounced and expected James to take them in. She hadn't cared for the Haverstocks' opinion at the time, and she still didn't. But now she suddenly saw her actions through her husband's eyes, and she realised how selfish she had been. The last thing she wanted to do was make more trouble for James.

'I'm sorry,' Carrie spoke up. 'It was only a day out. I've been going to the galas since I was a bairn. I didn't realise it would cause so much trouble.'

'Which only goes to show how stupid you are, doesn't it?' Sir Edward snapped.

Something changed in James' manner. He rose slowly to his feet, towering over them.

'That's enough,' he said. 'It's bad enough that you come here and insult me. But when you insult my wife . . . ' He took a deep breath, and Carrie could see him fighting to keep his temper. 'I would like you to leave,' he said.

Eleanor gave a little squeak of dismay. Sir Edward stared at him. 'You're throwing me out?'

'No, Sir Edward, I am asking you to leave. But I will throw you out if I must?'

Sir Edward's eyes turned to ice, and for a terrible moment Carrie thought that it might come to that. But then he seized his walking stick and got to his feet. 'Come, Eleanor, we won't stay where we're not wanted.'

'But, Father . . . '

'I said, come! Or are you going to defy me too?'

Eleanor looked into her half-finished cup of tea, then quickly set it down and stood up.

Sir Edward looked James up and down with an expression of contempt on his fox-like face. 'I'd expected more loyalty from you,' he growled.

James lifted his chin. 'You pay for my loyalty while I'm at the pit,' he said. 'But that doesn't give you the right to come to my home and issue orders and insults.'

'Your home? May I remind you, this house and everything else in this village belongs to *me*.'

'In that case, perhaps you would like me to leave?'

Carrie held her breath. For a long moment the two men stared at each other, toe to toe. Then Sir Edward sneered.

'I thought you were your father's son, but you're nothing like Henry Shepherd and you never will be.' He nodded towards Carrie. 'You're no judge of character, either. You did yourself no favours when you married that minx. I told you you'd live to regret it, didn't I? It looks as if she's already bringing you down. And when she's taken everything, she'll go back to her own and forget about you.'

He stormed out, leaving Eleanor fluttering in his wake.

'He doesn't mean it,' she whispered to James. 'He's just upset, that's all.'

'He's not the only one,' James said grimly.

'Just give him a chance to calm down,' Eleanor went on. 'You know how he can be . . . '

'Eleanor!'

'I'm coming, Father.' She shot another quick, helpless glance at Carrie, and then was gone.

Sir Edward's departure seemed to have sucked all the air from the room, leaving Carrie breathless. She stared at the door long after they had heard the Haverstocks' car pulling away.

'I'm sorry,' she said again. 'I truly didn't mean to cause so much trouble.'

James stared at her, as if seeing her for the first time. 'You've got nothing to apologise for. You've done nothing wrong. It's that monster who should be saying sorry.' A muscle flickered in his jaw. 'How dare he come in here and insult you!'

'I've never heard you speak to him like that before.'

'Perhaps I should have done it a long time ago.'

Carrie stared at him. Once again, she barely recognised the man before her. 'But you don't want to lose your job,' she reminded him.

'I'd rather lose my job than lose you.' He turned to face her, his expression softening. 'Oh, God, Carrie, I've been so wretched. I know I've changed since this lockout started, and I don't blame you for hating me.'

'I don't hate you. I've never hated you.'

'I've hated myself.' The strength seemed to go from his body and he sank down on to a chair, his face buried in his hands. 'Some of the things I've done – I told myself I was doing them for the right reasons, to keep the pit going.

But I was really just trying to prove I was as tough as my father.' He looked up and gave her a bitter smile. 'I was trying to earn Sir Edward's respect. And in doing so I lost yours.'

'Oh, James!' Carrie took his hands in hers. 'It wasn't all your fault. You were just trying to do your job, to provide for your family the same as everyone else does. Sir Edward's right, I should have been more loyal to you.'

'Don't you dare say that! That old goat is rarely right about anything.' James stood up, gathering her into his arms. 'Perhaps we've both made mistakes,' he conceded. 'I hope we can put them behind us now.'

'I'd like that.' She lifted her face to his for a long, lingering kiss. As his mouth found hers, Carrie felt as if a weight had been lifted from her shoulders. All her doubts, and any thoughts of Rob Chadwick, vanished from her mind.

'God, I've missed you so much,' James whispered, his face pressed to her neck. 'Can I come back to our bedroom? I hated sleeping in my study.'

'The sooner the better.' Carrie smiled at him. 'In fact . . .' She glanced towards the door. 'Why don't we go up there now?'

James gazed down at her. 'You know, perhaps Sir Edward was right about something,' he said.

'Oh, yes? What's that?'

He smiled slowly. 'You are a minx,' he said.

Chapter Thirty-Six

Eric Wardle was getting worse.

Abscesses had formed in the cavities of his spine where TB had eaten away the bone. Left untreated, they had slowly begun to spread their poison through his body. His liver, his intestines and all the other organs of his body were all slowly surrendering to its effects.

And now it was starting to affect his kidneys. Agnes almost didn't have to check the urine sample she had taken. She knew it would surely contain albumin even before she saw the white ring forming in the test tube.

She tried not to allow her feelings to show as she carefully made her notes. But there was no fooling her patient.

'It in't good, is it, Nurse?' Eric Wardle asked her.

Agnes turned to him, her usual bright smile in place, ready to say something suitably soothing. But the words died in her throat when she saw his face.

'It's all right, Nurse, you don't have to put it on with me. I know I in't got much time left. How long, d'you reckon? Weeks or months? Or days?'

Agnes took a deep breath. Poorly as he was, Eric Wardle looked like the kind of man to sniff out a lie.

'Weeks, Mr Wardle. I'm so sorry.'

He waved her words aside. 'Nay, Nurse, don't you take on. I always knew this blasted TB would get me in the end. I count myself lucky I've lasted as long as I have. There was a time, just after I came back from t'war . . . ' He paused, drawing in a deep breath. 'Anyway, I reckon

I'm ready to meet my maker.' He tapped the Bible at his bedside. 'But I'd be obliged if you'd keep it from the rest of the family. I know how my Kath worries, and I don't want to put any more on her shoulders than she needs to bear. It'll be our little secret, eh?' He winked at Agnes.

'As you wish, Mr Wardle.' She managed a smile, wondering if she could ever be that courageous, knowing the end was coming.

But she couldn't think about that. She owed it to her patient to make him as comfortable as possible for as long as she could.

She bathed him carefully, and powdered under the edges and straps of his brace, checking for any signs of plaster sores. He was painfully thin, his bones jutting under papery, yellowing skin.

'You're not eating, Mr Wardle?' she asked him.

He shook his head. 'It upsets my stomach, Nurse. Besides, I don't fancy food much.'

'All the same, you should try to have something to keep your strength up.'

'What do I need my strength for, if I can't even get out of this bed?' A look of despair crossed his face, a moment before his determined smile was back in place. 'I'm sorry, Nurse, you don't want to listen to me moaning, do you?'

'You moan as much as you like, Mr Wardle. I don't mind.'

'Nay, but I do. I'm not one for complaining usually. But I do miss going up to my allotment.' He turned his gaze towards the window. 'Them carrots and parsnips will need watering, else they'll dry out with all this sun.'

Agnes saw the longing look in his eyes. 'I see no reason why you shouldn't go there,' she said.

Hope lit up Eric Wardle's face. 'Do you mean it, Nurse?'

'Why not? The fresh air will do you good. As long as you promise not to start digging?' she warned him.

'Nay, my Carrie will do all that for me. It'll just be nice to be out in the sun, instead of being stuck in here.' He grinned. 'Thank you, Nurse. That's just the tonic I needed!'

The memory of the smile on his face stayed with her all the way back to Dr Rutherford's house. It was good to be able to cheer him up. Eric Wardle was such a nice man, Agnes wished she could have nursed him to better effect.

Those abscesses must have been festering inside him for years, she thought. Amyloid disease was very slow to take hold. Why hadn't Dr Rutherford noticed the signs? If he had aspirated the abscesses, or cut out the infected tissue, then perhaps Eric Wardle might not be dying now.

She tried not to allow herself to judge. But she couldn't help thinking that if Dr Rutherford put as much energy into his patients as he did into his garden and his fishing trips, the people of Bowden might be a lot better off than they were now.

She heard the voices drifting down the drive as she cycled through the open gates.

'Go away! Go away, I said! Shoo! Off with you.'

'I in't going anywhere till I see t'nurse.'

Agnes pedalled faster, rounding the sweeping bend in the drive, past the high hedge so that the front door came into view. There she was met by the curious sight of Mrs Bannister on the front steps, wielding a broom like a weapon while little Elsie Stanhope stood her ground below, arms folded across her chest.

Agnes jumped off her bicycle. 'Elsie? What's going on?'

Elsie ran to her. 'Nurse, you must come. It's our Christopher. I think he's dying!'

'Dying, indeed!' Mrs Bannister rolled her eyes. 'Don't be so dramatic, child.'

Elsie turned on her. 'He is dying!' she insisted. 'He's

311

got a pain in his belly so bad he can hardly stand it. Aunt Hannah reckons it's down to all the sausages and cake he ate at the gala but I've never seen him as bad as this. I don't know what to do!' she wailed.

'Surely you should go and fetch your aunt, rather than bothering the nurse?' Mrs Bannister said.

'I in't going into the woods, they're haunted. Besides, she'll only tell him it's his own fault. Please, miss?' She turned back to Agnes, wringing her hands. 'Will you come and look at him? I'm that worried about him.'

Agnes glanced at Mrs Bannister, still standing on the steps, her broom in her hands, ready to lash out.

'All right, I'll come.'

As soon as she saw Christopher Stanhope, Agnes knew he was suffering from more than indigestion. He was curled up in a ball on his bed, groaning in pain.

Agnes felt for his pulse. It skittered under her fingers. 'Christopher, where does your belly hurt?'

'Everywhere,' he mumbled, face pressed into the pillow.

'Where is it worst?' Agnes put her hand on his abdomen. The muscles felt rigid to her touch. 'Is it here? Or here?' She moved her hand to McBurney's point, between the umbilicus and the anterior superior iliac spine. Just as she had feared, Christopher let out a yelp of agony.

'How long has he been like this?' she asked Elsie over her shoulder.

'Since this morning. Aunt Hannah gave him some of her peppermint tea, but it didn't do any good.'

'And where's your father?'

'Down at t'pit gates with the rest of the men. Then he'll be off to the Working Men's while closing time, unless he decides to come home for his tea.'

'Does he know his son is sick?'

'Aye,' Elsie said. 'But Aunt Hannah told him it were

nowt to worry about. Not that he'd worry about us anyway,' she added in a low voice.

Agnes pushed down the surge of anger she felt. 'Go and fetch him.'

'I can't. He'll be angry.'

'I said, go and fetch him!' Agnes cut across her sharply. 'If he's angry then he can take out his temper on me.' She was more than ready for Seth Stanhope.

Elsie must have seen the expression on Agnes' face because she hurried off, slamming the door behind her.

Agnes took off her coat and hung it up on the peg on the back door. She found some clean sheets of newspaper, which she spread out on the table before she put down her bag. She had just finished washing her hands when Billy appeared in the doorway.

'Where's Elsie?' He stood in the shadows watching, his eyes round with apprehension.

'She's gone to fetch your father.'

'Our Chris is being sick.'

'Oh, Lord!'

She tipped the water from the bowl and rushed into the other room, but Christopher was already hanging over the side of the bed, retching on to the bare wooden floor.

'He's going to get a wallop for that,' Billy whispered, by her side.

'We'll soon clean it up.' Agnes handed him the bowl. 'Fetch some more water and a flannel for me, would you? There's a good lad. And some more newspaper, if you can find it.'

Billy took the bowl and hurried off.

Christopher finished retching and flopped back against the pillows, tears running down his cheeks.

'Here.' Agnes took the glass of water from the table at the side of the bed and held it to his lips. 'Try to drink this.'

Christopher took a sip then gave up. 'Oh Nurse, I feel awful!' he groaned.

'I know, pet. But we'll soon have you better.' Without thinking, Agnes tenderly pushed back the damp tendrils of dark hair from his perspiring face. Young tearaway that Christopher was, at that moment he was nothing more than a child in pain.

Billy returned with the water and the newspaper. Agnes dampened the flannel and wiped Christopher's face, then set about clearing up the mess on the floor. She had already made up her mind what needed to be done for the boy. Now all she had to do was wait for his father to come home.

She had lit a fire and was burning the newspaper when the back door opened. Agnes turned, expecting to see Seth Stanhope, but instead found herself staring into the cold black eyes of Hannah Arkwright. She carried her dusty old carpet bag in one hand, and a cooking pot tucked under her arm. It was black and heavy cast iron, like a cauldron.

'What's going on? What are you doing here?'

Agnes pushed down the surge of dislike she felt. 'Elsie asked me to come. She's worried about her brother.'

Hannah gave an angry sigh. 'She had no business getting you involved. I told her there's nowt wrong with the lad.' She dumped her bag on the floor and set the pot down on the table. 'Anyway, I'm here now. So you can be on your way.'

Agnes stood her ground. 'I'm not going anywhere until I've spoken to Mr Stanhope.'

'You think he'll want to speak to you?'

'I don't care what he wants. His son is very sick and needs to see a doctor.'

Hannah looked scornful. 'For belly ache?'

'I think it's more than that.'

'Aye, well, that shows what you know, doesn't it?' Hannah opened her bag and started rummaging through it. 'Another dose of peppermint tea is all he needs.'

'He needs a doctor,' Agnes repeated quietly.

'His father won't want that fool Rutherford coming here, I can tell you that now.' Hannah pulled a small brown paper packet out of the bag. 'A bit of peppermint will sort our Chris out in no time.'

She made a move towards the other room but Agnes stepped in front of her, blocking her path.

'No,' she said.

Hannah's thick brows drew together in a frown. 'What?'

'You can put your potions away. I'm not letting you treat him.'

Hannah towered over her, and for a moment Agnes thought she was going to be attacked, but she stood her ground.

'Out of my way,' she growled.

'No.'

'I won't tell you twice!'

'Hannah?'

The back door was open and there stood Seth Stanhope, Elsie behind him. He looked from one to the other of the women. 'What's going on?'

Agnes found her voice first. 'Mr Stanhope, your son is very ill,' she said, as calmly as she could manage.

'It's nowt, Seth, honestly. Just a touch of indigestion, like I said,' Hannah put in. 'There were no need for you to come home. I don't know why Elsie had to go and fetch you.' She scowled at the little girl.

'Hush, Hannah.' Seth looked at Agnes. 'What's the matter with him?'

'I think your son may have acute appendicitis.'

Seth's face blanched. 'Appendicitis?'

'Appendicitis, indeed!' Hannah scorned. 'As if—'

'I said, hush!' Seth snapped. His gaze didn't move from Agnes. 'What's to be done?'

'The doctor will need to see him. If he agrees with me, Christopher may need to be moved to hospital.'

'Hospital now, is it?' Hannah shook her head. 'Take no notice of her, Seth. I can put him right. I've always taken care of the bairns in the past, haven't I?'

There was a long silence. Agnes could feel the tension in the room like a band pulled tight, ready to snap.

Then Seth spoke at last. 'Fetch the doctor, Elsie,' he said over his shoulder.

'Seth!' Hannah let out a cry of dismay.

Agnes' knees sagged with relief. 'I'd best go myself,' she said, remembering how Mrs Bannister had greeted Elsie the last time. 'I can explain what's wrong.'

'Aye.' Seth glanced towards the other room. 'Will he be all right while you're gone?'

'I'll be as quick as I can.' Agnes didn't look at Hannah, but she could feel the other woman's dark gaze boring into her back as she put on her coat.

As she closed the door, she could hear Hannah's voice rising furiously.

'Why are you listening to her and not me ... I know what I'm doing, you know that ... The lad doesn't need a doctor, Seth ...'

Evening surgery had just finished by the time she returned to Dr Rutherford's house. Agnes caught the doctor as he was leaving his office.

'Miss Sheridan. Whatever is the matter?' He gave her a bemused smile over the rim of his spectacles. 'You look all of a fluster!'

'Doctor, you must come. The Stanhope boy is very unwell. I think he may have acute appendicitis. He's been

316

vomiting, and there is severe abdominal pain on the right side that has been steadily getting worse, and—'

'Slow down, Miss Sheridan, please!' Dr Rutherford shook his head. 'You know I can't see the boy. What would the Haverstocks say?'

'But Christopher is very ill, Doctor. I believe there's a strong chance the appendix might burst, if it hasn't done so already.'

'But the Haverstocks . . . '

'Did you hear what I said, Doctor?' Agnes fought the urge to grab him by his tweed lapels and shake him. 'The boy might die. Do you really want that on your conscience?'

She saw Dr Rutherford hesitate, the flicker of doubt in his eyes.

'You took a vow,' she said. 'When you became a doctor. You promised to help the sick, no matter who they were. Surely that means something to you?'

Dr Rutherford's mouth thinned, and for a moment she thought she had gone too far.

'Very well,' he said tautly. 'I will see this child. But I want you to know I don't appreciate your tone, Miss Sheridan. Nor do I like being placed in a difficult position like this.'

'No, sir.'

'Please be assured I will have words with your Nursing Superintendent about this matter.'

'I understand, sir.' Agnes was sure Miss Gale would be staunchly on her side once she found out what had happened. But at that moment, she didn't care if she was hauled up in front of the District Association and stripped of her badge, if it meant saving Christopher Stanhope's life.

At the cottage, they found Seth pacing the kitchen. He swung round to face them, and Agnes caught a glimpse of the raw dislike in his eyes when he looked at Dr Rutherford, before the mask came down.

'Thank you for coming, Doctor,' he said gruffly.

Dr Rutherford's gaze skimmed past him towards the parlour. 'Is the child through there?' He addressed himself to Agnes, ignoring Seth.

'Yes, Doctor.'

Hannah was sitting by Christopher's bedside, sponging his face with a damp flannel. Agnes hoped she hadn't slipped the boy one of her concoctions while she had been away.

Agnes was afraid Hannah might try to cause a fuss but she set down the flannel and moved aside to allow the doctor to examine the boy. Agnes could feel Hannah's resentful glare fixed between her shoulder blades while he did so.

Dr Rutherford examined the boy. As he did, his expression changed from one of irritation to a look of grave concern.

'Well?' Seth said.

'You were quite right, Nurse, the boy is showing signs of acute appendicitis.' Dr Rutherford still addressed himself to Agnes. 'I'll make arrangements to admit him to hospital immediately.'

She caught Seth's sharp intake of breath. From the corner of the room, Hannah gave a grunt of disgust.

Dr Rutherford put away his stethoscope and straightened up. He looked directly at Seth for the first time.

'I take it you have the money to pay for his treatment?'

Seth glared back at him, eyes so dark with fury Agnes feared he might strike the doctor.

'I'll find it.' He took a deep, shaky breath, his eyes moving to the still figure on the bed. 'Just save my lad,' he said quietly.

Chapter Thirty-Seven

Carrie could hardly see the beans she was plucking from the stems for the thick veil of tears in her eyes.

Over in the corner of the allotment stood her father's old wooden chair, which they had dragged up from the cottage a week earlier. Every day for the past week he had come to sit there, watching her work. Sometimes he sat quietly, reading his Bible, only looking up to offer advice on what she was doing. Sometimes they talked, about how things were growing or the world in general. But most of the time he would just sit, his face turned up to the sky, enjoying the warmth of the late August sun on his face.

But today Carrie had had to come alone, as her father didn't have the strength to get out of bed.

Her mother had tried to reassure her. 'He's just having a bad day,' she had said. 'It's only to be expected some-times. You'll see, he'll be up and about again soon.'

Carrie had smiled and nodded to make her mother feel better. But deep in her heart she knew Eric Wardle would never sit in his old chair and feel the sun on his face again.

A tear plopped on to the leaf of the bean stalk, and Carrie dashed it away. She went on plucking the pods, yanking savagely at the stems and dropping them into the basket at her feet. She knew her father would have told her off for not doing it properly, but she didn't care. All she wanted was to finish the job, run away and never come back to the allotment again. Nausea churned in the pit of her stomach. There was no joy in it any more, now she was alone.

But then she realised she wasn't. Looking around, she saw Rob Chadwick standing by the fence.

Carrie hadn't seen him since the gala, the previous week. So much had happened after that, with her being reunited with James and then her father taking ill, that she had barely thought about Rob.

'I saw you from down the lane,' he said. 'You looked as if you needed some company.' He climbed over the low fence. 'Anything I can do?'

She was going to say no, but didn't have the strength to argue. She stepped to one side, nudging the basket towards him with her foot.

'If you like.'

He started to pluck at the beans, pulling them from their stems. 'I heard about your father.' Carrie said nothing. 'I'm sorry.'

'Thank you.'

'I always liked him,' Rob went on. 'He was a good man. One of the best at the pit.'

'Was?' Carrie turned on him angrily. 'Why are you talking about him as if he's gone?'

'I'm sorry, I didn't mean—'

'My father is alive,' Carrie said, turning back to her picking. 'He's alive,' she repeated quietly. She couldn't allow herself to think about anything else.

'Aye.' Rob looked awkward. They carried on picking in silence, standing side by side. Carrie wondered that she could stand so close to him and not feel anything. Once upon a time, she would have trembled at the nearness of him. But now she was barely aware of him, his shoulder brushing hers.

As they worked, she was aware of Rob's silence. It

wasn't like him to keep so quiet, she thought. Usually he chattered nineteen to the dozen, cracking daft jokes and trying to make her laugh. But today he looked as if he had the weight of the world on his shoulders.

She didn't ask what was troubling him. She had enough worries of her own not to need to burden herself with anyone else's.

Finally, he spoke up. 'I've been thinking.'

'Oh, aye?'

'The baby's mine, in't he?'

Carrie's busy hands froze and for a split second the world seemed to tilt on its axis, spinning in front of her eyes. Nausea crawled up her throat and she wondered if she was going to be sick.

Calm. Be calm.

She forced her hands to start moving again, but her fingers felt strange, as if they didn't belong to her.

'I don't know what you're talking about,' she said flatly.

'I'm no fool, Carrie. I've worked it out. The bairn was born in April, nine months after the gala. We lay together a couple of weeks before you got married.'

Be calm.

'The baby arrived early—' she started to say, but Rob cut her off.

'You might be able to pull the wool over that fool Shepherd's eyes, but it doesn't work with me. That was why you didn't want me to know how old the boy was ... because you knew then I'd find out. I'm right, in't I?'

Carrie opened her mouth to deny it, but the words clogged her throat, refusing to come out. She stared at the blurred green of the bean stalk in front of her, longing for something to happen, some magic that would whisk her away so she wouldn't have to face this.

But deep down she knew it was inevitable. Part of her

had known it since the day Rob Chadwick came back to Bowden. Sooner or later, the secret she had kept so carefully would be revealed, and her world would start to fall apart.

'I knew it.' She heard the triumph in Rob's voice. 'And Shepherd has no idea?'

'You think I'd tell him?' How could she ever admit something like that? It would break James' heart, and hers with it.

Shame washed over her. She had wanted to tell him. When she first found out she was pregnant, shortly after they were married, she had wanted to come clean and admit everything. But then she had thought about it. Why should she allow one mistake, one stupid, unguarded moment, to ruin her whole life? She and James were happy and in love. Why shouldn't it stay that way forever?

And they had been happy. But the secret had always been there, casting a long shadow over her marriage.

'You should have told me,' Rob said, interrupting her thoughts.

Carrie turned on him, anger flaring inside her. 'And what would you have done?'

He looked taken aback. 'I would have done the right thing by you,' he mumbled.

'You wouldn't know the right thing if it hit you in the face!'

'That in't fair!' Rob straightened up, defending himself. 'I could have proved mysen to you, if you'd given me the chance. I could've married you.'

'And what kind of life would that have been for both of us?' Carrie shook her head.

'We could have made a go of it.'

'For how long? How long before you started to resent me and the bairn for tying you down?'

Suddenly her head was clear, all the girlish, romantic notions she had held on to for so long disappearing like threads of mist. She had always imagined fondly what her life would have been like if she had married Rob. But now the reality of it hit her for the first time. She saw herself at the doorway of a dreary pit cottage, staring up the lane and wondering when he would come home, or if he would go straight to the Working Men's Club to spend all his earnings again. She saw the endless tears, and the arguments, and slamming doors.

Rob Chadwick was a charming, handsome man, but he was not the marrying kind, she realised. He would never take kindly to having his wings clipped.

'If you'd wanted to marry me you would have done it years ago, instead of leaving me first chance you got,' she said.

Rob nodded slowly. 'Happen you were right – once,' he conceded. 'I wasn't ready to settle down when I left Bowden. But I'm a changed man, Carrie.' He looked at her, his hazel eyes full of appeal. 'You've seen for thysen how much I've grown up in the past couple of years. I've realised what I've been missing all this time. And now I want to make things right.'

Carrie stared back at him warily. 'What do you mean?'

'I want us to be together. You, me and our son.'

Our son. Fear washed over her, making her feel sick. 'But I'm married!'

'Leave him.' Rob made it sound like the most simple thing in the world. 'I can't stand the thought of you being with Shepherd, of him bringing up my boy. I don't want him to grow up like James Shepherd. I want him to be a man . . . '

'James is more of a man than you'll ever be!'

'He isn't the boy's father!' Rob shot back. He must have

seen the anger on Carrie's face because he softened and went on, 'Look, I don't blame you for marrying him. I walked out on you, and you were desperate, I understand that. But I'm back now, and I want us to be together.'

And what about what I want? Carrie thought.

'I know it might be difficult for us to stay here.' Rob was still talking, words tumbling over each other. 'But I've been thinking about it, and I reckon we should go away somewhere, start afresh. I could get a job at another pit, or on a farm – anywhere as long as it's away from this place.' He looked at her, his eyes shining. 'It's what I want, Carrie. And it's what you want too, in't it? It's what you've always wanted.'

As he went on talking, a picture filled Carrie's mind. James at last year's gala, carrying the baby in his arms, his face full of love and pride.

'No,' she said.

Rob stopped speaking abruptly, his brows drawing together. 'What?'

'I don't want to be with you, Rob. I love James.'

'No, you don't. You can't.'

'I do.' Suddenly she had never been more sure of anything in her life. 'I love James with all my heart. He's my husband, and Bowden is my home, and this is where I want to stay. With him.'

'You don't mean that.'

'I do mean it. And I want you to go away and leave us alone.'

Rob's mouth twisted. 'You expect me to walk away, knowing I have a son?'

'Henry in't your son. James is the one who brought him up. He is his father—'

'He'll never be my lad's father!' Rob made a grab for Carrie, his powerful hands digging painfully into the soft

324

flesh of her arms. The dangerous anger in his face frightened her. 'I won't let you do this,' he said. 'I won't let you take my son away from me!'

'Let me go!' Carrie started to wriggle free from his grasp. Rob seemed to realise what he was doing and released her abruptly, his hands dropping to his sides.

'I'm sorry,' he started to say. 'I didn't mean to frighten you. I was just so angry, I didn't know what I was doing. Forgive me, Carrie.'

'Leave me alone!' She snatched up the basket at her feet. 'Stay away from me and my son, do you understand?'

He started to follow her, but Carrie spun round to face him, her anger stopping him in his tracks.

'I said, stay away from us!'

She walked away, her heart thudding in her chest. Her legs felt so weak she wasn't sure they would carry her.

Thankfully, Rob didn't try to follow her, although she could feel him watching her as she reached the border of the allotments. It was only when she started down the lane that she heard his ominous warning called after her as she hurried away.

'This in't over, Carrie. You should know I don't give up that easily!'

Chapter Thirty-Eight

'Mr Shepherd, you must come and see what's happening in the yard!'

James glanced at the clock on the wall, his heart sinking. Two o'clock in the afternoon, and the next busload of blacklegs would be arriving for their shift. He could already hear the roaring of the men at the pit gates as the bus rumbled past them.

'If it's another fight, get Sergeant Cray to sort it out,' he sighed, going back to his papers.

'I'm not sure as how you'd call it a fight, sir. Not a fair one, at any rate.' His secretary Miss Molesworth stood in the doorway, her face alight with excitement. 'Truly, Mr Shepherd, you'll want to see this!'

Curious, James rose to his feet and went to the window overlooking the yard and its outbuildings. Below him, the men were getting off the bus, ready for their shift.

Miss Molesworth came to stand beside him. 'Over there, sir. By the gates.'

He lifted his gaze to where she was pointing, at the picket line beyond the gates. Sure enough, there was some kind of riot going on. The men were shouting, shaking their fists, all converging on something, or someone, in the crowd – what it was James couldn't make out. Through the window, he could hear them screaming abuse.

'Traitor!'

'Blackleg filth!'

'Should be ashamed of thysen!'

James had grown used to hearing curses uttered at the gates, but this time they seemed more angry and venomous. He could see fists punching, legs kicking out, blows raining down . . .

'What on earth . . . ?' He was just about to go down and stop the fight when the pit gates swung open. James realised what had stirred up the men on the picket line when a lone figure emerged from the crowd and walked through the gateway.

'My God,' he murmured.

'I told you, didn't I, sir?' Miss Molesworth sounded triumphant. 'I saw him from the yard. They've been having a right old go at him this past five minutes, and he didn't even try to fight back. Just stood there taking it. Funny that, don't you think?'

James hurried down to the lamp room, where the men were lining up to collect their checks.

'Stanhope?'

The man on the end of the line turned slowly to face him, and James gasped. Blood oozed from the cut on his lip, and a purple bruise was already blossoming along the ridge of one cheekbone.

But it was the wretchedness in his eyes that truly shocked James.

'What are you doing here?'

'I've come to work.'

'But I don't understand.' James glanced towards the window that looked on to the pit yard. He could still hear the jeering of the men beyond the gates.

'Nothing to understand,' Seth said shortly. 'I'm here to work, if you want me.' His mouth clamped shut and James knew he would get nothing more out of him. He stared at Seth's battered, swollen face.

'Why didn't you come in on the bus with the other men?'

Seth's lip curled. 'I don't belong with them blacklegs.'

'You could have saved yourself a lot of trouble.'

'Happen.' Seth fixed his gaze on the middle distance.

James frowned. Seth Stanhope was the proudest, most stubborn man he had ever met. 'You should go to the first-aid room, get someone to look at that eye for you.'

'Nay, I'd rather get to work, if you don't mind?' Seth glanced towards the dwindling line of men waiting to step into the cage.

'Very well,' said James. Then, as Seth turned away, he said, 'Thank you. For coming back.'

Seth met his gaze for the first time, his eyes cold with loathing.

'I in't doing it for you,' he said.

James climbed the stairs back to his office, still picturing Seth as he walked through the pit gates. He didn't know what had driven the man to break the lockout and betray his friends, but he knew it was not a decision that had been taken lightly. Whatever his reason, James knew life would never again be the same for Seth Stanhope, not after this. He would be a pariah in Bowden, along with the other men who had been forced back to work in order to survive.

James knew he should be feeling elated that one of the main ringleaders of the lockout had given in, but instead he felt utterly downcast. What a dreadful situation they had created – one where men who were formerly good friends were forced to turn on each other. The lockout would be over one day, but it had created rifts in the community that would probably never heal.

Miss Molesworth looked up from behind her typewriter when he walked in.

'There's someone to see you, sir,' she said.

'Thank you.' James hoped it wasn't Sir Edward. The

way he felt, he wasn't sure he could face him at that moment. Fortunately for him, Sir Edward still seemed to be sulking since the argument over Carrie and the gala.

But when James opened the door and saw Rob Chadwick waiting for him, he suddenly thought that a visit from the pit owner might be preferable after all.

Chadwick was leaning back in James' chair, feet up on the desk, looking very pleased with himself.

'Y'know, I've often wondered what it would be like to be in charge of this place and sit up here all day,' he said, looking round at James. 'Turns out it in't that much after all, is it? Nowt more than a poky little box, when you think about it.' He nodded towards the portrait on the wall. 'I see you've got the old man watching you. I follow in my father's footsteps too, but I weren't so lucky as you. No silver spoons for me, just a pickaxe and a life down t'pit to look forward to.'

'What do you want?' James asked coldly.

Rob gave him a slow smile. 'Now don't be like that. Happen I've come to ask for a job.'

'I wouldn't have you. You were too much of a trouble-maker last time.'

'Beggars can't be choosers, can they? Anyway, I wouldn't take a job now if you gave me one. I'm no blackleg scum.'

James thought about Seth Stanhope, and the injured pride on his battered, bloodied face.

'So why are you here?' he said. 'And you can stop playing stupid games, I'm not in the mood.'

'Oh, I in't playing games, believe me.' Another slow, insolent smile spread across Rob's face. 'I'm here to talk about Carrie.'

James' blood ran cold, but he forced himself to remain calm. In the back of his mind, in the dead of night, he had thought about this scenario, played it out in his head, rehearsed for it many times.

He was ready.

'And what could you possibly have to say about my wife?'

'Your wife!' Rob echoed the words mockingly. 'She was my girl first.'

'Is that what you've come to tell me?'

'No. I've come to tell you I want her back.'

James said nothing. He had heard those words so many times in his nightmares, they hardly came as a surprise to him now.

'I daresay you know we've been seeing a lot of each other lately, since I got back to Bowden?' Rob went on. 'Although come to think of it, you probably don't, do you? It's all been going on behind your back, you see. She even helped me get away from the police when I was stealing coal from the yard. Mind you, she were up to no good hersen, delivering food parcels in secret. Bet you didn't know that either, did you? Nor that she's been pawning the jewellery you gave her to give money to the Miners' Welfare.' He laughed. 'Aye, Carrie's always been loyal to her own.'

Sir Edward's warning came into James' mind.

And when she's taken everything, she'll go back to her own and forget about you. The words carried a proper sting now.

'Anyway, as I said, we've been seeing a lot of each other lately. And we've decided we want to be together.'

James laughed. It was a nervous reaction, but it still took Rob aback.

He sent him a guarded look. 'What's so funny?'

'You are, you fool. You really think you can just walk in here and demand that I give up my wife to you?'

'The bairn is mine.'

James stopped laughing. The words seemed to echo around the office.

Rob looked satisfied. 'I thought that would wipe the smile off your face. Who's the fool now, eh?' He leaned forward, rubbing his hands together. 'It happened two years ago, after the gala. A couple of weeks before she were due to marry you ... can you imagine that? Poor Carrie, she were in such a state, not sure if she were doing the right thing. Well, it weren't like you were her first choice, was it? I was always the one she really wanted, as well you know.' He smiled. 'I daresay it was me she was remembering on her wedding night, too. Or did you think you were the first—'

James sprang towards him, his fists clenched. Rob didn't flinch.

'Go on, then, hit me,' he taunted. 'A real man would have knocked me flat a long time ago. But you in't got it in you, have you? Not even when I come in here and tell you I fathered that baby you've been bringing up as your own!'

James uncurled his hands. 'Get out,' he hissed.

'Is that the best you can do?' Rob mocked. 'You in't going to fight for your wife? But then, I s'pose there's no point, is there? I mean, you always knew this would happen, didn't you? You knew you weren't man enough to keep a girl like Carrie. I daresay she wouldn't have stayed with you this long if it hadn't been for the bairn.' He shook his head. 'Anyway, I'm back now. And I reckon it's only right that we should be together. A proper family.'

'If you think I'm giving up my wife and son to someone like you, then you're wrong.' James found his voice at last, spitting out the words like venom.

'My son,' Rob reminded him. 'He's my boy, not yours.'

Nausea rose in James' throat, choking him. 'Get out.'

'Don't worry, I'm going. I reckon we've said all we've got to say to each other.' Rob rose to his feet. His burly frame seemed to fill the small office. 'But I in't leaving Bowden, not without Carrie and the bairn.' He smirked. 'I daresay we'll be seeing a lot of each other, from now on.'

James stayed at his desk long after Rob had gone, staring down at the papers on his desk as if he no longer recognised them. Nothing seemed real to him any more.

And yet he wasn't shocked. Deep down he had always known he was lucky to have Carrie, and that one day his luck would run out.

He understood that Rob Chadwick was the love of Carrie Wardle's life. He had watched them together often enough, seen the way she lit up whenever he was around her. It was the same way James felt whenever he saw her.

And then Rob had gone, and Carrie was heartbroken. And slowly, carefully, James had put together the pieces of her shattered heart, and made her smile again. It didn't matter to him that he was second best, because he knew he had enough love for both of them. And sometimes when Carrie looked at him, he could even imagine that her eyes lit up the way they used to do for Rob.

But in his heart of hearts, he had been waiting for this day, when Rob came back to claim what was rightfully his.

And he knew Carrie had been waiting for it too.

James moved like an automaton through the rest of the afternoon, hardly knowing what he was doing. When the clock struck five and Miss Molesworth tapped on the door to tell him she was going home it took him completely by surprise. Had it really been three hours since Rob Chadwick sat here in this office, taunting him?

He half expected Carrie to be gone when he returned

home. James opened the door tentatively, bracing himself for the maid to appear and tell him his wife had left, complete with the baby and all her bags.

When he heard Carrie's voice drifting down the stairs, he didn't know whether to laugh or cry.

He crept up and watched them for a moment through the half-open nursery door. Carrie was sitting on the floor, her skirt pooled around her, singing a funny little song to the baby while she bounced him up and down on her knee.

'This is the way the farmers ride . . . '

The sound of Henry's gurgling laughter went through James' heart like a dart.

He took a step back, and the floorboard creaked under his feet. Carrie looked up.

'James? Is that you?'

He took a deep breath, pinning a smile to his face, and forced himself to walk into the room.

'You're early.' She put the baby down and got to her feet. As she approached to kiss him, James held himself rigid.

It was too much to hope she wouldn't notice. 'Are you all right, my love?' She pulled away from him, frowning.

'I'm fine, thank you. Just a headache.'

'Can I get you something? Some aspirin?'

'No, thank you.' He saw the genuine concern in her eyes. She seemed to care for him, but that wasn't the same as love, was it?

Looking more closely, he could see the lines of strain in her face. She had been so preoccupied over the last few days. He had put it down to worry about her ailing father, but now he wondered if she was deciding how to tell him about Rob.

'Dada!' Henry cried out, toddling towards him, his

chubby arms outstretched. James automatically went to pick him up, then stopped himself.

'James?' Carrie was staring at him, her frown deepening. 'Don't you want to hold your son?'

But he was already gone, closing the nursery door behind him.

Chapter Thirty-Nine

'Have you heard the news? Seth Stanhope's crossed the picket line!'

Agnes kept her eyes fixed on the thermometer she had just used to take Eric Wardle's temperature, but her attention shifted to the other side of the room where Eliza and Hattie Wardle and their sister Carrie were busy with the baking around the kitchen table. The aroma of freshly baked bread filled the cottage.

'They were all talking about it when I went to fetch the water from the pump this morning,' Hattie went on, up to her elbows in the bread dough she was kneading. 'Mrs Morris said the men gave him a terrible time when he walked through the gates yesterday. Alec Morris even blacked his eye for him.'

'And he didn't fight back? That don't sound like Seth Stanhope!' Eliza said.

'Nurse?' Agnes looked round to see Mrs Wardle watching her anxiously. 'Is everything all right?' she asked. 'My Eric's temperature in't gone up or owt, has it?'

Agnes looked back at the thermometer, almost forgotten in her hand. 'Not at all, Mrs Wardle, everything is just as it should be.'

She made a careful note of the number on the chart, her head half turned to catch the girls' conversation on the other side of the room.

'Serves him right anyway, whatever they did to him,' Eliza declared from over by the range, as she prodded at some newly risen dough with her fingertip. 'Blacklegs deserve all they get. In't that right, Father?'

Eliza turned to her father, looking for his wisdom as usual, then her face fell as she remembered that he was too ill to reply. Agnes caught her crestfallen expression and her heart went out to her.

'All the same, they didn't ought to treat him like that.' Kathleen Wardle spoke up for her husband. 'Seth Stanhope's still one of us, when all is said and done. And I daresay he's got his reasons. In't that right, Nurse?'

Agnes nodded absently. But all she could think about was Seth Stanhope walking in through those pit gates.

'He was the last one I expected to break the lockout,' Eliza said, pushing the loaf tins back into the oven and closing the door. 'Everyone thought he was going to be the last man standing.'

'Aye,' Hattie agreed. 'Mrs Morris reckons that's why the other men are so angry with him. With Mr Stanhope back at work, it's only a matter of time before the rest of them give in too.'

'I bet your James will be pleased about that?' Eliza said to Carrie.

She looked up from the cake batter she was stirring. 'What?'

Eliza sighed. 'Honestly, Carrie, you're in a world of your own. All this time we've been talking, and you haven't been listening to a word. And you've beaten all the air out of that batter, too. It won't be fit for baking now.'

Carrie stared down blankly at the wooden spoon in her hand. Poor girl, Agnes thought. She looked as if she had the weight of the world on her shoulders.

She wasn't surprised. Out of the four Wardle girls, Carrie was the closest to her father. It must be hitting her hard, knowing what was to come.

Agnes cleaned the thermometer then finished examining Eric, checking under the straps of his brace.

'There's a place here that's starting to look a bit red,' she said. 'I'd better put some powder on it before it turns into a sore.'

Kathleen looked distraught. 'But I've been washing and drying him carefully, just like you said.'

Agnes looked at the woman's anxious expression. Eric Wardle could not have had a better set of nurses than his wife and daughters. Kathleen and the girls attended him constantly. They had even moved his bed into the main room of the house so that they could keep their eyes on him all day.

'I don't want him to feel as if he's on his own, stuck in the other room,' Kathleen had explained. 'He always liked to know what was going on.'

Agnes knew as well as she did that Eric Wardle was past noticing what was happening around him. But she understood how important it was for Kathleen to feel as if she was doing something that would make a difference. That was why Agnes had taught her how to give him a proper bed bath and how to clean his mouth out with a moistened cotton wool swab on the end of a piece of stick.

'It isn't your fault, Mrs Wardle,' she assured her now. 'Sometimes these things happen in spite of our best efforts. I'll treat it now and then see about getting his splint adjusted so it doesn't cause him any discomfort.'

'Thank you, Nurse.' Kathleen glanced at her husband. 'Are you sure I'm looking after him properly? I've been doing everything just as you showed me, but I wasn't sure—'

'I couldn't have done it better myself, Mrs Wardle,' Agnes reassured her.

Kathleen looked gratified. 'I just want to do my best to make him comfortable while . . . ' Her voice trailed off.

Agnes read the desperation in her eyes. Kathleen Wardle knew she wouldn't be able to hold on to her husband for much longer.

Once she had made sure Eric was comfortable, Agnes went to wash her hands in the bowl his wife had set out for her on the scrubbed wooden draining board. Behind her, Eliza had set the first batch of freshly baked loaves on the table to cool, while Hattie divided up the dough into tins for the next lot. Carrie had put her cake in the oven.

'I'm going up the allotment,' she announced to her mother. 'The potatoes and onions need to be got in before the cold weather sets in.'

'Oh, but surely it's too early for that?' her mother protested.

'All the same, I'd like to get it done. And Father would want the fruit bushes tied in, too.'

'Yes, but—' Kathleen started to say, then stopped herself. 'Just as you like, love,' she answered quietly.

Kathleen and Agnes looked at each other. They had both seen the look of fierce determination on Carrie's face. It didn't matter to Eric Wardle any more whether the fruit bushes were neatly tied, or the potatoes and onions harvested. But Carrie needed to do it all the same, for her own sake more than his.

'I have to pass the allotments on my way to my next call,' Agnes said brightly as she dried her hands and put away her towel. 'Perhaps we could walk together?'

'Aye, if you like.' Carrie nodded, but she seemed too preoccupied to take in what Agnes was saying.

They walked up the lane in silence, Carrie pushing Henry in his pram and Agnes pushing her bicycle over the cobbles. Usually Carrie would be talking, about the baby or her father, or anything at all. But today she seemed quiet and edgy. As they walked, she kept looking around her, as if she expected someone to jump out on her at any moment.

Then Reg Willis greeted them both from the front door of his cottage, and Carrie flinched as if she had been struck.

Agnes turned to face her. 'Are you all right, Mrs Shepherd?'

'Aye, why shouldn't I be?' Carrie turned on her, her blue eyes snapping.

Agnes blinked, taken aback by her ferocious reply. 'Oh, I beg your pardon.'

'No, it's me who should be sorry.' Her shoulders slumped. 'I'm not feeling mysen just now.'

'I'm not surprised,' Agnes said. But she had the feeling it wasn't just her father that was causing the young woman concern.

If she didn't know better, she could have sworn Carrie Shepherd was trying to avoid someone.

They reached the allotments. It was a grey, overcast day with a stiff wind blowing down from the hills, and for once there was no one else tending their land. Agnes looked over the neat patchwork of brown and green, admiring the vegetables growing in their regimented rows. It appealed to her sense of order.

'Which one is your father's allotment?' she asked.

'This one, closest to the fence.' Carrie eased the pram through the gateway and parked it on the narrow strip of grass that separated the allotment from its neighbours.

'You've kept it up very well,' Agnes observed.

'Aye.' Carrie looked around. 'It's what Father would have wanted.'

'It must be very satisfying, growing your own vegetables. But I'm not sure I'd have the patience for it. I wouldn't know where to start, either.'

'I grew up here,' Carrie said. 'I've been helping Father on the allotment for as long as I can remember. I even looked after it by mysen while he was away in the War . . .' She glanced at the old wooden chair that stood forlorn in the corner of the plot, then turned away again. 'These days I like to come up here when I want to be on my own, to think.'

Agnes regarded her carefully. 'And is there anything in particular you need to think about at the moment?'

Carrie didn't reply. She took a trowel out of the pocket of her sacking apron and bent down to dig at the potatoes, loosening the earth around each straggly green plant.

'You know you can always talk to me, if there's something troubling you?' Agnes ventured.

'I in't ailing.'

'No, I can see that. But I like to think I can help with other matters, too.'

Carrie ignored her. She finished loosening the soil and carefully pulled out the plant, revealing three or four potatoes growing at its root.

Agnes sighed. 'I'll leave you in peace. But don't forget, if you ever want to talk—'

She started to walk away, but Carrie called after her. 'Wait!'

Chapter Forty

Agnes turned around slowly. Carrie had straightened up to face her, the plant hanging limp from her hand. Her expression was troubled.

'You're right,' she said. 'There is summat on my mind. I need to tell someone before I go mad, but I can't talk to anyone else.' She looked around her across the empty patchwork of allotments, as if checking they were truly alone. Then she turned back to Agnes. 'Can you keep a secret?' she asked in a low voice.

Agnes tried not to smile at the question. If only Carrie knew how long she had been keeping her own secrets. 'You can trust me,' she said.

Carrie paused for a moment, and Agnes could see her weighing up her words, wondering how to say whatever it was she had to say.

Finally, she spoke. 'Out there, on the lane ... I was worried about meeting someone.'

'Who?'

Carrie hesitated, then said, 'Rob Chadwick.'

Agnes wasn't surprised. She should have realised that arrogant young man would have been somewhere at the bottom of it.

She hoped Carrie hadn't done something foolish, for her own sake.

Carrie must have seen the expression on her face, because she said quickly, 'Nay, it's nowt like that. At least, not on my part. Not any more.' She lifted her chin. 'I love James,' she said firmly.

'But the young man won't take no for an answer?' Agnes guessed. She could just imagine Rob Chadwick refusing to accept that any girl was immune to his charms.

Carrie hung her head, looked down at the plant in her hand. 'He wants me to go away with him,' she said quietly.

Agnes was shocked. 'But you're a married woman!' she exclaimed.

'That don't mean owt to Rob. If he wants summat, he don't like anything to stand in his way.' There was a trace of bitterness in Carrie's voice.

'You told him no, I take it?'

'I tried, but – it's more difficult than that.' She looked wretched.

'In what way?'

'He knows something about me, a secret. He says he'll tell James . . . '

'What kind of secret?'

Carrie pressed her lips closed, as if she was trying to force the words back, to keep herself from saying them out loud.

Finally she lifted her haunted gaze to meet Agnes'. 'Henry in't James' son,' she said.

'What?'

'It was a terrible, stupid mistake.' Once Carrie had started speaking, her words tumbled out in a torrent. 'I was going to marry James, but I wasn't sure – when Rob came back, I thought I still loved him . . . ' Her blue eyes pleaded with Agnes for understanding.

Agnes stiffened. 'Did he take advantage of you?'

'Nay, it weren't like that. I were as much to blame as he was. I thought—' Carrie shook her head. 'No, I don't know what I was thinking, truly I don't. But straight afterwards, I knew I'd made an awful mistake, that it was James I wanted. I felt so ashamed, I nearly called off the wedding. I didn't want to marry him feeling so dirty and wrong ... '

'So why didn't you tell him?'

'I wanted to,' Carrie insisted. 'But then I thought if I said anything it would make it – I dunno, more real, I suppose. I just wanted to forget all about it, to bury the whole thing and pretend it had never happened.'

'But then you found out you were pregnant?'

Carrie nodded. 'I didn't know what to do. I knew straight away it must be Rob's baby. I decided it were God's way of punishing me, making sure I'd never be able to forget what I'd done.' She shuddered at the memory. 'I were beside mysen, I didn't know what to do. I even thought about going to Hannah for one of her cures ... '

A trickle of ice ran down Agnes' spine. She had dealt with the terrible aftermath of such cures often enough back in Quarry Hill. She wasn't surprised someone like Hannah offered help of that sort.

'But then James guessed,' Carrie went on. 'He was so happy, so delighted he was going to be a father, there was nothing I could do about it. I hoped and prayed it might turn out to be his baby. Months and months I worried about it. Everyone thought I was just anxious because it were my first. They said that was why Henry was born early.' She looked up at Agnes, her eyes bright with remembered hope. 'I wanted them to be right. I wanted so much for him to be James' son. But deep down I knew the truth.'

She looked so forlorn, Agnes' heart went out to her. 'And James has never suspected?'

'Why should he? He trusts me.' Carrie sounded bitter, full of self-hatred. 'Not that I deserve it, after the way I betrayed him.'

'You said yourself, you made a mistake.'

'Aye, and I'm paying for it now, in't I?' Carrie chewed her lip. 'He'll never forgive me for this. I've lost everything. I wish Rob Chadwick had never ever come back to Bowden!'

She burst into tears, and Agnes hurried through the gate to put her arms around her, comforting her. 'Don't cry, pet,' she tried to soothe her. 'I'm sure it will be all right.'

'How can it be all right?' Carrie pulled away from her sharply. 'Rob's going to tell James, and everything is going to be ruined. Rob reckons my husband deserves to know the truth, and happen he's right. He'll hate me, and it's no more than I deserve.'

She fell sobbing into Agnes' arms again. She felt as fragile as a child. Poor girl, Agnes thought. There might be some who would say Carrie had got what she deserved, but Agnes was not one of them. She knew only too well what it was like to go through life burdened with a terrible secret.

'It seems to me there's only one thing you can do,' she said. 'You must tell James yourself.'

Carrie pulled away from her again, her face mottled from crying. 'I couldn't do that!' she gasped.

'What choice do you have? He's going to find out anyway, and surely it's better coming from you than Rob Chadwick?'

Carrie was silent for a moment, taking it in. 'It will break James' heart,' she said.

Agnes nodded. 'Perhaps. He's certainly going to be angry and upset that you didn't tell him the truth sooner. But if he loves you —'

Carrie shook her head. 'How can he love me after this?'

'I don't know,' Agnes admitted. 'But I do know this is the only chance you'll have to put things right.'

Carrie looked at her, blinking back her tears. 'Is that what you'd do?'

Agnes hesitated for a fraction of a second. 'It's the best thing to do,' she said firmly.

Carrie looked agonised. 'You're right,' she said. 'I suppose I will have to tell James. He deserves to know the truth, and he deserves to hear it from me.' But even as she said it, Agnes could see the courage ebbing from those blue eyes.

Agnes left Carrie on the allotment and returned to her rounds. As she cycled away, she looked back over her shoulder at the forlorn little figure sitting on an upturned bucket in the middle of the patch of ground.

Poor Carrie. She was about to lose her father, and now perhaps she was going to lose her husband too. Agnes wondered if his wife would ever find the courage to tell James the truth.

God knows, she herself had never found the courage to tell Daniel.

If she had, would things have turned out differently for them? she wondered. Perhaps they might have been married by now, and she would be holding her son in her arms instead of mourning him alone.

But even as the thought came to her, she knew it was a foolish thing to imagine. She could never have told Daniel the truth, because that would have meant answering questions she didn't want to answer, bringing to light secrets that she wanted to be kept deep in the dark where even she did not have to think about them.

I just wanted to forget all about it, to bury the whole thing and pretend it had never happened . . .

Carrie's words had struck a painful chord inside her. The poor girl had to confront her past now, but Agnes wasn't sure she would ever be prepared to do the same.

The sound of a horn behind her startled her out of her reverie. Agnes wobbled on to the grassy verge, pedalling to stay upright as the bus rumbled past, taking the next shift to the pit. She looked up at the men's faces through the windows. Their expressions were grim, defiant, but there was a wretchedness about them, too. They looked as if they hated themselves as much as the men on the picket line hated them.

She heard the roar of the men at the pit gates, like animals baying for blood. Then she thought about Seth Stanhope, marching resolutely through the crowd, submitting to their curses and insults and blows, all for the sake of his son.

She paused for a moment, making up her mind. Then she turned her bicycle and followed the bus down towards the colliery gates.

Chapter Forty-One

The hooter sounded for the end of the shift, and Seth set down his pick and straightened up slowly. It was months since he had hewn coal from a seam, and every muscle in his body protested painfully, no longer used to spending hours bent double, wielding a heavy pickaxe. He longed for home and a hot bath more than he ever had in all the years he had worked down the pit.

Around him, the other men set down their tools, as silent as they had been all day. Seth had never known the pit to be so quiet. Usually, they would be laughing and joking amongst themselves as they worked the seam, all pals together. But apart from one or two familiar faces, most of the men around him were strangers.

It made him uneasy. Coal miners usually worked in tight teams. They depended on one another, trusting one another to do their job properly and keep the rest of the team safe. But he knew none of these men, and trusted them even less. How could he put his life in the hands of someone who was prepared to betray his fellow pitmen . . . ?

He stopped the thought dead.

But it wasn't just the other men who worried him. There was something about the seam itself that felt wrong.

The props groaned above his head, as if the ground was waking up from a long sleep. The air was hot and thick, pressing against his skin, and the coal face refused to yield under his pick. The seam had lain idle for so long, gases had built up and several times during the shift the deputy had had to call them off until it could be made safe again.

But this was more than fire damp. After nearly twenty years down the pit, Seth had a sixth sense for when things were going wrong. He had tried to talk to the deputy about it, but he wouldn't listen.

'After making trouble again, Stanhope?' Arthur Marwood had said. He was one of the few Bowden men to be working down the pit, and one of the first to go back to work. Seth held him in special contempt, and Marwood knew it. 'None of the other men have complained.'

'They don't know this pit like I do.'

Arthur Marwood's mouth curled. 'Think you're so special, don't you? Get back to work and keep your mouth shut, if you know what's good for you.'

When the shift was over they travelled up in the cage to the surface, crammed in together, reeking of stale sweat. They lined up to hand their checks over the counter in the lamp room, then emerged into the early evening. It was a grey, miserable day but the light still hurt Seth's eyes, making him blink.

'Not coming on the bus with us, lad?' one of the men, a stranger from up Middlesbrough way, asked. Seth shook his head.

'Look at him, reckons he's better than the rest of us,' Arthur Marwood mocked. 'Thinks he's going to walk out of them pit gates a bloody hero. Well, let me tell you, you in't no hero now, Stanhope. Not in their eyes. You're a blackleg, just like the rest of us.'

'Never,' Seth muttered.

'Oh, aye? And what makes you so special?' Another local man, John Chambers, taunted him. 'You think those men at the gates are going to welcome you with open arms, just because you're the great Seth Stanhope?' He shook his head. 'They're going to give you the same welcome I had from you when I went back to work to feed my family.'

If only it was as simple as feeding them, Seth thought. If it was only a matter of going without, he would willingly have starved himself rather than let down his fellow pitmen.

But his son needed treatment, and hospitals cost money.

'It was greed that sent you back to work, John Chambers,' he said. 'You and your family could've lived hand to mouth, just like the rest of us. But you decided to betray your mates instead.'

'And you think your mates will care that you're doing this for your sick lad? D'you think their hearts are going to bleed for you?' John sneered. 'You're going to hear the same insults you shouted at me when I first went through them pit gates. And you're going to deserve them because you're twice the traitor I am.' He squared up to Seth. 'They all expected more of you, Stanhope. And you let them down.'

'What's going on here?' Suddenly James Shepherd was shouldering his way between them, his smart suit a stark contrast to their blackened, sweat-soaked pit clothes.

'It's him,' John Chambers started to say. 'He said—'

'I don't care who said what. Stop it, both of you.' James turned to Seth. 'Get on the bus, Stanhope.'

'Nay, I won't.'

James Shepherd stared back at him. He looked like a boy, his body all gawky angles. Seth had seen more meat on a butcher's pencil.

'Please, Stanhope,' he said. He shot a worried glance towards the pit gates. 'I can't allow you to walk out of those gates. Not after what they did to you yesterday.'

'Aye, and they'll probably do the same to me again today.' The blackened skin around his eye still pulsed painfully, even after Hannah had put raw meat on it to draw out the swelling. 'But I'll not skulk away on a bus to the middle of nowhere. I still live in this village, and sooner or later I'll have to face them.' Better to let them take their revenge now than have them smashing his windows late at night, frightening the bairns.

James sighed. 'Very well,' he said. 'Watch yourself, won't you?'

'I hope they tear you to pieces,' Arthur Marwood called back over his shoulder, as he followed the other men towards the waiting bus.

Seth could see the men's faces pressed up against the bars of the pit gates as he walked towards them. Their mouths were open, roaring with anger. A few days ago he would have stood with them, shoulder to shoulder. He would have called them his friends. Now he barely recognised them, their faces twisted with rage and spite.

The gates swung open and Seth walked out, into the baying mob. He kept his head up, looking straight ahead of him as the men closed in on him, nearly jostling him off his feet. A gob of spittle hit him and ran slowly down his cheek. Seth's fists clenched at his sides, but he made no move to wipe it away.

'You're a bloody traitor, Seth Stanhope!' He heard the voice of Tom Chadwick in the crowd.

Poor Tom. Seth knew the hardships he had been through to keep his family together. Barely a month ago, Seth had stood on this very spot and urged him not to give in, even though his bairns were suffering and his wife was terrified of what was to become of them.

And now look at him. Tom had every right to feel hurt and betrayed. Seth deserved all their scorn and anger. Because no matter how much they hated him, it could never match how much he hated himself.

'Hope tha's proud of thysen, Stanhope! You've let us all down!'

The fist came out of nowhere, driving into his belly, winding him. Seth doubled up, just in time to see the second fist coming towards his face. It caught his jaw, snapping his head sideways and knocking him off balance. He hit the ground and curled up into a ball, his body tense, waiting for the kicking he knew would come.

Through the ringing in his ears, he suddenly heard a voice calling out, clear and cold, 'Let me through!'

He felt a boot connect painfully with the small of his back, sending darts of pain down his legs.

'Stand aside! Let me through, I say!'

It was a woman's voice. Seth felt a shadow fall over him.

'Mr Stanhope?'

He squinted up at the blurry outline of a woman looking down at him. As the picture swam into focus, he made out a cap perched on top of chestnut hair, and a pair of beautiful, bright brown eyes, full of concern.

'Mr Stanhope?' she repeated. 'Can you hear me?'

He tried to speak, but only a groan came out. Warm blood oozed from the cut that had opened up again on his lip, still badly swollen from the previous day. He could taste it, metallic on his tongue.

He tried to struggle to his feet, but a bolt of pain in his ribs caught him off guard and he hissed in pain.

'Where does it hurt?' Miss Sheridan asked him.

'I'm – all right.' He managed to bite out the words.

'I can see you're not.' Miss Sheridan's arm went around his shoulders, trying to pull him to his feet. She turned to the other men, a blurred ring of faces standing around them. 'Help me get him up.' No one moved. 'Isn't anyone going to lend a hand? He's supposed to be your friend.'

'He in't no friend of ours,' someone mumbled.

Agnes stood up. 'How could you? For pity's sake, you're no better than animals!'

'She's right.' Another voice, this time one Seth knew well. The crowd parted and he saw the tall, familiar figure, dressed in a man's overcoat, her broad shoulders swathed in shawls.

'Hannah . . .' He tried again to get up, but his head swam.

'You ought to be ashamed of yourselves.' He heard Hannah's voice rise as she addressed the crowd of men. 'You reckon you're such heroes, don't you? But I bet there in't one of you who would have the courage to face up to him if you were on your own!'

She turned back to him. 'Come on,' she murmured, hooking her strong hands under his arms and hauling him to his feet. 'Let's get you home.'

'Here, help me get him into the chair.'

The lass was stronger than she looked, Hannah thought. She was only a slip of a thing, but she had taken more of Seth's weight than Hannah had expected as they half carried him all the way back to Railway Row.

Of course, Seth had protested all the way home that he didn't need their help, but every time they released him he staggered like a drunkard.

'Concussion,' Agnes declared, as they lowered him into the chair. 'He must have hit his head when he fell.'

'Nay, I'm fine,' Seth mumbled through swollen lips. 'Stop fussing over me, and leave me alone.'

'Aye, happen we should have left you alone by them pit gates,' Hannah said as she filled a bowl with cold water from the jug on the sill. 'Those lads might have knocked some sense into you.'

Seth glowered back at her but said nothing.

'I don't understand,' Agnes Sheridan said. 'Why didn't he get on the bus with the other men?'

'Because he's got some daft notion that he owes it to his mates to let them knock him about.'

'But that's ridiculous!'

'Aye, it is.' At least they agreed on something, Hannah thought as she dipped a cloth in the water. 'I know what I'd do if I could get my hands on 'em.' She wrung out the cloth as if it was a scrawny neck.

She carried the bowl across to where Seth sat and set it down on the hearth beside him.

'Right,' she said, 'let's get you cleaned up. And I don't want to hear a word about it,' she added, as Seth opened his mouth to protest.

She thought Miss Sheridan might try to step in and take over, but to her surprise the nurse stood back and let her get on with cleaning Seth's wounds.

Hannah glanced at her out of the corner of her eye. Agnes was watching Seth, chewing her lip worriedly. When Seth flinched in pain, she seemed to flinch too.

Hannah couldn't get over the sight of Agnes, her shoulders squared and chin lifted, facing down that mob.

'It took a lot of guts to do what you did,' she said quietly. 'There in't many who would stand up to a load of angry pitmen.'

'I didn't stop to think about it,' Agnes looked at Hannah. 'But I'm glad you came along when you did.'

'I thought I'd best walk over to meet him. I had a feeling he might need some company after what happened to him yesterday.'

Hannah dabbed at the painfully swollen flesh around Seth's eye, the skin already blossoming purple. Lord, how she hated those men for what they had done. She wouldn't forget, either. Their faces were marked in her mind forever now.

She glanced up at Seth. He had gone very quiet, his face turned away from hers.

'You reckon he might have concussion?' she said to the nurse.

'It's possible. He did get a nasty blow to his head.'

'And what's the treatment for that, then?'

She saw the surprise on Agnes' face. Hannah was surprised at herself, if truth be told. But she had made a terrible mistake with Christopher, and she didn't want to take any chances. Even if it meant swallowing her pride and accepting that she might not always know best.

'It really depends how bad it is. If he loses consciousness or starts to vomit—'

'I in't got concussion,' Seth growled.

'We don't know that yet,' Agnes said. 'Here, let me check your eyes.'

She started towards him, but Seth jerked away from her.

'I'm telling you, I'm all right.' He gasped, his teeth clenched together in a hiss of pain.

'It looks as if he might have damaged his ribs,' Agnes said. 'I'll have to get them bandaged up.'

'Hannah can do it.'

'But—' Agnes Sheridan started to protest.

'I said no. If there's any nursing to be done, Hannah can do it.'

Hannah sat back on her heels, the damp cloth in her hand. Seth's face was turned away, but she could read his obstinate profile. Suddenly she understood.

'He's right,' she said to Agnes. 'I can manage.'

Agnes Sheridan looked from her to Seth and back again, her expression bemused. She opened her mouth to argue, then closed it again.

'Very well. If that's what you want,' she said.

But Agnes insisted on giving Hannah a clean bandage and instructions on how to apply it, and Hannah patiently resisted the urge to point out she was helping her mother strap up men's broken bones long before Agnes put on her smart nurse's uniform.

All the while, Agnes kept looking past Hannah's shoulder at Seth. But he refused to meet her eye, his moody gaze fixed stubbornly on his boots.

It wasn't until she was leaving that Agnes whispered, 'I don't understand . . . Did I do something to offend Mr Stanhope?' She looked so lost and bemused, Hannah almost felt sorry for her.

'You shamed him,' she said shortly. 'Earlier on, at the pit gates.'

Agnes frowned. 'I only tried to help him!'

'Exactly. You saw him when he was weak, and he won't be able to stand that.'

Hannah saw Agnes' frown deepen as she struggled to take in what she was hearing. 'But he lets you help him?'

'I'm family.' *And I don't matter to him*, a voice inside her head added silently.

'But I don't think any the less of him for what happened.'

'Nay, but he thinks less of himself. He's a proud man, Miss Sheridan.'

'Too proud for his own good, if you ask me,' Agnes said curtly.

'If you think that, then you don't understand Seth Stanhope.'

Agnes glanced back over Hannah's shoulder at him. 'No,' she sighed, a hint of sadness in her voice. 'I'm beginning to realise that.'

Hannah watched her cycling away, her head down. The nurse was gone, and Hannah knew this time she wouldn't

355

be back again. Miss Sheridan had managed to drive a wedge between herself and Seth, just as Hannah had always hoped she would.

Hannah knew she should have been elated, but she actually felt rather sorry.

Seth looked up as she went back inside. 'Has she gone?'

'Aye.' Hannah took one last look up the lane as she closed the door.

'Good. Best if she doesn't call any more.'

'She saved you from a beating, Seth.' Hannah had a sudden recollection of the young girl, facing down the crowd like an angry lioness.

'There was no need,' he said. 'Anyway, as I said, best if she doesn't call any more. We've no need of her.'

Hannah looked at his battered, stubborn face. The nurse was right: sometimes he was too proud for his own good.

Chapter Forty-Two

As everyone predicted, by the middle of September all the men of Bowden Main had returned to work.

Sir Edward Haverstock made one of his rare visits to the pit as they arrived for their first shift. He stood in the yard with James, rubbing his hands together with unconcealed glee, and watched them clocking on.

'Well, my boy. We won, didn't we?' he laughed, clapping James on the shoulder. 'I told you they'd have to come crawling back sooner or later. And on our terms, too.'

James held himself rigid, his arms clamped to his sides to stop himself from punching Sir Edward's smug face. He wished he didn't have to stand there and enjoy their defeat. The looks on the men's faces filled him with guilt. He wanted to crawl away and hide from the shame of it all.

And then he spotted Rob Chadwick sauntering across the yard towards him, that big knowing smirk on his face.

James stiffened, instantly wary, like an animal ready to fight.

'Hello, who's this?' Sir Edward said at his side. 'One of our men?'

'No, sir.'

It had been two weeks since Rob had come to his office. James had not seen or heard anything of him since that day, and he had begun to allow himself to think that the danger had passed. But now all his fears came flooding back at the sight of him.

Rob was standing in front of them now, that insolent grin still plastered all over his face.

'Good morning, Mr Shepherd,' he greeted him.

'What do you want, Chadwick?' James blurted out.

Rob paused for a moment, his smile widening. He was enjoying himself, James could tell.

'I came to ask, sir, if there was any work going?'

James stared at him. 'Here?' He was so shocked he could barely take in what he was hearing. 'You're asking for a job here, at the pit?'

'Aye, sir. I'm not needed on the farm now the harvest's done so I thought I'd ask here, since it looks like I'm going to be stopping on for a while.' He held James' gaze while he said it.

'You've worked at this pit before?' Sir Edward asked.

'Aye, sir. I was brought up to it. I worked at Bowden Main since I were fifteen years old.'

'Well, in that case—'

'No,' James said.

Sir Edward turned to face him. 'I beg your pardon?'

'There are no jobs going at Bowden Main. Not for the likes of this man.'

Sir Edward stared at him in astonishment. 'What are you talking about, Shepherd? Only yesterday you were telling me how short-handed we are, since so many of the men have left the village and found other work. And here we have an experienced pitman looking for work, and you want to turn him away? It makes no sense to me.'

'Nor me, sir.' Rob looked back at James boldly.

James found his voice. 'This man is a known trouble-maker, sir,' he said to Sir Edward. 'The last time he worked here . . . '

'The last time I worked here I were nobbut a lad,' Rob said. 'I'll admit I were a bit wild back in those days. But

I'm a grown man now, and I'm hoping to have a family to support soon.' He sent James a sly look. 'I'm ready to buckle down, for their sake.'

'There you are, then.' Sir Edward nodded, satisfied. 'You heard the man, Shepherd. Let's give him a trial.'

'But, sir—' James started to say. Sir Edward held up his hand.

'That is my final word on the subject,' he said.

'Thank you, sir.' Rob bowed his head, trying to look humble, although James could still see that insolent glint in his eye. 'I'm much obliged. I won't let you down, I promise.'

'See that you don't.' Sir Edward turned to address James. 'Take him up to the office and get him started, Shepherd.'

'Yes, sir,' James replied through tight lips.

'That's you told!' Rob laughed as he followed James up the wooden stairs to his office. 'Call thysen pit manager? We all know who really gives the orders round here, don't we? I can't say as I'd let the old man talk to me like that. But I suppose you're used to it, in't you, being his lackey?'

James closed the office door and turned on his tormentor. 'I thought I told you to leave Bowden and not come back?'

'And I thought I told *you* I weren't going anywhere without Carrie and my son?' Rob shot back. He looked around. 'Well? In't there some papers or other I've got to sign?'

James went to the filing cabinet and took out a form. 'Here,' he said, shoving it across the desk towards Rob. 'Fill this in. That is, if you can write?'

He smirked at the insult. 'Oh, aye, I can write.' He snatched the pen from the inkstand. 'You reckon you're better than I am, don't you? But let me tell you summat. For all your fancy education, it's still me Carrie wants.'

'Then why hasn't she left me?'

359

It was the hope James clung to in the dead of night when he lay awake, despairing. Every day when he returned from work, his heart was in his mouth, waiting to see if she was still there. And as time went by, he had started to allow himself to hope that Rob had been lying.

Rob's mouth tightened, his smile disappearing. 'Aye, well, happen she's too soft-hearted. She feels sorry for you. And I suppose she feels as if she owes you summat. After all, you have been bringing up another man's child all this time. But you must know how unhappy she is?'

James was silent. The truth was, things had been strained between them lately. He'd sensed Carrie had something on her mind, and several times had caught her watching him and known she was on the verge of saying something. But coward that he was, he had always managed to distract her, because he was so afraid of what he might hear.

Rob must have read his troubled expression. 'You see? You do know what I'm talking about, don't you?' He put down the pen. 'Anyway, the way I see it, we should sort this out honourably, man to man—'

James laughed. 'What do you know about honour?'

'I know I'd never cling on to a woman who didn't care for me!' Rob settled back in his chair. 'But either way, the truth will come out.'

James stared at him. 'What do you mean?'

'If you don't leave her, I'll make sure everyone knows Henry is my son.'

'You mean you'd shame Carrie?'

'Oh, Carrie and I can always leave the village, start a new life together if we must. It'll be you everyone will be pointing the finger at, you who have to live with the gossip and the humiliation. I don't suppose you'll be able to stand that, will you? You won't be able to hold your head up in

Bowden again.' Rob smiled nastily. 'It's your choice,' he said. 'Let her go like a real man, or hang on and see what happens.'

James thrust the piece of paper at him. 'You forgot to sign this.'

Rob picked up the pen and scrawled his name. 'You never know,' he laughed. 'The pit roof might fall on my head and that will be the end of me.'

James glared back at him. 'I could never be that lucky,' he muttered.

He sat at his desk, simmering with anger, long after Rob had gone. Out of the corner of his eye he could see his father glaring down at him. His mouth was curled, and he seemed to be sneering at his son's humiliation.

Suddenly James was a boy again, knocked flat on his back in the dust by another local lad, with his father standing over him.

You're too soft, that's your trouble.

Henry Chadwick would not stand to have his shame paraded around the village. His father would hit first, and hit hard.

It was a long, frustrating day. James tried to concentrate on the ground surveys he had commissioned for the sinking of the new shaft, but he was aware of trouble going on outside. Several times the men surfaced due to fire damp, and there were fights in the yard as they waited to go back underground. The mood at the pit was tense and unhappy, nothing like he had ever known.

Usually it would have been a relief to go home, but this time James returned to William Street with a heavy heart, knowing what was to come. By the end of this evening, one way or another, his life would not be the same.

His heart lurched into his mouth when he saw Carrie waiting at the gate. Even though he had been preparing himself for this moment all day, the reality of it caught him like a blow.

She saw him and started to run to him. As she drew closer, he could see she had been crying.

He wanted to run to her, but his feet were rooted to the ground. He could taste fear in his mouth.

'Oh, James!' She launched herself at him and he forgot himself, his arms going around her, holding her trembling body close to his. Her skin was soft against his cheek, her hair freshly washed with a fragrance of lemons. James breathed it in, knowing he would never smell it again.

'What is it, my love?' he murmured

Carrie pulled away from him, her blue eyes shimmering bright with tears. 'It's Father . . . ' she whispered.

Chapter Forty-Three

The whole village turned out to pay their respects to Eric Wardle.

The tiny Methodist chapel where he had often preached was filled to overflowing with friends and neighbours. Carrie could see their bowed heads as she walked slowly behind her father's coffin with her mother and sisters, baby Henry in her arms and James at her side.

It was a warm day, and the sun streamed in through the high windows. The perfect Indian summer day, Carrie thought. Her father would have been out on his allotment, soaking up the last rays of the sun before autumn came, planting lettuces for the following spring and some late turnips for their green tops. How he would have scolded them for wasting such a glorious day indoors.

Gertie, her youngest sister, was in floods of tears, but Carrie, Eliza and Hattie were all determined not to cry in front of everyone. All the same, Carrie was thankful for James' supportive arm around her. He was like a tower of strength beside her, holding her up when her legs started to buckle.

After the burial, they all made their way back to Coalpit Row, where her mother and sisters had prepared a spread. As was customary in the event of a miner's death, the Haverstocks had made a small contribution, but Eric Wardle had put aside some money of his own to pay for his funeral.

Carrie set Henry in his pram for a nap, then helped her

sisters arrange the sandwiches, sausage rolls and dainty cakes on plates, while her mother made a pot of tea.

Carrie was taking the damp tea towel from over a plate of sandwiches when she saw Rob outside the back door, smoking a cigarette in the lane and talking to a few of the other men.

Her heartbeat quickened in her chest. She hadn't seen him during the service, although she hadn't really been aware of anything in the chapel but the blur of many faces. She could only hope and pray he would behave himself. Surely even Rob Chadwick would have more respect than to cause trouble at her father's funeral?

Thankfully, he stayed away from her, and Carrie began to relax. But later, as she was speaking to the minister with James, she saw Rob approaching out of the corner of her eye.

Carrie felt James stiffen by her side.

'Carrie,' he greeted her, his voice sombre. He looked like a stranger in his ill-fitting suit. 'I'm sorry for your loss.'

She nodded, hardly trusting herself to speak.

'Your father was a good man. He was always very kind to me.'

Carrie thought about Rob, coming to visit when they were courting. Her father always treated him politely as a guest in his house, but Carrie remembered the strained smile on Eric's face when Rob showed off at the table, pulling faces and making her and her sisters laugh.

Eric Wardle certainly hadn't been particularly sorry when Rob left the village.

'Happen it's for the best, lass,' was all he had said. 'That lad's too restless for his own good.'

Carrie was too heartbroken to listen at the time, but now she understood the wisdom behind her father's words.

'He was kind to everyone,' she managed to say.

The silence lengthened. 'Have you heard, I'm working at the pit now?' Rob said.

Carrie looked at him sharply. 'Since when?'

'I started four days ago. In't that right, Mr Shepherd?'

James nodded without speaking. Carrie caught the look that passed between the men. Nausea rose in her throat.

'Excuse me.' She pushed past them, out of the door, across the lane to the earth closet. She barely had time to close the wooden door and fall to her knees before she was sick.

She stayed there for a long time, her face pressed against the damp, whitewashed brickwork with its blossoming patches of green-black mould. The hot, reeking air of the privy stirred her stomach again, but she couldn't bring herself to leave the sanctuary of the closet. For the moment, she was safe.

Finally she emerged, to find Miss Sheridan waiting for her, looking concerned.

'Gertie heard you and came to fetch me,' she said. 'Are you all right?'

'Yes, thank you.' Carrie forced a wan smile.

'Are you sure? You look rather peaky. You're not sickening for something?'

'Nay. It's just today . . . It's all been too much for me.'

'Of course.' Agnes Sheridan's brown eyes were full of sympathy. 'Would you like me to walk you home?'

'No, thank you. I ought to stay.' Carrie looked past her shoulder into the cottage. 'My mother needs me. I'll walk home with James later.'

'Oh, but your husband has already gone.'

'Gone?'

Agnes Sheridan nodded. 'I saw him leaving a short while ago. I'm sorry, I thought you knew. ' She blushed.

'No. No, I didn't.'

'He seemed in rather a hurry. Perhaps he'd had word of a problem at the pit?'

'I expect that'll be it.' But it was Rob's doing, Carrie was sure of it. She had seen the way they had looked at each other. Rob had probably insulted James.

But all the same, it wasn't like him to go off in a huff. It was her father's funeral, and her husband had abandoned her without a word of goodbye.

'Forgive me for asking, Mrs Shepherd, but is everything all right with you?' Agnes Sheridan was watching her carefully. 'I wouldn't usually pry, but since that conversation we had—'

'Yes. Yes, everything's fine,' Carrie replied absently, her gaze still fixed down the lane.

'So you told him?'

Carrie hesitated. 'No,' she admitted. 'No, I didn't. I've thought about it, but – it never seemed to be the right time.'

How could she ever find the words to say such a thing? She had tried, several times. Sometimes she lay awake in bed, going through it over and over in her mind, trying to think of the right words to say that wouldn't make him hate her.

But she had failed.

'I see.' Agnes Sheridan nodded. Carrie saw the reproach in her eyes. She doubted if the nurse would ever be so weak. But then, she would probably never be foolish enough to get herself in such a mess in the first place.

Carrie's mother didn't seem too troubled when she found out James had gone.

'I expect he's too upset,' Kathleen said. 'They were very fond of each other, you know. Your father used to say the lad hadn't had an easy time of it, with that bully Henry Shepherd.' She smiled weakly. 'Eric had a lot of time for James. He always used to look forward to his visits.'

Carrie frowned. 'What visits?'

'Didn't he tell you? James used to come and sit with your father some afternoons, after he was taken ill and couldn't get up and about. He would read to him, and they would talk. They'd go on for hours, the two of them.' She looked confused. 'I'm surprised James didn't mention it to you?'

'So am I,' Carrie said. She was beginning to wonder if she really understood her husband at all.

'But I suppose that's just like him, isn't it?' Kathleen Wardle said. 'Such a modest young man. Never one to show off or make a fuss about anything.'

'No.'

'Anyway, I must go and see what's keeping your sister,' her mother went on. 'I told her to go and make another pot of tea hours ago, and I still haven't seen a sign of it. People are getting parched.'

She bustled off. Carrie watched her go. Her mother was doing her best to keep busy, occupying herself by making sure everyone's cups were kept filled and there were enough sandwiches to go round. Carrie feared for what she would be like later, when the guests had gone home.

And then she saw something through the window that made her forget James, and her own grief and her mother's.

Rob Chadwick was sitting on the low wall by the coal shed, with little Henry in his lap.

He was singing him a song. Carrie could see him pulling faces as he bounced the baby up and down on his knee. There were people all around him, watching and smiling.

Carrie felt the blood drain to her feet, leaving her light-headed.

She pushed her way through the guests and rushed outside. Rob looked up at her, grinning.

'Look, here's your ma,' he said, turning the baby round to look at her. Henry gave her a toothy grin.

'Give him to me!' Carrie hurried towards them, holding out her hands, but Rob shifted the baby away from her.

'I was just keeping the little lad entertained. He was sitting up in his pram, wondering why he were missing out.' He jiggled the lad on his knee. 'He's a bright little thing, in't he? Handsome, too. Just like his father.'

Carrie glanced round at the other people listening. Rob was deliberately taunting her.

'Give him to me!'

Henry seemed to sense her tension. He burst into tears. Carrie made a grab for him, pulling him right out of Rob's arms.

'You had no right,' she muttered.

'I have every right,' he reminded her in a low voice.

Carrie glanced around her, then turned and walked off down the lane, rocking Henry in her arms to calm him.

She hadn't gone far when she heard Rob's footsteps behind her.

'Why are you following me?' she said, without looking round. 'Go back inside.'

'Why? Are you afraid your mester might see us? Oh, no, I forgot. He's gone, in't he?' Rob tutted softly. 'Fine husband he is, leaving you all by thysen at your father's funeral. I mean, what kind of a man does that?'

She sensed Rob approach, to stand close behind her. 'If it had been me, I wouldn't have left your side for a minute,' he said softly. 'When I saw you in that chapel, all I wanted was to take you in my arms and comfort you.'

His hands came down on her shoulders and Carrie jerked out of his grasp.

'Don't!' she snapped. 'Don't touch me.'

Rob stood, his hands in the air. 'I only wanted to make you feel better,' he said. 'What are you so worried about, Carrie? Everyone will know about us sooner or later.'

'Us?' Carrie glanced past him up the empty lane. She could hear voices coming from her parents' cottage and she longed to be there, in the safety of the crowd, with her mother and sisters. 'How many more times do I have to tell you, there is no us?'

Rob's confident smile faltered. 'You don't mean that,' he said. 'You're just upset over your father, that's all. Once you've had a chance to calm down—'

'I don't want to be with you,' Carrie interrupted him. 'I love James. I want to stay with him.'

'I told him about us.'

She stopped dead, staring at Rob. 'What do you mean?'

'Just what I said, I told him about you and me – and the bairn.'

He smiled at Henry and reached out to touch his hand, but Carrie pulled away.

'You – you didn't. You couldn't—'

'I had to do summat. I knew it would be better coming from you, but when you didn't say anything, I thought it must be down to me. So I went to see him in his office.'

'When? When did you go to see him?'

'A couple of weeks ago. Ask him thysen if you don't believe me.'

Carrie stared at him, trying to take it in. All that time and James had said nothing to her. Or perhaps he was waiting for her to say something?

She looked back at Rob. 'Why?' she whispered. 'Why would you try to ruin everything?'

Rob looked offended. 'What do you mean? I did it for you. I thought you'd be pleased.'

'Pleased?'

'I meant what I said when I told you I wanted us to be together.' He took a step towards her, his arms outstretched. 'I only want to look after you and our—'

369

'Don't!' Carrie clenched her teeth together to stop herself screaming out the word. 'Don't you dare call him your son. I swear, if you say it one more time I'll swing for you!'

He took a step towards her, entreating her. 'Carrie—'

'Don't touch me.' Carrie shrank away from him. 'How many more times do I have to tell you, I don't want you? I don't want to be with you and I never will!'

He blinked at her. 'I don't understand. I thought we—'

'No,' Carrie cut him off. 'You thought, Rob, not me. It's always been you. What you think, what you want. You're so busy making plans, you've never once listened to what I want.'

'But you love me?' He sounded so plaintive when he said it, for a moment she almost felt sorry for him.

'I don't,' she said, more calmly. 'I thought I did, once. But I was young and very foolish then. It wasn't until I met James that I realised what true love really is.'

Rob stared at her. He looked like a lost little boy. 'You don't mean that,' he whispered, but there was no conviction behind his words.

'I do, Rob. You must believe me.'

'And what about my son?'

She felt her anger rekindling. 'He isn't your son. James is the only father Henry's ever known, and ever will know.' If he'll still have me, she thought silently.

Rob straightened up, squaring his shoulders. 'I won't stand for it,' he declared.

'What will you do? You can't make me love you, Rob. Any more than I could make you love me once.'

He went on staring at her, but she could already see the defeat in his hazel eyes. 'What do you want me to do?' he asked.

'Go,' she said. 'Leave Bowden, and leave us alone.'

For a moment she thought he was going to give in.

Then his chin lifted. 'I in't going to give up,' he declared. 'I in't going to be cheated out of my—' He saw Carrie's face and stopped. 'This in't over,' he warned.

That was the difference between them, Carrie thought as she headed home later. Rob Chadwick couldn't believe that anyone couldn't love him, and James couldn't believe that anyone could.

But now all she could think about was finding him, and putting things right. If he was prepared to give her another chance, then she would gladly spend the rest of her life proving how much she loved him.

Her heart was pounding as she parked the pram outside the front door and let herself in.

'James?' Her voice echoed in the silence.

She heard a sound coming from the end of the passageway and started to move towards it, only to stop dead when she saw the maid emerging from the kitchen.

'Where is Mr Shepherd?' she asked.

'He's gone, ma'am.'

She saw the softness in the other woman's eyes. The maid made no secret of how much she despised Carrie, so for her to feel any kind of pity towards her . . .

Panic flooded through Carrie but she managed to keep herself calm. 'Gone? Gone where?'

'I don't know, ma'am. But he left you a note.' She took an envelope from her apron pocket and handed it to Carrie.

'Thank you.' It took every scrap of dignity she could muster not to fall on the letter and rip it open. Instead, she managed to give the maid instructions to look after the baby, and then took herself up to her room.

It was only then, sitting on the window seat with the curtain pulled across to shroud her from view, that she allowed herself to open the letter and read what James had to say.

Dear Carrie

By the time you read this, I will be gone. I think it's best for both of us if I move out for a while. I will spend the night in the colliery office, then find lodgings in Leeds while I consider what is best to be done.

You mustn't blame yourself, my love. It was my fault for trying to hold on to you for so long. But when I saw you with Rob Chadwick today, I suddenly realised where your heart belonged. But thank you for letting me share it for a short time.

You have made me so very happy. Now it is your turn.

With love,
James

The heartache she had fought so hard to keep at bay finally overcame her in a crashing wave. By the time the maid brought her a cup of tea half an hour later, Carrie lay sobbing on the bed, all thoughts of dignity long forgotten.

Chapter Forty-Four

That night the harsh clang of the calamity bell cut through Agnes' dreams, startling her awake.

She sat bolt upright, her heart racing at the sound. A sliver of moonlight crept through the crack in the curtains, slicing across the bare wooden floor.

She was fumbling into her dressing gown in the darkness when she heard the knock on the door, followed by the sound of Mrs Bannister's footsteps going down the stairs.

As Agnes went out on to the landing, she could hear voices below. She recognised the gruff tones of Sam Maskell, one of the overmen at the colliery.

'There's been an accident at t'pit. The doctor needs to come.'

'Dr Rutherford is away visiting his son in Leeds. We're not expecting him back until tomorrow afternoon.'

'Not here?' Sam stood on the doorstep, wringing his cap between his fists. 'So what's to do, then?'

'I'm sure I don't know,' Mrs Bannister said. 'I suppose you'll have to send for Dr Joseph in the next village.'

'But there in't time ... There are men trapped down there.' Agnes saw the despair on Sam Maskell's face.

'I'll come,' she said.

'You, miss?' Sam looked doubtful.

Mrs Bannister turned on her scornfully. 'And what could you do? You heard what Mr Maskell said, they need a doctor down there.'

'And he also said there wasn't time to send for one.'

Agnes already had her bag open, checking its contents. 'At least I can try to help while we wait for Dr Joseph to arrive.' She turned back to Sam, not waiting for an answer. 'I'll get dressed, then follow you down to the pit,' she said.

Sam glanced at Mrs Bannister, and Agnes could see him making up his mind.

'I'll tell 'em you're on your way,' he said.

A crowd had gathered at the pit gates, men and women, all waiting for news. This time Agnes was allowed to pass through them and in through the gates. The yard was busy, with lamps blazing and men going back and forth. Over by the cage, she could see the silhouetted figures of the rescue team, preparing to go down below ground.

James Shepherd strode across the yard to meet her.

'Sam has explained about the doctor's absence. Thank you for coming, Miss Sheridan.' He looked dishevelled, his shirt rumpled and his tie missing.

'I'm glad to be of help. What's happening?'

'It's bad.' James' face was grim. 'The sick room wasn't big enough to take all the injured men, so we've moved them to one of the workshops. Follow me.'

The bright light of the workshop hurt Agnes' eyes after the darkness outside. The machinery had been pushed aside to make room for lines of chairs where the injured pitmen slumped, nursing their various injuries.

Agnes surveyed the rows of men. Blood dripped from gashed heads and hands, limbs were held at unnatural angles. On the seat nearest to her, she glimpsed the bloodied nub of broken bone that had pierced through the flesh of the man's arm.

She took a deep breath and forced herself to stay calm. 'Is this all of them?' she asked James.

He shook his head. 'I've got a man counting the checks to see who's missing, but we know there are at least six others not accounted for. The rescue party are on their way back down there now to look for them.'

James looked worn out, Agnes thought. His face was drawn and grey with exhaustion.

She looked back at the rows of men, counting them in her head. Then she made up her mind and turned to a frightened-looking boy, nursing an injured hand close by her.

'Are you well enough to walk?'

'Aye, miss.'

'Good. Then go down to the gates and see if Miss Arkwright is there. Tell her I need her help.'

'Aye, miss.'

He touched his cap with his good hand and hurried off.

'Hannah Arkwright?' James gave her a quizzical frown.

'I don't have any choice,' Agnes said. 'I can't leave men to sit in agony while they wait for me to tend to them.'

She washed her hands, then filled another bowl with water to wash the men's wounds. She was setting out all the disinfectants and swabs and dressings she needed when the door opened and Hannah appeared, wrapped in her old overcoat. Agnes was glad to see she carried her bag with her.

She looked around at the men, then at Agnes. 'You sent for me?' There was a hint of doubt in her voice.

'I need your help,' Agnes said. 'All these men have to be treated, and I can't manage by myself.'

She tensed, waiting for Hannah to make a smart reply. The other woman looked around the room again, her gaze travelling slowly over the rows of faces.

'Tell me what needs to be done,' she said shortly.

'Thank you.' Agnes tried not to wince when Hannah set down her dirty old carpet bag on the table beside the nurse's leather Gladstone. 'There are wounds to be cleaned and dressed, and each man needs to be checked for fractures and concussion. I thought perhaps you could start at one end and I'll start at the other?'

'And never the twain shall meet, eh?' Hannah gave the slightest of smiles.

They worked in silence together, speaking only to the men they were treating. Neither of them said a word, nor even looked at each other. They worked steadily and methodically, an oasis of calm while all around them chaos raged.

Agnes could hear the shouts of the men in the yard as they went back and forth. From what she could gather by talking to the injured men, there had been a major collapse in the mine. The rippers had been working as usual on the face overnight, blasting out the rock to expose the coal seam for the hewers to start on in the morning. But either the roof hadn't been propped enough, or they had not accurately predicted the weight of the ground above, and the newly exposed seam had caved in.

Most of the men had managed to claw their way out to the air road, the main tunnel that provided the ventilation for the shaft, but the men working on the furthest end of the seam had been cut off.

It was those men the rescue team had gone back to find. But it was a risky business as the rest of the roof could go at any time.

'Seth is one of the rescue men.'

Hannah murmured the words so quietly, Agnes wasn't sure she had heard her at first. She looked round at the woman who now stood beside her. Hannah's broad, plain face gave nothing away as she wound a bandage carefully around a man's fractured arm. But Agnes could see the fear in her black eyes.

Agnes' heart hitched in her chest. Seth was down there.

She looked around desperately. 'Is there any sign of Dr Joseph yet?' she called out.

'We've sent a lad to Overthorpe to find him,' Sam Maskell replied. 'But we've had no word back as yet. Have we, Mr Shepherd?'

But James Shepherd wasn't listening. He was staring down at a list one of the men had given him. Agnes saw what little colour he had drain from his face and knew straight away it was bad news.

'Mr Shepherd?' she prompted him.

He looked up sharply, as if seeing her for the first time. Agnes went over to him. 'What is it?' she asked. 'What's happened?'

He lowered the piece of paper, his expression dazed. 'We've had word back from the rescue team. They've managed to get through to the men who were trapped, but they're badly injured.'

Agnes swallowed past the sudden dryness in her throat. 'How bad? Can they bring them up?'

'They can move a couple of them, but at least one needs a stretcher ... ' He looked down again at the piece of paper in his hand. Agnes caught sight of six scribbled names. The men who were trapped, she guessed.

She made up her mind. 'I'm going down there,' she said.

Everyone stared at her. She could feel Hannah's intense gaze boring into her back.

'Nay,' Sam Maskell said. 'It's the doctor's job.'

'Yes, but the doctor isn't here, is he? And we don't know when he'll arrive.' Agnes appealed to James Shepherd. 'If those men are too injured to be moved, I might be able to help them, or at least ease their pain.'

James looked around the room. 'But what about these men?'

'We've already treated most of them. Hannah can look after the rest, can't you?'

Hannah gave a curt nod. 'Aye,' she said.

'You can't allow it, sir,' Sam Maskell was saying. 'It's too dangerous—'

'She's right,' James cut him off. 'She might be able to do something for those men.'

'But how's she going to get down there on her own? Once she gets to the pit bottom, she'll be lost.'

'I'll go with her.'

'You, sir?' Agnes heard the doubt in the overman's voice. 'Begging your pardon, Mr Shepherd, but you in't familiar with them tunnels . . . '

'Of course I am. I study maps of them all the time.'

Agnes could see the pained look on Sam Maskell's face as he struggled to find the right words. 'But that in't the same as seeing 'em every day, sir. And if you'll excuse me for saying it, you know what you're like when it comes to being underground.'

'Nevertheless, I'm going,' James said firmly. 'These are my men, and it's my duty to make sure they're safe.' He turned back to Agnes. 'We could take a couple of stretchers down with us, to bring them back to the surface.'

But even as he spoke, Agnes could see the apprehension written on his face.

She gathered up her bag and gave Hannah some instructions for treating the men. The other woman remained sullenly silent, and Agnes wasn't sure if she was even listening. But as she left, she felt Hannah's hand on her arm, her grip as strong as a man's.

'Bring him back safe, won't you?' she murmured.

There was no need to ask who she meant. Agnes looked into her dark eyes, mute with appeal. I'll do my best,' she promised.

378

Chapter Forty-Five

Agnes' courage almost failed her as she stepped into the cage with James. Sam Maskell pulled the door across, and it clanged shut with a deafening finality. The next second the cage jolted into life and they were plummeting downwards, the cold air rushing up, whistling past her ears.

She glanced at James. She could feel the waves of fear emanating from him. He clung to the stretchers they had brought with them, his knuckles white. In spite of the cold, his brow gleamed with perspiration.

After what seemed like an endless time, they finally bumped to the ground. James yanked at the door with shaking hands, rattling it across, and they stepped out into the bowels of hell.

The air was hot, dense with so much dust and smoke Agnes could not see more than a few inches in front of her. From somewhere out of the darkness came the terrified screams of the pit ponies.

Agnes stood for a moment, too afraid to move, until she heard James' voice close beside her.

'This way. We'll carry the stretchers between us, if you can manage them?' They plunged into the smoky gloom, each holding one end of the stacked stretchers. The lamp James held in his other hand barely pierced the gloom.

Water splashed around Agnes' ankles, soaking her shoes. Yet more dripped from the roof on to her head, running down her face. She could hear scurrying sounds in the darkness.

'Listen. Even the rats are leaving,' James said grimly.

On they went, until the cage was far behind them, lost in a warren of tunnels which seemed to get narrower and narrower, closing in on all sides. Above their heads, the roof creaked and groaned.

Agnes remembered James' warning that it could all come down at any time, and gripped her end of the stretchers, fear clawing at her throat. If she lost him now, she knew she would never find her way back.

'Watch your head, the tunnel gets quite low here. But it should widen out again soon.' James was doing his best not to show his fear, but Agnes could hear the quiver in his voice.

Finally, as James had promised, the tunnel opened out and Agnes felt a rush of fresh, cold air.

'The air road,' James said, sounding relieved. 'We should be able to find the others from here.'

'I think I can hear them . . . ' Agnes stopped, cocking her head in the darkness. From somewhere further up the tunnel she could just make out the murmur of men's voices.

They followed the sound down the air road for a while and then turned down another short stump of tunnel.

'Hello?' James called out, swinging his lamp high.

'Not so loud! D'you want to kill us all?' Seth's voice growled back out of the darkness.

They found the men hunched at the end of the tunnel, amid a tumble of fallen rocks and boulders and broken pit props.

The first thing Agnes saw was Seth, crouched beside a man who lay shuddering on the ground. As her eyes grew used to the dusty air, she saw the man's legs were an ugly mass of blood and bone and mangled flesh. Shock snatched the breath from her throat, and it was all she could do not to recoil.

Seth looked up, his expression changing when he saw Agnes.

'What's she doing here?' he said.

Agnes ignored him. She forced herself forward to examine the injured man. He was shuddering and twitching like a puppet.

Seth moved aside reluctantly to let her attend to him. 'Been doing that ever since we got here,' he said.

'Shock,' Agnes said. 'We need to keep him warm.' She dropped her bag on the ground and shrugged off her coat to drape over him. Seth immediately took his off too and handed it to her.

Agnes felt for the man's pulse, his hand cold and clammy in hers. It fluttered as lightly as a trapped butterfly under her fingers.

'Reckon he's beyond help,' Seth muttered. He still bore the scars of his beating, purple bruises around his eyes and a swollen lip.

Agnes looked down at the man. He had already lost so much blood, she could almost see the life draining out of him. 'At least I can give him something for the pain,' she said.

'Where's the rest of the rescue team?' James asked, looking round.

'Three of them have gone up the drift to take the other injured men to safety,' Seth said. 'We reckoned it were too dangerous to take the cage up to the surface again. The vibrations could bring down more of this place.'

'We came down in the cage.'

'Aye, I know. We felt it.' He looked grim. 'I said I'd stay behind with these two. It's a long walk up the drift, and we didn't reckon they'd make it. One's gone already.' He glanced to the far corner of the tunnel, where Agnes could make out a figure lying on the ground, covered in a make-shift shroud of tarpaulin.

381

'Who is it?' James' voice was flat.

'Reg Willis.'

Agnes stopped, her hands fumbling with the hypodermic needle she was trying to put together in the dark. She had a sudden picture of the day she first arrived in Bowden, and little Reg Willis sitting behind the table at the Miners' Welfare Committee in his stiff, uncomfortable collar.

She was suddenly aware Seth was watching her keenly. She pulled herself together and finished giving the injection.

'How many men did they take up to the surface?' James asked.

Seth frowned at the question. 'Three, I think. Aye, there were three.'

'And what happened to the other man?'

'What other man?'

'I had the checks counted. There were six men down here. With these two, and the three that have gone up to the surface, that only makes five.'

Seth looked around. 'You must have got it wrong. We searched everywhere.'

'What about the tailgate?'

Seth shook his head. 'That were the first to come down. If he were down there I doubt if there's much left of him by now.'

'What were the names of the men who were taken up to the surface?' James demanded.

Seth's frown deepened. 'Geoffrey Frisk, I think. Aye, and his brother Percy . . . '

'What about Rob Chadwick? Was he one of them?'

Agnes looked up sharply at the name.

'Nay, I've not seen him.' Seth looked from James to the far end of the tunnel. 'Why, do you think—'

'I don't know,' James said. 'But I'm going to find out.'

He started back towards the air road, but Seth stopped him.

'It's too dangerous,' he said. 'There's nobbut a couple of props holding it up, and they could give at any minute.'

'I need to find him,' James insisted.

'Aye, we will. When the others get back.'

'But it might be too late by then!'

'I daresay it's already too late.' Seth's voice was sombre.

For a moment James looked as if he might argue. Then his shoulders slumped. He sat down on a rock a short distance away, hidden in the shadows, his head in his hands.

Agnes turned her attention back to the man on the ground. He had lapsed into unconsciousness, his chest rising and falling as his breath came in quick, shallow gasps.

'How is he?' Seth asked behind her.

'It's not good.' Agnes forced herself to think, pressing her hands to her temples. 'If there was some way I could raise his hips above his head, I might be able to keep the blood flow going ... '

'What about these rocks? We could pile them up, make a bit of a platform. Would that work?'

'It might.' She held up the lamp while Seth searched around, groping in the gloom. He found some loose chunks of rock and Agnes set down the lamp beside the man's head and together she and Seth piled up the rocks, forming them into a crude plinth.

Seth sat back, breathing hard. 'Now what?'

'Now we have to lift him on to it.' Steeling herself, Agnes slid her arms under the man's hips and tried to move him towards it. He was a dead weight in her arms and she could feel the muscles in her back straining as she struggled to lift him. She tried again but her arms slipped and she found herself holding on to the bloody, mangled pulp of his upper thighs.

'Do you think it will help?' Seth asked.

'I don't know,' Agnes admitted. 'But I can't think of anything else to do.' She wiped her forehead, and felt sticky blood smear from her sleeve across her brow.

They sat in silence for a moment. Then Seth said, 'I never thanked you – for what you did for our Christopher.'

Agnes stared at him, taken aback. It was the last thing she had been expecting. 'How is he?'

'They reckon he'll make it. But he could have died. Another few hours . . . ' Seth's voice trailed off.

'I know.' As she had thought, Christopher's appendix had been on the point of bursting when the operation took place. 'But he's having the treatment he needs now, and that's the main thing.'

'I don't think I could have coped with losing someone else.' Seth's voice was bleak in the darkness.

'You mustn't think like that,' Agnes said. 'Christopher will recover. He's a strong young man.'

'Aye. You were right about summat else, too,' Seth said after a brief silence. 'I haven't been a good father to those bairns.'

'I'm sure that's not true.'

'Yes it is, and you know it. Haven't you taken me to task about it often enough over the past few months? But I never listened to you. I told mysen you were interfering, just like I told mysen I was doing my best for them by going to work every day and keeping a roof over their heads.' He shook his head. 'But I wasn't, and that's the truth. I didn't take care of them. I just gave up and let Hannah do it all. And this is what happened.'

'You couldn't have stopped Christopher from falling ill,' Agnes said, but Seth hardly seemed to be listening.

384

'I knew it was wrong,' he said. 'I knew it wasn't what their mother would have wanted, either. But the fact is I couldn't face being a father to them. So I stayed out and kept mysen busy with the union and the Welfare Committee and everything else, and acted like I was doing something important, all because I couldn't face going home knowing she weren't there.'

Agnes stared at his shadowy profile. It was as if the darkness had allowed him to reveal his deepest fears.

'Grief does strange things to people,' she said.

'Aye, and I let mine take me over,' Seth said. 'I was so wrapped up in how I felt, it never occurred to me that the bairns were missing their mother too. They needed me, and I let them down. And I don't think I'll ever forgive mysen for that.'

He slumped forward, his grief so raw Agnes felt helpless in the face of it. Without thinking she reached for his hand.

'It isn't too late to put things right,' she said. 'You still have a family. Billy, Elsie, Christopher – they still need you.'

'You're right,' he said. 'If we get out of here, things are going to be different. I'm going to be different, I can tell you that.'

'You mean, when we get out of here?' Agnes said.

Seth was silent a moment too long. 'Aye,' he said quietly.

Agnes was suddenly aware of his rough, callused hand holding hers. How did that happen? she wondered. She was about to pull away but then realised how much she needed the reassurance of his fingers curled around hers.

Then she remembered James, sitting in the darkness. He must be utterly terrified, poor man. If anyone needed reassurance, he did.

'Are you all right, Mr Shepherd?' she called softly. There was no reply. 'Mr Shepherd? James?'

Seth's hand slipped from hers. 'Mr Shepherd?' They were both silent, listening. All Agnes could hear was the steady plop of water dripping down.

'Where is he?' she whispered. She turned to Seth in the darkness. 'You don't think – ?'

'I think the damn' fool's gone off on his own to look for Rob Chadwick.' Seth muttered a curse under his breath and shifted beside her. 'I'd best go and find him.'

'I'll come with you.'

'Nay,' Seth said. 'You stay here and look after him.' He nodded towards the man on the ground. 'The others should be back soon, and they can take him by stretcher to the surface.'

'But I might be able to help.'

'Nay, I said!' Seth turned on her, and she saw the glint of fear in his eyes. 'If that roof goes, I don't want to have to pull your body out as well.'

They were both silent for a moment, staring at each other, making out each other's faces in the gloom.

'Be careful,' Agnes pleaded.

A shadow of a smile crossed his face. 'Aye. And you. Sit tight until the rescue party comes back.'

Agnes listened to him clawing his way slowly through the darkness, clambering over fallen rocks, coughing in the dust, until the sound faded away and she was quite alone. In a distant part of the pit, the ponies were still whinnying in fear, sensing danger. Agnes prayed they would be safe.

She prayed they would all be safe.

She turned her attention back to the man on the ground. He was barely breathing now, in spite of her efforts.

Agnes was reaching into her bag to find a cloth to wipe his face when she heard a distant rumble of thunder from somewhere above her.

She snatched up the lamp and looked about her, but the sound had faded away, replaced by the pitter-patter of what sounded like rain falling around her.

Agnes put her hand up to her hair, expecting it to be wet, but it was still dry. Puzzled, she looked up, and caught a face full of dust and tiny fragments of pebbles showering down from the ceiling.

There was another rumble, and an ominous cracking sound above her.

'Seth!' She screamed out his name without thinking as a rumbling tide of rocks began to fall. Agnes dived for cover, her hands over her head, while the world began to crumble around her.

Chapter Forty-Six

Carrie went down to the pit as soon as she heard the bell. Even though she had no reason to fear for her own loved ones any more, the sound of the calamity bell always woke up something inside her. She dressed quickly, roused the maid and told her to take care of the baby, and then hurried down to gather with the other women.

It was only when she saw them all standing at the gates anxiously waiting for news that she realised why she had come. In times of crisis like this, Bowden became one family, sharing each other's pain and fear.

She looked for her own mother and sisters, but there was no sign of them. Carrie wasn't surprised. Her poor grief-stricken mother was probably too exhausted to cope with anyone else's heartache today. She hoped Eliza, Hattie and Gertie were taking proper care of her.

Then Carrie spotted her friend Nancy, flanked by her mother and Ruth Chadwick. As Carrie pushed her way through the crowd, she could see the two older women had hold of Nancy's arms, propping her up on either side.

Fear seized her. Oh, God, not Archie? They had been married such a short time.

She hurried towards them, calling out Nancy's name. Her friend looked up, saw her and burst into tears.

'Oh, Carrie!' Nancy fell into her arms, sobbing. 'What am I going to do?'

Carrie consoled her, stroking her soft hair. 'Shhh now. Don't take on, Nancy.'

'But it's been so long, and we've had no news.'

'He'll be safe, don't you worry.' Over her friend's shoulder Carrie caught a glimpse of Ruth's tense face. Jinny stood with her mother, looking after the other children.

'They should never have put him on the night shift,' Nancy wept. 'He's always hated it. He says he never likes to leave me – oh, Carrie, I can't lose him. Not now!'

'She's just found out she's expecting,' Mrs Morris explained to Carrie, with a worried glance at her daughter. 'You need to calm down, Nancy lass. This in't doing that bairn any good.'

Carrie looked at the woman's taut face. Mrs Morris, like Ruth Chadwick, had been through too much in her life to let bad news overwhelm her. The pitmen's women had a tough, practical philosophy. Whatever life landed you with, you just had to get on with it and muddle along as best you could.

But there was nothing tough or practical about Nancy. Her emotions consumed her, good and bad. She was either singing or sobbing, as her mother would say.

And now her heart was breaking. Carrie felt utterly helpless in the face of Nancy's storm of grief. All she could do was go on holding her, trying to comfort her.

'Shhh, love. Your mum's right, you'll do thysen no good.' She rubbed Nancy's heaving back. 'Archie will come back to you, you'll see. The Lord won't take him away from you, not now ... '

Nancy pulled away from her sharply. Her pretty features were so red and puffy from crying, Carrie barely recognised her. 'The Lord took Harry Kettle away while Ellen was expecting!' she snapped. The next moment her face crumpled and she was crying again. 'Archie might never see his baby, just like Harry.'

Carrie glanced at Ruth's stoical expression. With Nancy's

grief so all-consuming, it was easy to forget the other poor woman was waiting for her son.

Then Ruth spoke. 'Rob is down there too,' she said quietly.

Carrie looked back over her shoulder, towards the pit, trying to take in what she was hearing.

Rob Chadwick was lost underground.

She braced herself, waiting for the pain to tear at her heart, just as it tore at Nancy's. But nothing came.

She was worried for Rob, just as she was concerned for Archie and all the other men. She hoped and prayed for their safe return. But more than that, there was nothing. Certainly none of the grief and despair that were ripping Nancy apart.

'Archie will come back,' Carrie murmured, turning back to comfort her friend. 'They all will.'

'Look!' Jinny Chadwick was pointing towards the gate, her face lit up with excitement. They all swung round to look at the figure limping across the yard towards them.

'It's my son.' Ruth's words were faint, as if she couldn't quite believe them enough to say them out loud. 'It's my Archie.'

'Archie!' Nancy screamed out. She broke away from Carrie and pushed her way to the gates, waving madly.

'Look at her,' Mrs Morris said, shaking her head. 'I reckon she'll climb them gates if they don't open them soon.'

The gates opened and Nancy launched herself into Archie's arms, nearly knocking him off his feet. Carrie felt a pang as she watched them embracing, holding on to each other fiercely, as if they never wanted to let go again.

She thought about James and what she had lost, and a desperate yearning went through her.

By the time Nancy returned, leading Archie through

the crowd by the hand, Carrie had managed to put on a brave face. Her friend looked so radiantly happy, it was impossible not to smile.

Archie was smiling too, but his eyes were troubled as he explained what had happened. The roof had collapsed on them, shutting off part of the seam and burying some of the miners under rubble. Carrie shuddered as he described how they had dug themselves and each other out, clawing away the rocks. Then they had tried to find their way out, some of the injured men crawling on their hands and knees, until they were met by the first of the rescue party.

'And what about Rob?' Ruth Chadwick asked.

Archie's face grew sombre. 'I don't know,' he said. 'I were working on the maingate, and he was down t'other end from me. The second rescue party were on their way down when I came up, so I daresay they'll find him . . . ' He looked at Carrie. 'Your mester's gone down with 'em, and that nurse.'

Carrie stared back at him, bemused. 'But – you must have got it wrong.' She shook her head. 'James hates the pit, he would never go down there.'

'I heard them talking, while I were waiting in the workroom to get my leg seen to. Mr Maskell tried to tell him not to, but Mr Shepherd were most insistent he should go.'

'He wouldn't do that. He wouldn't . . . ' Carrie stared past Archie into the pit yard. Pools of lamplight illuminated figures going back and forth.

He wouldn't go down there. He was too afraid. Unless . . .

Unless he thought he was doing it for her.

'He'll be all right, Carrie.' She felt Nancy's hand on her shoulder. Now it was her turn to be the comforter. 'He won't be in any danger. He's the pit manager,' she added.

Carrie stared at her blankly. What was she talking about? As if being the manager would somehow shield James from danger! Would his smart suit save him from a crumbling roof and falling rocks?

She wanted to shake Nancy, shout at her for being so stupid. But then she saw her friend's kind, open face and realised she was only trying to help, as Carrie had just done for her.

'Carrie?'

She turned around, her heart lifting with relief at the sight of her mother and sisters.

'What are you doing here?'

Kathleen Wardle frowned at the question. 'Where else would we be? We can't stop at home at a time like this.'

Carrie fought the urge to hug her mother. She looked more frail than Carrie had ever seen her, and some of her indomitable spirit had died with her husband. But at least she was here.

'James is down with the injured men,' Carrie blurted out.

Her mother's face creased in a frown. 'Why?'

'I don't know.' But it was a lie. Carrie knew very well what had driven her husband to put his life in danger.

And if he died, it would be her fault.

'I'm going to find out what's going on,' Eliza said, slipping away from them into the crowd.

Kathleen Wardle laid her hand on Carrie's arm. 'It will be all right,' she said.

'I know.' Carrie smiled back. But she didn't mean it, any more than her mother meant what she had said.

Eliza returned a few minutes later with news that more injured men were being brought up to the surface through the drift mine, but at least one had already died.

Panic seized her like a fist in her chest, twisting her heart. Her mother asked the question that she daren't.

'Who is it?'

'Reg Willis.'

'Oh, no, poor Reg. And poor Ida.'

Carrie was silent, hating herself for the relief she felt. Somewhere in the crowd, Ida Willis' world had collapsed around her. She thought about their daughter, her friend Betty, always laughing and smiling behind her counter at the Co-op. The poor girl would be devastated.

They stood for a long time, waiting for more news, but none came.

'You should go home and rest,' her mother said. 'You're doing thysen no good standing here.'

Carrie shook her head. 'You can go, if you like. I'm stopping here.'

'I'll stay with her,' Eliza said.

'And me.' Hattie turned to their youngest sister. 'Gert, you go home with Mother. We'll stay with our Carrie.'

'Aye.' Kathleen Wardle nodded. 'Come on, Gertie. Look after her, won't you?' she said to her daughters.

Carrie was grateful to her sisters for rallying round her as the long hours of the night stretched on. They found a spot close to the pit gates, and spread out their coats to sit on. They huddled together against the chill of the night and for a while they talked, making conversation about nothing, until Eliza and Hattie both drifted off to sleep, one on either side of Carrie, their heads lolling on her shoulders.

But Carrie stayed awake, keeping a lonely vigil, her gaze fixed on the yard. Every time there was a movement at the pit head she jerked upright to look.

Gradually, more men emerged from the workshop, nursing bandaged wounds, all with a story to tell. Carrie watched as they greeted their loved ones, so joyful to see each other again. Then they headed home, their arms around each other, and the other people at the gates huddled closer, watching and waiting for news.

And all the time, the rumours kept circulating. There

had been another rock fall, more men were trapped, one was dead and then he wasn't . . .

Gradually, the sky turned an opaque indigo colour, heralding dawn. Thin threads of pink light had begun to appear on the horizon when Eliza stirred.

'What time is it?' She stretched and yawned.

'I don't know.' Carrie had stopped counting the hours a long time ago.

Eliza looked around. 'Where is everyone?'

'They all went home.' Now they were alone, sitting on the cobbles by the pit gates. The last person to emerge had been Hannah Arkwright. She had come through the gates shortly before dawn, nodded to Carrie and headed off down the lane.

'Is there any news?'

'Not yet.'

Hattie woke up shivering. 'I'm cold.'

'Perhaps we should go home?' Eliza ventured.

Carrie shook her head. 'I in't going anywhere.'

'But Carrie—'

'I said, I in't going!' Carrie turned on her. 'Not until I've seen him with my own eyes.'

She caught the worried glance that passed between Eliza and Hattie. 'You go, if you want,' she said, more gently. 'But I can't leave, not now.'

Footsteps approached, coming up the cobbled lane from the rows. Carrie looked round to see Hannah Arkwright marching up the lane, huddled in her old overcoat, a flask in her hands.

She approached them. 'I thought you might be in need of this?'

Carrie stared dumbly at the flask she held out to her, too befuddled by weariness to understand what was being said to her.

'It's tea,' Hannah said shortly. 'Don't worry, I in't trying to poison thee.'

'Thank you.' Carrie took the flask from her. 'I'm very grateful.'

Hannah shrugged. She looked embarrassed by her own kind gesture. 'It's only tea.'

Eliza took the flask from Carrie and poured the tea for her. Carrie wrapped her hands around the cup, feeling the warmth seeping into her chilly fingers.

'No news, then?' Hannah nodded grimly towards the gates.

'Nay.'

The woman hesitated. 'Seth's down there,' she said. 'And t'nurse. And your mester.' She looked sideways at Carrie. 'They went to help another one who was trapped further down the seam, but the roof caved in and blocked the way back out. They're down there clearing the way now, trying to get to them.'

She didn't attempt to console Carrie, who was oddly grateful for that. She was tired of listening to people telling her that everything would be all right, and that they would get everyone out safely. Carrie knew they were only trying to be kind, but she didn't need false hope.

But Hannah knew the truth. It was written there, in her bleak expression. She knew as well as Carrie did that the longer they were down there, the less chance there would be of anyone coming out of the pit alive.

And so she and Hannah stood, side by side in silence at the gates, and watched. Carrie felt reassured by the other woman's tall, solid presence beside her. Hannah was an odd one to be sure, but somewhere inside her she had a heart.

And her heart was breaking, just as Carrie's was.

Dawn light flooded the sky, flushing the yard with a soft pinkish-purple colour.

'Why don't you go home?' Carrie said, turning to Hattie, who leaned against the fence, her eyes half closed, drooping with weariness. 'You should be in bed, not—'

'There's someone coming out,' Eliza interrupted, her gaze fixed beyond Carrie towards the pit head. 'I can see a stretcher, look. And there's more. One, two, three . . . '

Carrie and Hannah both swung round. Sure enough, men were emerging, carrying stretchers between them.

'Who is it?' Carrie heard Eliza saying. Her voice seemed to be coming from a long way away, growing fainter every minute. 'I can't make them out from here.'

'Nor me,' Hannah said.

'I think the second one's a woman, but I can't see James.'

The last stretcher appeared, shrouded in a tarpaulin canvas. The sight of it took away what was left of Carrie's strength, and her legs crumpled from under her.

'Carrie!' she heard her sister scream. The last thing she remembered was Hannah's strong arms around her as she sank to the floor.

Chapter Forty-Seven

Everyone reckoned Seth Stanhope should have died at the bottom of the pit.

The rocks that rained down should have shattered his bones and crushed him, just as they had poor Reg Willis and John Porter. But instead he had escaped with nothing more serious than a dislocated shoulder.

'He must have the luck of the devil,' they said.

And perhaps he had. Hannah had invoked every spell and incantation her mother had ever taught her as she kept vigil during that long, lonely night.

She was still keeping vigil now as she sat at his bedside in the cottage, watching him sleep. His poor, battered face was more bruised from the beating he had received earlier than it was from the rock fall.

At least the accident at the pit had put a stop to all that nonsense. All morning the other men had been calling at the cottage to see how Seth was and offer their thanks for what he had done. Suddenly he was a hero again in their eyes.

Hannah hadn't allowed them over the doorstep, of course. She wasn't touched by their humbleness or their contrition. Seth might be willing to forgive and forget in time, but she knew she never would.

He stirred restlessly in his sleep, his lips moving. Hannah watched him, drinking in every detail of his face: his strong jaw, the shape of his mouth, the delicate fringe of his eyelashes, the way his hair fell across his brow.

Without thinking, she put her hand out and touched his bare shoulder. His skin was surprisingly soft, compared to the hard, unyielding muscle beneath.

'What . . . ?' He jerked at her touch, struggling to sit up before he was fully awake.

Hannah snatched her hand away. 'It's only me, Seth.' He turned sharply to look at her, and she saw the remembered fear in his grey eyes and knew that for a moment he was back there, lost in the darkness and the swirl of choking dust.

Then the fight seemed to go out of him and he settled back against the pillows.

A stray lock of hair fell into his eyes. Hannah fought the urge to reach out and push it back.

'How are you feeling?' she asked.

'Like I've been put through a mangle.' He winced in pain as he shifted his weight against the pillow.

'Here, let me.' Hannah reached over and adjusted the pillow for him. 'You had quite a jolt. It's bound to be painful.'

Seth looked past her towards the door. 'Where are the children?'

'They're at school. Where else would they be at two o'clock in the afternoon?'

'Two o'clock?' He frowned. 'Surely I've not been asleep all this time?'

'Aye, and I'm not surprised. You were exhausted.'

'I was sure I was awake.' Seth's eyes fluttered closed again. 'I must have been dreaming.'

'You were. And talking in your sleep, too.'

His eyes flashed open. 'Was I? What did I say?'

'I don't know, I couldn't make it out,' she lied. She didn't want to tell him he had been crying out Agnes' name.

He was quiet for a long time, and Hannah could see him steeling himself, preparing to ask the question.

'How are the others? John Porter? Did he—'

Hannah shook her head. 'Dead before they got him to the hospital, poor lad. And Reg Willis, too. But Rob Chadwick's alive, thanks to you and Mr Shepherd. You were heroes, the pair of you.'

'Fools, more like,' Seth said grimly. He looked at Hannah. 'How is he – Mr Shepherd, I mean? He were right in front of me when the rocks came down. He took the worst of it.'

'He's in hospital.' Hannah lowered her gaze, thinking of poor Carrie Shepherd, shivering at the pit gates all night. 'But as to what will happen to him – I don't know.'

Seth nodded, his face sombre. Once again, Hannah knew he was reliving those last dreadful moments in the pit, when he thought his life was going to end.

Then he said, 'What about the nurse? Have you seen her?'

He made it sound like a casual question, but Hannah could see the intent in his eyes.

'Nay, but I heard they'd taken her to the hospital. Just to be on the safe side,' she added, seeing the panic on Seth's face. 'She's all right, from what I can make out.'

He nodded. 'That's good, then. Y'know, she surprised me, when we were down that pit. Never lost her head, not even for a minute. She's a tough one, that girl. Tougher than she looks.'

'Aye, she is.' Hannah pushed down the pang of jealousy she felt at the admiration in his voice. 'Now, why don't you get some more sleep? You'll feel better for it.'

'I don't need any more sleep. It's time I was up and about.' He started to throw back the bedclothes, only to let out a sharp hiss as the pain caught him unawares.

'You see? You in't going anywhere till that shoulder's

healed, Seth Stanhope. Now settle down and get some rest.'

'I told you, I don't want to sleep!'

Hannah sighed. He was going to be a difficult patient, she could tell. 'At least promise me you'll stay in bed while I make you a nice cup of tea?' she said.

'If I must.' Seth rolled his eyes. 'Then I'm getting up.'

'Just as you like.'

She took her time putting on the kettle and making the tea. By the time she returned with the tray, Seth was sound asleep again.

It was the middle of the afternoon before Agnes finally managed to convince the staff of the Leeds General Infirmary Casualty department that she was not suffering from concussion.

'I told you, I'm really quite well,' she insisted several times. But they refused to believe her, and insisted on putting her to rest in the Admissions ward for a few hours, so they could keep an eye on any developing symptoms.

Agnes could scarcely hide her irritation. She had always known how insufferable doctors could be when they thought they knew best, but she had never realised nurses could be just as bossy and overbearing. She made up her mind there and then that she would try to listen to her own patients more, instead of always believing herself to be right.

Finally the young doctor accepted that her pupils were not dilated, she had not been sick, nor did she have any headaches, dizziness or bleeding from her ears. She was also well enough to be able to scold him when he turned up to shine his torch in her eyes and ask her if she knew the name of the Prime Minister.

'Yes, well, I think you can go home,' he mumbled, blushing to his ears.

But Agnes had no intention of going straight home. Instead she went up to Male Surgical to visit Christopher Stanhope. It occurred to her that he might be wondering why he had had no visitors that day.

Naturally, he was worried when he heard about the accident, but Agnes was able to reassure him that his father was quite well.

'I daresay he or your aunt will be in to see you as soon as they can,' she said.

'Thanks, Nurse.' He grinned sheepishly at her, no doubt remembering how mercilessly he had teased her in the past. Strange how none of that seemed to matter now.

After she had finished visiting Christopher, Sister Surgical invited Agnes to her sitting room just off the ward for a cup of tea. They discussed the boy's progress, which Sister was very pleased with, and then she asked about the accident at the pit.

'I understand you were quite heroic, Miss Sheridan?' she said.

'I don't know about that.' Agnes thought about poor John Porter and Reg Willis, and how she had followed as their bodies were brought to the surface, shrouded in old pieces of sacking.

She remembered Ruth Chadwick telling her a similar story about her brother when she had first come to the village, but it only struck Agnes now what a humiliating end it was for a proud miner.

She looked up at Sister Surgical. 'May I ask how you know about the accident, Sister? I didn't think the news would have spread all this way?'

Sister smiled and put down her cup. 'Have you forgotten, Miss Sheridan, one of your Bowden men was admitted to my ward this morning?'

'So he was.' Agnes shook her head. How could she have

forgotten that? Perhaps that young doctor was right and she was concussed, after all? 'How is Mr Shepherd?' she asked.

Sister's expression clouded, and Agnes recognised the look she knew only too well from her days as a trainee at the Nightingale Hospital.

'The operation was a success,' Sister said, choosing her words carefully. 'The surgeon managed to stop the internal haemorrhaging and stitch up the rupture in his abdomen, but his injuries were severe and he lost a great deal of blood . . . ' Her brow furrowed. 'Of course we remain optimistic that he will make a full recovery, but the next few days will be critical for him.'

Agnes set down her cup. 'May I see him, Sister?'

'Of course, although I must warn you he still hasn't fully come round after the operation. His wife is with him now. I've put him in room three, off the main ward. For peace and quiet,' she said.

Agnes' heart sank. The private rooms were generally given to patients who had little chance of recovery.

Carrie Shepherd sat at her husband's bedside, clutching his hand above the white coverlet. She looked around sharply as Agnes opened the door, then her face relaxed.

'Oh, Miss Sheridan, it's you. I thought it might be one of the staff nurses, trying to chase me away again.'

'How is he?'

'He woke up a few hours ago, which they said was a good sign. But he's been sleeping on and off all the time since then.' Carrie looked up at her. 'They said it was nothing to worry about, but I'm not so sure . . . what do you think, Nurse?'

Agnes looked down at James Shepherd. His face had the pale sheen of candle wax against the linen pillowcase.

'He has lost a lot of blood,' she said, choosing her words

just as carefully as the ward sister had. 'It will take some time for his body to regain its strength.'

'But he will regain it, won't he?' Carrie's eyes pleaded with her. She looked so fragile, like a child.

'I . . . 'Agnes started to speak, but then they heard a groan as James stirred.

'He's waking up again!' Carrie released his hand abruptly and jumped to her feet. She took a step back from the bed, colliding with Agnes, who caught hold of her.

'What's wrong? Don't you want him to wake up?'

'Of course, it's just—' Carrie dropped her gaze. 'I don't want him to find me here.'

'Why not?'

'You know why!' Carrie's voice was pleading. 'He won't want me here, not after what happened. Please, Miss Sheridan, I have to go!' She pushed past Agnes and fled the room, closing the door behind her just as James opened his eyes.

He looked dazed to see Agnes standing over him.

'Miss – Miss Sheridan?' He frowned. 'Where am I?'

'You're in hospital, Mr Shepherd.' Agnes automatically slipped into nursing mode, smoothing down his covers. 'You've had an operation, do you remember?'

He gave the slightest of nods. 'I – I think so.' His frown deepened, and Agnes could see him slowly piecing everything together. 'Yes, I remember. But I thought . . . ' He looked around him. 'Is Carrie here? I thought I heard her voice.'

Agnes glanced over her shoulder at the door, willing Carrie Shepherd to return. 'There's only me here,' she said.

'Yes.' He sounded forlorn. 'Of course. I don't suppose she would be here, would she?'

'How are you feeling?' Agnes asked, to distract him. 'Are you in pain?'

'A little.' His ashen face told a different story. 'I'm very thirsty. Might I have a drink?'

'Not yet, I'm afraid.' Agnes went to the stand beside his bed, checking the steady drip of saline. 'This might need adjusting. I'll speak to Sister about it.'

She turned to go, but James said, 'Wait. I need to know – are you all right?'

'Oh, yes, I'm quite well. Just a couple of cuts and bruises, nothing serious.' She touched the dressing on her brow.

Agnes made light of it deliberately, not wanting to think about those hours she had spent lying in the dark, her face pressed into the thick, gritty dust that coated her mouth and throat, afraid to move in case she set off another rock fall.

'And the others?' James' voice was tentative, as if he hardly dared ask the question. 'Stanhope and – and Chadwick? Did they survive?'

'Seth Stanhope has a dislocated shoulder. But that didn't stop him helping to carry your stretcher!'

'I'm surprised he didn't abandon me, after I defied him.'

'I think he was relieved you managed to find Rob Chadwick. They might have given up on him if it hadn't been for you.'

'So Chadwick's alive, then?'

Agnes nodded. 'He has a fractured femur, so he'll need a few weeks in hospital, but – yes, he's alive. Thanks to you.'

The slightest shadow of a smile crossed James' face. 'At least I did something right.'

Agnes hesitated, wondering if she should ask the question that had been haunting her ever since that dreadful moment down in the pit.

'Why did you risk your life to rescue him?' she asked finally.

He frowned. 'I did it for Carrie, of course.'

Agnes sat down at his bedside. 'I saw her waiting at the pit gates,' she said. 'She waited there all night for news.' He winced, but said nothing. 'It was you she was waiting for, James. Not Rob Chadwick.'

He shook his head. 'No, you've got it wrong. She loves him. I know she does. I saw them together at her father's funeral.'

'Then why has she been sitting by your bedside all this time, waiting for you to wake up?'

He looked confused. 'I don't understand – where is she now?'

'I'm here,' Carrie said, from the doorway.

Chapter Forty-Eight

The first thing Agnes noticed was the way James' face lit up when he saw her. He still loved his wife, Agnes could see it as clear as day.

She only hoped Carrie could see it too.

'I wasn't sure you'd want to see me?' Carrie said shyly.

James seemed genuinely surprised. 'Why not?'

Carrie couldn't look at him. 'I know Rob told you – about the baby . . .'

'Ah.'

'I'm so sorry, truly I am. I wanted to tell you myself, you don't know how often I tried, but every time I couldn't bring myself to do it because I was so afraid of losing you—' Her words came out in a rush, tumbling over each other.

James looked dazed. 'You were afraid of losing me?'

'Of course. I love you.'

Her words hung in the air and Agnes found herself willing James to speak.

'I love you too,' he said.

Carrie looked up at him. 'But how can you, after what Rob said?'

'About Henry not being my son?' James smiled. 'He thought he was playing his trump card with that one. But he wasn't telling me anything I didn't already know.'

'You – you mean, you knew?'

'I've always known.'

Carrie looked blankly at Agnes, then back at her husband. 'But I don't understand.'

'I was very ill when I was a child,' James said. 'Parotitis. Or, as we usually call it . . . '

'Mumps,' Agnes finished for him. A thought began to stir in her brain.

James smiled knowingly. 'I can see Miss Sheridan understands, don't you?'

Agnes looked at Carrie. 'Mumps can sometimes leave a man sterile.'

'You mean you can't father children?' Carrie looked back at James. 'Why didn't you tell me?'

'Because I was afraid you would leave me. I feel so ashamed when I think about it. I know I should have told you, I know how much you longed for children . . . I deceived you every bit as much as you deceived me.' He looked regretful. 'But I hoped that the doctors might be wrong. Some men have mumps and still go on to father children, so I've heard. So I prayed for a miracle.' His mouth twisted. 'And then a miracle happened, didn't it?'

Agnes glanced at Carrie. The poor girl looked dazed as she struggled to take it all in.

'So you knew about Rob and me . . . '

'I guessed. After that day at the gala, you started acting so strangely . . . you seemed so remote. I began to think that you had changed your mind about marrying me.'

Carrie shook her head. 'Of course I wanted to marry you. But I didn't know how I could. I felt so guilty and wretched about what I'd done.' She covered James' hand with hers. 'How could you do it?' she whispered. 'How could you take on another man's son as your own?'

'Because I wanted us to be happy,' he said simply. 'It didn't matter to me, truly. And once Henry was born, it didn't matter that he wasn't my son, either. The moment I saw him, I loved him with all my heart. He's always been my son as far as I'm concerned, and he always will be.'

Agnes looked at him with new respect. She had always known James Shepherd was a good man, but she had never realised how kind and honourable he truly was until that moment.

'But then Rob came back,' James went on. 'He told me he wanted you and his son, and I just assumed you would want the same.'

'But why?' Carrie asked. 'Why would you even think that?'

'Because I always knew I was second best,' James said. 'I wasn't the one you really wanted. I suppose I always knew in the back of my mind that my happiness couldn't last, that one day you would wake up and realise you didn't want to be with me.'

'I always wanted to be with you. I love you.'

'I love you too.'

Agnes edged towards the door, although she had the feeling that they had forgotten all about her a long time ago.

'But what about Rob?' Carrie said. 'What if he tells everyone the truth?'

'Let him,' James said. 'Let him tell whoever he likes.'

'But the rest of the village . . . the Haverstocks . . . '

'Can all go to hell as far as I'm concerned. As long as we're together, I don't care what anyone else thinks. We are together, aren't we?' He sent her a searching look.

Carrie smiled. 'Always,' she said.

Agnes smiled, closing the door on them.

She went back down to Casualty, being careful to avoid the bossy nurse who had been so insistent about her concussion that morning, and sought out Sister Casualty in her office.

'I was wondering,' Agnes said, 'about the men who were brought in after the pit accident this morning?'

Sister put down her pen. 'What about them?'

'I know one of them went up to the Surgical ward, but what happened to the other one? The fractured femur?'

Sister Casualty rolled her eyes. 'Oh, him. He went up to Orthopaedics. And not a moment too soon, either,' she said crisply. 'He drove me quite mad, flirting with my nurses.'

Agnes smiled. 'That sounds like Mr Chadwick!'

'Anyway, he's Orthopaedics' problem now, and good luck to them. I hope the sister there has better luck keeping him in order than I did.'

The moment Agnes opened the doors to the Orthopaedics ward, she realised Sister Casualty's fervent hope had been in vain.

Sister Orthopaedics was not on the ward, but Agnes could hear Rob's laughter coming from behind a curtain pulled around his bed.

As she approached, a young student nurse emerged, smiling. She stopped dead when she saw Agnes, a tide of colour sweeping up from her collar to the edge of her starched cap.

Agnes nodded towards the curtains. 'I've come to visit Mr Chadwick.'

The nurse recovered her composure. 'Visiting hour ended ten minutes ago.'

Agnes leaned in towards her. 'I'll tell you what,' she said sweetly. 'If you don't tell Sister I'm here, I won't tell her about you giggling behind a curtain with a patient.'

The student blushed again. 'Five minutes,' she said tightly, then hurried off, her head down, shoes squeaking on the polished floor.

Rob's grin widened when he saw Agnes. 'Hello, Nurse. Fancy meeting you here.'

'Hello, Mr Chadwick. I see you're feeling better?'

He shrugged his broad shoulders. He had lost a little

of his devilish charm, dressed in blue striped pyjamas, his leg held up in a complex arrangement of splints and pulleys. 'You've got to do summat to keep your spirits up, in't you? Is that why you're here? To cheer me up?'

'No, Mr Chadwick.'

'Pity.' His grin widened. 'I could do with some entertainment. I'm already bored to tears in this place.'

'You'd best get used to it,' Agnes said. 'You're going to be in here for a long time.'

'How long, d'you reckon?'

'It depends. It can take weeks for a femur to heal. And then you'll have to do your exercises, to build up your muscles again.'

'Weeks?' Rob looked despairing. 'I'll die of boredom long before then.'

'I wouldn't joke about dying if I were you. It nearly happened, remember?'

His face darkened. 'How can I forget? Every time I close my eyes . . . ' He shuddered. 'I don't mind telling you, Nurse, I really thought I was going to meet my maker in that bloody pit. Pardon my language,' he added quietly.

'James Shepherd nearly did,' Agnes reminded him.

'Aye.'

She waited, but Rob stayed silent. 'Well?' Agnes prompted him. 'Aren't you going to ask how he is, since he was the one who saved your life?'

Rob shifted uncomfortably. She was glad to see his conscience was pricking him. 'How is he?'

'He'll live. His wife is with him now,' she added.

Colour flared in Rob's face. 'Aye,' he mumbled. 'I suppose that's where she belongs.'

'Are you quite certain about that?' Agnes sent him a narrow look. 'You're not going to try and ruin things between them?'

'What's the point? She's already made it plain how she feels about me. I'm not one to hang around where I in't wanted.'

'And what about your son?'

Rob looked so downcast, Agnes almost felt sorry for him.

'Henry'll be all right,' he said. 'He's got a father, he doesn't need me. And I don't need him, either,' he said, his chin lifting. 'I've been doing some thinking. I reckon once I get out of here I'll head out of Bowden, go down south. Thought I might try my luck down there, on a farm. It's best if I'm not tied down.'

He was putting a brave face on it, Agnes could tell.

'No more mining?' she said.

He shuddered. 'Not any more. I reckon I've used up all my pit luck.'

Agnes understood how he felt. She wondered how long it would be before she ever willingly ventured under-ground again.

The curtain swished aside and there stood the student nurse, who had now recovered her composure.

'Five minutes is up,' she said. 'And Sister's on her way back to the ward.'

'Thank you.' Agnes turned back to Rob. 'I'll leave you then, Mr Chadwick, Take care, won't you? I wish you well.' She was surprised to find she meant it. His charm had won her over.

'And you, Nurse. And if you fancy a change of scene, you can always come down south with me?'

Agnes shook her head. 'You're incorrigible, Mr Chadwick.'

'I'll take that as a compliment, shall I, since I don't know what it means.'

As she was leaving, he called after her, 'Nurse?'

'Yes, Mr Chadwick?'

'I've been thinking, trying to work it out. Why do you think he did it?'

'Did what?'

'Carrie's mester. There's never been any love lost between us, so why did he put himself in danger to save me?'

'Because he's a good man,' Agnes said.

'Aye.' Rob Chadwick thought about this, taking in what she had said. 'A better man than me, at any rate. The best man won, eh?'

Agnes smiled. 'Let's hope so, Mr Chadwick.'

Chapter Forty-Nine

It was late December, and Dr Rutherford had decided to retire.

Mrs Bannister had organised a tea party at the house for him, to bid him farewell. But no one had turned up, not even his good friends the Haverstocks. Agnes couldn't help feeling sorry for him as the three of them made awkward conversation in the parlour.

'It's an atrocious day,' Dr Rutherford said, looking out of the window. 'I daresay that's what's kept them away. Sir Edward does suffer very badly with his chest in the winter.'

'Yes, I expect that's it.' Mrs Bannister held up a plate. 'Another slice of cake, Doctor? It's Victoria sponge, your favourite.'

She was tight-lipped, doing her best to hide her emotions. Agnes thought she was probably the only one in Bowden who was truly sorry to see him go.

At least the new fishing rod Agnes had given him as a leaving present had cheered him up. She had tried to pretend that everyone in the village had contributed towards it, but even though Dr Rutherford had commented on their generosity, she could tell he wasn't really fooled.

In spite of everything they had been through, Agnes thought it a shame he should leave in this way. It wasn't much to show for more than twenty years as the village doctor. But he only had himself to blame. If he had shown any kindness or compassion to his patients, perhaps they might have done the same for him.

She wondered if this thought was occurring to him too, as he stared out of the window, like a faithful but long-abandoned hound waiting for its master.

'When is the locum arriving?' Agnes asked, trying to distract him.

'He's due from London this evening,' Dr Rutherford said. 'Or he should be, if the weather doesn't close in.' He peered out at the dirty grey sky, heavy with the promise of snow.

'Do you know anything about him?' Agnes asked.

Dr Rutherford shook his head. 'Only that he's a young man. But I daresay he will have lots of new ideas like you, Miss Sheridan.'

He made it sound like a criticism. Agnes smiled sweetly. 'Then I look forward to meeting him.'

'Well, he needn't think he'll be bringing any new ideas into this house. I won't have it!' Mrs Bannister declared.

Dr Rutherford's eyes twinkled behind his spectacles. 'I'm sure you'll be able to set him straight if he tries anything, Mrs B.'

'I'll do my best, Doctor.'

Agnes looked from one to the other and wondered how Dr Rutherford had never noticed the housekeeper's secret yearning for him for all these years. It was obvious to Agnes and she had only been living under the same roof a matter of months. She couldn't help feeling sorry for Mrs Bannister, too. The poor woman was clearly devastated at losing her precious Dr Rutherford, and fearful of all the changes that his departure might bring.

But at least Dr Rutherford had promised to send for her once he was settled in his new home up in the Highlands, so there was hope for them yet, Agnes thought. In the meantime, the housekeeper had agreed to stay on until a new doctor could be found to take over the house and the practice.

The doorbell rang.

'I wonder if that's the Haverstocks?' Dr Rutherford turned hopefully towards the door, only to sink back in his seat again when it opened and Jinny appeared, a piece of paper in her hand.

'A boy brought a note for you, Miss Sheridan,' she said.

'A note?' Mrs Bannister held out her hand. 'Give it to me.'

Jinny's eyes darted from the housekeeper to Agnes. 'Please, miss, he said only t'nurse was to see it.'

Agnes could feel Mrs Bannister's displeasure. She took the note from Jinny and read it. She could barely make out the badly scrawled marks on the paper, but she understood their meaning.

She slipped the piece of paper into her pocket and turned to Jinny. 'Tell the boy I'll come straight away,' she said.

'Well?' Mrs Bannister demanded, as soon as the door was closed. 'What did it say? Who was it from?'

Agnes got to her feet. 'If you'll excuse me, I have to go and call on someone,' she said.

'Who? Who do you have to call on?' Mrs Bannister twitched with annoyance. 'I disapprove of secrets. This is the doctor's house, and he has a right to know—'

'It's quite all right, Mrs Bannister.' Dr Rutherford raised his hand to quieten her. 'Do you think you might need my help, Miss Sheridan?'

Agnes looked at him. How many times had she begged for his help and he had refused? All those poor people who had gone on suffering because he wouldn't lift a finger.

She was tempted to remind him of it when she saw the wistful look on his face. She knew then that she didn't

415

need to say a word. He was already counting the cost of what he had done.

'It's all right, Doctor,' she said kindly. 'You enjoy your rest. You're retired, remember?'

'Aye.' Dr Rutherford looked sad. 'Aye, so I am.'

Outside, a bitter wind howled through the streets, ripping at the bare trees. It was scarcely three o'clock in the afternoon, but already the sky was darkening.

Even through her gloves, Agnes' hands were raw with cold as she clutched the handlebars of her bicycle. She could feel the first icy spots of snow stinging her face.

On her way up the hill out of the village, she passed a man and a woman, with a small child between them, heading down the lane. The woman had hold of the child's hand while the man dragged an enormous Christmas tree behind him.

Agnes overtook them, then pulled in to the kerb and stopped to wait for them to catch up with her.

'Merry Christmas!' she called out to them, her words carried away on the whistling wind. 'My goodness, what a big tree!'

'My son chose it.' James Shepherd gave her a mock grimace. 'I only hope I'll be able to get it in through the front door!'

Agnes looked down at Henry's beaming face, rosy with cold. Now he was losing his baby softness Agnes could see he was starting to look more like his father, with his deep set brown eyes and wisps of brown hair poking out from his thick woollen hat.

If Rob Chadwick had stayed in the village a few more months, he would have been in no doubt that James Shepherd was Henry's father. It looked as if James had got his miracle after all.

Or perhaps it wasn't such a miracle, she thought, looking

at Carrie Shepherd. It was still early days, and her slender figure showed only the slightest curve under her coat, but she already had the radiant bloom of a pregnant woman.

'Have you heard our news, Miss Sheridan?' Carrie said, smiling. 'James has left the pit.'

'No!' Agnes looked from her to James and back again.

'Aye, it's true. Now Miss Colley's left to get married, he's taking over as the junior teacher up at the school.' She beamed proudly at her husband.

'That's wonderful news. I'm so pleased for you. I think you'll make a very good schoolmaster.'

'I don't know about that.' James looked rueful. 'I'm not sure what Miss Warren will make of me!'

'Surely she can't be any worse to work with than Sir Edward?'

'That's true.'

Agnes could already see the relief on James' face. He looked as if the weight of the world had been taken off his shoulders.

'I'm very pleased for you,' she said.

'Aye.' Carrie reached for her husband's hand. 'It's a new start for us.'

Agnes saw the look of love that passed between them, and felt a pang. If anyone deserved a new start, it was them. And with Rob Chadwick now long gone from the village, and James his own man at last, perhaps that was what they would get.

'Where are you going on this terrible night?' James asked.

'I have an emergency call to make.'

'Well, I hope you haven't got too far to go. The snow's going to be coming down soon.'

'Snow!' Henry cried out, jumping up and down with excitement.

'Yes, indeed, young man.' James smiled down at him.

'We shall have to see about building a snowman in the morning.' He looked at Agnes. 'Be careful, won't you, Miss Sheridan? I don't envy you being out in this weather.'

Agnes glanced up the lane, where the first flakes of snow were beginning to swirl and drift, carried about on the hectic wind.

She wasn't looking forward to it, either.

'I didn't think you'd come,' Hannah said when she opened the door, her bulky frame blocking out the dim lamplight from the room behind her. For a moment she stood there staring, then she remembered herself and shifted aside to let Agnes in.

Inside the cottage the air was hot and stuffy, reeking of smoke and cats. But even though the cottage was warm, it was still bare and cheerless. What furniture there was seemed old, worn out and unloved.

A scrawny ginger cat dozed on a threadbare chair by the fireside. It raised its head to look balefully at Agnes as she set her bag down on the table.

'How is she?' Agnes asked, taking off her coat.

'Ailing,' Hannah said shortly. 'She's been bad for a few days but she's got worse since this morning.'

'Why didn't you send for me earlier?'

'I didn't want to send for you at all. She were the one who wanted you, not me.' Hannah jerked her head towards the doorway that led to the other room.

'Why? I've never met her.'

'I don't know, do I?' Hannah snapped. 'Mother has her own ways of going about things.'

She looked put out about it, and Agnes could understand why. Over the past couple of months, she and Hannah had reached an uneasy truce. They tolerated each other, as long as the managed to keep out of each other's way.

'Is that her?' a thin voice croaked from the other room. 'Has she come?'

'Aye, she's come.' Hannah kept her unfriendly gaze fixed on Agnes. 'Tha'd best go in,' she said. 'She don't take kindly to being kept waiting.'

Agnes wasn't sure what to expect of Nella Arkwright. She had heard enough tales of the fearsome witch who lived up in the woods, who cast spells and consorted with demons and who murdered her husband by magic when he said a wrong word to her.

But it was nothing more than a frail old lady she saw lying in the bed, her shrunken frame almost lost under the patchwork quilt. Her white hair was fanned out in sparse strands over the pillow, framing a tiny, wizened face like a dried apple.

She cackled, 'I told you she'd come, didn't I?' Nella turned her dim gaze on Agnes. Her eyes were opaque with age, but Agnes had the uncomfortable feeling she could see more deeply without them. 'She said you wouldn't. But I knew you better than that.' Her mouth stretched, exposing a dark, toothless hole. 'Oh, yes, I know you very well.'

Agnes stepped back from the bed. 'Your daughter tells me you're not feeling well,' she said briskly, fighting to regain control. 'Let's see what we can do for you, shall we?'

'You can put all that away, you'll only be wasting your time,' Nella said as Agnes opened her bag. 'I'm dying. My time has come, and that's all there is to it.'

'In that case, why have you sent for me?'

'Because I wanted to see you.' She raised a hand to beckon Agnes to her. 'Come closer, and let me look at you.'

Agnes glanced at Hannah, who stood like a sentry by the door, her face expressionless.

'Well, come on!' Nella snapped impatiently. 'Don't worry, I in't going to eat you. I suppose that's what you've heard, in't it? That I go out hunting in the woods to find bairns for my cooking pot?'

'I'm sure I don't listen to such nonsense,' Agnes dismissed.

'So you won't mind coming closer, will you? Just into the light, where I can see you better. My old eyes in't what they were.'

Agnes edged closer to the bed. This was ridiculous, she told herself. She had nothing to fear from an old, dying woman. But she still felt a wave of revulsion wash over her as Nella looked her over.

'Aye, just as I thought. You're a pretty little thing. She's got a look of my Sarah about her, don't you think, Hannah?' Nella nodded to herself. 'No wonder you caught Seth Stanhope's eye. Men always like a pretty face.'

Agnes saw Hannah's stricken expression out of the corner of her eye.

'So what seems to be wrong with you?' Agnes said.

'I told you, I'm dying. Stop asking foolish questions and let me be – ah!' Nella stiffened with pain.

'Mother!' Hannah rushed to her side, but Nella turned away from her.

'No! Don't you touch me. You're too clumsy with those big, rough hands of yours. Have you seen her hands, Nurse? Like shovels, they are. I ask you, d'you think any man would put a ring on a great big paw like that? They'd never get one to fit!'

She gave a harsh, rasping laugh. Agnes glanced at Hannah, waiting for her to react. But she shrank back, her head hanging low, like a scolded child.

'Your daughter's hands are very skilled, Mrs Arkwright,' Agnes said. 'I've seen how gently they can dress a wound and bring a baby into the world.'

Hannah looked up, and Agnes saw the look of surprise and pride that flashed across her face.

'So you two are all friends together now, are you?' Nella's voice was caustic. 'It won't last, it never does. Who'd want to be friends with a big, ugly lump like her?' She turned to Hannah, cowering like a whipped dog in the shadows. 'Don't just stand there, girl. Make thysen useful and bring me a cup of tea. I'm parched.'

'Yes, Mother.' Hannah scuttled off.

Nella's toothless mouth curled in derision. '"Yes, Mother,"' she mocked her daughter's girlish lisp. 'What kind of cruelty is it, to give a monster like that such a pretty voice? It makes you wonder about the world, doesn't it?'

'Leave her alone.'

Nella turned her head to look at Agnes. 'And who are you to tell me what to do in my own house?'

'I can always leave, if that's what you want? Unlike your daughter, I have better things to do with my time than dance attendance on you.'

Nella cackled. 'Listen to her! In't you afeared of me, lass?'

Agnes lifted her chin. 'Certainly not.'

'Happen you should be.'

Before Agnes could reply, Hannah returned, carefully carrying a chipped bone-china cup and saucer in both hands.

'Here you are, Mother.' She set it down on the night-stand, then carefully lifted her mother's frail body upright and held the cup to her wrinkled lips.

Nella took one sip then spat it out, straight into her daughter's face.

'It's stewed!' She snatched the cup and hurled it at the wall with surprising strength for one so frail. It shattered, splashing the faded rose wallpaper with an ugly brown stain.

421

Agnes gasped, her hands flying to her mouth, waiting for Hannah to explode with rage. But the other woman laid her mother back down and stood up.

'I'm sorry, Mother,' she said quietly, wiping her face. 'I'll make some fresh.'

She left the room. Agnes stared after her, shocked by what she had seen.

'You don't like it, do you?' Nella taunted her from the bed. 'You think I treat her badly.'

I think you're an absolute monster. The words were on the tip of Agnes' tongue, but she knew she must not say them. Nella was trying to anger her, but Agnes would not give her the satisfaction.

'It's not for me to say,' she said. 'Now, you seem to be in a lot of pain. Would you like me to give you something?'

Nella turned her face away. 'I in't afeared of pain,' she said coldly.

'In that case, I'll leave you to rest.' Agnes smiled to herself, sensing Nella's frustration and fury. Agnes was refusing to play her game, and Nella didn't like it one bit.

Agnes turned on her heel and went through to the kitchen, where Hannah stood at the range, making the tea. Agnes could see straight away the other woman had been crying.

She turned away from Agnes sharply, sniffing back tears. 'How is she?'

'She's resting.'

'Would you like a cup of tea? I've made a fresh pot.'

Agnes glanced at the window. The snow was falling more heavily now, thick flakes drifting against the glass. She thought longingly of Dr Rutherford's warm, clean house.

'Thank you, but I really should be—' Agnes was about

422

to refuse when she saw Hannah's desolate face. 'That would be very nice,' she finished instead.

Hannah took her mother another cup of tea and then she and Agnes sat together in the flickering firelight, listening to the wind howling outside.

'What a dreadful night,' Agnes said.

'Aye. Mother allus said she would die on a night like this, when there was snow in the air.' Hannah's voice was flat as she stared into the flames.

'Why do you let her speak to you like that?'

Hannah shrugged. 'Mother don't mean anything by it,' she said. 'Besides, she's right. I am big and ugly. Can't argue with that, can I?'

Agnes turned back to look into the fire.

'My mother could be harsh too, sometimes,' she said.

She could feel Hannah looking at her. 'Why?'

'I was – am – a disappointment to her, I suppose.'

'You?' Hannah sounded disbelieving. 'I can't imagine that. You couldn't be a disappointment to anyone. Not like me.' The scrawny cat jumped into her lap and she stroked its long, sinuous back. 'You got any other family? Brothers and sisters?'

'One sister. Vanessa.'

'Older or younger?'

'Two years older.'

'Sarah were younger than me. The bairn.' Hannah's mouth twisted. 'She were always the favourite.'

So is Vanessa. Agnes thought about her mother and sister, off for afternoon tea or on another of their endless shopping trips. It never ceased to amaze Agnes how long they could spend talking about shoes, or gossiping about people they knew. She was more like her father, with her nose always in a book.

'Mother allus preferred Sarah to me,' Hannah's lisping voice interrupted her thoughts. 'She's even told me it would have been better if I'd died instead.'

Agnes stared at her in shock. She couldn't imagine even Elizabeth Sheridan being cruel enough to put such a thought into words.

Poor Hannah. No wonder she was so desperate to find someone to love her.

They went on sitting together in silence, both lost in their thoughts. Agnes wondered if Hannah had fallen asleep, but when she looked to the side the other woman was wide awake, staring into the flames.

Gradually, the fire died down and Hannah roused herself to build it up with more logs from the basket. The cat sprang from her lap and came to wind himself around Agnes' legs.

'You haven't been to visit the Stanhopes lately,' Hannah said.

'I've not had any reason to come. Christopher has made a full recovery, there's no need to check on him any more.'

'All the same, I thought you might have called.'

'Why?'

'To see Seth.'

Agnes reached down to stroke the cat's skinny flanks. The last time she had seen him was two months earlier. Christopher had come out of hospital, and Agnes had been to visit him as part of her duties.

She was just packing away her things when Seth had come in, black from the pit. Billy followed at his heels, chattering away.

Seth had stopped dead when he saw her, the smile freezing on his face. 'Nurse,' he nodded, whipping off his cap.

'Mr Stanhope.' Agnes was surprised to find herself just as tongue-tied. 'How is your shoulder?' she asked.

'Mending nicely, thank you.' He glanced past her towards the bedroom. 'How's our Chris?'

'He's doing well.' She could feel a blush creeping up from underneath her starched collar.

For a moment they stood awkwardly, looking everywhere but at each other, until Billy broke the tension.

'Can you play football, Dad?' he asked.

Seth started shaking his head, and for a moment Agnes thought he might refuse. But then he said, 'You'll have to wait till I've had my bath, lad.'

Agnes felt her face growing hotter, remembering the time she had walked in and caught him in the tub. Her gaze strayed to the fire, thinking about it, then she pulled herself together.

'Right, well, I'd best leave you to it,' she said briskly, gathering up her bag. 'I'll call again tomorrow.'

'Aye.'

But she hadn't seen him since. Every time she called on Christopher after that, Seth somehow contrived to be out of the house. Agnes knew it was no coincidence. He might have stopped avoiding his children, but now for some reason he was trying to avoid her.

'He went back down the mine,' she said.

Hannah nodded grimly. 'What else could he do? He's got to earn a living. Besides, mining's in his blood.'

'I suppose so.' Agnes wondered if he had the same nightmares she did. Did he wake up gasping for air, fighting off the bedclothes, imagining they were rocks landing on him?

Once more, they fell silent. The fire hissed and crackled as it consumed the new logs.

'I was jealous of you,' Hannah said at last.

Agnes frowned. 'Why?'

'I've always loved him, you see. But then I lost him to Sarah.' The firelight flickered on Hannah's face. 'Then when she died, I thought I might have another chance with him. But then you came along, and—' She stared down at her hands in her lap. 'I hated you. I blamed you for taking away what I felt were mine. But I were wrong, just like I were wrong about him and Sarah. She didn't take him from me.' She turned to look at Agnes, her eyes dark pools in the firelight. 'Seth Stanhope were never mine, and he never will be. It's you he wants.'

The idea was so absurd, Agnes nearly laughed. Hannah wouldn't have said that if she had seen the way he'd treated her that day in his cottage! 'You're wrong,' she said. 'He has no interest in me.'

'Of course he does. He'd never admit it, but I can tell. God knows, I've watched him enough to know what's going on in his heart,' Hannah said bitterly.

Agnes remembered that very first day at the Miners' Welfare, Seth scowling at her across the table. She had been attracted to him even then, she realised.

She pushed the thought from her mind. 'Even if it were true, I wouldn't be interested,' she said. 'I'm too busy with my work.'

'Work?' Hannah sounded incredulous. 'You mean to tell me you'd rather tend to people's bunions and bedsores than find a man to love you?'

Agnes gazed into the fire, feeling its heat against her face. Once she might have said yes without hesitation. But now she didn't know what to think.

Before she could manage a reply, Nella let out a loud cry from the other room.

'Mother!' Hannah was gone before Agnes had even risen to her feet.

Nella was curled up under the quilt, whimpering like a wounded animal. She was so lost in pain, she didn't even push Hannah away when she went to her.

'Mother?' Hannah brushed a wisp of hair from her mother's damp face. 'I in't seen her like this before.' She turned to Agnes, her dark eyes desperate. 'Can't you do summat?'

'No.' Nella found her voice. 'I'm near my time and I want—' She stopped talking, flinching as the pain swept over her again. 'Leave us. I want to speak to the nurse. I've got summat important to tell her.'

Agnes could feel Hannah looking at her, and willed her not to go. Suddenly she didn't want to be alone with Nella Arkwright, or to hear what she had to say.

The door closed softly behind her, and then they were alone. As soon as her daughter had gone, Nella seemed calmer.

'That's better,' she said. 'The pain has passed now. I can feel the shadow of death watching over me, waiting . . . ' She sighed, and the glimmer of a smile crossed her face. 'It won't be long now.'

'Perhaps I should fetch your daughter.'

Agnes started for the door but Nella said, 'Wait. Don't you want to know what I've got to tell you? I've had a vision.'

Agnes held herself rigid. 'I'm not interested in fortune-telling.'

She went to turn away, but Nella grabbed her hand, her grip shockingly strong for one so old and weak.

'You'll see him again,' she hissed. 'You think he's gone from your life, but he is not dead to you.'

'I – I don't know what you're talking about.'

'Yes, you do. You know.' The old woman's opaque eyes were suddenly blazing. 'You think about him all the time.

He's in your dreams. The one who is dearest to your heart. And he'll come back to you one day. One day . . . '

Agnes snatched her hand away, but as soon as she did, Nella's arm dropped limply to the bed and she lay back, staring glassily up at the ceiling.

'Hannah!' Agnes cried out. But she knew it was already too late.

Chapter Fifty

Afterwards, Agnes offered to help lay out the old woman, but Hannah refused.

'Nay, I'll do it mysen,' she said. 'It's what she would have wanted.'

Agnes could see she needed to mourn her mother alone, so she didn't argue.

Hannah watched her as she packed up her bag. 'You ought to call round to the Stanhopes', you know,' she said. 'I know the bairns would like to see you, especially little Elsie. She often talks about you.'

Agnes smiled. 'We'll see.'

She put on her coat and prepared to go into the night. As she opened the door, a rush of icy air blew in, bringing a flurry of snowflakes with it.

'It's settled,' Hannah remarked, looking out. 'Deep, too. Tha'll never get your bicycle through that. Why don't you stay till the worst of it's over?'

'Thank you, but I need to get back sooner or later. I have my rounds in the morning.' And if she was honest, the idea of spending the night at the Arkwrights' old farmhouse with Nella dead in the room next door did not appeal to her.

'Then I'll fetch the horse and cart, give you a lift.'

'I'll be all right, honestly.' Agnes glanced towards the bedroom door. 'You need to be with your mother,' she said.

Hannah looked as if she might argue, then she shrugged her broad shoulders. 'Well, at least take this shawl to keep you warm. And these boots.' She picked up a pair of men's boots from where they sat by the hearth. 'They'll keep out some of the cold.'

Agnes looked at the boots, at least three sizes too big for her, then back at her own shoes. They were stout black leather, but no match for the deep drifts of snow. 'Thank you,' she said.

As she watched Agnes pulling on the boots, Hannah suddenly said, 'What made you come?'

Agnes frowned up at her. 'You sent for me.'

'Yes, but why did you come? You could have just ignored my note. No one could blame you, after the way I treated you.'

'It's my job,' Agnes said. 'I'm a nurse and I have to look after people, whether I happen to like them or not.'

Hannah's mouth twisted. 'My mother taught me to wish ill on anyone who crossed me. She certainly wouldn't have had me make them better.' She looked at Agnes. 'Happen that's the difference between us, in't it?'

'Happen it is,' Agnes said.

She was glad of the boots as she stepped out into the freezing night. The snow had settled in drifts, far too deep for her bicycle to manage. In the end Hannah abandoned it by the Arkwrights' back gate and made her way through the woods on foot. Even with the lamp Hannah had given her to light her way, it was dark and forbidding. The wind howled and whistled, reminding her of Nella Arkwright's rasping cackle. It was almost as if the old woman's spirit was there in the trees, watching her . . .

Superstitious nonsense, Agnes told herself briskly. There are no such things as ghosts. But even so, she couldn't stop herself screaming when the bare branch of a tree caught her, clawing the cap from her head.

The snow was deeper than she had expected, and her

feet sank with every step. It was an effort to pull her heavy boots out of the thick drifts, and by the time the woods thinned out and the lights of Bowden Main Colliery came into sight, Agnes was stumbling with exhaustion.

Once she had found the path down, she allowed her thoughts to wander. And as usual whenever she had an idle moment, her mind wandered towards Seth Stanhope.

After what she had been through, she'd never imagined she would feel the pull of attraction towards a man again. And to be attracted to Seth was the last thing she wanted, or needed. It was hopeless, the worst match she could imagine.

And yet . . .

Hannah had told her that Seth was too proud to admit how much he liked her. Perhaps the same was true of her?

You think about him all the time. He's in your dreams. The one who is dearest to your heart. And he'll come back to you one day. One day . . .

As she stumbled in through the back door of Dr Rutherford's house, into the darkness of the kitchen, all Agnes could think about was being warm. A cup of tea, or perhaps even a glass of brandy. Then into her bed, pulling the quilt around herself until her body had thawed out.

The range was still warm. Agnes dragged a chair over to it and sat down to pull off the wet boots, but she was too tired and her hands were too numb with cold to manage the laces. She was still struggling with them when a man's voice called out, 'Who's there?'

The next moment the kitchen light went on. Agnes flinched, shielding her eyes from the sudden brightness.

'What the—'

'Agnes?'

His voice stopped her dead in her tracks. Agnes lowered

her hand and stared, blinking, into a face she'd never thought she would see again.

'Daniel?'

For a moment they could only look at each other. He looked so absurd in his dressing gown and pyjamas, wielding a poker. Agnes could only imagine what she looked like, bundled in a tattered shawl and men's boots, her hair hanging in wet rats' tails about her face.

He lowered the poker. 'I thought you were a burglar,' he said. She would have laughed if she had been awake. As it was, she was certain she must be in the middle of a strange dream.

But then she felt melted snow dripping down her face in icy drops. Surely this couldn't be a dream?

Daniel looked as dumbstruck as she felt. 'I can't believe it – it's really you.' He shook his head. 'What are you doing here?'

'I'm the district nurse.'

'I thought you were in London?'

'It's a long story,' Agnes said. She looked him up and down, taking him in. Tall, slim, black hair and dark brown eyes – it was really Daniel Edgerton. 'I thought you were in Scotland?'

'Another long story.' He was staring at her as hard as she was staring at him. 'Agnes Sheridan. I can scarcely believe it.' He ran his hand through his hair, making it stick up on end. 'God, I think I need a drink!'

'Me too,' Agnes said.

She yanked off the boots and padded barefoot over to the cupboard where she knew Mrs Bannister kept her medicinal supply of brandy.

She couldn't find any glasses, so she took out two teacups instead.

'Reminds me of the old days at the Nightingale,' Daniel

said. 'All those illicit parties at the doctors' house – but look at you. You're trembling.'

'It's just the cold,' Agnes said, although she knew it was more than that. Her whole body felt as if it had gone into shock. 'I've just walked three miles through the woods.'

'In this weather? My dear, you must be positively hypothermic. Here, come and sit back down by the range. And take that wet coat off.'

'I c-can't,' Agnes said through chattering teeth. 'I'm too cold.'

'Have this.' Daniel slipped off his dressing gown.

It was all too absurd, Agnes thought as she sat with her stockinged feet up on the range and Daniel's dressing gown draped around her shoulders. Her former fiancé had reappeared in her life five minutes ago, and she was already wearing his night apparel.

Any minute now, she would definitely wake up.

But she could smell the faint aroma of his cologne from the dressing gown, and feel the warmth of his body seeping into hers. It was all too real to be a dream.

The one who is dearest to your heart. And he'll come back to you one day. One day . . .

'Were you with a patient?' Daniel asked, breaking into her thoughts.

Agnes nodded. 'She died.'

'I'm sorry.'

She glanced at him. Daniel had always been very caring, not like the other junior doctors who could tell a patient's family that their loved one had died one minute and be off laughing with their friends the next.

Daniel. The man she had once loved with all her heart. The man she had abandoned with barely a word of explanation.

433

'So you're the new locum?' she said.

'So it seems.' Then he looked at her over the rim of his teacup. 'This is all rather awkward, isn't it?'

'Yes, it is rather,' she admitted.

'I'd never have accepted this post if I'd known . . . '

'I'm sure you wouldn't. I daresay I'm the last person you'd want to meet?'

'Oh, no, not at all,' he said hurriedly. 'I was thinking more of you, actually.' He looked rueful. 'It can't be much fun for you, coming face to face with me? Especially after you fled to the other end of the country to escape me.'

He was smiling when he said it, but Agnes felt the sting of his words. 'It's not easy for either of us,' she said, gazing into her brandy.

'Perhaps I should say I've changed my mind?'

'Do you want to?'

'I don't know.' He considered it for a moment. 'I must say, I was looking forward to a stay here. In my last practice I was working with a father and son who bickered constantly, so I rather liked the idea of being on my own for a while. And it is only for a few weeks . . . But the last thing I want to do is make things difficult for you?'

Agnes thought about it. Her first instinct was to say that it would be hard for them to work together, but she didn't want to be churlish. She had already put Daniel through enough.

'I'm sure we can manage,' she said. 'As you say, it is only for a few weeks.'

'Are you sure you can bear it?' He looked relieved.

'I can if you can. And I'd hate to leave the people of Bowden without a doctor.' God knows, they deserved someone decent after so many years.

'Then let's give it a try,' Daniel said. 'After all, it's been a long time, hasn't it?'

'Yes.'

'And I'm sure there must be another chap on the horizon by now?'

A picture of Seth came into her mind.

'No,' she said.

'Really? You don't seem very certain about that?'

She caught his speculative look. 'It's probably best if we don't discuss it, if we're going to be working together,' she said.

'No, of course, you're quite right.' Daniel nodded. 'We'll keep it all strictly professional.'

'I think that would be best.'

He looked back at her, smiling sheepishly. 'Well, well. Who would ever have imagined this would happen?'

Agnes thought about Nella Arkwright, lying on her deathbed. *The one who is dearest to your heart. And he'll come back to you one day. One day . . .*

'Who indeed?' she said.

The Nightingale series

On call in the 1930s

The Nightingale Girls
Donna Douglas

'Fans of Call the Midwife will enjoy this'
Woman's Own on The Nightingale Girls

The Nightingale Sisters
Donna Douglas

'Fans of Call the Midwife will enjoy this'
Woman's Own on The Nightingale Girls

The Nightingale Nurses
Donna Douglas

A Nightingales Christmas Story
A Child is Born
Donna Douglas

ebook only

'Fans of Call the Midwife will enjoy this'
Woman's Own on The Nightingale Girls

Donna Douglas
Nightingales on Call

'Fans of Call the Midwife will enjoy this'
Woman's Own on The Nightingale Girls

Donna Douglas
A Nightingale Christmas Wish

Donna Douglas
Nightingales at War

'If you like Call the Midwife, you'll love this warm-hearted tale'
Press Associate on the Nightingale series

'Fans of Call the Midwife will enjoy this'
Woman's Own on The Nightingale Girls

Nightingales Under the Mistletoe
THE SUNDAY TIMES TOP TEN BESTSELLER
Donna Douglas

A Nightingales Short Story
Little Girl Lost
Donna Douglas

'Fans of Call the Midwife will enjoy this'
Woman's Own on The Nightingale Girls

A Nightingale Christmas Carol
THE SUNDAY TIMES TOP TEN BESTSELLER
Donna Douglas